r every purpose under heaven . . .

He could pretend he was simply being paranoid, but the depth of what was happening to him denied him that luxury. It would only be a matter of time before the *Post* accused him directly of killing Mary Jacobs, and he had to get to the bottom of this long before that happened, long before he became even more guilty by acclamation.

It was still early; only 7:30 in the morning. He had a gun in his pocket, that in itself was a crime, and he would not hesitate to use it if he had to.

Time to get into the game, Richard.

BLOWBACK

"Fullilove seems to have a true insider's knowledge of Washington and the devastating threats that lie just around the corner for America."

Kyle Mills, *New York Times* bestselling author of *Storming Heaven* and *Burn Factor*

"A great read."
Denver Rocky Mountain News

D0556863

ADVENTURE

SUSPENSE

ATTENTION: ORGANIZATIONS AND CORPORATIONS
Most HarperTorch paperbacks are available at special quantity discounts for bulk purchases for sales promotions, premiums, or fund-raising. For information, please call or write:

Special Markets Department, HarperCollins Publishers, Inc., 10 East 53rd Street, New York, N.Y. 10022–5299.
Telephone: (212) 207–7528. Fax: (212) 207-7222.

ERIC JAMES
FULLILOVE

BLOWBACK

HarperTorch
An Imprint of HarperCollinsPublishers

This is a work of fiction. Names, characters, places, and incidents are products of the author's imagination or are used fictitiously and are not to be construed as real. Any resemblance to actual events, locales, organizations, or persons, living or dead, is entirely coincidental.

HARPERTORCH
An Imprint of HarperCollins*Publishers*
10 East 53rd Street
New York, New York 10022-5299

First HarperTorch paperback printing: February 2003
First Amistad special printing: October 2001
First Amistad hardcover printing: September 2001

HarperCollins®, HarperTorch™, and ❦™ are trademarks of Harper-Collins Publishers Inc.

Printed in the United States of America

Visit HarperTorch on the World Wide Web at www.harpercollins.com

10 9 8 7 6 5 4 3 2 1

To my extended family, the Fulliloves, Wingoods, Whites, Blands, and Jenkinses: Some ties are thicker than blood and will last longer than time

BLOWBACK

1

Salim hopped out of the back of the canvas-covered truck as the convoy squealed to a halt on rusty brakes. He was a mechanic, and the lead troop carrier had been farting and misfiring for a half a klick. The stark sounds of the engine backfires echoing through the dense vegetation had gotten on everyone's nerves. *Probably just need to adjust the timing*, he thought, as he lit a Turkish cigarette and strolled casually toward the front of the convoy.

They had left Pakistan two days earlier fully packed with minimal instructions from their superiors. Even Salim had a weapon, although he was not trained for combat. He hoped if they met any Indian troops he wouldn't shoot himself in the foot with the fucking thing. He hated guns.

He waved to a friend of his in the back of one of the troop carriers and continued at a leisurely pace toward the lead vehicle. Someone with rank was shouting at him, but the officers were always yelling, yet he, Salim, was the only one who could reliably fix the problem, so they could go fuck their mothers for all he cared. He took a heavy drag on the cigarette, feeling the nicotine make him a little light-headed. Someone on his truck had shown him a small stash of opium and a pipe, but Salim had shaken his head. These kids didn't know what they were getting into, thinking that this was some kind of a damned camping trip. But Salim had been in the Kashmir before, and he knew that many of the fresh-faced kids wouldn't be returning home if what he thought was going to happen, happened.

He blew a cloud of smoke at the officer screaming at him, saluted, then scratched his crotch. Several of the troops watching hooted and hollered at his seeming show of disrespect, but that was his reputation with these children, and he wanted to show them that he feared no one. He snapped off a more rakish salute at the officer's back, then slid halfway under the front bumper of the troop carrier at the head of the convoy. He could hear the clanking of one of the ancient tanks the Pakistani army had brought along because the new ordnance couldn't be squeezed through the narrow passages they were hoping to navigate in Kashmir.

He lay in the rutted dirt of the rough road, the coolness of the mud and packed dirt at his back somehow soothing. There was nothing underneath the truck that he needed to see, but it gave him another opportunity to stick it to his superiors and take his time.

Opium pipes, indeed. What the children packing the trucks didn't realize is that the job of the infantry is to die for their God and country; there was dying, and there was the horror of slow death and the greater horror of being maimed. Salim had seen men unscathed by bullets and bombs but tortured by the carnage they'd witnessed on the field of battle. In that regard, none of them would escape unharmed, none of them would return home exactly as they'd left. For these children, these virgins of infantry combat, what they had been to their wives and lovers and family had begun dying the moment the trucks had rolled across the border into Kashmir.

They just didn't know it yet.

Okay, he'd fucked around long enough. He latched onto

the right front wheel of the truck and turned himself sideways so that his head was staring at the sky right under the
cab's passenger door and his feet still protruded from under
the hood. It was a clear sky with a wisp of cloud, but there
was a contrail of some kind almost directly overhead.

There was shouting and pointing as others noticed the
long arc of white vapor seeming to point right toward them,
and Salim looked at it with curiosity, not fear, thinking that
maybe his stupid government had announced to the world,
somehow, where they were and what their intentions were.

Unless it was an attack of some sort. He tried to think of
a prayer, but none came, his faith too rusty to provide even a
moment of comfort. Others saw the contrail and were stu-
pidly raising weapons as if they could shoot the thing down,
but even Salim could see that it was much too high in the
sky. A few rifles chattered even as the officers were yelling
at the men to cease firing. . . .

And then the contrail ended in a brilliant flash that he saw
for perhaps a second before his retinas burned away, and he
was blind, and people were screaming, and he felt his face
flush with unaccountable heat from nowhere but the sky; the
ground shook slightly as the concussion wave swept down
on him, and a roar unlike anything he'd ever heard thundered. He tried blinking to clear his eyesight but couldn't,
and then the screams died down into silence and his exposed
lower legs began to feel like jelly. He tried to push himself
from under the troop carrier but it was as if his arms had
turned to mush, so he crawled away from what he thought
was the truck, passing at least two inert forms that he assumed were the prone bodies of his comrades. He had no
way of knowing that a heavy dose of gamma radiation was
destroying the tissues in his torso and legs, while his thorax,
which had been underneath the truck, had received a dimin-
ished, but still fatal dose because it had been partially
shielded by the vehicle.

He rolled over and his insides heaved and bloody liquid spewed from his mouth and bloody discharge rushed noisily from his disintegrating bowels. He lay still, listening for sounds from the thousand or so men that were within earshot and heard nothing but wind through the trees and an angry swarm of black flies, and a little time passed as he refused to believe that he was to be the last to die, alone.

WASHINGTON, D.C., SEVERAL HOURS LATER

A steady soaking rain was falling as Richard Whelan tailed his girlfriend's battered Volvo to her apartment, the snick of his Porsche's wipers barely intruding on his thoughts.

Ex-girlfriend, he corrected himself. As of forty-five minutes ago. Give or take.

He was tapping his fingers on the steering wheel to the hard rhythm of Lenny Kravitz's "Fly Away" coming softly out of the radio.

It was a year of your life, he thought. *Are you really ready to write it off?*

Do you have a choice?

Maybe he was better off leaving this particular vortex behind. An easy rationalization—she's white, you're black; *well, there's a first time for everything. . . .*

But it wasn't that simple, was it?

You work for the president of the United States. She's Marty Jacobs's daughter, *the* Marty Jacobs, legendary entrepreneur and fund-raiser for a president who was anything but happy with this particular stunt.

You tiptoed into this relationship under heavy fire, now what?

Tiptoe out and use a pair of rusty pliers to pull the bullets out of your ass?

Is that even possible?

You didn't need this particular occupational hazard, Rich. You didn't need it, and you went ahead and busted the taboos anyway without giving a damn about the consequences.

Piss off the leader of the free world?

Check.

Piss off your family?

Check.

How about random black people—*what are you doing with a white woman?*

Double check.

He saw Mary make a left onto the East-West Highway, and he flipped the turn signal up to follow her.

Do I just get my stuff and fly away like the song says? Or spend a last night together as a way of saying good-bye? Or maybe they would reconcile one last time.

Or—*oh, the hell with it.*

And what about your issues? The typical pattern in your relationships? Richard Whelan, the intense loner, national security adviser to the president, by all accounts brilliant, life expectancy of his girlfriends, six months, a year at the outside.

Good looking enough to be a ladies' man, at least that's what people said (Whelan couldn't see it when he looked in the mirror but he'd take it), six foot two, in good shape, dark skinned, the antiplayboy who somehow had a playboy reputation.

Or were the women attracted to his résumé? Ivy League, Marine Corps Reservist who served in the Gulf War . . .

Or maybe the attitude. Right on the smooth edge, baby, right in the hot seat.

"President Roswell brought me into this administration to cut through the crap and stop the intelligence failures that have plagued his first year in office. My definition of compassionate conservatism? Very simple. If you screw up I'll notify next of kin after I go upside your head with a baseball bat. From now on the rules have changed."

Christ, had he really said that all those months ago? Had he been that stupid?

Except that you were right, Whelan. You took the heat, too, most of it coming from the intelligence community, most of it because you were right and didn't bother covering your ass. Your gasoline-drenched hoped-like-hell-you-were-fireproof ass, and in dances Mary Jacobs asking if you have a match.

Mary Jacobs who was very white, very blond, very connected, and very much in love with one Richard Whelan.

Houston, we have . . . *Whelan flambé.*

And something more, something she'd said at the cocktail party earlier, something that was disturbing the orderly, slow destruction that usually occurred in his relationships, because Mary had a secret or secrets, something with a gravity all its own. She professed to love him, and he thought he loved her, but that dark *something* prevented any real discussion of, for example, marriage, even though there were plenty of reasons (read that as *her father*) why marriage was a difficult proposition at best.

Ahead of him, Mary made a left onto Montgomery. Her apartment building was on Wisconsin, a short drive from Rock Creek Park. Richard turned to follow her, poking along in the rain even though he was accustomed to driving much faster regardless of the weather.

But there was Mary, ahead of him, her asymmetrical taillights (one was broken and had red masking tape over the naked white bulb), driving that funky Volvo of hers as slow as possible because it was slippery, and let's ignore for a moment that her family had more money than the Catholic Church and could buy her any automotive toy she wanted.

She just wasn't into material things.

And that was one of the things he liked about her. *Dammit*. Like the way she'd grabbed his arm at the cocktail reception tonight and whispered in his ear about how she wanted to jump his bones right then and there, and could they maybe find a spot so she could hike her skirt?

Gotcha, Richard. The look on your face is priceless. For a badass, you're such a prude.

Or the thoughtful way she looked at him when he was making a complicated point about foreign policy. Marveling at and understanding his intellect at the same time—she'd told him he was the smartest man she'd ever met the first time they went out to dinner.

She stroked your ego and you fooled yourself into thinking that this time it'd be different. Yeah, it's different all right: *infinitely worse*. Because you can be justified in your anger, but what's the justification if you end up alone? That you were right? That you had issues?

That you took heavy damage to be with her?

A year of your life, man. Are you really ready to just let it go?

Two cars behind Richard Whelan's black Porsche the driver of an unmarked police car glanced at his watch and checked their location. He nodded to his partner, who pulled the red dome light from the glove compartment and flicked it on as the driver activated the halogen strobes hidden in the grill of the vehicle. They passed the Chevy between them, got right on Whelan's bumper, and hit the siren.

The driver nodded to himself as the Porsche obediently pulled to the curb; he slid the unmarked car right in behind him.

He checked his watch again.

"Call it in," he said to his partner, and then climbed out of the car.

Richard Whelan saw the red lights on the roof and the strobes in his rearview mirror. The rain intensified a bit as he pulled over, certain that he'd been obeying the speed limit and hadn't made any of his usual aggressive driving moves. Mary Jacobs had just turned onto Wisconsin, and he was reasonably sure that she hadn't seen the cop pull him over.

He hoped this was just a misunderstanding, because he didn't want Mary to think that he'd peeled away from her in anger. *You tiptoed into this relationship, you have to tiptoe out as well.* He rolled down his window, fishing in his hip pocket for his wallet and the requisite license, registration, and insurance card.

The driver waited until his partner made the radio call before stepping out and approaching the Porsche.

"Sir, please turn off the engine and step out of the vehicle with your license and registration," he called to Whelan. His partner stayed on the passenger side of the Porsche.

Aw, shit. When they want you to get out of the car they think you're some kind of drug dealer. Damn. He carefully got out of the car, keeping his hands visible at all times, his wallet in his right hand. He pushed the door shut with his hip.

"Is there a problem, Officer?" he said as politely as he could through gritted teeth. *Really not in the mood for bullshit right now*, he thought.

The plainclothes cop in front of him looked like a football linebacker, and his partner was even bigger. Both were white, which was a bad sign. He took in the dark hair and the mustache as the cop approached him, and he also saw that the man's service revolver was drawn, probably from a holster in the small of his back, and that the cop held the gun not quite pointed at him, but not completely pointed at the ground, either.

"Nice car, Midnight," the cop snorted derisively. "Out for a little joyriding?"

"No, sir, just following my girlfriend to her house." Whelan knew the drill. Be polite, show respect, even if it was only for the gun, and don't make any sudden moves that would turn into a shooting.

"You were following someone? In this neighborhood?"

He's dense. Not good.

"My girlfriend, Officer. She turned off just before you stopped me."

"Sure she did. You got a license and registration for this thing?"

"Yes, *sir*. In my wallet. I'll just take it out . . ." Richard Whelan moved to take his papers out of his wallet.

"Freeze, asshole!" Now the cop had the gun pointed at his face. "Rudy, pat him down."

The other cop came around the front of the Porsche. He patted Whelan down quickly and expertly.

"He's clean."

"Is there something I can help you with, Officers? Was I speeding or something?" *The next thing I ask is whether I'm under arrest; if not, they can go screw themselves.*

"Shut the fuck up, nigger. Gimme the wallet."

Whelan offered the wallet. But the cop grabbed his wrist and studied his watch.

"Well, looky here, Rudy. Son of a bitch is wearing a Rolex."

Rudy just whistled. "Drivin' a hot car, wearin' an expensive watch, huh. Think he's dirty?"

"I smell *something* on this jiggaboo motherfucker, that's for sure. Been drinkin', Midnight? Got any weed on you?"

Oh, screw this. "My name is Richard Whelan. I work for the president of the United States."

"Oh, yeah? The president needs a nigger like you? For what? To shine his shoes?"

Both cops laughed at that one.

"Look," Richard Whelan said, "I don't want any trouble." *And you don't want any part of me.*

Mustache looked at his partner. "Oh, he doesn't want any trouble, Rudy." Mustache came up to Whelan and got right in his face. "Well, pal, I think trouble just found you."

Mary Jacobs pulled up in front of her apartment complex, curious that Richard was no longer behind her. That was odd. She'd just checked in her mirror and seen the distinctive headlights of his ridiculously phallic sports car just a second ago, it seemed. She got out of the Volvo, locked it, and scanned the street.

Must've gotten caught in traffic, she thought. She took one last look and went into her building.

Whelan said nothing and stared calmly into the cop's eyes. *Two against one. Fair fight once I disarm one of them. . . .*

"Get on your knees, asshole."

Whelan hesitated. "Look, I've done nothing wrong. Why don't you just check my license and registration and I'll forget this ever happened." *Well, your Honor, I'm supposed to be this arrogant nigger, and I thought kicking the cop's butt was more consistent with the stereotype than "Have a nice day, motherfucker. . . ."*

The cop stepped back and shoved the barrel of his gun in Whelan's face. "I said on the ground, now!"

Before Whelan could react, the other cop had stepped in behind him and swept his legs out from under him, and Richard tumbled onto the ground.

Mustache kicked him in the side, and Richard groaned and rolled over onto his stomach.

IOU a deluxe double ass-kicking, Whelan thought through the stabbing pains.

One of them, Rudy, he thought, put plastic restraints on his wrists and tightened them. Mustache went to kick him again, but for some reason his partner stopped him with a look.

"Okay, Midnight. Let's have a look at the trunk." With that, the first cop leaned into the driver's side of the Porsche and pulled the hood release.

Mary Jacobs hesitated as she stood in front of her apartment door. *Is it really over?* She thought about the cocktail party—going had clearly been a bad move on her part because she'd known that one of her father's single business associates was going to be there, and the man wouldn't take no for an answer even though she'd been with Richard. She and Richard had been coming from different social engagements, hence the two cars. That had also probably been a mistake.

And then there was Bettina Freeman. Richard had had a brief fling with her before she'd met him, and he'd been honest about that when they discussed going. And she had to admit, they were a natural. Bettina Freeman, deputy undersecretary of state, an attractive bourgeois black woman with a lot of class. *Accent on black.* Richard Whelan, also attractive, and attracted to Ms. Freeman if she'd read the signs right. *That was always the question with them, always part of the dynamic.*

She shook her head. What had happened next was almost as predictable as the sun rising in the east.

She took out her keys and went into the apartment.

"It's clean."

"Yeah, Rudy, I can see that." The cops were standing in front of the Porsche, looking into the trunk space under the sloping hood. The Porsche's engine was in the back of the car, behind the driver, and the less than spacious trunk was under the hood.

"What do you want to do about him?" The one called Rudy jerked his head in Richard's direction.

"Let him go. Fuck it."

Whelan was angry and soaking wet, lying facedown on

the ground with the fine rain soaking his back. One of the cops, the one with the mustache, yanked on his wrist restraints and pulled him to his knees.

The cop named Rudy knelt behind him and cut the wrist restraints off.

"Sorry for the inconvenience, nigger," the cop in front of him smiled. Just then Whelan heard the radio in their patrol car squawk, and the cops exchanged a glance.

The pistol across his face, when it came, happened so fast that Whelan didn't have time to react, and the barrel of the gun scraped a thin ribbon of flesh from his cheek as he went down backward next to the left rear tire of his car. *That's a triple ass-kicking I owe you now, buddy.*

As soon as she opened the door she realized there was something wrong. The front hall light was out, and she could tell even in the dim ambient light that her apartment had been ransacked.

But the door had been locked, she thought as she fumbled in her purse for her cell phone to call the police.

So whoever came in had a key?

And then a gloved hand clamped over her mouth, and she realized that whoever it was had been waiting for her.

"Unit two, be advised we have a code fourteen, over?"

Mustache was about to kick Whelan in the ribs again when his partner pulled him away.

"That's enough. We got the call. Let's get the fuck outta here."

"C'mon, you saw the way he looked at me. Let me kick his ass a little more."

"Nick, you heard the radio. We gotta go."

Whelan was disoriented from the blows to his face and torso. Rain blurred his vision. He saw one of the cops, probably the one with the mustache, lean over him.

"You have a nice day, nigger," the cop whispered to him. "You lucked out this time."

And then the cop wheeled and went back to his car.

Whelan rolled to his left as he heard the car doors slam, but he didn't catch the license plate of the unmarked cruiser as it peeled rubber pulling away from the curb.

It was some minutes before he could hoist himself into his car. He'd checked carefully, nothing seemed broken, but those two cops were going to be in a world of hurt once he contacted his lawyer and the D.C. Metro Police. He'd call 911 when he got to Mary's house and then Chuck O'Shay, White House chief of staff.

You should have kicked that bastard's ass, he thought angrily.

Well, I'll get my day in court. The one called Rudy had called mustache Nick, and they were both big men. Shouldn't be too hard to find.

In two minutes he pulled in behind Mary's Volvo, ignoring her usual female parking job that nearly took up two scarce spaces on her street. He got out, locked the car, and let himself in with his front door key, finding it odd that the doorman was not around. As he got into the elevator he explored his cheek and chin gingerly with his hand and came away with fresh blood and cursed again.

He got off on Mary's floor and strode quickly to her front door. He rang the bell and waited impatiently.

No answer. She's probably in the shower, trying to avoid me.

He used his door key. Something heavy held the door back, and when he could get it open a crack, he saw that the hall light was out. He reached in and flicked the switch, leaving a bloody smear from his cheek on the pastel-colored wall, then pushed the door open against the resistance.

And stopped cold. Frozen with surprise, a certain kind of fear, a little frosty bastard with a chilly voice whispering in his ear. Whispering unwanted intuition as he looked at Mary Jacobs's lifeless body with her head lying at an impossible angle in the vestibule of her apartment, a little whisper of trouble, big trouble with a capital *T* in River City—

She may be dead, God help her, he thought, *but somehow, some way, this is going to end up being about you.*

2

A drop of his blood rolled down his cheek and onto the parquet floor as he stared at Mary's body.

He knelt down to feel her ankle for a pulse, the flesh still disturbingly warm, her heart silent in her chest.

Whelan stood up.

Pulled his cell phone from his pocket. Dialed 911.

"Nine-one-one Operator."

"I'd like to report a murder."

"Address?" *Happens every day*, he thought as he listened to the operator typing into her workstation.

"Twenty-seven ninety-five Wisconsin Avenue. Apartment forty-five."

"Are you at the scene now?"

"Yes."

"Is the assailant, or assailants, still in the vicinity?"

"Not that I can tell."

"Sir, your name?"

"Richard Whelan."

"And the deceased's name?"

"Mary Jacobs."

"Your relationship to the decedent?"

"I was . . . a friend."

"Sir, I have units with an ETA of ten minutes inbound.

Please wait for the police to arrive. I'm sure they will have questions."

"Thank you. Do you need my number?"

"No sir, your phone number shows up on my screen whenever I'm connected."

She rang off.

Within ten seconds, his phone rang again.

"Yes."

"Richard, this is Chuck O'Shay. We have a situation."

Chuck O'Shay was the president's chief of staff, and his words gave him pause.

"Where are you?"

"In the room. With the man." That would be the Situation Room, with the president. Neither of which O'Shay would say on an open phone line. "Members of the NSC are en route. I suggest you get here as quickly as possible."

Richard Whelan hesitated. Translation: Members of the National Security Council are on their way. Additional confirmation that something very serious had occurred.

And I should be there.

The 911 operator had requested that he stay put. Leaving the scene of a murder, could he possibly construe that as executive privilege?

"Did you hear me, Richard?"

"Yes, Chuck. I should be there within twenty minutes."

"See that you are. This one looks serious."

"Right. On my way."

He folded the phone and put it in his pocket. *This one looks serious.* In an environment where crisis was the norm, O'Shay's words were an ominous signal.

Should he report the assault by the two police officers as well? he wondered.

He looked down at Mary. *She's dead, Whelan. Nothing you can do for her now, except grieve. Harden your heart.*

Leave her.

He looked at his watch. He was supposed to be at the White House in nineteen minutes, and at this juncture, time could be of the essence.

With a force of will he turned away from Mary Jacobs's body, pulled the door to her apartment closed, but did not lock it, and hurried to the elevators.

When he reached the lobby he jogged out past the startled doorman without comment, crossed the street to his car, and drove off.

The doorman hadn't seen Richard Whelan come in because he'd gotten a phone call that someone suspicious was hanging around the dumpster in the back of the building. He'd gone to check it out but had found nothing, even though he'd spent several minutes prowling the alleyway.

But he knew Whelan, had seen him accompany Ms. Jacobs up to her place many times. And he did notice that Whelan appeared to have been in a scuffle, and that he peeled away from the curb as if he was in a terrific hurry.

And then the white police cars pulled up, and serious-looking Metro D.C. cops climbed out.

He crossed himself when he saw the van marked CORO-NER double-park on the street in front of the building.

It took Whelan seventeen minutes to reach the White House and park his car in the secure lot. This was one of the many times he was thankful that he hadn't gone for the government sedan and driver because he'd come close to bending the Porsche several times in his hair-raising ride from Mary's apartment. He was also thankful that he'd been able to avoid most of the Sunday traffic in Georgetown. He showed his ID and pass to the Federal Protective Services guy at the gate, who admitted him without comment.

At least, until he got a good look at Richard Whelan's face.

"Hey, Mr. Whelan! You cut yourself shaving?"

"What?" Richard hesitated. "Yeah, something like that."

"Here's a tissue. Better get that cut looked at, sir. It's a nasty one."

The guard handed him a tissue, and Richard dabbed at his cheek.

"Thanks." Whelan winced as his bruised ribs reacted to him reaching up to dab at his face.

"No problem," the guard said, watching as Whelan's face contorted with pain. He noticed the president's national security adviser touch his right side gingerly. Man looked like he'd been in a fight.

Whelan made his way into the interior of the White House.

Detective Bill Johnson unfolded himself from his black Chevrolet Caprice (affectionately called "bathtubs" by the hoods on the street because they were big and slow and easily outrun in a car chase) in front of 2795 Wisconsin Avenue. Johnson was a big man, easily six feet five inches tall, clean shaven, with short black hair and a stoop in his shoulders from perpetually shrinking his frame to move through crime scenes.

His partner, Bobby Steinway, was the shorter part of the Mutt and Jeff team. Steinway fairly bounded out of the other side of the car, a lit cigarette dangling from his lips. D.C. cops had the street cordoned off, and the coroner's people were already on-site. All he and Steinway had to do was work the crime scene before four hundred bodies trampled it.

Yeah. Right.

"We know anything about the vic?" he asked Steinway.

"Name, rank, and serial number, that's it. Died in her apartment. Once we get some particulars we can pull all the relevant data from wherever—motor vehicles, banking, credit cards . . ."

Johnson shook his head. "Look at this building. Doorman, locked front door, nice neighborhood. I doubt very seriously this woman got mugged. We need to look at who she knows and who was here."

One of the beat cops securing the scene approached them as they walked into the building. *All these boys want a detective's shield,* Johnson thought.

"Yeah, Officer . . . ," Johnson looked at the cop's name tag, "Donaldson, you got something?"

"Doorman says he saw the victim's boyfriend leave out of here in a hurry just before the cavalry pulled up. You might want to talk with him."

"Got it. Thanks, Donaldson."

He looked at Steinway. "You do the doorman. I'll do the crime scene. Then we switch, okay?"

"Got it."

A Marine Corps corporal snapped to attention, then held the door open to the Situation Room located under the Oval Office in the White House. Whelan had managed to stop the bleeding on his cheek and hated himself for having to shove Mary's murder from his mind. There would be hell to pay for leaving her apartment, that much he was certain of. But duty was calling.

He entered the Situation Room.

There was a hubbub of voices that immediately grew quiet when he walked in. Whelan took in the scene immediately—maps of Kashmir, the disputed territory between India and Pakistan, overlaid with the latest estimates of the disposition of each country's armed forces. That gave him both the *where* and the *who*. He surveyed the occupants of the room, gathering as much intel as he could about the situation based upon who was there.

The president looked grave and was whispering something to Charles O'Shay, who sat to his right. Mike Monroe, the DCI, or the director of the Central Intelligence Agency, was seated on the other side of the president. Next to him was Phillip Erskine, Monroe's number two at CIA.

Farther down the table were most of the Joint Chiefs of Staff for the armed forces, led by Steadman Dennis, an air force four star who was the group's chairman. At the other end of the table was Ron Dempsey, the secretary of state. And next to him, surprise, surprise, was Bettina Freeman, which was logical, because southern Asia was one of her areas of expertise. The secretary of defense was out of town, he recalled, otherwise he would have been in attendance as well.

On the front wall was a satellite photo. A man he didn't recognize had been talking when he came in. The briefer would presumably supply the *what*.

"Mr. President," Whelan said simply. He took a seat at the end of the table, next to Bettina Freeman, because it was the only one open.

The analyst in the front of the room had a laser pointer, and he cleared his throat in an effort to recapture everyone's attention.

"As I was saying . . . ," he began, but Richard Whelan raised a hand to stop him.

"Could someone please bring me up to speed?"

The gathered group looked at each other, no one wanting to deliver a synopsis to the president's national security adviser because of the justifiable fear of Whelan picking up something that the group hadn't noticed and being made to look foolish because of it.

Chuck O'Shay waded in.

"India exploded a nuclear device over a disputed section of Kashmir approximately two hours ago. They claim they caught a platoon of Pakistani soldiers making an illegal incursion into Indian territory. Pakistan is up in arms, naturally, and the Chinese and even, interestingly, the Russians have lodged protests over what they call India's latest act of aggression."

"Did you say a nuclear weapon, Chuck?"

O'Shay nodded. The analyst introduced himself, then picked up the theme from there.

"I'm Sam Hennings. Not just a nuclear weapon, Mr. Whelan. We think it was an enhanced radiation weapon, a.k.a. a neutron bomb." Hennings was about five-nine, slender, with thinning sandy hair.

"How recent are these images?" Whelan nodded at the screen in front.

"This is a still from one of the Keyholes covering the area. We pulled it down less than forty-five minutes ago for this briefing, just before the satellite passed out of range."

Mike Monroe cleared his throat. "Richard, we just started the briefing, so perhaps your questions will be answered if we let Sam here continue." He looked at Whelan expectantly.

There were a million questions on the tip of his tongue, but Richard held back. He nodded at Monroe.

Monroe nodded at Hennings.

"As we said, it appears that Indian forces detonated an enhanced radiation weapon over a column of Pakistani troops making an incursion into the disputed territory of Kashmir, approximately two hours ago. One of our special Keyhole satellites monitors the region because of the spate of nuclear testing both countries engaged in back in 1998. So we saw the flash, confirmed that it appeared to be a nuclear detonation, and the readings from the watcher indicate that it was an enhanced radiation weapon to boot."

He pointed at the image on the screen. "As you can see from this photo, the area irradiated by the blast does not exhibit the typical characteristics of ground zero of a conventional atomic or thermonuclear airburst. The fact that you can still distinguish vehicles and bodies at ground zero is indicative that it wasn't a conventional or tactical nuclear detonation."

He used the laser to circle clumps of bodies on the screen. One poor bastard was off by himself, near a troop carrier.

"As you can see from the casualties, these people died pretty much where they stood, presumably victims of a massive dose of gamma radiation. For those of you who are not aware of the difference in the technology, neutron weapons are designed to kill people without the residual blast effects of a conventional nuclear attack. And they are designed to kill quickly, within minutes or seconds of the detonation of the weapon. Depending upon the yield, you can expect one hundred percent fatalities within the effective range of the blast.

"The Pakistanis were caught in the open, by themselves, so it's difficult to tell from these photos what the effective kill radius of the weapon was, and therefore how big it was. And the Indians, so far, have played their cards close to their vests about how the weapon was deployed."

"What do we think?" Whelan asked.

"We think it was launched by an air breather. We detected no launches from India's nuclear-capable missile forces, and their state of readiness does not indicate that they were even in a position to launch such an attack." The term *air breather* denoted an aircraft.

"And we think that the Indians attacked this formation because it was making an incursion into Kashmir?"

"Correct. These troops were hit just inside the border of Kashmir, and their direction of travel clearly indicates that they came from Pakistan. Moreover, this was an organized military force of some size and strength, not a supply convoy of insurgents intending to arm freedom fighters in Kashmir, as has been Pakistan's cover story in the past for these kind of troop movements."

President Roswell: "So the Indians decided to catch them

with their pants down, is that the current thinking from Central Intelligence?"

Mike Monroe looked at Whelan, hesitant to commit himself to an assessment in the national security adviser's presence. "We think that explains why that particular type of weapon was used, Mr. President. They wanted us to see that it was a combat-ready force, that it was clearly in Kashmir, and that they were justified in their actions."

"Justified, Mr. Monroe?" This from Bettina Freeman, next to Whelan. "I'm not aware of any *justification* for the aggressive use of nuclear weapons. Are you?"

"No ma'am, I'm not. But I'm not the sonofabitch who pulled the trigger on this one. For those answers, you'd have to ask the Indian prime minister."

"But you do believe that this was about show-and-tell, Mr. Monroe?" Bettina insisted.

"I can't see any other reason why they would do this in this fashion, yes."

"Mighty large price to pay to make a point, wouldn't you agree, Mike?" This was Whelan, and everyone turned to look at him.

"Do you have another explanation, Rich?" Monroe said dryly. Everyone in the room knew there was no love lost between the DCI and the president's national security adviser.

"Not right now. But I don't need one to know that your dog don't hunt. What I think State is trying to say is that the Indians are going to incur a tremendous international outcry over this, and your show-and-tell theory doesn't provide nearly enough justification for this kind of action."

Everyone started speaking at once, but it was Richard Whelan who quieted the assembled group.

"Let's not jump to conclusions, everyone," he said with a pointed look at the DCI. "I think we need to know which troops were killed and what each side's response has been."

Sam Hennings broke in. "We've been rechecking our assessments of the disposition and combat readiness of India's and Pakistan's troops, focusing, obviously, on Pakistan's response. We should have some answers within hours."

"Then there's nothing else that we can do right now, is that correct?" Whelan said, ignoring the throbbing of his cheek and ribs.

"State thinks you should get both leaders on the phone ASAP, Mr. President, and try and initiate a diplomatic solution before they start lobbing bombs at each other."

"Already in process, Bettina," Chuck answered for the president.

"Then I suggest that we adjourn until we have new information, or at least some gauge of the reaction from the president's phone calls," Whelan said.

They all looked at him resentfully, the Johnny-come-lately who was calling the tune, but they all agreed.

Whelan stood a little too quickly and winced.

Bettina Freeman was right there with another tissue. "What the hell happened to you? Did that fight with your girlfriend get physical?" She dabbed at his cheek.

Whelan shook his head. "Much worse than that," was all he would say.

It had been easy for Detective Bill Johnson to determine which way to go once he got off the elevator on Mary Jacobs's floor. There was a uniformed officer at the doorway to her apartment and another trying to shoo the victim's neighbors back into their apartments. Johnson flashed his shield at the uniform and stepped over the threshold into the apartment.

He paused to take in the scene. The place looked like it had been hit by a tornado, but it wasn't the kind of damage that a thief does when he's looking for things to steal. No, Mary Jacobs's apartment looked like she'd had a knock down, drag out fight with whoever killed her. Johnson pulled on a pair of latex gloves and examined the locks on the front door.

There were no scratches on the locks, and no splintering of the wooden jamb of the doorway. The door certainly hadn't been forced, and if she was smart, Mary Jacobs probably wouldn't have entered an apartment with the door broken half off its hinges, anyway.

He took out a small notepad and jotted down his observations. He noted the blood on the light switch and wall, and the single drop of blood on the floor near the body. One look at Mary Jacobs made the cause of death reasonably clear—her neck had been violently broken. So the blood on the floor wasn't likely to be hers.

Which meant it could be the perp's.

He went through the two rooms of the apartment. Besides the living room near the entrance foyer, the rest of the apartment was undisturbed. There was a jewelry case in plain sight on her dresser, and Johnson lifted the lid with the cap end of his pen.

And whistled. Whoever Mary Jacobs was, she certainly had expensive taste in jewelry. And it looked like everything was there, because both trays of the case were full of expensive pieces.

He went back out to the foyer where the body was. He bent down to examine the victim's arms and ears.

Right wrist still had an expensive watch. Couldn't read the label because the watch face was too damn small, but he could see that it was encrusted with jewels that looked like diamonds.

And she had what looked like expensive gold earrings studded with tiny diamonds in her ears, as well.

"Anybody here find her purse?"

One of the uniforms inside the apartment spoke up. "I think I saw it near the living room sofa."

"Is that where it was when we got here?"

"Yup. We didn't touch anything except to have a quick look around."

Good, he thought, assuming he was telling the truth. He yelled to the photographer who was shooting pictures of the body, "Did you shoot the living room yet?" The police photographer nodded that she had. He didn't want to disturb anything that hadn't been catalogued and photographed.

He went over to the living room, noting that the lamp closest to him had been knocked over and the shade crushed. The pocketbook was on the coffee table in front of the couch, unopened. He also noticed that the stereo was on, but the sound was down.

He pinched the clasp of the pocketbook with a gloved hand and fished out a wallet with the tip of his pen.

Cash, credit cards, everything looked intact.

Certainly doesn't look like a robbery, he thought.

Richard Whelan occupied prime office space on the floor below the Oval Office in the White House. He walked quickly past his secretary's empty workstation into his office, sat down, and shut the door. Hard to believe it was a Sunday, and that in just a few hours his life had turned upside down.

There would be a million things to do and look at because of the international crisis, but he couldn't focus, couldn't get a grip on India and Pakistan, because he kept thinking about Mary. All through the meeting in the Situation Room he'd kept thinking about her and the way her body had been sprawled out in her apartment, her neck twisted at an obscene angle, her flesh cooling to his touch.

And he'd left the scene of a crime. The first thing he should do is call the police. Or maybe tell O'Shay what had happened. It would be far better if the president's right-hand man heard it from him and not from somewhere else, because Whelan had his share of enemies in the Roswell administration.

Yeah, O'Shay was the priest for this one. Whelan picked up his phone to request a confessional.

"Whatcha got?" Detective Bill Johnson was talking to his partner in the lobby of 2795 Wisconsin Avenue.

"Boyfriend. Name of Richard Whelan. Left out of here in a hurry right after nine-one-one got the call, apparently."

"Is this Whelan the one who called it in?"

"Not sure. We don't have the synopsis of the call yet from the ops center."

"Hmm. This info about Whelan came from the doorman?"

"Yup. Said he thought Whelan looked like he'd been in a fight or something. Guy drives a Porsche, and the doorman said he laid some rubber down getting out of here."

"That ties."

"Ties with what?"

"No forced entry, no sign of a burglar, apartment in some disarray. Looked like a fight, wallet, including cash and credit cards intact in the living room. Jewelry in the bedroom, expensive stuff, easy to fence, all intact it looked like. I make it that they were in the living room when it started, then it escalated into the hallway, and he snapped her neck. What's this Whelan look like?"

"Well built, about six-two. Worked out, according to the doorman, because when he stayed over here he liked to jog in the park." Steinway was smiling at him.

"And?"

"And Whelan is black, *bro*."

"So?"

"This Mary Jacobs is connected." Steinway rubbed his thumb and forefinger together. "Father's some kind of rich geezer. White girl, black guy who is suspect number one. Remind you of anything?"

"Don't go there, Bobby."

"C'mon, it's like the O.J. case all over again, except this time the vic has the dough. Tell me this Whelan guy hasn't got 'perp' written all over him. Probably has a history of domestic violence."

"O.J. was found not guilty by a jury of his peers. You say Mary Jacobs has family money?"

"A shitload, according to the doorman."

"Then who's Whelan? Stud of the month?"

Steinway shook his head. "Nope. Whelan works for the president of the You-Nighted States."

He saw Johnson's surprised look and added, "and I'm tellin' you, Bill, O.J. is guilty. Just like this guy."

"Thank you, Lance Ito."

Whelan was just finishing his phone call with a very unhappy Charles O'Shay when there was a knock at his door.

"Come."

Bettina Freeman was standing in the doorway. "Busy?"

"Sort of. I'm due in the Oval Office in five minutes." And how unpleasant a meeting would that be, he wondered.

Bettina stood in the door, blocking it as if she were afraid he'd run away. "I'm sorry about what happened at my cocktail party, Richard."

"Which part of it? You flirting with me, or the big blowup with my girlfriend?"

"Both. Well, less sorry about you fighting with your white girlfriend."

Whelan stood up. Yes, his *dead* white girlfriend. Whom he had to tell the president about in three minutes. Who would want him to get on the phone with Mary's father, who despised him, but was close to the president.

"No response?"

Whelan shook his head. He wanted to tell her, but couldn't find the words, even though he'd have to tell Edgar Roswell those very words in a few moments.

But Bettina was still blocking the doorway, and he caught her scent, the same scent that she'd been wearing at the cocktail party a few hours before. He was facing her, less than a foot between them, and he could see, what, longing? in her eyes, but now wasn't the time.

"Excuse me, Bettina. I have to go."

"Okay, but promise me you'll call me about the India-Pakistan thing, okay? I need to talk to someone outside of the gnomes at State."

"Fine. I'll call you later."

Whelan made his way up to the Oval Office, expecting and finding Chuck O'Shay and the president waiting. From the look on Edgar Roswell's face it was clear that O'Shay had already given POTUS a heads up.

"Richard," the president said in greeting as they sat down. POTUS, or President of the United States, was approximately five foot ten, with the looks of a retired news anchor and the deep voice of a skilled orator. O'Shay, on the other hand, looked like he could be a good toady, even though he was much sharper than people gave him credit for. O'Shay was five foot seven on tiptoes and favored tweeds and bow ties, thinking it made him look professorial. His dark hair was peppered with gray.

"Mr. President. I take it Chuck has filled you in on what happened."

"Briefly. But I wanted to hear it from you."

"I was following Mary Jacobs back from Bettina Freeman's cocktail party. I was stopped by two plainclothes police officers—"

"For what? Speeding?" the president asked; Richard's driving habits were well known by the administration.

Whelan shook his head. "No, sir. Mary drives, um, drove, a Volvo, and since I was following her, I was well under the speed limit."

"Then why were you stopped?"

Whelan shrugged. "I'm not sure." He debated telling the president that he'd been stopped simply because he was "driving while black" but decided against it.

"Anyway, Mary went ahead. I don't think she saw them stop me. I got to her place and she was . . . dead. Sprawled in the middle of the floor of her apartment. I called it in, then Chuck called me in for the meeting in the Situation Room."

"Wait a minute. That means you left the scene?"

"I didn't have a choice, sir. So yes, I left the scene."

O'Shay piped in next. "But these police officers, the ones that stopped you. Did you get any names? Badge numbers?"

"No. They were in street clothes in an unmarked car."

"License plate number, then?"

"I didn't notice it at the time, Chuck."

"The cops that stopped you, they might be keys to your alibi."

"I don't think so," he replied, thinking, *alibi?* "Mary must have been killed as soon as she entered her apartment, which would have been within minutes of me being stopped. They can't determine a time of death that precisely, so it's of absolutely no help in that regard."

President Roswell regarded him thoughtfully and reached over to get a cigar from his humidor. "Chuck here told me that there was a huge row at the cocktail party between you and Mary."

"There was."

"But you didn't kill her."

"Of course not." Temper, temper, Richard.

"Calm down, Richard. You realize that there's going to be hell to pay with Marty on this, don't you?"

"Mr. President, Mary Jacobs is *dead*. Whatever else happens, that's what's foremost in my mind right now." And he fixed Roswell with a stare.

"Of course. Richard, of course. I think you should call

Marty, though. And then I think you should get out of here. You look like hell."

"But the India thing—"

"Will keep for a few hours. Without you. Besides, I'm going to need you at full strength once we get something to evaluate. So I want you to make that phone call, then go home and get some rest." POTUS raised his hands against Richard's protest. "That's an order, son. Go. Chuck and I will hold the fort for a few hours. Okay?"

"Yes, sir."

Both he and O'Shay stood to leave. Richard shook Edgar Roswell's hand and then he and O'Shay turned to leave.

"Chuck?" the president said. "Could you stay behind for a minute? I want to talk to you about the phone calls to India and Pakistan."

"Sure, Mr. President. Richard, I'll catch up with you later."

Edgar Roswell watched his national security adviser depart and then turned to his chief of staff. The smile had vanished from his face.

"Chuck, what the hell is going on?"

O'Shay shrugged. "You know as much as I do, Mr. President."

"What I know is that he looks like he was in a street fight. And I don't want to think about the phone call I'm going to get from Marty Jacobs when he finds out that his daughter, who was dating my black national security adviser, is dead."

"I understand, sir."

Roswell ran a hand through his silver mane of hair. "And this dustup in India on top of everything."

"You could just suspend Whelan pending the outcome of the D.C. police's investigation."

Roswell looked at him. "Does that mean you think he did it?"

O'Shay shrugged. "It's not him I'm thinking about, sir.

It's you. And your administration. We can't afford to be distracted right now, because if we drop the ball, India and Pakistan could go all the way to an all-out nuclear exchange."

"That's what I'm worried about, too. The only problem is, the best defense against that happening just walked out of the Oval Office. Monroe and his boys may sniff about him, but, dammit, Whelan is the best pure intellect in this dump. And everyone knows it."

"So what are you going to do?"

"There are two problems, really. Whelan and Marty Jacobs."

"Okay," O'Shay said, not really understanding how Marty Jacobs could be a problem. "Two problems, then. What are you going to do?"

Roswell shrugged. "Did you see that look Whelan gave me when I mentioned Marty? I know that look, Chuck. It's spelled 'Loose Cannon.'

"So this is what I'm going to do. Contain them, Chuck. Contain them."

3

He was at the initial release point some sixty miles away from the target at Angels 35, or thirty-five thousand feet. The missile was spun up and ready for launch.

He keyed his mike.

"Strike Seven is at the IP, over."

"Strike Seven, you are confirmed as 'weapons hot.'"

"Say again, control."

"Strike Seven, you are confirmed for launch and immediate turn to heading one three zero."

Confirmed. He checked the missile once again; everything green.

He selected missile on his weapons options and toggled until he had selected the modified Lancet 3 under his right wing.

Best to get it over with. He pressed the control stud. His MiG-27 shuddered as the missile left the rails. He saw the plume of exhaust from the solid fuel engine as the missile separated from the fighter and turned straight up. The flight path programmed into the missile's computer would take it to eighty thousand feet before it turned down onto the target.

Singho keyed his mike. "Fox one, control. Missile away. Turning to course one three zero."

He turned the stick and rolled the fighter into a tight turn and headed for home. He could see the clouds rolling into the area from the mountains to the north.

Weather front, he thought.

Captain Amjad Singho of the Indian Air Force finished rereading this last section of his report. He was in his office adjacent to the pilot's lounge with the door closed. He wondered if any of the pilots in his squadron suspected the truth about his solo 'training mission.' He hoped not. He had a hard time dealing with it himself.

He sat back in his chair listening to the rain drumming on the roof. There would be no public damage assessment from the strike, but he'd been told that the missile had performed flawlessly. His identity was a carefully guarded secret; the flight controller as well as the ordnance specialists that had loaded the missile onto his fighter had been quietly transferred to another facility and were confined to their quarters.

He looked out the tiny window at the rain slashing across the runways. The weather had closed in an hour ago. He'd been well over one hundred miles away from the target when the weapon exploded, but he still harbored the irrational fear that he'd picked up some radiation from the detonation. He looked at his hands, held them steady over the desktop to see if he still had the shakes.

Muslim blood on his hands. He couldn't see it, but he could sense it, and it was never going away.

Duty Before Self, he thought, the code of the Indian Air Force.

WASHINGTON, D.C., THE SAME TIME

He was in the cockpit approaching Baghdad, flying low and slow to get Iraqi air defenses to paint him so that the stealth fighters could nail them. His A-10 was lightly loaded, with HARM antiradar missiles and the ubiquitous twenty-

millimeter chain gun in the nose. He was in the zone, thinking and reacting in six dimensions—altitude, attitude, airspeed, controls, weapons, threats. . . .

A threat tone growled in his ears, and he pushed the
throttles to full military power. Compared the flight plan in
his head, the intelligence estimates of where Saddam's guns
and SAMs were supposed to be to his current position.

The threat was early. Mobile battery—maybe more out
there . . .

Push the nose down out of reflex and without thought, get
some more airspeed, he thought, and he dove down toward
the city below.

And straight into antiaircraft fire. His plane bucked once,
then twice, then shuddered as something vital was hit, and
the controls became a little mushy. Still he continued down,
trying to get below the AA fire, so he could park a few missiles of his own in Saddam's backyard. Airspeed, altitude,
nose down attitude, performance envelopes of his missiles
versus the range and accuracy of the AA . . .

Another Iraqi air-defense radar came up, and he
punched off a missile, then made a sweeping left turn to get
the hell out of Dodge before the air force guys blasted the
targets that were so nicely lighting up the midnight skies
over the city with their emissions.

A bang, somewhere near the tail of the aircraft, warning
lights, hydraulics were going, and the controls seemed to go
limp for a second. He flattened out three hundred feet over
Baghdad, knowing that he was too low to afford losing control, and too low to eject.

You'll just have to bring it in, Whelan, he thought, but
then the cockpit began filling with smoke. Vectors home
falling short in his mind's eye. He pulled back gently on the
yoke to bring the nose up, hoping the turbofans were still
turning enough to get him some altitude.

I'm twenty-two years old, he thought, much too young to

buy it in the desert. C'mon, motherfucker, climb out, climb out, and suddenly he was clear of the city and turned back toward Allied lines, fifteen hundred feet high with a trail of black smoke that vanished into the night behind him. He needed fifteen minutes to get close to his guys, and far enough away from Saddam's Republican Guards, because he was too handsome to be beaten to a pulp by those assholes, no, no, no.

His seat began to get hot right about then, and the smoke made it impossible to breathe. Either you punch out or get barbecued, my brother, he thought, and he broke radio silence to tell the world that his airframe was in a world of hurt, and that he was going down. Blew the canopy, and the flames leaped up around him, hungry for the rush of oxygen, pulled the handle and blasted away from his doomed craft, the slipstream threatening to tear his face from his head as he lifted up, up, and away.

As the chute deployed and he raised his helmet visor, he realized that he'd never been so damn scared in his life, and never so alive as he sniffed the desert air and singed neoprene of his flight suit.

He woke with a start, the sheets damp with his sweat. A dream, just a dream, and then he looked at his nightstand and saw a picture of him and Mary Jacobs, and realized he'd wakened into a nightmare.

He checked his watch. Three o'clock, Monday morning. The Iraqi desert faded from his senses, and he felt the silver-dollar-shaped scar on his right thigh from when he'd been burned sitting in the cockpit of his doomed A-10.

He set the picture of him and Mary facedown on his nightstand and got up to make some coffee, the memory of his first night of Desert Shield reminding him of what the analyst, Sam Hennings, had said in the Situation Room hours earlier. Some poor bastard in an air breather, an aircraft, probably a MiG from what he recalled of India's air force, had launched a gleaming tube of death at an unsuspecting column of Pakistani troops. The first and only nuclear weapon launched in anger since Hiroshima and Nagasaki, and somebody had to look in the mirror and be responsible. He didn't envy the pilot, if what Hennings said was true, because even in the performance of his duty he'd disgraced the uniform of all the armed forces, everywhere.

And they'd used a neutron bomb, of all things. A genocide weapon.

Why? Why now?

Bill Johnson and Bobby Steinway had convinced a judge that they had enough to go after Richard Whelan. They had an eyewitness who placed him at the scene, they had no evidence of a break-in, and they had what they hoped was his blood on the wall and the floor of Mary Jacobs's apartment. Moreover, the detectives argued, because of his position he was a definite flight risk. They also had what they thought was a motive, gleaned from Mary Jacobs's answering machine. The judge listened, sitting in his living room in a bathrobe, agreed, and signed an arrest warrant.

"God help you if you're wrong," was all the judge said as he scribbled a signature.

They left the judge's home at 3:15 in the morning. Johnson was tired, having catalogued the evidence from the scene until he and his partner were convinced they had enough to go to a judge.

Johnson and Steinway climbed into their Chevy. "So, you think Whelan owns a Bronco?" Steinway asked, laughing.

"What, are you looking forward to a low-speed chase? I hope so, because with the way you drive, anything higher than low speed and I'm getting the hell out."

"Very funny. You just refuse to see the similarities, my friend. I was hoping you could tell me why the brothers have such a thing for blondes. And necks."

"Necks?"

"Nicole gets hers cut, Jacobs gets hers broken. Face it, Billy-boy, there's a racial and cultural pattern here that's bigger than the two of us."

"Steinway?"

"Yeah?"

"Just shut up."

Whelan sat on the bed for a moment before he put his shoes on to head into the White House. He debated calling O'Shay to see if anything else had happened, but thought better of it. He had to review the raw intelligence for himself to make sure he understood what India's strategy was and, he had to admit, to see if there was something that everyone else was missing.

He turned on the stereo—Lee Ritenour playing Wes Montgomery tunes. And for a few moments he allowed himself to think about Mary's death. He should have O'Shay coordinate with the White House counsel's office to march in for questioning before the police decided to drag him in on their own. That way he'd have an attorney on the government's dime, not his, just in case he needed it. Still, he couldn't shake the feeling that there was something more to Mary's death than met the eye. He would be under a cloud until it was cleared up.

Whelan, the president's arrogant national security adviser who had the audacity to date the most politically sensitive white woman he could find who was now dead.

And he still hadn't called Marty Jacobs. The longer you wait, Whelan, the worse it will be.

He also thought about Bettina Freeman. He had the feeling that she knew exactly what she was doing at her reception when she'd walked up to him and kissed him right in front of Mary, a nice full kiss on the lips that had lingered a beat too long. And he'd let it linger, too, because Mary had pissed him off with that friend of her father's.

Perhaps they'd both been guilty of dishing.

But that didn't explain who killed her and why.

The doorbell rang, and Whelan slipped his feet into a pair of loafers and went down to answer it, expecting it to be something messengered from the White House.

He was surprised at the two detectives and the uniformed cops behind them at his door.

"Richard Whelan," the tall black one intoned. The other one grabbed his shoulder and turned him around to apply handcuffs. "I'm Detective Bill Johnson of the D.C. Metro Homicide Division. You're under arrest for the murder of Mary Jacobs."

THE WHITE HOUSE RESIDENCE AT THE SAME TIME
Michael Monroe, director of the Central Intelligence Agency, folded his frame into a couch opposite the president in the sitting room just outside of the president's bedroom. Monroe was just under six feet tall, somewhat heavyset, with sandy blond hair and wearing a suit. He'd thickened at the waist in recent years, and his disdain for exercise had made it more difficult to keep the pounds off. As long as the suits still fit, though, he thought, he wasn't going to worry about it.

He didn't need to look at his watch to know that it was four in the morning. The president's summons had reached him at home in Bethesda less than an hour ago, and he'd hurriedly dressed to meet with his boss.

The president was wearing a jogging outfit. A steward left a coffee service on the table between them and quietly closed the door.

"It's four in the morning and you look like you're dressed

for a funeral, Mike," the president remarked dryly as he poured himself a cup of coffee.

"I plan to go into Langley after we finish and see what fresh intel we've turned up on India and Pakistan, Mr. President."

"Yeah. But I didn't call you out because of the international crisis, Mike."

"I didn't think so, Mr. President."

"Have you heard about the Whelan mess?"

"Meaning Mary Jacobs's murder? There have been a few whispers, Mr. President. It's impossible to keep a secret in this town."

He studied the president, who sipped coffee in silence. Something was bothering POTUS, and when something bothered him he called Mike Monroe. In his mid-sixties, President Edgar Roswell was in the second year of a difficult presidency. Roswell had risen from state politics to the Senate based upon his oratory skill, his savvy about how to appeal to big money donors, and the fortuitous failures of his rivals.

"What do you know about the Whelan thing?" the president said finally, looking at the thin folder Monroe had carried in with him.

Monroe opened the folder. "On short notice I called in a few favors, sir, got some information about it, and I have to say that it's a mess, Mr. President."

"Anything involving Marty Jacobs is a mess."

"I also had one of my best people do some snooping. As you know, Whelan and Jacobs had been going out for about a year. The relationship was rocky, in part because Marty Jacobs wasn't thrilled about it. Apparently Jacobs kept trying to fix his daughter up with men he felt were more . . . appropriate for her. Several people indicated that they had a huge row at Bettina Freeman's cocktail party yesterday evening because a friend of Marty's kept trying to hit on Ms. Jacobs."

"Your assessment?"

"I think Whelan will be arrested soon. She was killed in her apartment in a good neighborhood. Whelan was ID'd leaving the scene. Depending upon what forensics the D.C. police can turn up, they may have a very good case against him."

"Shit."

"It gets worse, sir."

"How could it possibly be any worse?"

Monroe paused to carefully consider his response.

"How far do you and Richard Whelan go back, Mr. President?"

"I've known him since he was a high school kid. He was a classmate of Skipper's."

"Right. Prep school, if I recall."

Edgar Roswell nodded. "And then Skipper was killed. Richard was very . . . kind."

"Kind enough to land his current job twenty years later?"

Roswell shrugged. "He has all the credentials. Harvard, Tufts, intelligence work, think tanks. Shot down in the Gulf War, where he was flying tank busters as a reservist, for God's sake. The personal connection only put him on my radar screen when Belton resigned. Nothing more. At the time, he was the perfect replacement."

Arna Belton had been the president's national security adviser but had resigned for health reasons within months of Roswell's inauguration.

"I need to know, Mr. President, because there's something even more disturbing about this."

"You keep saying that. What've you got?"

"Well, obviously, sleeping with the white daughter of a major defense contractor does not suggest top-shelf judgment. But we think there may have been something more unholy between them."

"Like what?"

"Whelan may have compromised national security."

Roswell sat up straighter. "With Mary Jacobs?"

Monroe closed the file. "It may have been inadvertent. It may have been simply a lack of judgment. But we have inklings that Mary Jacobs may have been in possession of classified materials directly linked to your national security adviser."

"Damn." Roswell slapped his thigh. "Why would she be interested in anything crossing Whelan's desk? Defense Department procurement stuff I could understand. But secrets?"

Monroe shrugged. "We're investigating, Mr. President."

"Investigating?"

Monroe pulled a memo from the file. "There are obviously limitations in our charter, Mr. President. This is more rightfully the purview of the FBI. We will need a presidential finding to pursue this in the interest of national security."

Roswell glanced at the memo, pulled a pen from his suit coat, and signed it.

"Keep the FBI out of this, Monroe. Christianson," the head of the Fibbies, "is a fucking Boy Scout who has forgotten which administration appointed him."

"Yes, sir."

The president looked at his DCI. "What about Marty Jacobs? He involved in this?"

"Doesn't appear to be. But who knows? By all accounts he's devastated over the loss of his daughter. So far."

Roswell looked again at the memo authorizing the CIA to violate its charter and investigate U.S. citizens on domestic soil. Monroe was smart; Roswell didn't want the FBI nosing around in Marty Jacobs's affairs. *Sleeping dogs and Boy Scouts don't mix.* He'd nearly pulled the trigger on both the attorney general and her lap dog, Christianson, over the preposterous notion that they revive the independent prosecutor statutes to look at his campaign financing. If the FBI started nosing around Marty . . .

"Fine. Keep Marty out of this. Keep him clear. More than the presidential finding, I want you, Mike, to personally make sure that Marty Jacobs stays clear of any of the dirt. Understand?"

"Yessir, Mr. President."

D.C. METRO HOMICIDE DIVISION

They led Richard Whelan into an interrogation room and sat him down.

"Coffee?" The white detective was short, perhaps five foot nine, and skinny as a rail, with telltale yellow nicotine stains in the creases between his fingers. "Name's Bobby Steinway." He shook Richard's hand.

"Coffee works," Richard said. Steinway nodded and left the room.

The other detective, the big black guy, easily six foot five and close to two sixty, was reading from a file. As Steinway left he looked at Richard, then resumed his reading for a moment.

When he spoke, he had a deep gravelly voice: "Brother," he said looking down at the file, "you're in a whole lot of trouble."

"No, I'm not."

"Oh, a tough guy, huh?"

Whelan shrugged. "I probably need to have an attorney present, Officer—"

"Detective. Johnson. Bill Johnson."

"Maybe the White House counsel can convince you this is all a mistake."

"Am I supposed to be impressed? Well, I'm not. We know who you are, Whelan. And before you get on your high horse, let me say this. We have you at the scene at or around the time of death, we've got motive, and you, quite frankly, look like you've been in a scuffle, presumably with the deceased. Maybe you can cop a plea to manslaughter if the White House counsel can argue that it wasn't premeditated. But not even God is going to get you out of this one."

"Maybe not God, Detective. But a couple of D.C. cops can explain my injuries."

Bobby Steinway had just returned and set a cup of coffee in front of Whelan.

"What's this about D.C. cops?"

"The suspect was just about to enlighten us, Bobby."

They both looked at Whelan.

"I was following Mary Jacobs home and I was stopped by two undercover cops in an unmarked car." He looked at Steinway. "Two white cops."

"Yeah, so what?"

"I drive a Porsche. I was well under the speed limit. In a nice neighborhood."

Steinway snorted. "You mean you were 'profiled'?"

Whelan nodded. "Complete with racial slurs and an illegal search of my car."

"In Washington, D.C.? You claim that you were 'profiled'? C'mon, Whelan, that bullshit's so thin it's nothin' but a fart."

"You keep radio logs, right?"

Johnson replied: "Yup."

"Then check your records. Two white cops, Rudy and Nick, stopped me at eight o'clock yesterday evening, give or take a few minutes, in the vicinity of Rock Creek Park."

Johnson looked at Steinway. "Go check it out, Bobby."

"Will do."

"And then I want to speak to my attorney."

Marcus Blaze took an hour to get to the station house where Whelan was being held.

Marcus had made a name for himself as a criminal defense lawyer in the D.C. area by defending a homeless subway pushing suspect by claiming that it was society's fault that this particular man had ended up on that particular subway platform to push that particular white woman to her death. During the criminal trial, he'd announced the filing of a multi-million-dollar civil suit against the Washington, D.C., Division of AIDS Services on behalf of both his client and the deceased, on the grounds that the policies of that organization had illegally denied his client necessary access to housing and services and medical care for his psychosis and HIV infection, and that had he been housed and on his meds he would never have pushed the deceased into the path of a subway train.

He'd nearly been disbarred for his grandstanding. His client lost the criminal case and was in jail, but the city had quietly settled the civil suit, and Marcus's take had made him a modestly wealthy man. His oft-quoted comment about the turn of events—"Shit, if I can bat five hundred I can play in the majors"—had not endeared him to the D.C. legal establishment, but he had a booming practice.

Blaze also knew how to enter a room. Dark blue suit, sky blue shirt, and a monochromatic tie to match. He looked angry as he swept into the interrogation room.

Detective Johnson started to protest, but Marcus waved him off. "I need to confer with my client. Get the fuck out." And just looked at Johnson as if to say *you don't want any part of this*. Johnson knew Marcus Blaze by his reputation and his distinctive television commercials—"Marcus Blaze is on FIRE for YOU!"—and wisely decided he didn't need the gratuitous aggravation.

Attorney and client shared a slight smile at the response as they watched Johnson leave.

Their smiles vanished at the same time as the door closed.

"Why the hell did you call me at four o'clock in the morning? Don't you have some white-shoe Ivy League sons of bitches to do this?" Marcus said.

"I figured this was more up your alley, *bro*."

Blaze looked at him sharply but said nothing for a moment. "You mean a homicide is more my thing, is that it? Be even better for me if a drug dealer was involved?"

"Well if the shoe fits—"

"Don't," Blaze exploded, "don't even go there. I'm not the one in jail, bitch."

"Yeah, but you know the turf, don't you, Marcus?"

"Well you sure as shit don't. The high and mighty Whelan in the slam. Picture that."

"Stop screwing around, Marcus. I need to get out of here, and I need to get out PD-fucking-Q."

"So you need me, is that it?"

"I don't need shit. If you can't or won't, the phone book's full of shysters."

"Oh, so I'm a shyster, huh?"

Whelan turned away. "I thought that kinder than 'low-rent Johnny Cochran.'"

"Aw, shit, now you talkin' trash. I should just kick your whiter than white ass right now."

Whelan smiled. "I'm sure you would. If you could."

"You were lucky that time," Marcus said defensively.

"And the time before that. And, if I recall correctly, the time before that, too."

"Yeah, well that Kung Fu–Ju Jitsu crap isn't fighting; this ain't *The Karate Kid* and you ain't Ralph Macchio. And you didn't answer my question, *bro*. Why call me?"

"Because this setup stinks. I get stopped by some stupid cops and my girlfriend turns up dead. If this is going to be a street fight, I need a street fighter."

The two of them looked at each other warily.

"If you weren't family, I'd let your ass rot."

"You're just jealous because Mom loved me better."

"You want me to walk out, don't you?"

"No, dammit, I want what's between us to get *behind* us.

I'll admit that I haven't been much of a brother. . . ."

"Half brother. If you're going to kiss my ass, you'd best get it right."

Whelan sighed. "Fine. Half brother. But I'm still family."

Blaze shook his head. "Funny how the family gets religion when the boogie motherfuckers get in trouble. Funny how you want me to put years of your bullshit off to the side like it's nothing because you need something."

"Marcus, I work for the president of the United States."

"Yeah, the great Richard Whelan. Went to the finest schools, had the finest career up there in the Ivory Tower with the white folks. Got so white you had to dip one of 'em, and I hate to say I told you so, but I tried to tell you that they weren't going to let a brother get all the way into their drawers."

"As if I didn't know I was playing with fire. Gimme some credit, Marcus."

"No, no, no, Rich. Give *me* some credit. You called me because you need me for once. Let's forget about all the times I needed you and you were like, Marcus-motherfucking-who, okay?"

"Fine, Marcus. Let's just call a truce for now."

Marcus sat on the edge of a chair. "Because, and I wanna hear you say it, bro, because you need me."

Richard Whelan sighed. "Okay. Because I need you."

"See? Wasn't so hard. Now let's just hear what the cops say, and for once, let the street fighter work the game, 'kay Harvard?"

Richard nodded.

"Lemme go get Big Foot and bring him back in."

Marcus turned back toward Richard as he started to the door.

"And just remember something. I'm still about six seconds away from kickin' your lousy ass, 'family' or not, okay? So fuck the cozy shit and let's get the light work over with."

Johnson and Steinway came back into the interrogation room. "My client has agreed to listen to what you have to say. And, if you two are good little boys, he may even answer some questions," Marcus Blaze said as he looked them over. Then he waved his hand dismissively. "Proceed."

Johnson turned to Whelan. "First, consider yourself Mirandized, okay?" He looked at Blaze. "I don't want any legal bullshit coming down about this."

"Fine," Blaze said, studying his nails like he didn't care. Richard was concerned that Marcus might throw this one to teach him a lesson, but he didn't say anything.

"We took a quick look at the victim's apartment and we found a hidden storage area."

"So? What's your question?"

Bill Johnson retrieved something from the file and handed it to him.

"We found this sheet of paper at the scene, like it had been left there by mistake. This your work?" he asked.

Richard looked at the document in front of him. It said

CHINESE NUCLEAR ESPIONAGE AGAINST U.S. WEAPONS
LABORATORIES: A SUMMARY OF PUBLIC AND CLASSIFIED
DAMAGE ASSESSMENTS

By
RICHARD WHELAN
National Security Adviser to the President of the United States

It was stamped TOP SECRET.

Richard, stunned, looked at it. It was only the cover page, but that was more than enough to piss him off.

"This is mine, but since there's nothing attached, it's meaningless."

Bill Johnson smiled. "Nice try, Rich. Meaningless? Even

your lawyer would say that the theft of top-secret documents could play into motive." Johnson looked Blaze in the eye and dared him to say something.

"Then I'd say this is a plant and I'm being set up."

"By who? Why?"

"I don't know."

Johnson and Steinway exchanged a glance. Steinway opened a little notepad and consulted his notes.

"There was a message on Ms. Jacobs's answering machine. From an Alan Someone, last name unknown. Do you know if she was seeing someone named Alan?"

A second jolt, although this one left Richard indignant. "Mary and I were dating. She wasn't seeing anyone else."

"I'm afraid the message left a pretty graphic impression that she was seeing this Alan guy, that they were, well, involved."

"Bull." Richard's voice had turned cold.

"And you were not aware of it?" Steinway was looking at him. Johnson said nothing.

"She wasn't seeing anyone but me, okay? I know that for a fact."

"I hate to break it to you, Richard, but if she was, it suggests a decent motive on your part, you being the jealous suitor and all."

"I wasn't jealous." Richard said a little too loudly.

Johnson spoke next. "Then there's the little scene that occurred at the cocktail party just before Ms. Jacobs was killed. Care to tell us about it?"

"We had an argument. That was it."

"Caused by?"

"We had an argument. That's all."

"We talked to several people who were there, Richard. They said it appeared that Ms. Jacobs was flirting with someone at the party."

"I didn't think she was flirting."

"But this someone was a friend of her father's, correct?"

"I guess."

"Who happened to be white. And wealthy," Steinway said.

Blaze, indignantly: "You're white, too, pal, and we ain't holding that against you, are we?"

Steinway ignored Blaze. "Was this guy at the party named Alan?"

"No."

"So your girlfriend flirts with this guy at a party. She has a message from some other guy on her answering machine. Do you get the impression that Mary wanted to play the field a little bit?"

"Not at all."

Johnson: "And how did your argument at the reception conclude?"

"What do you mean?"

"We talked to someone who overheard her say, 'It's over, Richard, just follow me back to my place and get your stuff.' Did Ms. Jacobs say that to you?"

"We'd had a fight. Emotions were running high."

"High enough for you to snap her neck, Mr. Whelan?"

"You're out of line, Detective," Blaze said. "Rich, don't even dignify that with an answer."

Johnson sat back. "Okay. Let's go over your supposed traffic stop again. Tell us exactly what happened."

Richard Whelan repeated the story about the two white cops, Nick and Rudy, who'd assaulted him and then let him go.

"And you're sure you heard the radio mention something about a 'code fourteen'?"

"Yeah. Then they drove away."

Steinway and Johnson exchanged a glance. Blaze couldn't resist jumping in and needling them.

"So what's a code fourteen? Dunkin' Donuts is having a sale, all units respond?"

Steinway looked at Whelan. "There's no such thing as a code fourteen."

"Well that's what I heard. Have you pulled the tapes of radio traffic from last night?"

"That will take some time, but quite frankly, Mr. Whelan, we don't need to."

"Why the hell is that?" Marcus asked.

"Because the duty logs don't show any Rudy and Nick in an unmarked car in that part of town. D.C. Metro doesn't even put unmarked cars on traffic patrol. We strictly do marked cruisers with uniformed officers."

"Maybe they were undercover narcotics detectives. They seemed to think I had drugs in the car."

Steinway shook his head. "In an unmarked car? With strobes in the grill? Whelan, when we send people under cover, they go under cover. The homies would spot two big white guys in an unmarked car a mile away in this town."

"But these guys were cops."

Johnson: "No they weren't, Whelan. Duty rosters are posted electronically these days, and we had someone search the records. No white D.C. police officers with first names Nick and Rudy worked under cover together last night. It didn't happen."

Richard Whelan was taken to a courtroom to be arraigned at 9:00 A.M. He sat chained with several other miscreants from the city lockup while the cases before him were dealt with. Judge Harold Timmons was adjudicating his case, he saw from the nameplate on the judge's raised bench.

The bailiff called the case: "People versus Richard Whelan, aggravated assault, murder in the first degree."

Richard was brought forward.

"How do you plead?" Judge Timmons asked, looking at something laid out in front of him.

"Your Honor!" Marcus Blaze jumped up. "My client is

being held on purely circumstantial evidence. There are no eyewitnesses that place him with the defendant at the time of her death, and the police refuse to research evidence that is critical to my client's defense. I hereby make a motion for dismissal."

Timmons looked over the top of his bifocals at the prosecutor. "Has the state established a case against Mr. Whelan, counselor?"

The assistant D.A., Jerome Henry, was brand new, and still wet behind the ears. He fumbled for a moment with his papers wondering, *Who could ever keep up with all this crap?*

"Yes, Your Honor, uh, the defendant was placed at the scene by a call to police emergency. He stated during the nine-one-one call that he was in the victim's apartment. Standard operating procedure is for nine-one-one to request the caller to remain at the scene until the police arrive if there is no imminent danger, but the defendant was seen fleeing the scene shortly after placing the nine-one-one call. That, plus the physical evidence that the defendant had been in an altercation at that time constitutes probable cause; we also have other circumstantial evidence that implicates the defendant."

"Do you have the report from the arresting officer?"

"Uh, no, Your Honor. I just got this file about five minutes ago. What I have is a written synopsis from the detectives on the case with a formal arrest report to follow."

"Then how am I to rule on the defendant's motion to dismiss?" Timmons asked.

The judge looked at the P.D. and at Assistant D.A. Henry.

The bailiff handed the judge a note. The judge looked at the note, then looked at Richard. Then he looked at the note again.

Then he looked at Marcus Blaze. *Something just went down*, Blaze thought. *Something important.*

"Motion to dismiss denied," the judge said. Then he continued: "Given the severity and heinous nature of the crime, I'm ordering bail set at one million dollars, and the defendant is remanded to custody until trial. Bail is subject to reconsideration pending the development of additional evidence by the prosecutor's office." He banged his gavel. "Bailiff, call the next case."

Richard, stunned, was hustled out of the courtroom without getting a chance to say a word. Marcus hurried after him.

"Officer," he said to the cop escorting the prisoners to a waiting van, "can I have a word with my client?"

The cop looked at him sourly. "I got six prisoners here. And a schedule."

"Won't take but a minute," Marcus beamed a forty-thousand-watt smile at the cop, who shrugged.

"Make it quick."

Marcus pulled Whelan as far away from the other prisoners as he could.

"Looks like you could be the poster child for the 'Having a Bad Day' club. But don't sweat it."

"Did you call the White House and tell them what happened?"

"Better. I called Bettina. She talks the lingo and said she would get a message to this O'Shay character."

"Don't get her involved in this!" Whelan hissed.

Marcus, angry, thought, *When it comes to you, Rich, she's about up to her pretty ass in involvement.* "Look, let your friends help you out for once, okay?"

"I need to make bail in a hurry."

"I'm on it, Harvard. If I say I'm on it, I'm on it."

"My tax attorney has all my financial records. It'll be a stretch, but I can come up with the money."

Marcus stepped back. "Damn, government sure pays better than it used to when my pop worked for the post office."

"I didn't always work for the government, Marcus, and I've made some decent investments."

"Be that as it may, Rich, putting up ten percent of the bond in cash or assets will spring you. And let me worry about that, because if I move some stuff around it might be quicker."

"Okay. And Marcus, I know it looks bad, but I didn't—"

Marcus shook his head. "Look, Mr. Goody Two-shoes, I know you didn't do it. And something funky just happened with the judge. Did you notice the note the bailiff passed him?"

"Yeah. So?"

But the cop was looking at his watch. "Guys, we need to get back to the station house. I'm sorry, but you have to wrap it up."

"Something in that note made him take a hard line. I didn't even get to give my 'upstanding member of the community' speech. So you hang tight."

"Ready?" the cop asked. Blaze nodded.

Richard held out his hand and Marcus looked at it for a second.

They shook hands slowly, a new sensation for both of them, and Whelan was led off to a waiting police van.

Richard was thinking about Marcus as they led him back to his holding cell. His mother's son by a failed first marriage, Whelan hadn't even known about his half brother's existence growing up because his father, a strictly upright physician, had expressly forbidden contact between his wife's new family and the old.

It wasn't until college that he'd discovered he had an older brother that he'd never known, and Marcus came on like a street thug. It was a huge embarrassment when he just showed up at his Harvard dorm with a six-pack of beer and a couple of reefers.

"Moms told me where to find you," Marcus had said sim-

ply as the white boys in his quad had looked at the shades
and chains in disbelief.

"You must be . . . Marcus?" Whelan had said. The letter
had come a week ago, and Whelan hadn't believed it ini-
tially, although he could believe that his father would keep
his mother's past a secret.

And he'd expected someone more like . . . him. A preppie
college boy with a suntan and rhythm, someone who knew
the white world and the black world.

"Wassamatter, you ain't down?" Marcus had challenged
him.

"Hey, Rich," Knox, one of the guys on the floor had
asked, "everything okay? This guy hassling you?"

Marcus had pulled down the shades to get a close look at
the skinny white kid who was offering to protect his half
brother.

And did a double take. "You buggin,' right?"

"Excuse me?"

"Say, Rich," Marcus said in his best Poindexter voice,
"this fellow bothering you? Shall we have the rugby team
pummel him?" Marcus turned to Knox. "Get outta here,
punk, I'm talking to him, not you."

Knox looked at Whelan, a question on his face.

"It's okay, Knox."

His white classmate shrugged and moved away.

"So can we go someplace and fire up the weed, bro?"

"Uh, not a good idea."

"Don't tell me you Ivy League boys don't get high."

Whelan shrugged. He'd learned in high school that afflu-
ence and drugs were the yin and yang of upper-middle-class
white existence. "Nobody here is gonna be shocked by the
smell of reefer. But I don't smoke."

"Cool." Marcus handed him a beer. "You get busy with
the brews, and I'll light up."

* * *

"So you're at Northeastern."

"Junior year."

They were sitting in Richard's dorm room with the windows open to let the smell of marijuana smoke out. Richard had kicked his white roommate out with a look and a subtle shake of his head.

"I gotta tell you, Marcus, I . . . well, I was kinda surprised at my mom's letter."

"She's my mother, too, Rich. Unless that accidentally on purpose slipped your mind."

"Hey, no beef, okay." Richard shrugged and put his hands up in a defensive gesture. "But why come here? Why now?"

Marcus looked at him like he was nuts. "You're family."

"Not for the first nineteen years or so of your life."

"When Mom told me you were up here, y'know, it was like, oh, shit, I have family for once in my life. My pops is dead, and I don't get to see Mom too often, so I'm on my own."

Marcus took a deep drag of the reefer. "Family, man. You probably take it for granted, but to me . . . shit, this is like something I've been looking forward to my whole life. So when Mom told me you were right across the river—"

"You decided to stop by. With a six-pack and a couple of joints."

"Well damn, man, I didn't fuckin' know you was up here in Whiteyville and don't git high and don't drink, from the pussy sips you've taken from that malt liquor. I thought, hey, family gonna be like me."

So did I, Whelan had thought.

". . . and them Radcliffe bitches? Oh, niggah, please."

They both laughed at that one.

"Oh, wait Harvard, I know the fuckin' temple for you boys is Wellesley. Y'all got cars, can get out there with your little Crimson windbreakers and them bitches probably fall all over themselves."

Marcus seemed to be into impressions, and he hiked his voice up an octave. "Oh, that Richie is a nice boy. His father's a doctor. And if you look at him, Betty Sue, I'll scratch your eyes out."

And Marcus batted his eyes at him.

Richard, laughing almost in spite of himself: "Northeastern has some talent too, bro. Can't deny that. Big-assed school like that, she-e-it."

"Oh, we got some 'back' over there. No question. But, y'know, since we . . . gettin' acquainted, I wanna suggest a little 'xchange program. Check it out. I'll introduce you to some cute little numbers on my campus, and you show me some of them long-hair high-titty chicks you be banging."

And just like that, just as they were starting to relax with each other, something in Richard's look, or his hesitation, something that played right into the big chip on Marcus's shoulder, something about turning the hip street brother loose on the women he had crushes on but hadn't even had the courage to ask out yet . . .

And Marcus was smart and perceptive, because it was only a second of a young man's insecurities and the laughter caught in Marcus's throat.

Just like that.

His jailers were kind enough to let him listen to an all-news radio station while he sat in a holding cell. The Chinese ambassador to the United Nations was to deliver a speech to the General Assembly, and the commentators were sure that the topic was India and the extraordinary events of the past twenty-four hours.

Richard settled in to wait and listen, hoping Marcus could get him out of the pokey, his thoughts swirling around what the police had told him.

Why would Mary have a copy of the cover page to a white paper he'd done on the Chinese? That was question number one. Question number two was if the police hadn't stopped him Sunday night, who had? He didn't take Johnson and Steinway to be the types that would deliberately cover something like that up, particularly with Marcus on the case—Blaze would subpoena their dirty underwear if he thought it would reveal something.

No, too many things didn't add up. Mary hadn't been robbed, and there had been a space of only minutes between when he'd been stopped and when he'd gotten to her apartment. Minutes in which a killer had gained entrance to her place and killed her, presumably as she walked in the door.

And then there was his egocentric suspicion that this was about him, not her. A snippet of conversation came back to him:

"Maybe we don't know each other as well as we should."

"It takes time."

"Yeah, but what if there are things about you that I wouldn't like if I knew about them? What if there are things about me that you wouldn't like if you knew about me? I mean really knew?"

Like she was dating other people? And who the hell was "Alan," anyway? Not to mention the guy at the party. Mary had had to physically break away from him, actually take the beefy arm he'd had draped around her shoulder and walk away.

At least, that's what she'd done when he was watching.

And what about when you weren't?

Still, he hated coincidence. If he hadn't been stopped, he would have been with Mary when she entered her apartment. And she would still be alive, most likely, unless the person or persons waiting for her had a gun. And even then . . .

If he hadn't been stopped. By two cops who weren't cops

at all, but who got a coded radio message while they were kicking my ass.

Coincidence? Whelan shook his head. They roughed me up so it would look like Mary and I had a physical fight. After we'd had a heated argument at a function.

But if it wasn't coincidence, then could someone have pulled all of that together in the time it took for Mary and I to have the argument and leave Bettina's party? Isn't that a little absurd?

On the radio, the Chinese ambassador began his speech. He could hear the singsong Chinese in the background while the network broadcast a simultaneous translation.

"The People's Republic," the translator intoned, "is prepared to bring all of its military might to bear to repulse Indian aggression at our border and at the request of Pakistan, who we promise will not feel the boot heel of Hindu repression. . . ."

Whelan glanced at his watch. It was just before noon.

Judge Harold Timmons was in his chambers eating lunch and catching up on some reading. The newspapers were full of the Indian-Pakistan crisis, each one with a more garish headline than the other. Timmons thought most Americans didn't give a damn about someplace so far away, but headlines sell newspapers.

His clerk knocked on the door. "Come on in, Steven."

"I heard you had some excitement this morning, Judge."

Timmons shrugged. "How do you mean?"

"That guy, Richard Whelan, who was arraigned this morning? He's the president's national security adviser."

"Really? Wait, *that* Richard Whelan?"

"Yeah, juicy stuff, huh? I bet there'll be a big splash in the papers tomorrow about the case."

"Hmm. The president's national security adviser?"

"Yeah. Why?"

Timmons held up the paper. "Whelan picked a bad time to be accused of murder."

Steven scanned the headlines. "You know, I heard that on the radio, but I didn't think to make the connection. From what I've read, Whelan is pretty well regarded in the Roswell administration. Guy has an amazing background."

Isn't that interesting. Timmons began thinking about the note the bailiff had handed him in the courtroom. "Well, I would like to finish my lunch and get back out on the bench at a reasonable time. If you'll excuse me, Steven?"

"Sure, Judge. If you need anything, let me know."

As he heard Steven walk away, Judge Timmons went to his closet where his robes were hanging. He felt around the pocket of the set that he'd been wearing this morning and pulled out a crumpled piece of paper. He'd learned long ago that the machinations at the federal level were simply none of his business; you played ball and looked the other way if you knew what was good for you.

He smoothed out the piece of paper in his hand. It was the note that the bailiff had given him when Whelan's case came up. He looked at it again.

The Feds want him detained.

And then he crumpled it and threw it in the wastebasket.

4

At 2:00 P.M., Detective Johnson opened the door to his cell. Richard could see Marcus Blaze following close behind.

"You made bail, Whelan," was all Johnson would say.

"Hey, Marcus, thanks a lot."

Marcus wasn't smiling. "Wasn't me. You didn't even give me time to get in touch with your tax guy."

"Which means it must've been the White House."

"Really?" Blaze asked, brightening. Then he looked up at Johnson. "Yeah, uh-huh! Well! I guess if the Prez-E-Dent thinks my client is innocent, I believe that's a big 'Fuck You' to those of you who are keeping score." Blaze pulled a crisp hundred-dollar bill out of his pocket, reached up, and tucked it in the breast pocket of Detective Johnson's jacket.

"Just a little somethin' for your troubles, Lurch. Kindly bring my client's bags around front, 'cause we be checkin' out."

"What did you just call me?"

"Oh, I forgot to use your given name, Detective, what was it, Johnson?" Blaze theatrically motioned to the cell door. "After you, my good man."

Johnson took the hundred-dollar bill out of his jacket pocket, crumpled it, and threw it on the floor as he led the way out of the cell. Blaze bent over and scooped up the bill, whispering to Whelan as he passed, "Sasquatch-lookin' motherfucker."

If Johnson heard him, he gave no sign.

THE WHITE HOUSE

After he returned to his office, Whelan decided to bury himself in his work for a few hours. He began by reading the thick packet of intelligence data gathered about India's transgression in Kashmir.

Kashmir had been disputed territory between India and Pakistan since the separation of the countries from British rule in 1947. It was some of the most desirable land in the area, and it had a healthy Muslim population. Its first "ruler" had cast his lot with India, hence India had the "legitimate" claim to the area as its own.

But two wars had not quenched Pakistan's thirst for troublemaking. The last time there had been a major dustup had been in the late 1990s with heavy fighting between Indian troops and what Pakistan claimed were "freedom fighters" being supported by Pakistan's supplies. That conflict, thank goodness, had not gone nuclear, even though both India and Pakistan were nuclear capable. In addition, Pakistan had profited from China's help in the nuclear arena.

He meticulously went back through the satellite photos. CIA apparently had a Keyhole tasked to keep an eye on the region; the analyst, Sam Hennings, had said as much. The first sets of photos were commercial satellite shots of the Pakistan border—these showed the Paki convoy heading out of Pakistan into Kashmir. Whelan noted that the force estimates had increased since yesterday's briefing—now it was estimated that Pakistan had committed a full brigade of troops to the effort.

Whelan sat back for a moment trying to recall the last intel briefing on the readiness of Pakistan's ground troops. The last conflict with India had bled them pretty badly, if he recalled correctly. Only with massive amounts of matériel from the Chinese, who were seeking a buffer to keep India occupied, could Pakistan have rebuilt her capabilities in a few years. Still, a brigade-level force was significant.

Whelan turned on his computer and sorted through his statistical files until he found the one he wanted. CIA and British intelligence estimated that Pakistan had committed at most a couple of regiments to the Kashmir conflict at the end of 1999. Neither side had taken any of the telltale steps to prepare to deploy nuclear armaments in that conflict, saber rattling to the contrary or not.

He looked at the second set of images. These showed the Pakistani convoy clearly inside Kashmir, moving slowly through tough terrain. He checked the date stamp between the Comsat photo and the much greater resolution Keyhole photograph.

Not quite forty-eight hours.

He pulled out a magnifying glass and studied the photo. There appeared, to his untrained eye, to be a number of troops, both in vehicles, if he read the types of trucks he was seeing correctly, and on foot moving with the convoy. He counted the trucks to double-check the CIA's estimate of the size of the force.

Then he went back to the statistical files and looked at total Pakistani troop strength and readiness estimates.

India had found out, obviously, and acted decisively to stop the incursion. Richard sat back in his chair for a moment, thinking.

If I were invading India, what would I do? I've already lost a war, yet I really want the territory. No one believed the previous cover story about insurgents fighting to free the Muslim population from Indian atrocities. The government of my country is shaky, the last prime minister having been thrown out by the military.

Well, if I'm American, I believe in deploying overwhelming force. Desert Shield–Desert Storm being a good example. Overwhelming force with force multipliers if I have them, e.g., aircraft.

What do I do if I'm Pakistani?

He studied the photos again. No heavy artillery, a few older tanks from the look of it. Just men, lots of them.

Just men.

And how would India have known about this? India didn't have access to sophisticated satellite intelligence, not to the point where they could have identified Pakistani troops from space. Unless they had gotten lucky with commercial satellite photos of the region and tumbled to what the Pakistanis were doing. Which was unlikely.

CIA used Comsat photos after the fact, once they knew what they were looking for. Once something blows, you go out to the open market and get photos from a particular day, time, and latitude and longitude if they are available. Otherwise, it was prohibitively expensive to buy images from every minute of every day of every square inch of ground even if the target area was relatively small.

The more he thought of it, the more he thought that India had bombed a needle in a haystack with pinpoint accuracy.

With a neutron bomb, no less.

He went back to his files and pulled up HUMINT/PAKISTAN, or human intelligence assets in Pakistan. Counterintelligence was not a strength of either country, but the element of surprise Pakistan had achieved in the last war in Kashmir indicated that India, at least at that time, didn't have much high-level intelligence in either the civilian government at the time or the military.

And the government had changed. So a strike against a sizable force entering Kashmir had to have been forewarned by something other than informants in order for India to react.

And what the hell could that be?

He went back to the written summary and scanned a few paragraphs. CIA now thought that the bulk of India's conventional forces were engaged in exercises and downtime elsewhere and couldn't have deployed to Kashmir in time to stop so significant an invading force. According to the summary, India had wanted to catch Pakistan red-handed invading Kashmir with their own troops.

So Monroe is still sticking to the party line—the show-and-tell theory.

Significantly there was no mention in the CIA report about how India knew that Pakistan was moving troops into Kashmir.

He went to the photographs of the day of the event. CIA said it was a neutron weapon. Why?

Sam Hennings had indicated in the initial brief that the event had been recorded by a specially enhanced "watcher" Keyhole that had been baby-sitting the area since the last round of India's and Pakistan's nuclear tests in the late 1990s. The "watcher" series was specifically designed to help detect and collect intelligence on nuclear events. But watchers were expensive, and this one was not able to cover the region fully.

So how had CIA known it was a neutron bomb? He went back to the report and saw a graph of the output of the weapon as recorded by the watcher satellite. So many electron volts of radiation at this frequency, none at that frequency, reduced but distinctive seismic effects, yada, yada, and look at the "after" high-res photos of the effects the weapon had on the convoy; a conventional nuclear weapon would have blasted the vehicles and personnel off the face of the earth, even at fairly low kiloton yields, but the vehicles and the people were still clearly visible as the fireball faded away on the Keyhole's next pass over the area.

Richard went to the "after" pictures. This was the same

shot that Hennings had shown the president. Richard tried to imagine what they'd felt, perhaps surprise at the lone plane they'd heard overhead, perhaps a hurried command or two to take cover to try and hide just how massive an incursion they represented. And then the impossibly bright light and killing radiation, minimal blast effects from a high-altitude burst, but, according to the photos and CIA's follow on estimates, nearly 100 percent casualties.

He looked at the photos. A still life–still death study. Bodies lay on the ground, many struck down where they fell, clumps of them spilling from the canvas-covered troop carriers. In an instant, a Pakistani troop convoy had been turned into bloated, lifeless bodies and abandoned equipment; in an instant the dagger in India's soft underside had been blunted and turned against the aggressor. A brigade of troops decimated with a single stroke.

Richard went back to the "before" pictures, then looked again at the "after" pictures, imagining the bodies lying strewn across the road and in the vehicles, too hot to touch.

Yes, he concluded, *definitely an enhanced radiation weapon.*

Forty-five minutes later he decided he'd gleaned as much as he could from the summaries. He really wanted to talk with Hennings, the CIA analyst that had put the pieces together. He glanced at his watch. Four fifteen. He hoped he was in at this hour and not pulling a late shift.

He culled the number from one of the classified lists of CIA employees on his computer and dialed him up.

"Hello, this is Hennings, here comes the tone. . . ." Obviously not there.

Richard left a message and continued to review the latest intelligence about Pakistan's angry response. Which was a trap, he thought, because either they weren't Pakistani troops or they weren't in Kashmir where they had no business being. India had already overflown the blast site and taken extensive photos that proved that the casualties were from Pakistan. The only question was where the carnage had taken place, which Pakistan was disputing.

And that was the real danger.

Chuck O'Shay and Frank Moynihan, head of the Secret Service, came to see him a short time later. An odd pairing, Whelan thought.

"Hey, Frank. Chuck." He knew Moynihan from way back.

But Moynihan was all business. He dropped a copy of the late edition of the *Washington Herald* on Richard's desk. Richard only glanced at the headline, but his stomach contracted:

President's National Security Adviser
Arrested in Socialite's Murder

"We need to have a little chat," Moynihan said.

"Why?"

O'Shay responded, smooth as silk.

"It's SOP, Richard, in situations where a member of the president's staff is a suspect in a capital crime. It will help the president respond that he's behind you one hundred percent and is convinced of your innocence."

"Okay, but I'm in the middle of the Indian thing. Can we do this later? Or better yet, tomorrow?"

Moynihan was stern. "No."

"Look, Frank, I'm not some nut case."

"From this article, I'm not so sure."

Whelan sighed. "I know it looks bad, but I can assure you I'm innocent. Frank, we go back a long way. Do you honestly think I could have done this?"

"And you should know that what I think isn't important. My job is to protect the president, Richard. From internal, as well as external, threats to his safety."

"Look, if anyone in the White House gave this any credibility, why did Chuck arrange my bail?"

O'Shay just looked at him. "You think that we arranged your release?"

"Yeah," Richard said, suddenly not so sure. "Who else would have?"

O'Shay shook his head. "The first I learned about your arrest was from Bettina Freeman. She said your attorney had asked her to call, and that he was arranging for you to make bail. I talked to the president about it, as well as counsel, and everyone was of the opinion that the administration should stay out of it."

Then who? Richard asked himself.

"I'm not really concerned about your legal troubles, Richard," Moynihan said. "We need to go back to my office so we can ask you some questions about this incident."

"Why not just get it over with here?"

"Because this is a formal inquiry. Another agent will be present as a witness. And I want the conversation taped for later analysis."

"What?" *And I considered you one of the few friends I have in the White House. . . .*

"You heard me. This is by the book. So let's go, otherwise I'm going to have to ask you to leave the premises."

Whelan was angry, but he realized that they were just doing their jobs. He was the one with a pall of suspicion hanging over him, and if anything happened, there would certainly be congressional inquiries until hell caught a cold.

"Fine, let's get this over with."

"One other thing." Moynihan was looking at him intently.

"What?"

"Do you mind being polygraphed?"

"Are you serious?"

Moynihan said nothing; he was studying Richard's reaction.

The white boys always circle the wagons when some-thing like this happens. "Fine. Whatever you say. Polygraph me if you like." *Repeat after me: This isn't because you're black. . . .*

A few minutes later he was seated with Moynihan, an-other agent whose name was not offered, and a technical services type who was setting up the polygraph equipment. Obviously, this had been planned in advance, and Richard wondered what Moynihan would have done if he'd refused.

When they were settled in with the tapes turned on and the polygraph machine functioning, Moynihan led him through a series of simple, straightforward questions designed to cal-ibrate his presumably truthful responses for the machine.

"Your name is Richard Whelan?"

"Yes."

"You're thirty-five years old?"

"Yes."

"You were born in New Jersey?"

"Elizabeth, yes."

"Father's name?"

"Robert Whelan."

"Mother's name?"

"Samantha Whelan."

"Are your parents living or deceased."

"Dead. My parents are both dead."

Moynihan paused, looking at a file—presumably Richard's FBI dossier.

"Your file says you know something about weapons. Do you own any guns?"

This had always been a sensitive subject between him and Mary.

"Yes."

"More than one?"

He had a whole gun cabinet locked away at his shooting club. "Yes."

Moynihan looked up, intent on registering his surprise. In case there are questions later. Frank knew he was a sport shooter, hell, Moynihan had recommended the gun club he used. But Richard had seen that look in people's eyes before: *Gun nut.*

"Do you hunt? Is that why you own more than one weapon?"

"No. I mean, I hunted with my dad as a kid. Target shooting is all I do now."

Moynihan made some notes on a legal pad he'd brought to the questioning.

"Did you kill Mary Jacobs?"

Jesus, there she was on the floor, her head tilted at a crazy angle, her eyes open and staring into space. The apartment had been dark, and something had blocked the door. He pushed the door open, jarring the body from where it had fallen, although he didn't know it was her body, not yet, until he turned on the lights in the hallway where she lay.

He stops, frozen, surprised, and looks at her. In the few minutes that she'd been out of his sight someone had brutally killed her and left him with questions and no answers.

Moynihan was looking at him closely. "Should I repeat the question?"

And he couldn't understand why these things happen to people. Why Mary? Why him?

"Did you kill Mary Jacobs?"

He looked at Frank Moynihan. Steady and ice cold. "No." *But what if I'd gotten there a little sooner? A minute or two? Would she still be alive?*

"Did you have a sexual relationship with Mary Jacobs?"

"You're out of line, Frank," he said through gritted teeth.

"When it comes to the president, nothing is out of line, Richard. Did you have a sexual relationship with Mary Jacobs?"

They all looked at him expectantly.

"Yes." *Ignore the indignant glances; yes, she was sleeping with me, and yes, she liked sleeping with me. . . .*

"Was she seeing other men besides you?"

"No."

"Were you jealous of her dividing her attentions between you and others?"

"No. There were no others."

"Did you knowingly or unknowingly pass Mary Jacobs sensitive information that crossed your desk in the course of performing your job?"

"No." But based upon what Detective Johnson had shown him, he couldn't be sure.

Moynihan cleared his throat, and Richard tensed.

"You've known the president since you were in high school?"

"Yes. I went to prep school with his son. He was a state senator then, just before he ran for Congress."

Moynihan was writing. "And what happened to President Roswell's son?"

"He . . . died while we were in high school."

"Did you have anything to do with Skip Roswell's death?"

"Of course not," Richard snorted indignantly.

"How was Skip Roswell killed?"

"It was nearly twenty years ago."

Moynihan waited.

"He was killed in a car crash."

"Was he driving?"

"No. A fellow student was driving. I was not involved."

"And you didn't kill Mary Jacobs?"

Surprise! "No."

"Did you knowingly pass her classified information?"

"No. Nor was I the second rifle on the grassy knoll when JFK was killed. Nor have I been abducted by UFOs. And I had nothing to do with the assassination of Martin Luther King."

Moynihan looked at the polygraph technician, who nodded.

"That concludes our questions. Thank you, Richard. I suggest, in the interest of decorum, that you consider going home."

But Richard was already pulling the wires from his muscular frame.

"Thanks for the career advice, Frank. But I have work to do."

Richard was back at his desk when his phone rang.

"You're a hot news item." He recognized the voice. And the attitude. Bettina.

"I take it you've seen the papers?"

"The *Herald* is kind of hard to miss. How does it feel to push World War Three southern Asia–style off the front page?"

"Wonderful. But since I'm such a 'hot news item,' perhaps we shouldn't be talking. And if you're calling to tell me 'I told you so,' save it for a recalcitrant head of state."

"So that's the thanks I get."

"For what?"

"Posting your bail."

"That was you?"

"Do you trust me, or would you like to see the receipt from the bail bondsman?"

"I don't doubt you. I just don't understand why."

"There's a special bond between old friends."

"Ah, that's the current euphemism for it?" He hesitated. He and Bettina had been an item for a while.

"Um-hmm."

"So how much do I owe you?"

"Dinner and drinks would suffice. Especially since I asked you to call me and you didn't."

"Christ, Bettina, my girlfriend was just brutally murdered. Not exactly cheery topics of conversation."

"I just need a cross-check of something, Richard. Surely you can function long enough to do that for an old friend."

"Fine," he sighed. "When?"

"How about tonight?"

5

Charles O'Shay and Frank Moynihan made their way into the meeting with the president, who was reviewing some paperwork at his desk. They only had a few minutes, and the meeting did not appear on any of their official schedules.

The president looked up as they settled onto the couch. Moynihan the Earnest, dark crew cut, dark suit, standing over O'Shay by four inches. They were here to talk about Richard Whelan, and from the looks on their faces, the news was not good. He sat back in his chair for a moment, reflecting on how much he wanted them to know about his concerns.

Marty Jacobs had called him screaming for blood. The one Achilles heel in his career was Marty Jacobs. And his daughter was dead, and his national security adviser was implicated in her murder. A more dangerous set of circumstances he could not imagine, because Marty Jacobs could talk about things that should never, ever, see the light of day.

And in all the years he'd known the man, he'd never heard him as upset as he'd sounded on the phone. This little bottle of nitro had to be contained, and contained quickly.

Well, shit rolls downhill. "Gentlemen?" He did not rise from his desk, and did not join them on the couch.

"We polygraphed Whelan, Mr. President."

"And?"

Moynihan shrugged. "There was nothing that clearly indicated that he was involved in Mary Jacobs's murder, but the machine didn't exactly give him a clean bill of health."

Edgar Roswell waited. When it was clear Moynihan had spoken his piece, he said: "I wanted results, Frank, not equivocation. Either he's in it up to his ears and we get him out of here, or he's clear and should enjoy the full support of this administration. What you're saying is that you don't know, and dammit, you are paid to know."

"As I suggested, Edgar," O'Shay used the president's first name to try and lighten him up, "perhaps you can suspend him. As of today."

Roswell regarded O'Shay coldly. "Based upon what? He has certain Constitutional rights."

"But this is an extraordinary situation."

"That it is. I've got the congressional intelligence people screaming that we missed the boat on India and Pakistan. I've got two hostile powers damn near threatening to exchange nuclear weapons. And in the middle of that, you're suggesting that I fire my national security adviser? Jay Leno will be doing jokes about how we were too preoccupied killing Mary Jacobs to notice the bombs flying, and he'll be doing them for the rest of his life.

"And the alternative isn't particularly appealing. I will now have to issue a statement saying that not only did we not drop the fucking ball on India, which we did, but that I 'support' my troubled national security adviser."

He stared at the two men. "All because you people can't do your goddamned jobs."

"That's why a suspension pending the outcome of a formal inquiry—"

"Chuck, shut up. Need I remind you of the shockingly low percentage of black voters who pulled my lever in the election? The NAACP and every bleeding-heart liberal would be all over us in a second. Innocent until proven guilty. Whelan himself could rake us over the coals if he wanted to. *If he wanted to.* Let me tell you something, gentlemen. The president of the United States does not wish to be held hostage to this situation. And since you can't give me results, I suggest that you coordinate your efforts with Monroe at CIA. If you can't get results, maybe he can."

O'Shay and Moynihan looked at each other. *Monroe? Isn't there a little matter about violating the CIA's charter here?*

But did either of them care to bring that up at this juncture?

THE CAPITAL BISTRO, 7:00 P.M.

Bettina Freeman looked at her reflection off the big plateglass window as she approached the front door. She was fashionably late, which was good. Let Richard stew a little bit. She was worth it.

Although Richard didn't seem to notice. She was tall, at five feet eleven inches, and could easily get to six feet in anything but flats. She was light chocolate in complexion, and while she regretted her short hair, it was a necessity given her hectic schedule. And she'd long ago adjusted to the fact that she wasn't beautiful, just pretty. Striking, even. She more than made up for it in brains and career. But men didn't seem to notice that, either.

She found Richard sitting at a booth in a dark corner, studying a menu. She sat down unannounced, startling him.

"Is this out of the way enough for you?" she asked him.

Richard looked around. "Yup. A soul food restaurant in the northeast part of the city. Not many movers and shakers likely to be here. Unless this administration has a secret fascination with barbecue ribs that I don't know about."

Bettina settled herself and a waiter bustled over with a menu. He smiled at the two of them, thinking they were a couple.

She studied the menu, decided that she wasn't hungry, and put the menu down.

"So," Richard said, "I obviously owe you."

She played it off. "You were in trouble, and I was in a position to help."

"Blaze tipped you off?"

"Marcus told me the situation after you were arraigned." And wasn't it a surprise to get a call from attorney Blaze about Richard Whelan.

"For what it's worth, I asked Marcus to keep you out of it."

"So you would have preferred to rot in jail?" she said as sweetly as possible.

"No. I would have preferred to handle it myself."

"Maybe this is one of those situations where the Lone Ranger needs a Tonto, Kemosabe."

"Sounds like Marcus did more than tell you I was in trouble."

"What *is* it between you two? Look, it doesn't matter what Marcus said or didn't say, Richard. Whether you care to acknowledge it or not, you are in some serious trouble. And sometimes, even the great Richard Whelan needs a friend."

"The 'Great Richard Whelan'? That's the second time today I've heard that."

"That's what they call you. Whelan's a genius, Whelan did this, Whelan did that. Do you have any idea how many people in the administration, not to mention on the Hill, would love to see you taken down a peg or two? Are you that blind?"

Whelan shrugged. "I'm not about to compile an enemies list, Bettina. I refuse to live that way."

"And you refuse to let your friends help you." *Or women*

to love you. "I knew you were in jail. I have some contacts in the D.C. government. I found you, and I bailed you out. So excuse me."

"How'd you come up with the money?"

"How, or why?"

"How, first. My bail was set at a million dollars."

"Ten percent of the bond secures the bail. I have property from my parents down South. I pledged the property in exchange for the hundred thousand dollars necessary to spring you."

"And the why?"

Bettina just looked at him. "Your naïveté is charming. But I didn't come here to debate my largess. I'm here in part to protect my investment. And get some dividends out of it."

"No questions about what happened?"

"No questions about how you spent a year with the daughter of a major defense contractor and staunch supporter of the president? Who happens to be white? Why, Richard, why do you think I'd be curious about any of that?" she said, her voice dripping with sarcasm.

"Bettina, look, I don't want to fight old battles. Mary is dead. She died horribly. The police want to pin this bad boy on me. Isn't that bad enough?"

"I don't want to fight with you, Richard. I'm here because I need to talk to the Great Richard Whelan. And since I'm now a part owner of the franchise, at least until this is cleared up, I plan to keep tabs on you."

"Fine."

Their waiter came over and took their orders. Richard took a sip of water. The bistro didn't have a liquor license.

"So what did you want to talk about?"

"First, I think we should clear the air."

"Which means?"

"You're still the bright moody guy I dated. I always got

the impression that sometimes you were there, and other times . . ." She waved her hand in the air.

"Well you have to admit the social load was pretty steep, dealing with you."

She was immediately defensive. "Meaning what?"

He paused, not wanting to continue.

All the "proper bourgeois" crap that you dragged me to, Bettina. This party in Oak Bluffs, that cookout in Sag Harbor, this reception given by the Congressional Black Caucus, all those "see and be seen" things . . .

"Cat got your tongue?"

He was suddenly tired. "Maybe this wasn't such a good idea."

"Do you want to talk about her?"

He shook his head no.

"It might help."

Richard just looked at her.

"Flirting with me at your party didn't help, by the way."

"Um, hmm. So I'm to blame for your fight."

"I didn't say that."

"But it's in the back of your mind, Richard. And by the way, while I realize the experience isn't necessarily all it's cracked up to be, you didn't seem terribly disgusted when I kissed you."

"I was mystified as to why you'd do that in front of my girlfriend."

"Because she was locked up with that other guy for so long, and I could see the steam coming out of your ears."

"Oh, and a kiss was just what the doctor ordered."

"You came to me to peck me on the cheek, Richard, and offer congratulations." She sat back and smiled. "So I congratulated myself."

"Very funny."

"Suzy White Girl thought so."

"We broke up because of it, Bettina," Richard said frostily.

"Over a kiss, huh? In relationship terms, Richard, that's not even a misdemeanor. So don't blame me if the ice was already thin and you crashed through it."

Whelan said nothing, and Bettina realized that she'd gone too far. "I'm sorry, Richard. Really. We can talk about something else."

Like what? Dating a white girl? Feeling isolated in a relationship and lonely now that she's gone? The frustrations? Her sense of entitlement because she was white? Do you really want to know these things, Bettina?

Richard's food arrived, and they were silent for a few moments.

"Look, let's not rehash the past. I need to talk about current events. I'm trying to make some sense over what's going on."

"You mean India and the big boom."

She nodded. *Maybe I can get his mind off her.*

"I've only skimmed the intelligence, and this was the stuff that they passed around during the crisis meeting in the Situation Room, so you've seen it."

"Yeah, but we don't get it. They did the testing in 'ninety-eight, they fought with Pakistan over Kashmir in 'ninety-nine, but since then, it's been pretty quiet. We've been going back channel with them about the Nuclear Nonproliferation Treaty, and we thought we were making progress."

"I can see where a mushroom cloud over some Muslims would give you pause."

"No shit. And a neutron bomb, to boot. Do we even have any of those things in our arsenal?"

"Depends on whom you believe. Publicly, no. They were supposedly decommissioned sometime after our nuclear forces came off twenty-four-hour-alert status. During the

Carter administration the notion of using an enhanced radiation weapon was floated as a way of stopping a Warsaw Pact
invasion of Europe until the good guys could hustle over the
Atlantic. Use of enhanced radiation weapons was thought to
give us the opportunity to blunt an invasion and retake any
gains made by the Soviets and their proxies. But the notion
obviously wasn't too popular from a NIMBY perspective."

"You mean the Europeans didn't fall down with gratitude
that NATO would consider using high-energy weapons on
their turf."

"That's an understatement. And then–president Carter
misunderstood the psychological implications of the United
States even thinking about forward deployment of those
kinds of weapons."

"So why would India develop, deploy, and use a neutron
bomb?"

"We knew they had them, but why they would deploy one
is a mystery. After the flurry in the late nineties, I thought
everyone in the region had calmed down. I was, however, always concerned with how rapidly their nuclear capabilities
developed."

"Meaning?"

"I mean, they tested atomic weapons in the seventies,
that's been clearly proven by seismic and satellite data. And
then they make huge leaps to develop and test thermonuclear weapons. And there is some worry that they've up-
graded their delivery options for the weapons they have."

"You think this is more than basic research?"

"Almost has to be, although with proliferation the way it
is, they could have simply purchased their current capabilities. I'm told you can cobble together a supercomputer
based upon software and instructions on the Internet. With
enough computational power, you can design things that go
'boom.'"

"Well, forget about where they got it. State is worried that

India is trying to demonstrate winnable first-strike capability that would destabilize the entire region."

"The 'use it or lose it' scenario for Pakistan."

"Right. Can you imagine a thermonuclear explosion in New Delhi? Or Islamabad?"

Richard shook his head.

"And what's really pissing off Dempsey," Roswell's secretary of state, and Bettina's boss, "is that we've expended a significant amount of diplomatic effort pushing India and Pakistan toward signing the NPT. The White House has always backed us on this. But the reaction to this incident has been wishy-washy at best. It's like they want to scold the Indians a little bit and hope the whole thing goes away. We're thinking we need to force these two toward diplomatic negotiations and chain them to their chairs until the NPT is signed. The White House isn't buying it. And Monroe at CIA isn't helping."

"What's Monroe got to do with this?"

"With foreign policy, nothing. That's my point. It seems that on this issue, Monroe has the president's ear more than Ron Dempsey does. And that, as they say, is bullshit."

Richard was dismissive. "I wouldn't worry about Monroe."

"Why?"

"Because he's a hack. One of the president's investment-banking buddies who hit the fund-raising piñata in the campaign and out popped the DCI appointment. His approach to intelligence is to do it the old-fashioned way—CIA buys it. They have the best toys, the best informants, but there's no soul in the place anymore, from what I've heard. His biggest accomplishment so far is getting the president to agree to have the satellite boys, the National Reconnaissance Office, report directly to him and out from under joint control with NSA. Ironic, since his buddy Phil Erskine can't interpret satellite imagery worth a damn."

Whelan took a sip of water. "No, Bettina, having Monroe screw around in foreign policy is like having some dumb-assed kid try and launch the Space Shuttle by lighting a match underneath it."

"But I thought he had an extensive background in intelligence?"

"Post Vietnam, I think. Ancient cold war, domino theory stuff. Like I said, don't worry about him. The president is smarter than that."

"And what about you?" She started tapping the table with her finger.

"What about me?"

"Your legal troubles." *Tap, tap, tap. Your grief.* "Are you going to be okay?"

"I didn't do it. So, yeah, I'll be okay," Richard said, not looking her in the eye.

Tap, tap, tap. "I've got a lot riding on it, Richard. Just making sure."

"What's with the tapping?"

"Huh? Oh, sorry. When I get nervous I tap my finger."

"Sounded like Morse code."

Bettina looked sheepish. "I learned it as a kid."

"Right, I remember you told me that. Well, I appreciate the gesture. I'll get this sorted out in no time."

Richard got up to leave.

"So long, Lone Ranger."

Whelan smiled. "Heigh-ho, Silver. Away."

As they were leaving, Bettina Freeman watched Richard Whelan go to his car and go home. She decided she would walk for a bit, so she could think about things.

But try as she might, she couldn't get Richard out of her head. *He's handsome, smart, and a great kisser, and he doesn't even know how many women would throw themselves at him if he just said hello and smiled.*

But he doesn't care about you. So you should not care about him, not that way.

But I mortgaged my house to get him out of jail. She'd fibbed about that so that Richard wouldn't know just how much she had at risk in his brush with the legal system. And she didn't want to admit that she still wanted him and wanted him to the exclusion of everyone else.

With a sigh, she hailed a cab and went home.

6

Richard Whelan dropped his copy of the *Washington Post* on
his desk. He ignored the headline, which was about him, and
the grainy mug shot photo that accompanied the story. The
message waiting light was lit on his phone. He picked up the
receiver, hoping it wasn't more bad news.

"Hi, Richard Whelan, Sam Hennings, returning your call.
I'll be out of my office most of the day, be back around four.
Feel free to call me then."

Based on the time of the message he'd just missed the
CIA analyst. He was about to dial Hennings's number when
his phone rang.

"Richard Whelan."

"This is Doug Bristol with the *Washington Post*,
Richard. We're going to run a follow-up story tomorrow
concerning your relationship with Mary Jacobs, and wanted
to know if you had any comment about her untimely
death?"

Christ! "No comment."

"Fine, Mr. Whelan. Are you aware that there are allegations that your relationship with Mary Jacobs compromised
national security?"

"Allegations from whom?"

"Highly placed members of President Roswell's administration."

"Any such allegations would be categorically false."

"And has the president asked for your resignation yet?"

"Absolutely not."

"Thank you, Mr. Whelan." The phone went dead.

He softly wiped a bead of sweat from his forehead. "Highly placed" members of the administration were alleging that he'd compromised national security? What kind of crap was that?

He thought about Blaze and the first time they'd had a fight. *These assholes are starting to piss me off the way only family can.*

Unless they were setting him up to get rid of him. Think about it. They don't want to nail me as a suspect in a murder. But if they nail me as a security leak they can "disappear" me without a trace. And quietly blame the southern Asia crisis on my incompetence.

That's how Washington works, Rich.

Charles O'Shay stopped in. Is he in on this? Richard wondered.

"Yeah, Chuck. What can I do for you?"

"The president wants to meet about the Chinese UN announcement. This afternoon, probably around five. He wants from you a preliminary assessment of the implications of all the saber rattling from all sides. He'll get a current estimate from CIA about their military activity, and he'll get from State anything we can get going on the diplomatic front."

Richard was taking notes. He met O'Shay's eyes when he looked up from his pad.

O'Shay looked at him closely. "You up for this?"

"Why wouldn't I be?"

"Because of the murder. And your arrest."

And my mug shots in the Washington Post, Richard thought.

"I'm handling it fine. I think I'm close to getting everything resolved."

O'Shay looked dubious but said nothing. "Good. Very good. It's important to the president that you get it finished."

O'Shay turned to leave. "Oh, and Richard?"

"Yes."

"Let me see what you're going to give to the president before the meeting, okay?"

That was highly unusual. *What, doesn't he trust me?*

"Sure, Chuck. Anything you say." As he watched O'Shay leave he couldn't get the single question he had out of his head.

Why? Why? Why?

He asked the White House AV department to deliver a VHS tape of the Chinese ambassador's UN address to his office. He wanted to study it before he decided what it meant. Absently, he sketched out on a yellow legal pad what he would say to Roswell at the meeting:

1. How each nation's nuclear capabilities influenced current events: China, India, Pakistan.
2. Relationship between China and Pakistan.
3. Other tensions in the region, e.g., Taiwan.
4. History of China's relationship with India.

Of course he didn't know anything new about the Indian weapon used in the attack on Pakistan, but that would have to wait until he questioned the CIA guy Hennings. He began pulling together summaries about India's and China's nuclear capabilities to begin honing a brief for the president.

He also called Bettina to see if she knew who was going

to handle things from the State Department, but she wasn't in. He left a message asking her to get back to him.

He was studying the intelligence summaries when his phone rang again. He debated briefly whether to pick it up because it might be either the cops or the press trying to make his life miserable. But he picked it up.

"Richard Whelan."

"This is Marty Jacobs, Richard. I've been waiting for you to call me, but in the absence of a phone call from you, I thought I would go ahead and initiate a meeting."

Aw, nuts.

Marty Jacobs wanted him to come out to the house. That's what he called it. Whelan reflected that you didn't call it a shack when it was a mansion on several acres of manicured land with lots of hired help and alarm systems and instant-response private security guards and everything else rich people needed to feel secure. He'd managed to delay him until this evening because he just didn't have the stomach right this second to head out to Potomac, Maryland, and talk to Mary's mommy and daddy. And he had a stack of work to get through.

He might never have enough emotional strength for that, he reflected. Were they supposed to grieve together? Group hug? Or would Marty Jacobs just take out a pistol and blow his brains out for the supposed murder of his daughter?

Who needs this? he asked himself. He buried himself in his work for the president's briefing.

By three in the afternoon it was starting to come together. He was one of the experts in the current administration concerning China's nuclear capabilities and where they'd gotten them, so he had only to brush up on his own research about that. He could also easily detail China's history of supplying Pakistan with nuclear and other arms because he'd been up to speed on the Nonproliferation Treaty from dating Bettina and preparing congressional testimony on it.

As far as China and Taiwan, he had to go back through several months of CIA data to get a current reading. He knew it was still a sensitive topic, but it wasn't one of the things that he was in the loop about. He found it interesting that both the Chinese and North Korea had staged ballistic missile tests aimed at scaring the bejesus out of Taiwan and Japan, respectively.

He looked at the write-up of the tests. Diplomatic protests from Japan against the North Koreans had had no effect. Taiwan knew better than to waste time protesting anything that the People's Republic did. He wondered if Taiwan had held any off-the-record discussions with the administration as a result of the missile tests. He made a note on his growing to-do list: *Talk to Bettina about Taiwan.*

He glanced at his watch. Nearly 4:00 P.M. He went over his notes. Looked like he had enough. It would be good if he could get the CIA analyst on the phone. He dialed the number, and Hennings, surprisingly, picked it up on the first ring.

"Sam, Richard Whelan."

"Hey, Richard. So I finally get to talk one-on-one to the legend."

"Uh, yeah. I wanted to follow up about this India thing." *And I hope you haven't read the* Post *yet.*

"Sure. Haven't spent too much time on it since the initial brief, but I'm all ears."

"We're sure that it was a neutron bomb?"

"Yup. Radiation signature picked up with the Keyhole watcher satellite. Consistent with a high-energy weapon, which, in our CIA parlance, is a neutron bomb."

"When will we know how big the blast was? During the brief you indicated that you couldn't tell from the satellite images."

"Right. I wasn't specific because the size of the explosion has to be extrapolated from seismic data if we don't know anything about the design and can't extrapolate anything from the affected area, which we can't with an airburst inducing heavy doses of radiation. And the seismic data is the province of the pointy-headed scientists that run the various seismic networks that we turn to when something like this happens."

"Which networks?"

"Primarily KNET, which gives broadband coverage and is located in Kyrgyzstan. But we need to cross-index those readings with other networks, like GERESS, a German system, for example."

"So you expect to know something soon?"

"Beats me. Kiloton size of the weapon has not been a primary line of investigation. Besides, the neutron weapons don't have the same concussive blast effects that the city-buster nukes have, so it's tough to say what precisely the seismic data will tell us."

"What has been the primary focus of the investigation?"

"Nothing, since our official estimate suggests that India nailed the Pakis for a border incursion. Our existing intel suggests that India's armed forces are where we thought they were, so no follow-up has been done. As for the bomb, we know it was nuclear, we know it was an enhanced radiation weapon, and we know there are a bunch of dead Pakistanis. The DCI was explicit about not needing to know more than that."

"But why a neutron bomb? A tactical weapon, sure, but a neutron bomb? Not the kind of thing you want to be first on your block to detonate."

"I agree, but the official line from on high is the show-and-tell theory put forth at the initial brief. It may be a crock, but for the record, I yield to the superior breeding and culture of my betters. If you catch my drift."

Whelan did, and he was beginning to like Hennings.

"Next question: How did India know that there were troops invading Kashmir?"

Hennings shrugged over the phone. "Beats me. Not a clue."

"Okay. Have we compared the output of the weapon with other known neutron weapon tests to see if we can determine yield and design characteristics that way?"

"No. Like I said, no one cares."

"But I'm curious. Did they convert an existing weapon into an enhanced radiation bomb, or did they make one in the oven from scratch?"

"Good question, because then we might be able to figure out if they have any more."

"Yeah. So is there a way of analyzing the results that would tell us more about the weapon itself?"

"Let me think. See, there's a group in the National Laboratories, you know Lawrence Livermore, Sandia, those guys, that does advanced-computing stuff. Part of what they specialize in is something called 'visualization.' If we were to compare the Indian imagery and spectrographic data with existing or modeled weapon explosions we might have a basis to compare it to and make some assumptions. It's kind of a long shot, though."

"Look, I can't ask you for this directly, because you're obviously not in my chain of command, or even close to it. But I'd be curious, wouldn't you? To know as much about the design characteristics of the weapon? Because if and when the stuff starts hitting the fan, someone, the president, your boss, the Joint Chiefs, someone is going to want to know what they might be up against here. And they won't be lookin' at me for answers, that's for sure."

Hennings seemed to consider this for a moment. "Yeah," he said, exhaling, "you're probably right. I'll keep you posted on what I find out, if anything. It might take a while, though."

"Why?"

"Modeling this stuff is extremely complex. So trying to

compare an aerial detonation with data from underground tests is going to be very hairy for these guys."

"Maybe they'll see it as a challenge."

"Oh, I'm sure they will. But this is about scarce resources, though, and if I tell them on the sly that this is a matter of national security, someone, like my boss, may hear about it and get a wild hair up his ass about it, and by extension, me."

"Sam," Richard said, "just tread lightly, okay? Let me know if you get anything."

"Will do."

Bettina called just as Richard was gathering his things for his meeting with the president.

"Hey," she said, sounding just as rushed as he was, "are you in this briefing at five o'clock?"

"Yes. What's this, your cell phone?"

"Yeah. I'm on my way over. Listen, I was thinking . . . ," she hesitated, as if she wasn't sure about what she was going to suggest.

"Go on, Bettina, spit it out."

"I was talking to Blaze about your case."

Uh-oh. "And?"

"Do you think maybe there's something more to this than meets the eye?"

"Meaning?"

"The mystery traffic stop. Awfully convenient, given the timing. Maybe you should start looking for the phony cops."

"Way ahead of you, particularly since I'd like to put my foot up their collective butts. I'm just not sure where to start yet."

"Hey, you're the genius. You'll figure something out. Maybe start with ex-cops in D.C."

"I'll think about it."

"I gotta go. See you shortly."

"Okay."

"And call me later, okay? Maybe I'll have an angle on this."

Richard hung up the phone. *Interesting*.

THE SITUATION ROOM—5:00 P.M.

Richard Whelan walked into the brief like he owned the building, trying to shut the events of the last forty-eight hours out of his mind and focus on what he excelled at. The players were all there, Dennis of the Joint Chiefs, O'Shay, the president, Dempsey from State, Erskine of CIA. Bettina walked in just before he did.

They all looked up as he walked in, and Richard smiled tightly.

Mike Monroe folded a copy of today's *Washington Post* and put it on the table with Richard's mug shots faceup. Whelan shot him a murderous look but said nothing. Monroe only smirked.

The president ignored the slight. "Richard, you're first up. What've you got?"

Each and every person in the room glanced at the *Post* pictures before they met his eyes. He strolled to the front of the room, passing a packet of the information he'd brought with him to every person he passed. A few of them took the stapled pages as if they were faintly radioactive.

Bettina somehow managed to brush her hand against his knee as he passed.

It didn't help that he had no idea what he was going to say all of a sudden.

He was five, perhaps six, paces from the front of the room. There was a picture of a Pakistani military installation displayed on the front screen. It was an area he knew well because he'd studied it many times.

They'd stopped talking when he walked in. CIA had probably already briefed them, hence the photo. Erskine was

CIA's talking head at such gatherings, and he knew from Hennings what the party line was.

And Erskine couldn't interpret satellite intel worth a damn.

Three paces from the front.

India explodes a neutron bomb over unsuspecting Paki troops within a day or two of their crossing the border. A brigade of troops, much less than a major invasion force, but much greater than the nip and tuck of a typical border skirmish.

And India shouldn't have known the Pakis were there.

He reached the front of the room and faced the audience. "Gentlemen. Bettina."

There was some clearing of throats.

A neutron weapon. As he looked at them the pieces all fit together suddenly, the kind of epiphany that he was known for. He looked at Monroe and at his mug shots in Monroe's newspaper.

There's only one way to do this, he thought.

Trust your instincts. Go for broke.

"CIA has already told you that they believe India's aggression was intended to catch a border incursion by Pakistani troops."

He paused to look at every person in the room, and he lingered on Mike Monroe, then the president.

"That explanation is a crock of shit."

There was a murmur of voices, first and foremost among them Mike Monroe's. "They shouldn't have cut you loose from the district lockup, Whelan. Mr. President, we are wasting your time."

"Richard," the president intoned, "you want to explain yourself?"

Steadman Dennis, Chair of the Joint Chiefs, was thumbing through Whelan's information packet.

"Certainly, sir. General Dennis, the answers aren't in the information I distributed."

He leaned forward and placed both hands on the table. Bettina was smiling, and it was an effort to keep from winking at her.

"There are two critical questions, two answers that any explanation of the genesis of this incident has to supply.

"The first is how the Indian government knew that the Pakistani troops were in Kashmir. The second is why would India deploy nuclear munitions, in particular, an N-bomb, to stop them."

He turned to Monroe. "Mike," he said it so crisply that he nearly bit off the last two letters, "would you care to answer the first?"

Something in Monroe's face hinted that he suspected he was walking into a trap.

And something else suggested, *so be it*.

"We think that the Pakistanis were detected by Indian patrols in the area."

Whelan nodded. "My thinking exactly. Chairman Dennis, what's the current estimate on how long it takes for the Indian military to deploy nuclear munitions?"

"Their command and control functions are not robust enough to allow them to have the weapons lying about. The Indian government has assured us, and we have confirmed, that they keep their nuclear stores under lock and key in a centralized depot in a remote part of the country. The remoteness of the depot is designed to make it difficult to find and easy to secure and defend. The trade-off is that it takes time to requisition the weapons and make them battle ready. Our estimate, from the time the orders are given, is that it takes three to four days for them to deploy."

"Mike, how long after the convoy entered Kashmir was it hit?"

Monroe cleared his throat because he saw where this part

of Whelan's argument was going. "Less than forty-eight hours."

Whelan smiled.

"And that's problem number one. A scouting force would have had to have been on top of the Pakistan–Kashmir border and literally seen or heard the orders being given to the Pakistani troops to move out in order for India to have employed a nuclear response when it did.

"Which poses other problems. Why would India have troops so close to the border?"

Monroe: "Scouting patrol."

"Scouting for what?" Richard asked.

"I don't get what you mean, Whelan," Monroe said.

"What were they looking for? Why would they be so far away from any known base of operations that the Indian army has in Kashmir?"

Monroe shrugged. "We can't know that."

"Then let me ask another question. Pakistan has over sixty infantry brigades at its disposal. The military government tossed the supposedly corrupt civilian government in a bloodless coup. There have been numerous skirmishes with India over Kashmir, skirmishes that have ended in at best a standoff, primarily because the civilian government has never committed a sizable number of troops to the effort, making it a no-win situation.

"I would submit that we know something about governmental limitations in waging limited war; look at the difference between President Johnson's 'send them a message' bombing campaign in IndoChina to the massive military buildup for Desert Storm. Chairman Dennis, if you were a member of the military junta ruling Pakistan and you wanted to take Kashmir, would you send in an invasion force that represents a small fraction of the infantrymen you currently have under arms?"

Dennis: "No. Given the tactical difficulties of the terrain

and the history of losses, I'd hit them with everything I had."

O'Shay was looking through Richard's packet of materials. In it was the series of before and after Keyhole photographs of the Pakistani convoy.

"The satellite photos seem to indicate that they were giving it everything they had, Richard," O'Shay said. "Look at page eight of your package. The Keyhole photo clearly shows horse-drawn wagons in the middle of the convoy. If that isn't everything they had, what would be?"

Monroe was a man saved. "Yeah, I'd say if Seabiscuit is being committed to the war, that's an all-out effort."

Whelan's smile absolutely chilled him. "Is it? Taking horses through Kashmir, where the highest passes are choked with snow most of the year, in support of an invasion that you've presumably been planning for some time? Chairman Dennis?"

"Crappy logistics are the bane of any military organization, Mr. Whelan."

"Unless you didn't expect to take them very far. Crappy logistics may be the bane of the military, particularly if you're in a hurry."

Erskine: "You want to explain that, Whelan?"

"Sure, *Phil*. India has patrols close to the border with Pakistan that detect a convoy right after it crosses the border, patrols that are far from any known Indian military base. They find them, and then they employ a nuclear munition to kill them in an act certain to earn the Indian government the enmity of the entire community of nations, a retaliation that almost everyone, except my esteemed colleagues at CIA, thinks is way out of proportion.

"Naturally the question is why. And here's the answer.

"We may be looking at an imminent invasion, gentlemen, but not in the way we've been thinking about it.

"What we're looking at is an impending invasion of Pakistan. By India."

There was an explosion of voices as Whelan surveyed the room. He waited for them to talk themselves out. Then he cleared his throat.

"I started out by saying that the explanation for this incident had to answer two critical questions. How did India know the troops were there, and why did they employ an enhanced radiation weapon to take them out? CIA's answer is that the troops were detected by scouting patrols, and that the N-bomb was used to demonstrate to the world that Pakistan was guilty of a border incursion and they got what was coming to them."

He looked at his audience, knowing that he had them in the palm of his hand.

"Well, as a friend of mine once said, if you bat five hundred you can play in the majors. This time, CIA is half right. I believe that the Pakistani troops were detected by Indian Army scouting patrols, but that those patrols were covering for a much larger Indian force in the region. The sequence is this. India moves a large force into the region. There are plenty of Muslims living in the Kashmir, and I believe that Pakistan got wind of what was going on and hastily assembled the largest force they could muster to stop them."

He nodded at Dennis. "Crappy logistics are the bane of any military force, Mr. Chairman. Imagine trying to mobilize a brigade of troops to move into Kashmir on short notice? You bet your logistics are going to be crappy, but an army travels on its stomach, so they loaded up Seabiscuit and sent him to war when they ran out of trucks. They knew the Indians were close, so they didn't expect the horses to have to travel far, certainly not into the treacherous regions of the territory."

He paused, surveying the room.

"And why use a neutron bomb? That was the second question. As I said at the beginning, CIA's explanation is a crock. They didn't happen to have one lying around to blow away a column of enemy troops they just happened to stumble upon. Not less than forty-eight hours after they stumbled upon them. They executed a contingency in support of a carefully planned tactical position. They used an N-bomb, not conventional weapons, not even tactical nuclear weapons, because they had the Pakis at a choke point; a choke point that they wanted to move their own troops through with minimal loss to their own forces. This is not new military theory, gentlemen, Bettina. This is exactly the doctrine that we wanted NATO to adopt when President Carter suggested forward deployment of N-bombs in Europe. Peel the troops from their positions, and move in behind them without worrying about residual blast damage and radiation.

"Once the radiation dies down, the Indians will move their troops forward and into Pakistan. When their scouts encountered the enemy they took them out."

He cleared his throat. "Chairman Dennis supplied the rationale. If you're going to hit them, you go all out. Only a full-scale invasion of Pakistan would be justification enough to use a weapon of mass destruction in Kashmir. It is, in my opinion, a desperate gamble, but one which we have to believe that the Indian government is committed to heart and soul."

There was dead silence in the room. Phil Erskine spoke up. "While I'm not prepared at this time to respond to your theory, we haven't seen a proportional response on the part of Pakistan. That photo behind you shows heightened military activity, but not all-out mobilization."

Whelan turned around. "You're talking about this photo?"

"Yes, sir, I am."

"If I'm Pakistan, and I just lost a brigade of hastily sortied troops to an Indian nuclear weapon, what do I do?"

Dennis spoke up, a thoughtful look on his face: "If I'd lost all the troops I had closest to the border, I'd start preparing for bear."

"'Bear' meaning hitting the Indians with everything you've got, Mr. Chairman?"

"Yeah. That's exactly what I mean."

Whelan turned to Phil Erskine. "But you maintain that the photo behind me," he turned and pointed to it, "this photo, right? only shows heightened military activity. Not full-scale mobilization."

"That's precisely what it shows," Erskine said. "These facilities are the only ones where we see increased activity."

Whelan: "Right. Unfortunately, these facilities are not just any military facilities. I recognize these photos from a study we did a year ago about Pakistan's nuclear delivery systems.

"These happen to be launch facilities for the Hatf-1, Hatf-2 and M-11 missiles, which we believe are Pakistan's primary nuclear delivery systems. And this activity, gentlemen, would suggest that Pakistan has begun spinning up its missiles in anticipation of all-out war with India." Whelan placed his hands on the table and leaned forward in the direction of Erskine and Monroe. "The preparation of a possible nuclear response, and *only* a nuclear response, suggests that they are considering a decapitation strike against India, and makes this the gravest international crisis of this administration."

Whelan paused to look Mike Monroe directly in the eye. "And you bastards almost missed it."

Monroe jumped in. "Mr. President, we don't have anything that corroborates that theory."

Erskine seconded. "We don't have anything that suggests a major Indian force in the region. And without troops, this fairy tale falls apart."

The president, visibly angry, turned on Monroe. "If you don't have hard evidence of the disposition of Indian ground forces, I suggest you find them and find them PDQ. Fairy tale or not, I want to know the location and status of every single Indian military force. If we have to retask satellites, so be it.

"But I want it done. Now!"

Monroe broke in smoothly, seeking to do damage control. "We should have additional information within the next few hours. I suggest we reconvene tomorrow morning."

Bettina glanced at Richard and smiled so quickly he nearly missed it. The meeting broke down into a hubbub of conflicting voices. Richard breathed a sigh of relief.

He glanced at his watch, and he realized that he had to hurry or he was going to be late to his appointment to see Marty Jacobs.

NEW DELHI, INDIA

He left the restaurant with his wife, who was chattering away about the party they'd attended. A closed, private party for senior members of the government. He listened dutifully, his mind elsewhere.

It was nearly 6:00 A.M.

"Are you going into the office today?" she asked, a coded question to indicate her displeasure with the hours that he was working.

He shrugged. "I'm not sure."

"Surely the prime minister can let you have a single day to yourself."

"It isn't the prime minister that I'm worried about. It is to the state of India that I am dedicated, Sasha, not the men of its government."

"Then as one of your concerns, let me speak for the people. Stay home today."

He laughed, something that he had not done in many weeks. "We shall see, Sasha, we shall see," he said, even as he dismissed the notion in his mind.

He needed to talk to his nephew, Amjad Singho, a captain in the air force, although from the house it was difficult to talk without being circumspect. He had persuaded the young man to take on the delicate bombing mission and, in their single conversation since, he'd heard the terrible weight of guilt on his nephew's shoulders.

A guilt he shared, he reminded himself. An anonymous little man, he had been the architect of India's nuclear weapons program, not as a scientist, but as a strategist, arguing forcefully for the need of weapons and the willingness to use them. A new lexicon had entered India's government, the phraseology of what the Americans had called the cold war—MAD, or mutual assured destruction, first strike, and CEP, circular error probability. The code words for the nuclear winter of the soul, for he had no doubt that damnation was upon them for having committed what the world was condemning as an act of genocide.

That it was a war of destiny and wills that had been brewing since Gandhi's time was of no consequence. The mistrust between Hindu and Muslim was more ancient than Gandhi's fading memory, although he imagined that the Great One was sleeping with a troubled conscience. Certain precepts, such as nonviolence, paled against a world peopled with men far less altruistic than Gandhi, and Gandhi himself had been gunned down. Felled by his own greatness, he thought, so who would aspire to martyrdom now? Someone closer to the prime minister than he had said that India could skip the martyrdom and go straight to the dirty business of killing now that she possessed nuclear arms, and the prime minister had looked at him, the anonymous little man with strategic visions.

He had stood then, pacing the narrow room, looking at the speaker and seeing his challenge clearly. How far we have come, he'd said, was reflected in the pictures of atrocities perpetrated by Hindus and Muslims in Kashmir and available through the Internet to shock and disgust people all over the world. Martyrdom was overrated, he'd said, and the dirty business of killing was even dirtier when you were the victim, as opposed to the perpetrator.

The very concept of India and Pakistan having nuclear weapons would have been anathema to Gandhi and were the evidence not of technological achievement but of the truly regressive qualities of hatred and fear. He often wondered what Gandhi would have made of the world had he survived to see it, the horror of the nuclear flash that consumed so many cubits of dirt from far underground, and the chain reaction not of enriched uranium but of the governments of Pakistan and China in their rush to match if not exceed the destructive power held in New Delhi's hands.

And he feared, too, feared deep in his heart, that when you strike down a man you must kill his family and his children, too, lest they rise up and seek their revenge, not with the sticks and stones that children use to forcibly settle their arguments, but with atomic weapons.

But they had shared and liberated a nation together, the Hindus and the Muslims, and there were Muslims throughout India still.

So, he thought always, how does one kill the families and children of those who should be our brothers without killing ourselves?

WASHINGTON, D.C.

It was 7:30 before Richard got into his Porsche and began the drive out to the Jacobs residence in Potomac. Everything, all the uncertainty about her, came to the surface of his mind. Despite his turmoil about the day, the job, and the slam dunk he'd scored at the intelligence brief for the president, he still felt very uneasy going to visit Mary's parents.

Or at least, Mary's father. Marty Jacobs was a big florid man who looked and acted like he didn't take any crap from anyone. He certainly had not been shy about expressing his distaste for his daughter's relationship. This was not a small thing in Whelan's world. After all, the Marty Jacobses of the world had the ears of presidents and kings and king makers; piss these guys off and you could be unemployed permanently, at least in civilized parts of the world.

It began raining lightly, and he was glad because they needed the rain. He turned right onto Nebraska Avenue, carefully following the driving instructions he'd printed out from the Internet.

He stayed to his right onto Rittenhouse Street, noticing for a moment a pair of headlights that had stayed with him since his initial turn out of the parking garage. He made another right, then a quick left onto Bradley Lane. After less than a half a mile, he turned right onto Connecticut Avenue.

The headlights were still with him. At least he thought they were.

After a couple of miles he got onto the 495 Beltway heading into northern Virginia. From this he took I-270 north, toward Frederick, Virginia. He was cruising at well over the speed limit now, passing slower-moving traffic adroitly, watching his rearview mirror for any signs of pursuit, knowing that if he did see any, it had to be the work of amateurs.

Which disturbed him even more.

He got on Maryland Highway 187 headed into Potomac. The traffic had thinned out considerably, and the road behind him looked clear.

Breathe out, Richard. *Breathe.*

His cell phone chirped at him.

Bettina Freeman. "That was some stunt you pulled off today, Richard."

"I thought it was inspired."

"Well, Chuck O'Shay wasn't amused that you single-handedly turned the entire intelligence establishment on its ear without warning him. The president apparently gave *him* an earful about how *you* freelanced your way through that."

"What, does O'Shay cry on Ron Dempsey's shoulders?"

"Yup. While it was vintage Richard Whelan, you should

know better. POTUS doesn't like surprises. Surprises make him feel like he's not in control."

"You saw the way Monroe put the *Post* photograph on the table? I'd call that deliberate provocation."

"Regardless, you should have played ball nicely with the other kids and chatted with them about it out of earshot with the president. C'mon, Richard, that's Government 101. Never disagree in front of the chief executive."

"Since when have you known me to play nice with the other kids?" *Just ask Marcus about that one. . . .*

"Touché. But rarely have I seen you put a meeting into an uproar like you did today."

"If I'm right, they needed to be shaken up."

"If you're right. That's a big if. How the hell did you glean all that from the information they provided?"

"Because they provided *data*, Bettina. Useful intuitions from data, that's *information*. That's what I supplied. It just came to me right there in the Situation Room."

"Then remind me never to ask you to work a hostile room. Your legend as Richard the Great is secure once again."

"Very funny."

"Now if I could just figure out how to kiss the great man's ring," she said playfully.

Hmmmm.

"Where are you now?" she asked.

"On my way to the 'burbs."

"Oh." She sounded disappointed.

"Going to see Marty Jacobs, the legendary tycoon and father of my late girlfriend."

"Ugh. You really know how not to enjoy your fifteen seconds of fame, don't you."

"This was set up before the thing in the Oval Office."

"Well, if you don't get back too late, call me. Maybe I'll save you a slice of pizza."

They rang off.

Now that was interesting. Pizza, eh? And she was disappointed about where he was going, therefore . . .

Mary would always tell him that he was running away with himself when he started extrapolating like that. "*Come back, Richard, come back,*" she'd say, laughing.

Okay, stop it. Bettina Freeman is not interested in you anymore. Forget the kiss at the reception. And forget your response to it.

And if you think she's interested in you, all you have to do is jump bail and she says good-bye to 100Gs of property down south.

At that point he reached the driveway of the Jacobs estate. He took a deep breath and turned in.

Sam Hennings got off the phone with Enrique Gonzales, associate director of the ASCI program at Sandia National Laboratories. ASCI, or the Accelerated Strategic Computing Initiative, did high-speed computer modeling on everything from modeling nuclear weapons to assessing likely stresses on containment vessels used to test conventional munitions.

Hennings sat back, lit a cigarette, and scratched his head. Enrique was being a pain in the ass about using ASCI's test data to calibrate the Indian nuclear event.

"We can't just compare underground test data with aboveground events. We can't do it, Sam," Enrique had yelled into the phone. "First, we'd have to build a bridge from the actual blast data to conditions that we'd see in an underground test, make all sorts of assumptions, and then convert the data. That is a massive task, and we don't have the time or the resources to do it."

"This is a national security matter, Enrique," Hennings reminded him.

"Everything we do is a national security matter, Sam. Besides, I don't think you appreciate what you're asking us to do. An underground test is a carefully monitored event with telemetry measuring every possible variable that anyone can think of. What are we supposed to do with the missing data from an actual explosion? Make it up? What good would the results be if the conjecture we substitute for the actual data is what drives the conclusion? It's impossible, Sam. It's just impossible."

Hennings strongly considered going to his boss about this, and even going to Phil Erskine to see if he could move Gonzales off the dime. He pulled out a pad and started composing what he would say to Phil Erskine, but after a few sentences trailed off. Erskine was a bureaucrat, and he would want something in writing in quadruplicate before he would see him; worse, he'd want every intervening layer of management present in any meeting. Which would defeat the whole purpose of going to him.

Besides, Hennings knew the scientist type. You couldn't force these guys to do something they thought wasn't feasible, because they would drag their feet, do nothing, and then tell him that the results had been garbled by the flaws in the experimental design. Which would be scientist-speak for saying they bitched it.

No, he would have to build some other mousetrap to get them to play along.

He glanced at his watch. Man, it was late. There had been nothing from the big boys upstairs about them retasking any of the birds, although he knew for a fact from his connections at the NRO that a Keyhole had been redirected toward sites over India. And scuttlebutt had it that they were retasking the bird because none other than Richard Whelan had carved Monroe and Erskine a bloody new orifice in a brief to the president.

Whelan was certainly a player. The story from the brief had probably lit around Washington ten times by now, and Whelan's tag line, "You bastards almost missed it," struck at the heart of the patrician assholes that now ran CIA. There were people whispering in the halls about that one.

Which made today's *Post* story all the more inexplicable.

He was trying to accomplish what Whelan suggested because it just made sense. He knew in his heart that he should have no loyalty toward the man, not in this town, and so he would go so far but no farther. But even from the brief conversation on the phone, he didn't think Whelan was a killer. And cops were cops; when in doubt, they would arrest the closest person to a crime, guilty or not.

He called his wife, who was used to his unpredictably late hours, and told her he was coming home. Hey, maybe the brass was going to interpret the satellite data themselves and screw the professionals.

More power to them, he thought as he grabbed his keys and headed out the door.

Upstairs, Phil Erskine was fuming at his boss.

"God dammit, Mike, Whelan crucified us up there! The last thing I want is to get blindsided by a complete screwup like him!"

"Slow down, Phil. This is the future of the country at stake here, not some Army–Navy game. Whelan was right. We missed some things. We have a bird in place to go looking?"

"NRO says one's moving into position as we speak."

"Okay. Why not go home and get some rest?"

"What? Then how do we interpret the satellite data?"

"We get the analysts on it first, that's all. It was a big mistake bypassing them with the shots you showed the president."

"What about Indian movement in support of an invasion?"

"What about it?"

"Do we show it to the whole group or a subset if that's what we see?"

Monroe sat back. "We'll cross that particular bridge when we come to it."

His phone chirped. Monroe picked it up and listened for a moment.

"Yes, Charles, it was not our intention to look like idiots in front of the president. I'm sure the president is upset that we don't necessarily agree with his national security adviser on such matters, but the man had a point, and we're checking it out. And if he's wrong, I'm going to ram it up his black ass, just between you and me."

Monroe listened while Chuck O'Shay ranted about the president's reaction to the security brief.

"Look, Charles, hold on a minute. Whelan may have gotten lucky but he appears to have other problems. . . . Like what? Well, a source at the *Washington Post* says they're going to do a multipart story about his relationship with Mary Jacobs. Part one hits the newsstands tomorrow, and it isn't going to be pretty. So, yeah, we'll check out his scenario. But his time is going to come. Right. Good-bye."

"O'Shay?" Erskine asked.

Monroe nodded. "Gotta make another phone call."

Mike Monroe called Frank Moynihan. "Frank, the president told me about a conversation he had with you about his national security adviser. Well, FYI, there's going to be an article in the *Post* about him tomorrow. Don't know any details, but be on the lookout for it, okay?"

Erskine stopped pacing and sat down to wait his boss's phone call out.

The house was a sprawling Colonial on several acres of land. When he'd last been here, for lunch with Mary and her parents, he'd noted the swimming pool and tennis courts and the circular driveway and the lawn sprinklers that made the place look like a Colorado farm in the summertime. It must seem like cold comfort now, Richard thought, shaking his head. Cold comfort.

He raised the enormous door knocker and let it drop. He counted one one thousand, two one thousand, three one thousand, . . .

A butler opened the door. Big guy, looked Samoan or something, dressed in an ill-fitting black suit with a white starched shirt barely containing his massive forearms.

"Richard Whelan."

"Yeah. I know. Marty wants to see you right away."

And Richard was ushered into the darkened interior of the sprawling house.

Marty Jacobs was wearing a crimson Nike jogging suit and a scotch and soda. He lay on a couch in the basement in front of the deluxe entertainment center and stadium-sized television set watching Australian-rules football on ESPN 3. The look in his red-rimmed eyes indicated that he'd been wearing a hangover for just as long as he'd been wearing the jogging suit, which smelled pretty ripe. He reached for the remote to mute the football match and dropped it, which punched the volume up.

"Richard!" he screamed over the ESPN announcer who was cueing the "go-to-commercial" jingle, "Have a seat!"

Richard sat down. Marty was still fumbling with the remote. It looked as if his fingers had stopped working.

"How are you, sir!" Richard shouted, unsure of how to proceed.

"Fine! Helluva thing about my Mary!"

"What?"

"Helluva thing about my Mary!" but his fingers had found the mute button, and he yelled this into the suddenly silent basement.

Richard was silent for a moment. *She was lying there, in the foyer, staring into space. Her neck . . .*

"If I had been there it would have been different, Mr. Jacobs—"

A meaty hand waved the formality away. "Call me Marty."

Marty Jacobs stared at him hard as he said that, and his rheumy eyes liquefied just a little more.

"You and she . . . were . . . involved for about a year. I never thought my Mary would be with a . . . would have stayed with you as long as she did. Kids these days . . . can't figure them out."

With a what? A nigger? Go ahead, Marty, say it . . .
"Well, I, uh . . ."

"Your parents? Alive or dead?"

"Deceased. My dad about ten years ago, my mom a couple of years after that. They were married forty years." *And I have a half brother who thinks I'm not black enough. Course, I'm not quite the whiter shade of pale you were looking for, am I, Marty?*

"Forty years, huh? Your father was a doctor, right?"

"Yes. How did you know?"

Marty waved him off. "Doesn't matter, Richard. Nothing really matters at this point."

He stared into his drink.

"I bet you think you know something about how the other half lives, don't you? Private schools, Ivy League colleges . . ."

How the hell does he know all this? We never exchanged more than three words when Mary and I were dating, Richard thought.

"I'm not sure I follow you."

Marty sighed. "Look, Whelan, you've been close to money and power your whole life. But you can't know what it means."

Marty hesitated, searching for words.

"Hell, maybe I'm just a drunk old man, but when I make

a decision about something, it means something. It moves those pieces of the world that I influence. It's not just being part of the establishment, son, hell, it's *being* the establishment."

"I'm the national security adviser to the president, Marty. Of course I understand."

Marty shook his head.

"This was why I thought you were wrong for Mary. There are things you can't possibly know. About how things work."

Like she was seeing someone else? Someone Marty thought was more appropriate?

"I think I know all too well how the establishment works, Marty," Richard said between gritted teeth.

"I disagree. Family means different things when you're part of the establishment. Commitments are felt on a different level. What did your parents tell you about your career?"

"They said to find something I really loved, like my dad loved medicine."

Marty nodded. "Perfectly logical for your father to feel that way. But I never would have told Mary something like that."

"Why?"

"Because Rocketdyne Systems isn't just a job. It's part of my life and it had to be part of Mary's."

"She enjoyed working for you."

"Maybe. My point is that she didn't have a choice. If she'd been my only son instead of my only daughter it would have been different, more natural for her to take a place in the family business. But as my daughter . . ."

"As your daughter what?"

"Well, there were limits to what she could do. For me, I mean. For the company. And I think she resented it. I think she felt trapped on some levels."

"And this means what, sir?"

"There have been other . . . relationships that Mary's

mother and I didn't approve of, Richard. You weren't the first."

"Are you trying to tell me that I wasn't good enough for your daughter?"

"Oh, I'm sure you're a credit to your . . . what I mean is that for a . . . black man you've done quite well. But people should know their place, and Mary's place wasn't with someone like you." Marty sighed in frustration. "What I'm trying to tell you is that she rebelled when it came to dating. Perhaps you were part of that rebellion."

"I can't agree, Marty."

"Yeah, I'm sure you don't." Marty fell silent for a moment before continuing.

"Mary's mom hasn't been taking this too well, you understand, right? A parent should never outlive a child. It's hell. But I wanted the same things for my Mary that anyone would want. You understand that?"

Richard just nodded.

"I just wanted her to be happy. Maybe give us some grandkids . . ." He stopped, looked at Whelan as if the last thing he wanted on earth was mulatto brats sired by a black man, and then went silent for a moment.

"So you had a relationship with my little girl." Marty shook his head. "June fifteenth, of last year, I believe, is when it started."

"She told you?" Was June fifteenth the first time he and Mary had been intimate?

Or was that the first time she was with the other guy?

Marty shrugged. "A father knows these things."

"Did she tell you we discussed marriage?"

"I'm sorry?" Marty looked at him as if he was suddenly speaking Chinese.

"Marriage. Did your daughter tell you we had discussed getting married?"

"Oh, she was adamant about remaining single, Richard."

"Not with me she wasn't. But I didn't think we would last. As a couple." Richard laid it out there so that Marty could tell him that he wasn't the only one Mary was seeing.

"Really." Marty's voice was dead. "Then why did you stay with her?"

"I, um . . ."

"My Mary was a fine girl." Marty looked at him, daring him to say otherwise.

"She was. Like you, though, I just didn't know about the race thing," Richard said, just to get it out in the open. Since Marty didn't seem to think he was fit company for her, obviously race was the primary reason. . . .

Marty ignored the comment and staggered to his feet. "Want something to drink?"

"No, uh, no, thank you, sir." *Don't let it go. For God's sake, don't just let it go.*

"Did you hear what I said?"

Jacobs shrugged. "Sure. You don't want a drink."

"No. What I said about the race thing. It was a difficult thing for me, because Mary was white."

"Difficult. For you." Marty Jacobs looked at him, and Richard couldn't read his face at all.

"Because it's always a barrier. And it was obviously a barrier for you."

Marty retreated toward the bar in the basement, waving him off. "You sure you don't want a drink?"

"No." *No traction on that one*, Richard thought.

"Suit yourself. I just asked you to come out here so that you could tell me that you did everything you could to save my daughter." He said this while shuffling toward the basement bar; he was talking to the wall facing away from where Richard was sitting.

"Excuse me, sir?"

"I said," Marty turned toward him, "that I have powerful friends in this town. Hell, in every town. June fifteenth last year you started seeing my daughter. Then once or twice a week like clockwork. Now she's dead. Dammit, she's dead, and you're still here."

And I'm just some darkie, is that it? Well, I loved her, too, Marty. And I felt like a damned traitor because she was white.

"How do you know the date? Or how frequently?"

Marty Jacobs clinked some ice into a fresh glass, his watery eyes fixing Richard with his gaze. "A father knows these things. Otherwise he's not a parent."

A lover is supposed to know things too. Like what she was doing with another man. Why she had sensitive documents in her apartment.

Why she was killed. Why it's over without any real sense of closure.

Why it was falling apart.

Marty Jacobs poured some scotch into the tumbler with the ice, knocked it back, and threw the glass against the wall where it shattered.

"Shit. June fifteenth. I was surprised. When. I. Found. Out."

Let's try it again. "You know the precise date?" *That your daughter and I became intimate?*

"A father knows these things!"

"Was there anyone else?" He had to ask, had to. *Had to. Was it falling apart because there was someone else? Had she really loved him? Or was she simply using him?*

Marty Jacobs looked at him, his face flushing red.

"What did you say?"

"I asked you," Richard said, his own anger rising, "if she was seeing anyone else."

"How dare you!"

Anger and grief. You get close to someone, think about changing your whole life around, and then little by little you start finding out about the lies. And you want to deny it, I swear, Marty, I want to deny it and think better of her, but lit-

tle by little, the myth is peeling away, and I'm not sure I like what I'm seeing underneath it all.

"You said a father knows these things. So, Dad, was she sleeping with anyone else?"

"Get out," he growled.

"Tell me what I want to know, Marty." *I need the answers. I can't deny myself the answers. No matter how much it hurts, I need to know.*

"Get out!"

"Was she sleeping with someone else, Marty? You know, somehow, you know. So tell me. Was Mary sleeping with someone else?"

"Get the fuck out of my house!"

"No, God dammit! Tell me if Mary was seeing someone else! Tell me!" *If it was all a lie, then let me begin to get past all of it. Let me bypass that abyss and get on with my life and saving my career.*

"Get out of my HOUSE!" He threw the scotch bottle at Whelan's head.

Discretion dictated that he get out of there as soon as possible, so Whelan ran; he ran up the stairs, with other liquor bottles breaking around his feet, and sprinted past the Samoan butler.

The Porsche was parked near the front door. He climbed in, started it up, and was rolling down the long driveway toward the street.

Somehow, I have to find out what happened. And why. He owed himself that much even if there was no time to mourn. Even if the president and the world had to wait on him, for once, dammit, for once he would put his skills to work selfishly for himself, not the greater good.

He hit Potomac Drive and turned left.

A dark-colored Chevy Camaro parked down the street started up and came after him.

Sam Hennings was eating a bacon cheeseburger (there was no greater delicacy in Western civilization's empty-calorie menu, he'd decided) when he figured out how he could get Enrique Gonzales to help evaluate the Indian blast data. He glanced at his watch: 8:45 P.M. The guys on the West Coast might still be around, he decided.

He tried Enrique's number at Sandia National Labs. It rang five times and went into voice mail. Crap.

He retrieved his cellular phone, which had two hundred numbers stored in memory. He scrolled down the phone's display, looking for Enrique's cell-phone number, hoping that he'd stored it.

Aha! Found it. He hit the talk button and waited while it dialed.

Richard Whelan was fuming as he headed back onto MD-187 out of Potomac. The rain had just about stopped, and he killed his wipers as he slowed to merge into I-270 back to Washington. When he was angry he drove . . . faster. He jammed his foot on the accelerator and worked through the Porsche's gears. Punched a tape into the tape deck. Seal, "Kiss from a Rose," blared from the speakers.

Just as he accelerated onto 270 he noticed a set of head-lights shoot past an old VW bus and come up fast on his tail. Richard checked his speedometer, he was just passing sixty-five, nothing but a brisk walk in this car, so he hadn't blown through a speed trap with enough gusto to matter. Remem-bering the headlights from the trip out to Potomac he mashed on the accelerator some more and watched his speedometer leap toward eighty.

The car behind him continued to close. This guy must be doing close to ninety, Richard realized. He merged onto the Capital Beltway, with the mystery car right behind him.

And closing. In the endless American car–foreign car de-bate, Richard always conceded that for pure horsepower, American sports cars were tough to beat. But in the overall package, well, few people had enough automobile to catch him on anything but a straightaway. And from the accelera-tion his pursuer exhibited, Richard thought it had to be an American car with a fairly prodigious power plant.

It had stopped raining and the roadway was dry, allowing him to use the Porsche's superior handling. He pressed down harder on the gas. "Kiss from a Rose" mixed into Cream's classic "Sunshine of Your Love," a segue that un-nerved most people that heard it in his car, particularly since Whelan had a tendency to steer with his knees and beat the dashboard in time with Ginger Baker banging and crashing away on the drums.

The other car continued to press, pulling up to his bumper. Richard could see the hood scoop on the car, made it out to be a Camaro, of all things. A kid's street racer, maybe with some enhancements under the hood.

Let's see what he wants. Richard tapped his brakes, just enough to flash his brake lights, Eric Clapton lighting up the sound system with the classic guitar lick, Whelan's fingers rapping the steering wheel.

His pursuer overreacted, fishtailed, and pulled into the adjacent lane and accelerated until he was almost parallel to Whelan's car.

The passenger window was down. Richard glanced, and out of the corner of his eye saw the driver aiming a pistol at him.

Downshift! He worked the clutch and the gearshift to get some additional torque and shot ahead. Watching the speedometer climb past one hundred, he reached down and cranked the volume up on the stereo. The Camaro kept with him, and Richard changed lanes a couple of times to spoil his aim; he was focused now, humming lyrics to himself. But the Camaro kept coming, coming, pulling nearer and nearer until they got to a very straight section of the interstate.

Now it was a drag race. This was the one time when Whelan wished he'd opted for the turbo charged version of the car instead of the normally aspirated model he was driving. Although he could stay with the Camaro in terms of top-end speed, whatever his pursuer had under the hood was going to get him to the top end of his range quicker than Whelan's Porsche would get to his.

One ten. One twenty. Still coming. *Could drop a gear but I don't want to redline the engine.*

One twenty-five. The bass throbbing so much that his pant legs were vibrating. Still on a drag race, traffic sparse. They blew past a big green exit sign, eating up the blacktop so fast that the white lines were a blur. He had to fake this boy out, and fake him out quickly.

He darted into the center lane, forcing the Camaro into the third lane in order to pull parallel to get a shot off. They passed several cars of slower-moving traffic, Richard weaving the Porsche in and out and around slower-moving cars but still making sure he ended up in the middle lane with the Camaro to his left in the third lane.

Exit coming up!

There were two cars ahead and to his right, and even from half a mile back he could see that he wouldn't get past them to hit the exit ramp, and he couldn't risk slowing down and dropping in behind them to make the exit.

There was about fifteen yards between the two of them, and he guessed that they were poking along at the speed limit or a little slower.

The Camaro was gaining again. Ten seconds before he catches up, Richard thought. And he would have to bleed his excess speed to keep from flipping the car on the exit ramp. This was going to be very dicey. . . .

As he pulled alongside the slow movers he twisted the wheel. The Porsche turned nearly sideways, the Pirelli tires smoking away momentum, and he shot the gap between the cars in the right-hand lane. He sensed more than saw the Camaro start to try and dart in behind him, but he was too far away from the gap and overshot the opportunity.

Richard corrected into the direction of the skid as he smoked into the exit lane, sliding sideways on the pavement, the car trying to respond to his inputs and straighten out, him resisting the temptation to hit the brakes. He dropped a gear, the engine howling as the tires caught pavement and smoked some more, and the car began to straighten ever so slowly.

Richard looked out of the driver's-side window and saw the Camaro's brake lights as his pursuer fishtailed across two lanes toward the shoulder.

And he saw the sand-filled barrels guarding the abutment on the left side of the exit ramp rushing toward him at close to one hundred miles an hour, Ginger Baker pounding out the final beats to "Sunshine"; end of tape.

Norman, the driver of the Camaro, slid to a stop on the gravel lining the shoulder of 495 almost a quarter mile past the exit. He cursed, shifted into reverse, and spun his tires trying to get back to the exit ramp that Whelan had tried to take.

If he made it. Given the stunt he'd just pulled, Norm fully expected to hear the sound of a crash.

The Porsche began to straighten out, and Richard could see that the exit ramp sloped down and curved to the right. He jammed the gears again, watching the tachometer climb toward the redline, and stood on the brakes. The big disks at the front and rear wheels began to heat up, and he could feel the brake pedal heading closer to the floor as the brakes began to fade.

He straightened out twenty yards from the sand barrels.

Now all I have to do is keep the damn thing on the ground and make the turn, he thought. He was in second gear, and the governor on the transmission wouldn't let him destroy his transmission by dropping into first to use the engine to slow the car.

Nothing to do now but pray, he thought.

The Camaro reached the exit ramp in reverse. *No Porsche.* Norm came out of reverse and stomped on the gas, looking at the long trail of black skid marks Whelan had made down the ramp, amazed at the way the Porsche had made the turn in what must have been a murderous four-wheel drift. He drove as fast as he could around the bend until he came to a stoplight. There was no traffic around, and no telltale brake lights in front of him.

But there were skid marks. Whelan's Porsche had slid into a right turn.

The Camaro did the same.

Whoooeeeee, that was hairy, Richard thought as he slung the Porsche through a looping right turn onto a street at the end of the exit ramp. He'd cut the wheel hard as soon as he hit the downslope of the on ramp and hadn't gone airborne. He pointed the nose as perpendicular to his direction of travel as he could, which was into the right curve of the ramp, and applied the gas to keep more or less in the middle of the pavement as the car's four wheels drifted. Second gear, plenty of torque in the rear-mounted engine; the moment he'd felt the tail trying to get away from him into a spin he'd given it gas and turned as much as he could back in the direction of travel. Even with the heroics he'd managed to scrape the bumper on the guardrail as the ramp merged with the street; he was pointed into a right turn, anyway, and hit the gas and sped off.

Waiting for the headlights to come banging down the off ramp after him. He went a hundred yards in a straight line before he saw the wobble and wiggle of a pair of headlights come off the ramp behind him and make the same right turn.

He had no idea where he was. But he was on city streets. And he had no intention of traveling in a straight line.

Traffic was nonexistent, and the Camaro pilot saw taillights in the distance as he worked the gears and mashed the accelerator. He wanted to catch Whelan where his brute horsepower had an advantage, on a straight line, not through a series of turns. And he had to think about cops, too, because they'd been incredibly lucky until now. All they had to do was run through a speed trap or pass a local cruiser at high speed and things would get a lot more complicated. And since the message had only been to "teach the nigger a lesson," the driver felt perfectly justified in interpreting that as he saw fit.

As his hot rod began eating up the distance between the two cars, the driver saw Whelan's Porsche execute a damn near right angle turn onto a side street. He jammed his foot on the brake, working the gears, and slewed the Camaro around just in time to take the turn. He straightened it out, found he hadn't lost too much ground, and pushed down on the gas again.

Residential neighborhood, Whelan thought as he saw the Camaro's headlights swing into view behind him. Little shaky taking that turn, eh?

But this was a tract development of medium-size homes, and there were lights on and people about. He passed a Saab going the other way and looked at his speedometer. Sixty-five in a twenty-five zone.

Someone's going to call the police.

He squealed into a left turn, hoping he didn't run into a cul-de-sac.

The left put them on a long straight road bordered by a field on one side and half-finished houses on the other. The Camaro driver hoped that there wasn't a turn anywhere near, because he intended to conclude this little stunt before Whelan got them both killed in a head-on. He hit the gas and closed the gap.

Whelan saw the headlights gaining on him again. He didn't dare open the Porsche up again, not on this kind of road where he didn't know where the pothole was that would rip a wheel from his axle.

Instead he would set the Camaro up, if the topography of the road would cooperate. From the looks of it, there wasn't a right turn coming anytime soon.

That left only one other direction.

Norm leaned out of the driver's window, trying to see through the blast of wind whipping though his hair. He steadied the pistol, although he wasn't that good a shot, and decided he'd pull right up on Whelan's bumper before he began blasting.

The Porsche didn't increase speed as he walked in on it, engine and exhaust howling. *Just a few more seconds,* he thought. *Just a second more . . .*

There! He pulled the trigger. Once, twice, and then he lost count.

The back window blew out, and Whelan ducked, almost losing control of his speeding car. The Camaro was on his bumper, and Richard was certainly enough of a shot to know that he was going to take one through the seat back if he didn't move. He weaved to the left, then the right.

And then he saw salvation coming up fast.

He was still firing when the Porsche's taillights lit up, signifying "Brakes!" to his distracted brain. He hauled his head out of the slipstream and hit the brake pedal, but he still ran right up over the Porsche's bumper, the grinding thud and tearing metal jarring him. And just like that the Porsche disconnected and slewed into a left turn that he had way too much momentum to match.

And the friggin' road ran out right in front of him, and he threw his arms in front of his face as the Camaro blasted through a wooded fence and into the grassy field beyond.

There was nothing behind him. After a mile or two and several more turns, Richard stopped and inspected the damage to his car, keeping one ear cocked for the distinctive exhaust note of the Camaro.

His rear bumper had been torn off when the cars connected, and he had no rear window. But the engine was still purring, although he didn't have the heart to look closely at the tread on his tires.

What the hell was that all about? he thought.

His cell phone rang, and he nearly jumped out of his skin. He answered it as he climbed back into the driver's seat, pondering his next move.

"Hey, security boy, it's Bettina. Pizza's getting cold. Where are you?"

"Um," he said not wanting to tell her everything, "I'm on my way to my club. I'm going to pass on the pizza, unless you're talking about a slice with Letterman later."

"Is that some sort of a come-on, Richard?"

What a night. "Nope. Just don't want to piss you off, too, since that appears to be my specialty."

"What's at the club, anyway?"

"I think I need to carry some protection. I'll tell you about it when I get there."

9

Mike Monroe waited as his operations people brought in the first batch of new photos. He'd had them brought directly to him, no copies, none of the usual distribution. His desk was usually clear, anyway, and he laid the satellite images on his blotter one by one.

He wasn't trained in such things, but he wanted to see them himself. Before anyone, the analysts, Erskine, saw the images that he had before him.

He smiled as he looked at the first set of images—which were completely clear of any evidence of troops or vehicles—and thought about how big a stick he was going to ram up Richard Whelan's ass tomorrow.

After a million attempts, Sam Hennings finally got Enrique Gonzales on his cell phone. After calming the scientist down about haranguing him about "his impossible request," Hennings began selling his approach to the analysis of the data.

"Enrique, you've said that you can't take limited data from an atmospheric explosion and funnel it down into a meaningful comparison with data from your underground tests, correct?"

"Yes, yes, Sam, that is precisely the problem."

"What about expanding the existing data sets on underground tests to extrapolate how those designs would have 'performed' in an open-air detonation?"

"I don't follow you. What's the difference?"

"You already have complex visualization models that handle things like the propagation of fallout, blast radius, structural damage, and the like, right? You just plug in the parameters and run the models, pretty much?"

"An oversimplification, but essentially true."

"Then all I'm saying is to enrich those existing aboveground models with additional data from your underground tests. That shouldn't be too difficult, right?"

"You mean re-parameterize. But based upon what?"

"Worst case, you'd model what happens to an underground test if you remove all the constraints on blast and radiation propagation imposed by the fact that the weapon is six or seven hundred feet underground in Nevada. You calibrate those results with your existing aboveground nuke war models."

"And then?"

"See if the output from the various designs conforms with what the Indian explosion yielded. We're only talking about enhanced radiation weapons, Enrique. We're only talking about trying to fit your test data to fewer parameters. So rather than trying to extrapolate from the few to 'curve fit' the many, we extrapolate from the many to 'curve fit' the few. Should be much more robust."

"Hmm. Let me think."

"It's at least worth a shot, Enrique."

"And you want this done 'on the sly,' as you put it?"

"If we have to have your bosses talk to my bosses about it, World War Three will have already broken out and concluded by the time they collectively and bureaucratically say no."

Enrique laughed. "You're certainly right about that. Look, I have an idea. Someone's been interested in extrapolating new data from the existing models based upon some fairly new math that only three people in the world understand. This might be right up his alley."

"Will he do it on the sly?"

"Tsk, tsk, Sam. You're too paranoid, even for CIA. I'm sure that doing something that no one has ever done will appeal to this researcher's ego, and the lack of associated paperwork conforms with his utter lack of understanding of bureaucracy. Satisfied?"

"How soon can you have results?"

"It will take several days, perhaps as much as a week to do this, I'm not sure. Most of that is run time on the equipment, which is a competitive allocation between other projects that are not 'on the sly.'"

It's a long shot, anyway, Hennings thought. "Fine, Enrique. Let me know how it goes."

The Hunt Club was all the way in Silver Spring, which meant that Richard didn't get there as often as he liked. The unpredictability of his schedule was one reason, but the other, he had to admit, was that Mary hadn't liked his expertise with guns.

Works for a major defense contractor and doesn't like guns. He'd shaken his head many times about that one. So his time on the practice range had suffered.

He got there just as the last of the members were heading to their cars. He cornered Larry Fitz, the operations manager of the club and told him he needed to get to his locker before they kicked everyone out and turned out the lights.

"Richard Whelan. Haven't seen you in a while. How are things in government?"

"Top secret," Richard replied. "So can I get to my locker?"

"Sure, no rush. I was just about to go to the practice range for a bit before closing up. Care to join me?"

Richard shrugged. Since he thought he needed protection, he might as well take a few practice shots.

He went to his locker and retrieved a pistol, a Glock 9-millimeter handgun, and waited for Larry to meet him at the target range.

His father had taught him to hunt. He remembered it vividly, that day when he was thirteen that he and his father had gone on a hunting trip in upstate New York. He hadn't really bonded with his father even though he admired him; his father found Richard to be a complete mystery. So a hunting trip between just the two of them was not necessarily what the doctor ordered.

Dad had patiently gotten them into position to take down a deer. He told Richard to set up, making sure that he had a stable position from which to shoot his rifle, a big, awkward Remington Model 70 bolt action, making sure that the stock was braced so that the recoil wouldn't dislocate his shoulder. The gun had seemed too big and too loud, because although he was a healthy kid, he'd not yet experienced the growth spurt that would make him an athlete later on in high school.

So it was cold and awkward, and Richard looked through the telescopic sights and saw the deer. Magnificent animal. The crosshairs were centered. And Richard, almost without knowing it, took the shot just as naturally as his father might have, a gentle pressure on the trigger until he fired, surprising himself.

"Damn! You hit it!" His father had clapped him on the back, but when Richard looked through the binoculars he was anything but proud. The deer was down, fatally wounded, bleeding profusely and pawing the air and the ground trying to get up and get away.

"You're a natural, son." His father had said.

A natural? A natural what? Bambi-killer? he'd thought to himself.

"Way to go, son. Excellent shot from this distance. You have a real talent. You should be proud of yourself."

His eighth-grade teacher in the prep school that he attended, a Miss Larson, asked him if he was "proud of himself" when on an English test he'd outscored most of his white classmates, particularly the ones that were her pet projects. She'd slapped his test paper down on his desk, fourth-highest mark in the class (but still an A-) like it was a national disgrace, and berated the rest of her prized students for their performances.

Yes, I am proud of myself, he'd thought at the time, but it never meant the same thing that it meant for the white kids. Sometimes he wondered what he would have been if the finest education that money can buy had actually encouraged him to develop his skills, as opposed to merely tolerating his existence; he wondered why it was so taboo to do better than the white kids.

Because you aren't white. His father clapped him on the back. The deer was dead in a pool of its own blood. *This is their world.*

Richard went to Harvard despite the classmates who'd thought he was joking when he said he'd applied.

But I'm not bitter, he thought. I simply made it my business to be the best at everything I did.

But now Mary's dead and I'm accused of murder. Maybe good the world can accept, but great, at least from you, Richard Whelan, the world does not seem ready for.

Larry turned the lights on in the indoor practice range, and Richard looked at his watch: 10:00 P.M. He could do a few targets and still get to Bettina's in plenty of time for David Letterman. He rigged a target and sent it to the back of the shooting range, donned his ear protectors, and shoved a clip into the Glock.

Sighted.

Six shots, one, two, three, four, five, six, rapid succession, easy pulls on the trigger, rock steady on the aim, kept the recoil of the weapon under control.

He pressed the button to bring the target back to him.

Perfect. Head shots, with a spread so small it looked as if he'd fired a single large bullet through the paper. *Maybe the world isn't ready for "the Great Richard Whelan," he thought, but that's too damn bad.*

Fitz came over to look at his results and whistled. "Man, I need some of what you got," he said.

Oh no you don't, Richard thought.

Bettina met him at the door of her stylish Georgetown townhouse wearing a flannel robe and a bodysuit. Even though it was carefully concealed, Richard could see that extraordinary body.

"Letterman is in ten minutes," she said, showing him in. "Do you think pizza and microwaves go together?"

Still "cooking impaired," he thought. Not that Mary had ever demonstrated skills in that arena, either.

"Cold is fine. It's a guy thing."

"Cold, greasy pizza? It's a 'dead of heart disease' guy thing."

She led him into her living room. The big-screen television was turned to the news with the sound muted.

Richard picked up a slice of pepperoni and mushroom. "Not only is it a guy thing, but it is a guy thing that proves that it's a man's world."

Bettina snorted. "And how is that?"

"Because men don't need women. Cold pizza and warm beer and a football game and we're set. We are more advanced because we have fewer needs. QED."

"Oh, please. Have a seat."

He sat down, and for a guilty instant hoped that she

would sit next to him on the couch, but she sat opposite him in a matching wing chair.

She turned up the sound as the Letterman theme music came on.

"So what happened? And what is that bulge under your jacket?"

"I went to see the legendary Marty Jacobs. Had a screaming match with him, left, was followed by someone who took a few potshots at me while they chased me halfway to Baltimore. So I went to my club and checked out a gun."

"You have a gun? Here? In my house?"

"A little itty-bitty one, just because I know how sensitive you are. But perhaps I should rewind my synopsis. Someone put bullet holes in the Porsche."

"Wait a minute. You say someone put bullet holes in your car. As in, with a gun, *bang, bang*?"

"Yup."

"Things are piling up. Mary Jacobs was killed for a reason, and that reason appears to be related to you."

"That thought had occurred to me."

"Yeah, I'm sure it did. And now people are following you and shooting at you? You're the brilliant intelligence operative. Does all that sound like coincidence to you?"

"No, obviously not. Hence the weapon." He pulled open his jacket to reveal the Glock 9-millimeter automatic in a holster at his hip.

"You're mighty cool about this. And now you have to carry a gun. Which you, for example, presumably have a license for."

"Sort of." Well, maybe not as a concealed weapon . . .

"And you're out on bail for someone's murder."

"It's an event cascade," Richard said, shrugging.

"What?"

"It's an event cascade. The phrase relates to the rapid escalation of stuff that results in, for example, a plane crash.

Pilot spills coffee, systems short out, plane goes into a spin, wings fall off, then it crashes. This is an event cascade, where a bunch of smaller actions add up to result in something catastrophic. And whoever's doing this doesn't understand that the first catastrophe is that I'm going to kick ass until I get to the bottom of it."

"I don't think Mr. Macho is the right move, Richard."

Richard shook his head. "It's the only move. First of all, someone planted sensitive information in Mary's apartment. The cops mentioned it, and now the *Post* is about to go public with something as well. Second, there's the coincidence of being stopped by phony cops just in time for Mary to get killed and for me to show up afterward and look like the killer. Then there's the mystery surrounding my relationship with Mary."

"What mystery is that?"

"I always felt that there were things that she wasn't telling me about."

"Oh? Like why white women have no butts?"

"Very funny."

"So where do you start?"

"I have some ideas."

"Why don't you ask Blaze about finding the phony cops?"

"Blaze? Why Blaze?"

"Because," she said, patiently, like this was something that he should know, "your sometime friend Mr. Mojo knows people who know the streets. The man has defended every lowlife in this town. Maybe you weren't the first person these guys knocked around."

"Good idea, but that's not the one I was thinking of."

"Oh, are you going to tell me about it?"

He looked at her and smiled in a way that she found chilling. "I don't think you want to know."

10

Mike Monroe took the newspaper from the delivery boy's hand at 6:18 A.M. the next morning. He looked at the column in the lower-left-hand corner of the front page:

Questions Persist in Security Adviser's Role in Socialite's Death

He hurried in to call the president about this latest development with Richard Whelan.

President Roswell was already awake when the call came in. As he listened to Monroe's synopsis of the article he summoned the White House steward to get him a copy of the *Washington Post*. After listening to Monroe for a few minutes, Edgar Roswell cut him off.

"There are bigger fish to fry about this one, Michael," the president said softly, and Monroe instantly shut up at the president's use of his formal first name. "I got a deranged call from Marty Jacobs last night. Yes, Marty himself called me directly. I had no choice but to take the call."

"What did he have to say?"

"Well, it was obvious that he was drunk out of his mind, but what coherence I did get from him concerned Richard Whelan. Apparently he paid Marty a visit last night. Unsolicited."

"You're kidding."

"I wish I was. I had to listen to Marty Jacobs's drunken fuming about how 'that nigger fucked my daughter, and now she's dead.' " The president paused to let it sink in.

"I thought I charged you personally with keeping Marty Jacobs clear of this?"

"You did, but I never thought—"

"Michael, if I wanted you to think, I'd have made you a goddamned rocket scientist. I want you to cover my ass on this one. Particularly when it comes to Marty, okay? You understand how sensitive this could be, right?"

"Then why not can Whelan?"

"Things are too sensitive. At least right now. Besides, he certainly pulled your pants down yesterday. By the way, was he right?"

"Nope. Nothing on the satellite images that we can see. And NRO burned a lot of fuel repositioning a Keyhole and then moving it back. They're pissed that we chased a wild goose on this one because we already covered the area. It was a long shot that India was keeping forces under cover during our regular satellite passes."

"And your suggestion on how to proceed is what?"

"Talk to the Indian prime minister. Get them to tone down their rhetoric and pull back from any military maneuvers for at least six months. Tell the Chinese that's the stance you've taken. And hope it works."

"Hmm. Lousy advice, particularly since it echoes my conclusions. But to get back to Whelan for a moment, do you think he actually leaked documents to this woman?"

"It looks that way. But we can't be certain. Yet."

"Why the hell would Mary Jacobs be interested in anything Richard was working on? I just don't get it."

"Neither do I. But I'm telling you, Edgar. Whelan is bad news. You'd be better served to jettison him now than wait for something truly ugly to come bubbling up out of his past."

"I'll think about it," President Roswell said, then hung up in his DCI's ear.

. . . several White House sources have indicated that certain sensitive documents authored by Richard Whelan were found in Mary Jacobs's apartment after her death and that only decisive intervention by federal officials prevented the widespread release of these documents to the news media.

One document supposedly leaked to Jacobs chronicled the history of Chinese espionage at United States weapons laboratories, penetrations that many detractors have claimed increased during the Roswell years despite warnings about Chinese spying that go as far back as the Clinton administration. There have been persistent accusations that President Roswell ignored ongoing security breeches at U.S. weapons labs because of heavy support of his campaign by Chinese interests. Thus it is ironic that Whelan is alleged to have given his highly confidential report to the daughter of a major defense contractor who also appears to have been a significant contributor to President Roswell's reelection campaign.

Was Mary Jacobs's untimely death an accident? Or was she silenced by someone in the Roswell administration for simply knowing too much?

Richard read it and reread it, trying to stay calm. The other shoes are dropping. You expected it, get over it.

And damn well do something about it. If you don't, this particular aspect of the case will eat you alive. Just the article alone would be enough for the president to freeze him out of anything remotely concerned with national security, and how could he be the in-house adviser without access to information? Worked too hard to get here.

Too damn hard to fold without a fight.

The newspaper article played into what the cops had called his "motive" for Mary's death. And from the phone call from that reporter the other day, he knew that someone in the administration was feeding the newspapers *something*. More's coming, because whoever was behind this was being very thorough. They, whoever the hell they were, expected him to fold up and go away. Run along, nigger. Your services aren't needed anymore.

He pulled the Glock from under his bed. It was a big step to carry a weapon around. But someone shot at you. Is it self-defense if you shoot back? Or is there ever any justification for your anger? The only passage from the Bible that he'd ever memorized was Ecclesiastes, chapter 3:

To everything there is a season, a time for every purpose under heaven.

He could pretend he was simply being paranoid, but the depth of what was happening to him denied him that luxury. It would only be a matter of time before the *Post* accused him directly of killing Mary Jacobs, and he had to get to the bottom of this long before that happened, long before he became even more guilty by acclamation.

There was something that Marty had implied, that he wasn't good enough for her, that there was some unholy bond between daughter and father, or daughter and family enterprise. Maybe there was something that Marty could have gained by having Mary steal secrets from him, but he didn't know what.

But someone had killed her and someone wanted him to take the fall. If you need motivation, he thought, use revenge.

A time to weep, and a time to laugh; a time to mourn, and a time to dance . . .

No time to mourn anymore. She's gone, you're still around. You left her that night to do your job and your job isn't finished.

A time to cast away stones, and a time to gather stones; a time to embrace, and a time to refrain from embracing . . .

It was still early; only 7:30 in the morning. He had a gun in his pocket, that in itself was a crime, and he would not hesitate to use it if he had to.

Time to get into the game, Richard.

His first stop had to be Mary's apartment.

Bettina Freeman read the morning *Post* as well. The spin doctors were certainly laying it on thick. What was most frightening was that there weren't many people, short of the president or someone on his staff, who could pull this kind of thing off. So was the president involved? His chief of staff, Charles O'Shay?

And involved in what? Why had the girl died? Why were they so intent on framing Richard?

And how long would it take them, whoever they were, to come after her?

Susan Hennings tossed the *Post* onto the kitchen table, just missing her husband's bowl of Cheerios. Sam Hennings glanced at the headlines—China and India and Pakistan rattling sabers, then turned the paper over and saw the article on Richard Whelan.

He crunched through a couple of spoonfuls of cereal (this was his penance for bacon cheeseburgers) while he read the article. If Whelan had killed someone or had violated national security, why was he pushing so hard on identifying the precise design of the bomb the Indians had used? Didn't make any sense, while his explanations about why they would need to know made a lot of sense.

He'd been in Washington for fifteen years, and he knew that the press almost never got the whole story. They just got whatever story someone with an agenda wanted them to get. So whether Whelan was innocent or guilty of anything was never going to play out in a newspaper article or two.

And it was clear someone had an agenda to smear Whelan. And from the depth of the article and the height of the "unnamed sources" within the Roswell administration, it was clear that someone with some clout was doing this.

He thought about calling Enrique and pulling the plug on the computer work, but something about this setup didn't seem to make much sense. More data, rather than less, might shed light on things. And he hadn't made it an official request from CIA, and he'd emphasized to Enrique that he needed this investigation done quietly.

So maybe he was safe. He'd let things run for a while and see what happened.

Richard rolled up to Mary's apartment like he'd done a million times before but without the sense of anticipation that always came with his visits. Just to be safe, he parked a few blocks away and went in the rear entrance to avoid the doorman.

There was no police presence at her apartment house like he'd feared, and when he got to her floor, there was no police presence in front of her door. There was just yellow crime-scene tape blocking the entrance. The front door to her apartment was locked. He hesitated, not wanting to rekindle his memories.

·He opened the door with his keys. He carefully closed and locked the door behind him.

The apartment had been searched, there was no question about that, and her parents had not come to pack up her belongings. He stared for a moment at the chalk outline in the foyer that marked where Mary Jacobs had fallen when she'd died.

And what if the police return and find you rummaging around at the scene? He had a sudden chill at the thought of Marty Jacobs appearing in his crimson jogging suit with a drink in his hand, screaming obscenities at him. Well, if it happens, it happens.

He went room by room, nervously keeping an eye on his watch. CIA had rescheduled the brief for the president at 9:00 A.M. this morning. He had plenty of time. Keep looking.

The living room was fine.

The kitchen was fine.

The bedroom was fine. There was a picture of him and Mary in Rock Creek Park on her nightstand. It chilled him.

The bathroom was fine. *You're running out of real estate, dude.*

He went back to the living room. Think. What to do?

He went into the kitchen and opened every single cabinet. Dishes, kitchen stuff, piles of paper bags from the Safeway, spice rack, c'mon, hard to tell if he was skipping anything at the back of a shelf or not.

He went to the bedroom. Opened all the dressers, felt around in each drawer, then slammed them closed again. He went into the bedroom closet—

There, he'd just kicked something. A metal box with a clasp but no lock. He pulled it out of the bedroom and placed it on the bed. Opened it up.

It had files in it. All of them looked like they were classi-fied. Some had his notes scrawled on the documents inside the file folders. And they weren't copies.

These were originals. TOP SECRET and EYES ONLY stamped in red on the folders.

And there were dozens of them. All someone had to do was come in here and stumble upon them and it would be obvious that he was leaking documents to his girlfriend.

Well, he wasn't going to let that happen. He placed the documents back in the strongbox and closed it. He picked it up by the metal handle in the lid.

Walked to the door. Waited to see if a neighbor was coming down the stairs. When it was clear, he carefully opened the door, stepped into the hallway, and locked the door behind him.

Voices on the stairwell coming up!

"Where's the stuff?"

Someone talking on a cell phone or radio. Richard couldn't hear the response. Then, *"Right. Got it."*

The talker turned to his companion, and Richard recognized at least two sets of footfalls on the creaky wooden steps.

"It's supposedly in the bedroom closet. Metal box. You did bring your gloves, didn't you?"

"Course. Not that the D.C. police are going to dust for prints again, but you never know. And I brought the camera to take some nice photos of where we find the stuff."

Reflex action: Whelan pulled his gun. Then thought better of it. He fumbled his keys, trying to open Mary's door. They were one floor below him. In thirty seconds they would see him trying to get inside the apartment, anyway. They might already be able to hear him working the locks.

Can't worry about that. Thought again about the Glock pistol heavy in the holster at his waist. *You can carry a gun,* his father had been fond of saying, *but using a gun is something entirely different than carrying one.*

But these guys aren't the police. Let 'em come.

He was inside Mary's apartment. He shot the dead bolt and did the chain. Whoever was out there would know someone was inside, but it might give him a split second more to get out.

He went back into the bedroom. There was a fire escape

outside the bedroom window, but the window itself was painted shut. He'd joked with Mary that they'd die trying to get out if the place ever went up in flames.

It was not a joke now.

He undogged the latches and gave it a heave.

The window didn't budge. He could hear voices at Mary's front door.

He gave the window another heave. All that time at the gym had to be worth something, right? All that fast food forgone?

They unlocked the bottom lock on the front door.

C'mon, push!

The window didn't budge.

They unlocked the top lock; Richard could hear the dead bolt snap back into the door.

Another push on the window. Nothing. He was trapped; damned if he did, damned if he didn't.

They unlocked the middle lock and the door opened onto the chain.

"Shit. What's with the chain? Something's wrong."

He gave the window a mighty shove, but it wasn't moving. Not an inch.

"Did you hear that?"

"What?"

"The floor creaked. These wooden floors, any movement, any pressure, they creak. The floor just creaked. Someone is in there."

"Oh, you're just being paranoid."

"I don't want to go in there if someone's there."

"But this is a great story."

"I'm a reporter, not a daredevil."

He pushed up on the window. Move, damn you, move! Nothing.

"Look, you want the story? Or you want to tell your editor that today's column was a big fat whiff?"

Move! He pushed. Nothing.

MOVE!

"Fine, do it." They pushed past the chain so quickly that it simply snapped. Richard heard the door swing wide open and thud softly against the wall.

They're in.

Forget stealth. Get in the game, Richard.

He smashed the window and was out onto the fire escape in an instant.

"Washington Post. We just want to ask some questions!" they yelled from inside the apartment. Richard was boogying down the fire escape, trying to mentally gauge where his car was, hoping he didn't spill the contents of the box all over the rusted metal steps.

He was two stories below them now, he thought, which meant they wouldn't be able to identify who he was until he left the fire escape and headed toward his car. He toyed with the notion of leaving the vehicle, but whoever these people were, they might try to identify all the vehicles in the vicinity and ID him that way.

He reached the bottom of the fire escape and swung the last steps down to the ground. There were footsteps above him, coming fast.

He was on the ground. He would head the long way to his car, try and lead them away from the Porsche, and then double back and pick it up. . . .

"Hey, who the hell are you?" There was a flash from above him, and Richard heard the whine of a camera motor.

Photos, just what he didn't need. But there was still enough fire escape between him and the photographer that he wouldn't get a decent shot. Richard ran away from the building along the alley, away from where his car was parked.

Running footsteps behind him. His pursuer was working a camera, and a flock of pigeons burst into flight, startled by the flashes of light. Richard worried for a moment that he'd left fingerprints all over Mary's apartment, but wait a minute. His fingerprints had probably already been identified at her apartment.

He got to the corner, turned left, and accelerated, running as hard as he could.

By sheer force of habit he glanced at his watch: 8:15. Still plenty of time to get to the White House for the meeting with the president. . . .

THE OVAL OFFICE, THE SAME TIME

Edgar Roswell looked at his watch. Charles O'Shay did the same. The president leaned over to talk to his chief of staff: "You did tell Whelan about the time change, didn't you?"

"I left him a voice mail early this morning. Everyone else got it." The rest of the participants were here, with the notable exception of State, because if an intel failure had made them miss India's invasion plans, the president wanted to see the dirty laundry first.

"Mike? Let's not wait. What did the satellites tell us?"

Mike Monroe stood up and passed around a set of photographs. "Absolutely nothing, Mr. President. There is nothing unusual going on in that region of Kashmir, and we found nothing that suggests that anything out of the ordinary is occurring with India's other forces. And if Whelan were here, I'd tell him 'I told you so' myself."

The others let out a polite laugh. The president said nothing.

Bad sign for Whelan, Chuck O'Shay thought.

Richard came around the block, looking for any sign of pursuit or police activity.

He approached his car casually. Looked at his watch: 8:20. He'd just make it to the White House in time.

As he started up the Porsche he looked at the plastic covering the rear window and the glass beads still littering the rear seat. The gunshots through his rear window still made him angry just thinking about them.

As he pulled out, a black Chevy Camaro with a slightly bashed-in front end cranked its engine and moved into traffic to follow him.

11

As he pulled away from the curve, Richard dialed his voice mail at the office on his cell phone.

"*Hey, Richard, Sam Hennings here. I think the ASCI people at Sandia National Labs are going to help us on the Indian thing. Gimme a call, okay? Bye.*"

He deleted that message.

"*Mr. Whelan, Doug Bristol,* Washington Post. *Tomorrow's installment of your story is going to detail the transfer, by you, of sensitive government secrets to Mary Jacobs. Please call me if you care to comment. Good-bye.*"

He deleted that message with a vengeance. Was the "evidence" of his passing secrets to Mary the strongbox on his passenger seat? *Nice try, assholes. But I think you'll have to cancel tomorrow's article.*

"*Richard, Chuck O'Shay. That brief with the president has been moved up to 8:15 this* A.M. *The man has a conflict with a Girl Scout troop that he's meeting in the Rose Garden at nine. Eight-fifteen, new meeting time.*"

What? Richard risked a glance at his watch. It was already 8:25. Too late to even call and explain his absence. *Dammit.*

He was about to dial O'Shay's number when he reconsidered. What difference would it make? He was already in so much trouble that the only thing he would get from a phone call was grief in advance.

He listened to his last message.

"Whelan, Phil Erskine. The new satellite intel on Kashmir indicates nothing. No invasion force, nothing. You were wrong."

That one didn't feel right. He felt it in his gut, someone was missing the boat on this one. Maybe he could get Hennings to check it out for him. Maybe nose around and see what he could find out.

For a guy being publicly accused of giving away state secrets. Yeah, he'll jump at the chance.

Well, Hennings had called him with what appeared to be good news. Maybe he doesn't read the paper.

Still, it was worth a try. He glanced at his side mirror and saw an all too familiar sight.

A black Chevy Camaro with a hood scoop. This time he noticed the license plates—Maryland QXY 7740—right under the dented hood. Same car as last night.

Well, no more Mr. Nice Guy, he thought. He pulled the Glock out of its holster and headed for Rock Creek Park.

Bill Johnson was sitting at his desk drinking coffee when the call came in. He was studying a case file—a brutal slaying of a woman and her child, and trying to ignore the gruesome crime-scene photos clipped in the folder. He was happy to close the file and pick up the phone.

"Johnson."

"Detective, this is Richard Whelan. I think I have some information that has a bearing on my case. Can you run a license plate for me?"

"You're kidding, right?"

"Just do me a favor, Detective. Maryland plates, QXY 7740. Call me back at the White House and tell me who the car is registered to. Thanks, bye."

Sounded like he was on a cell phone in a car. Driving quickly from the engine noises in the background.

A red herring? Who knew? He glanced back at the double homicide case file. One of the crime-scene photos was peeking out of the manila folder, and all he could see was a limb, covered with blood, and from what he recalled it was the leg of the little girl victim.

He decided that he could spend a couple of minutes running down Whelan's license plate.

The East-West Highway was a hilly, curvy road that was unusually clear this time of the morning. Richard accelerated until he was afraid the car would go airborne over some of the rougher patches of the road. The Camaro stayed with him, running a few of the yellow lights and at least one red, nearly causing a spectacular collision.

Richard made the turns and entered the park, the engine growling as he worked the gears and slung the car through the tight turns, slowly increasing his lead over the Camaro, thinking ahead to how he could end this before someone called the police to report the two speeding cars.

Exiting the park, he turned left onto a tree-lined street that bordered the park; Richard knew that eventually this would turn into Oregon and begin a long downhill run with the park on his left and sprawling houses on his right. The Camaro quickly moved in to his bumper. *Let's just mess with him a little*.

Richard tapped his brakes, testing the other driver, who bumped him hard. Richard downshifted and leaned back on the gas, pulling away, then hit the brakes hard.

No turning back now, he thought. The Camaro came up on him, but at the last second Whelan swerved to the right, letting the Camaro pull alongside him. Richard pointed the Glock at the driver.

Pull over asshole! He motioned with his hand. He tightened his finger on the trigger.

The Camaro hit the brakes, smoking his tires, and both cars went airborne over a bump in the road. Richard stomped the gas, the bait finished, and pulled ahead as the Camaro came down hard, the front end pushing the shocks to the limit as the driver was a little late letting up on the brakes.

Richard crossed Military Road, reentering the park on Glover, passing the idyllic rest and parking areas as the road narrowed. The Camaro was catching up to him, which was fine, because once he hit Ridge Road he intended to take him down.

There were few cars in the park at this hour, and Richard mashed the clutch and worked the motor for as much torque as he could as he connected to Ridge. He made the dogleg right turn into the sharp left near a picnic area and let the back end of the Porsche loose, slamming the brakes as the car swung completely around.

Norm lost sight of his quarry as Whelan's Porsche whipped around the first curve on Ridge. He had to ease up on the gas to make the curve without spilling the car into the woods, and then there was a more acute left-hand curve coming up. He downshifted, hearing the rising note in the car's exhaust, and slung the Camaro into the curve. He was just about to stomp on the gas when he saw Richard Whelan, out of his car, a gun pointed at his windscreen, and the Porsche turned completely around, blocking his path.

Norm twisted his wheel, trying to use the shoulder to get around him.

As soon as he heard the Camaro's tires screaming through the curves, he tightened his finger on the trigger. For an instant, Richard Whelan stood frozen, his finger on the trigger, contemplating unleashing deadly force on another human being. The fluidity with which he tracked his opponent's windshield, the instinctual way in which his mind computed the trajectories, all of it was an automatic application of skills that he possessed but had never used. At least not like this. Maybe in an aircraft thinking in six dimensions at once, but not as some thug on a street corner asserting his manhood, not as some deranged lunatic bent on releasing some nameless rage.

Altitude, attitude, airspeed, controls, weapons, threats—he'd been cornered that night over Baghdad.

But he wasn't cornered now. *Dangerous, certainly.* Dangerous because he was crossing a line.

He dropped his sights down to the hood of the car, easy trigger pulls, the gun kicked, he dropped the sights, pulled the trigger, dropped the sights, a little bit of his anger discharged with each sharp crack in the morning sunshine as he methodically pumped bullets into the Camaro's engine block to kill the car's heart.

Just before the Camaro hit the shoulder and grass to pass him, he put one through the windshield on the passenger side, an attitude adjuster to give the driver something to think about, too.

The wounded engine coughed once as it labored to accelerate, tires spinning on the slick grass.

Whelan smoothly turned and dropped to one knee, pumping shots into the tires on the driver's side, little grunts from the smooth kick of the gun, totally on reflex, little grunts of breath—

Don't . . . *blam!*

Fuck . . . *blam!*

With me. *Blam, blam!*

But the driver was still giving the engine gas, and the blown rear tire screamed and shredded to the rim as the Camaro stumbled past the Porsche blocking the roadway and shuddered to a halt not ten yards past his car.

* * *

Norm was stunned by the flying glass from his shattered windshield but unharmed as the Camaro died on the shoulder. He was angry now. He pulled his gun and opened the door, intent on really teaching Whelan a lesson.

A park maintenance truck came down Ridge from the opposite direction, honking its horn and passing him on the shoulder.

Whelan wondered for a moment if it was possible that the Camaro had help, but he had to run the driver to ground before the situation got completely out of control.

He ran toward the Camaro. He was ten yards away when the door opened.

"Get out of the car, now!" he yelled.

He thought he saw movement, like the driver was going for a gun.

Reflex—threat. He snapped the Glock into position and put three shots through the rear window, shattering it before taking another breath. The parks department truck showed brake lights behind him, then accelerated as the driver realized what was going on.

"The next one is going right between your eyes! Get out of the car!"

He paused for the longest heartbeat in his life. He was exposed, peering through the shattered back window of the Chevy.

His chest heaved once.

If he saw threat, the driver was going to die, killed by the adrenaline pumping through his veins and the reflexes that he'd unleashed.

The driver broke out in a run, daring Richard to shoot him in the back.

Shit, I used to be a track star, Richard thought, and took after him.

* * *

It was a short race. To his left, the ground sloped downward toward a creek, and Richard took the Camaro's driver down with a flying tackle, and they tumbled to the edge of the shrubbery that fringed the picnic area. Richard clubbed the man with his gun, then hauled him out of the weeds and shoved him toward a picnic table.

They were both breathing hard. Richard jammed the pistol of his Glock into one of the thug's nostrils.

"Now why don't you tell me what this is all about."

The blond man raised his hands.

"That's a start. Who do you work for? Secret Service? Treasury? ATF?"

"I'm a private—if you don't take the gun out of my nose I'm going to shove it up your ass," he growled.

"Screw you. Answer the question."

Richard could feel the man's muscles flexing, like he was about to try something. He grabbed the man's right arm and pinned it behind his back and jammed his gun into his neck.

"I'm a private detective," the man said, panting from the struggle. "Marty Jacobs hired me to keep an eye on you."

"Say what?"

"Name's Norm. Private eye. I work for rich people who need someone who doesn't ask too many questions."

"And Marty Jacobs wanted you to follow me?"

"Yeah, asshole, and he wanted me to teach you a lesson."

"So the gunshots and the wild driving."

Norm said nothing for a moment. "He didn't say he wanted me to kill you."

"How long have you been following me?"

Norm said nothing, and Richard tightened his grip on his arm, and pinned it higher against his back. The private eye grunted in pain. "Not you. The daughter. Jacobs hired me to tap his daughter's phones, and wire her place for sound."

"From the beginning?"

"Over a year ago, yeah. Video, too."

"Did you say video?"

"Yes. Whenever she left the house."

"And Marty has the tapes?"

"Yes."

So Marty's had a front-row seat on her life, if he wanted it. Weird.

"How did he know when Mary and I got involved?"

"Dunno. Maybe she told him to piss him off."

But he had an idea. "Did anyone else show up on the tapes?"

"Fuck you. I've told you enough."

Richard yanked Norm's right elbow up toward his neck.

"Ahh, damn that hurts!"

"Answer the question."

"Sure. Lots of people."

"Going into her house? Coming out of her house?"

"No."

"Where are the tapes now?"

"Marty's house. In his basement. He keeps 'em in a foot-locker."

"Did you kill her?"

"No. You did."

Whelan tightened his grip, producing a groan. "Were you following her the night she got killed?"

"No."

"Why should I believe that?"

"Because the old man called me off a week ago. Now let me go, asshole."

"Okay, pal, get this straight the first time. If I ever see you again, if I ever see your car again, I'm going to hurt you. Understand?"

"Go . . . ," Norm said, ". . . and . . . fuck yourself."

"Whatever you say."

Richard glanced at his watch. It was after nine.

He let Norm go and backed away, just wanting to climb in his car and go to work. Assuming he still had a job.

But you're in the game now.

Once he was clear that Norm wasn't going to come after him, he climbed into his Porsche, cranked the engine, and steered his car out of the park.

It was after ten by the time he got to the White House. There was a nasty message from Chuck O'Shay on his voice mail. Yeah, too bad. He ignored the stares that he got from people he passed in the halls as he marched up to O'Shay's office still wound up from the shooting.

The president's chief of staff was on the phone when he barged in.

"Let me get back to you," O'Shay said to the other party on the phone and hung up.

He looked at Richard for a long time. "You look like something the cat dragged in. Where the hell have you been?"

"I need to talk to the president, Chuck."

"What?"

"I need to talk to the president about Marty Jacobs. I know he's a big supporter, but I think Jacobs may be trying to set me up to get back at me for sleeping with his daughter."

O'Shay didn't react for a moment. The words *Marty Jacobs* and *the president* used together in the same sentence gave him pause. O'Shay knew Marty was one of Edgar Roswell's money guys, but people weren't supposed to know how big a money guy Jacobs was for POTUS. The less said about it the better.

"Explain it to me." Whelan was keyed up, pacing on the balls of his feet like he was about to come across the desk and grab a handful of the president's chief of staff and lift him out of his chair.

Richard shook his head. "I have to talk to the president about it."

"Yeah, but given your track record lately, the road to the Oval Office runs right through my office. And where the hell were you this morning?"

"I was saving my ass."

"Saving it so that the president can fire it?"

"He won't, not after he hears what I have to say."

"You missed the brief."

"You left me a message changing the time. I didn't get it until it was too late."

O'Shay looked at him. "Did we change to banker's hours and nobody told me?"

Richard said nothing for a second. *Wind it down, Richard, wind it the fuck down.* "I was delayed coming in this morning."

"Because of Marty Jacobs?"

"Partly."

"Bullshit."

"Marty Jacobs set me up, Chuck. I know he's the president's big money go-to guy, but he set me up. This crap in the press? I bet it's coming from Jacobs."

O'Shay frowned, unconvinced. "I'll say it again. Bull-shit."

"Either I talk to the president or I talk to the press, Chuck. Your choice."

Charles O'Shay shook his head. You did not threaten the leader of the free world unless you had the balls and ballistic missiles to back it up. "I'll tell the president. Go back to your office and sit tight."

O'Shay watched Whelan leave. Then he picked up the phone.

"Sherrie? Get Frank Moynihan up here pronto."

* * *

Richard's office phone rang as he sat down at his desk. It was the Federal Protective Services cop from the main White House entrance.

"Mr. Whelan?"

"Yeah?"

"Hey, it's Ernie from the front entrance. I got two detectives here say they wanna come up and see you. Names of," he paused as if to look at the sign-in log, "Steinway and Johnson. Okay to let them up?"

Damn. The police. Here. *Not if he could help it.*

"Ask them what they want, Ernie, please?"

Whelan could hear Ernie place his hand over the receiver for a moment, then he came back. "They said they want to ask you some questions about a matter. That's what they said, 'a matter.' "

Several floors below, Ernie turned away from the waiting police officers. "Is this about the stuff in the papers, Mr. Whelan?"

" 'Fraid so, Ernie." Whelan looked around his office. He definitely didn't want them in here, particularly if O'Shay called him with a meeting time with the president.

Maybe he didn't have a choice. If he avoided them it would look bad. "Send them up, Ernie."

"Annie, can you get me a conference room?" he yelled to his secretary.

"For when?"

"Right now."

"Let me check." Annie was good, if underutilized. Whelan did most of his writing himself and managed his own schedule.

"Richard, I got you conference room D, as in David, downstairs."

"Thank you, Annie." He picked up a pad of paper to head the detectives off at the elevator.

He showed the detectives into the conference room and waited until they were seated.

"Can I have someone get you something? Coffee?" *A confession to discharging a weapon with deadly intent?*

Steinway and Johnson both declined, Johnson fingering the black soft-side briefcase he'd brought in with him.

"Is there a new development in the case?" Whelan asked as casually as he could.

It was Johnson, the big black guy, who responded. "I traced your license plates."

"And?"

Steinway: "Not so fast, Whelan. We have some questions we want to ask. So if you want our information, we want you to agree to answer some questions without that pain-in-the-ass attorney present."

Whelan shook his head. "I don't think so, gentlemen."

Johnson shrugged. "Then we'll bring you down to our house for questioning. Or we'll wait here until you can get your attorney down here. Either way, we need some answers, Mr. Whelan. The way it happens, well, that's up to you."

The conference room was equipped with a fancy conference call phone with a speaker.

"Maybe I can get Blaze on the phone." He fished in his wallet for Blaze's card, which had his cell-phone number. Richard leaned over the table to dial the number.

Blaze was on the line in seconds.

"Twice in one week, huh? Must be some kind of record. Am I on speaker?"

For some reason Marcus's voice calmed him down. "Uh-huh. I have Detectives Johnson and Steinway here. They want to ask me some questions. Can you participate by phone?"

"Yeah, but I don't recommend it. But go ahead. If the officers have questions, I'm here."

Whelan nodded to Johnson. "Go ahead. But I may get called into a meeting with the president at any time."

Steinway smirked. "We're so-o-o impressed."

But Johnson silenced him with a look.

"First things first. The plate you called in is registered to Norman Stallworth in Bethesda."

"Hmm. Okay, makes sense."

"You mind telling me what that was all about?"

"I was being followed. Guy said he was a PI and was working for Mary's father. Checks out, because the car he was driving had the tag I asked you to check."

"Why were you being followed?"

"I guess the old man didn't like the fact that I was seeing his daughter."

"Or blames you for her death."

"Whatever. What's your question?"

Steinway shook his head. "We pulled your late girl-friend's phone records."

Richard kept his expression neutral. "And?"

"Well, she calls you a lot." Johnson dumped the sheets of Bell Atlantic printouts across the table from his briefcase. "But up until three months ago she also calls another number quite a bit. We think this is the mysterious Alan who left the message on her answering machine."

Steinway pushed the phone records closer to Richard. "Recognize any of the other numbers besides yours?"

Richard looked. He noted Mary calling his number quite a bit. But there was a pattern as well. Several times she called a second number, 202-555-7678, right after she finished talking to him.

But last week was the first time in three months that she'd called the second number right after she'd called him. Richard thought back—last week seemed like last century. She called me Wednesday night, we weren't supposed to get together, so we didn't. I was working on some things at home.

He looked at the length of the call to him. Yeah, it was only a couple of minutes long.

Then he looked at the call to 202-555-7678. Two minutes. Did she see this mysterious Alan person after the phone call? Did she sleep with him?

What the hell had she been doing?

He realized that the detectives were studying the play of emotions on his face. He looked up and looked Detective Johnson in the eye.

"I don't recognize any of these other numbers." *Actually there was one he recognized, but he was damned if he was going to say so.*

"Are you sure?"

"Positive."

Steinway pulled his chair closer. "There is one number that you should recognize, we're told."

"Really? Which one?"

Steinway pulled the phone records to him, circled a number, then passed the sheets back to Richard.

"There. The circled number."

He looked at it. A 456 exchange. The White House. The fax number at his office.

"That's my office fax number," he said nonchalantly. *Why would she have called my office fax number?*

"Yeah, we understand that. But why is she calling your fax number from her home phone?"

"I don't know."

"She could have been faxing you something from her computer, right?"

"I never got a fax from her."

"Really. So sure?"

"Yup." And then a chill ran down his spine.

His computer was connected to the fax line as well. He used it to dial out into unsecured Internet service providers that were outside the White House intranet.

Could she have gotten into his White House computer? From the outside?

* * *

"Richard, she kissed you, and you kissed her back."

"It was innocent. My God, Mary, you knew Bettina and I used to go out. Maybe there's something there on her end, but . . ."

She'd turned away from him, and he'd scanned the crowd to see if people were watching them. They were in a protected area of Senator Hilden's Washington brownstone, where Bettina's reception was held.

"This isn't going to work," Mary said with some finality.

"Why not?"

"There's too much going on. Too much that's gone on."

"With that guy? That pal of your daddy's?"

"No. That's not what I'm talking about."

"Then what? What is it that's bothering you so much?"

And she'd looked at him, with what? Fear? Apprehension? Someone was coming toward them, O'Shay, from what Richard could see looking past Mary into the main dining room with the bulk of the guests. He'd looked at Mary, seen that look in her eyes. She'd said: "There's a file I transferred," but then O'Shay was on top of them, asking Richard a question, and the moment was lost.

Blaze, from the speakerphone: "Are you wasting my client's time just to talk about inconclusive phone records? Are you people ever going to build an actual case, or do you just want to play patty-cake?"

Detective Johnson looked at Whelan closely. "No. Someone who doesn't like you gave us a cassette recording of you talking to Mary Jacobs. We wanted to play it for you and get your reaction to it."

"How'd you get the tape?" Blaze asked.

"Anonymous benefactor," Steinway said.

"How do you know it's legitimate?" Blaze responded.

"We don't."

"Then why are you wasting our time?" Blaze said, clearly exasperated.

"Because this is still a homicide investigation, and your client is still suspect number one, that's why." Johnson pulled a cassette recorder from his briefcase, peered at it, then pressed its play button.

"Richard, look, I'm sorry about this."

It was weird hearing her voice, and Richard's heart turned over in his chest.

"Sorry isn't good enough."

"You should have known that I wanted to see other people."

"Well, that was never the understanding."

"Then let's make it part of the understanding going forward."

"No! This is all or nothing! Do you understand? All or nothing."

"That's not what I want."

"Then no one will ever want you again."

Johnson hit the stop button, and both detectives eyed him intently.

Richard was stunned. He had never had that kind of conversation with anyone, especially not Mary Jacobs.

"It's phony. Someone must have cobbled together a bunch of conversations between the two of us and between us and other people and spliced them together."

He looked at both detectives; neither one was buying it.

"So let me get this straight," Steinway says. "You claim that you never had this conversation? That this is part of some vast conspiracy to hang this one on you?"

"Rich," Blaze yelled from the speakerphone, "don't you dare answer that question. Detectives, you have to know how easy it is to put something like this together, right? And you surely know this wouldn't stand up in a court of law because you don't know where it came from. Right?"

Steinway shrugged. "As evidence it might not be the greatest, but it certainly puts things in a new light. Besides, if this is more than one conversation, that would mean someone was watching and recording the two of you for some time. Does that make sense?"

"Detectives, I swear to you I never had that conversation with Mary. Never." He looked from one to the other, suddenly concerned that they'd come down because they meant to rearrest him. "Obviously, someone has been watching us; for the tape to be legitimate it had to have come from surveillance."

"You mean the tape is legitimate?" Johnson asked him.

"Rich, don't say another word. Gentlemen, this conversation is over!"

Neither detective said anything for a moment.

Richard couldn't resist asking for one more bit of information. "Who is Alan, her supposed mysterious lover? Whose phone number is that?"

"We're not sure. The phone company has encountered a snag in releasing those records. But we'll find out eventually."

"What kind of snag?"

Johnson shrugged. "Not your concern. But we'll find out soon enough."

"Yeah, Whelan. Go back to work," Bob Steinway said.

And both detectives stood, signaling that the interview was over.

"Oh, and by the way, Whelan. I've requested some additional information. We'll get back to you when it comes in."

"Okay," Richard replied, puzzled by the oblique reference. "Call me if there's anything else you want from me."

Back in his office he sat down at his desk and pulled out the starched white shirt he kept in his desk drawer for emergencies and all-nighters. It was still wrapped in the plastic and cardboard backing provided by the laundry where he

had his shirts done. He had to admit he was tired of it all.
But he still had a job to do, although for how long he could
remain active on the president's staff with D.C. detectives
showing up at the White House, he didn't know.

He picked up the phone and dialed Sam Hennings.

Hennings was at his desk. "Sam, Richard Whelan."

"Richard, how's it going?"

If you only knew. "I got your message. How long do you
think it'll take the ASCI people to get some results?"

"If they are going to get results, you mean. It might not
work. They're using some new technique, so Enrique said it
might be as long as a couple of days. If it takes much longer,
then it probably means the methodology is flawed or there's
nothing in their data that closely matches the characteristics
of the Indian explosion."

"Um, hmm. Look, I need to ask you another favor."

Richard could sense his tone getting cautious. "Like
what?"

"First, you need to understand something. There have
been a couple of articles about me in the papers. If you
haven't seen them, you should read them, because they're
not exactly flattering."

"What does that have to do with anything?"

"Because I'm being framed, and I need to understand
why in order to make sure the 'who' I have in mind makes
sense. So I'm asking you to bend the rules just a little bit."

Sam Hennings was silent.

"Look, go find the *Post* article and read it. If you don't
want to help me, I'll understand," Richard said.

"I actually read the article this morning. Kind of hard to
miss."

"Then you know how this town works. Spin and innuendo is one thing, but whoever's behind this is trying to hang
me out to dry. I can't let it happen."

"Why'd you tell me about the article?"

"Because I wanted you to know what the risks are, and that you are dealing with a marked man."

"Yeah, and a man who takes absolutely horrid mug shots. I saw those in the *Post*. I wonder if they made them extra grainy on purpose? To make you look even more like a criminal?"

"Beats me."

"Well, depending on what you want, I'm willing to give it a shot. Every day someone in this town is trying to sell someone else a bill of goods. The sky is falling, the earth is flat, all you need is a cockeyed scheme and a press conference on the steps of the Capitol and you can get heard. So a simple misrepresentation of the facts to make someone look bad? CIA's done much, much worse."

Richard suppressed a sigh of relief.

"I appreciate the consideration, but here's what I want. Erskine and company supposedly had some hot photos taken of Kashmir yesterday, which came back clean. I want to get a look at those photos. Does your consideration stretch that far?"

"Does it make a difference one way or the other?"

"Yeah. In my gut I think something's wrong, and if we miss the boat, we miss it big-time. And I could use a save right now."

"I'm not sure if I can help you on that one but I'll nose around and let you know."

Frank Moynihan arrived at Charles O'Shay's office on the run. O'Shay motioned for him to shut the door.

"Whelan?"

O'Shay nodded.

"Something in addition to the *Post* article?"

"Yup."

"Spill it."

"Whelan had a run-in with Marty Jacobs, one of the president's closest friends. Totally pissed the man off, so much so that POTUS gets a call from the man last night."

"So Roswell isn't happy."

"It isn't about being unhappy, Frank. Now Whelan is convinced that Marty Jacobs is trying to frame him for revenge over his daughter's death. Came in here like a house on fire claiming that Jacobs is a racist who didn't appreciate Whelan sleeping with his daughter."

Moynihan shook his head. "Sounds ridiculous."

"Now here's where you come in, Frank. Whelan wants to meet with the president."

"About what?"

"He wants to accuse Marty Jacobs of setting him up. And I don't like it."

"You want Whelan out?"

Charles O'Shay shook his head. "Whelan threatened to go to the press. As if he needs more press at this point. But the administration certainly doesn't need any more press about Richard Whelan."

"So what do you want?"

"I want you to be in the meeting with POTUS and Whelan. And if anything, anything out of the ordinary goes down, I want Whelan thrown under some jail and the key lost for a hundred years. Think we can do that? As a matter of the president's security?"

"If he does anything, we'll move on him."

"Hang tight a second." O'Shay checked his computer and pulled up a copy of the president's schedule. He picked up the phone and called Roswell's administrative assistant who coordinated his schedule.

When he concluded the phone call he hung up. "The president will see us at two P.M."

Moynihan nodded and walked away.

* * *

Richard sat at his desk, drumming his fingers. He'd brought the metal strongbox in from his car and hidden it in one of his file cabinets. O'Shay called him and told him that they would meet the president in about two hours, at 2:00 P.M.

Okay, couple of hours to kill. What to do?

He closed his door and pulled the metal box from his file cabinet. He pulled out the sheaf of papers inside and placed them on his desk.

As he thought, the first document was an original of his classified assessment of Chinese espionage, minus the cover page. This was the rest of the document that the detectives had shown him when he was first arrested. He had several original copies of the paper in the files—he printed several at a clip because he did not want to photocopy sensitive material.

He took the original from the box and placed it back in its proper file.

The next set of documents concerned miscellaneous intelligence estimates concerning India and Pakistan.

Now that was interesting. *Coincidence?*

He hated coincidence.

He refiled those documents, thinking that there had to be someone in on this who had unrestricted access to the White House and his office. His office was locked when he wasn't there, and his cabinets were locked as well.

He peered at the cabinets themselves, looking for evidence that they had been rifled.

He didn't see anything out of the ordinary. The next document was something that he didn't recognize. It was stamped TOP SECRET on the top and said

PROJECT THOR

in bold letters, with a Department of Energy document number. He wasn't cleared for DOE stuff, which meant that the rest of it could be stuff he could be accused of having illicitly.

"Richard?" That was his secretary, knocking at his door. He quickly placed the rest of the classified material back in the strongbox and hid it in his file cabinet. He thought about it, and decided that if the rest of the reports were like Project Thor he wanted them out of his office. He'd take them out and put them in the Porsche.

As for the rest, he had a disquieting thought. What if these were distributed originals, and not his copies?

Jesus, that was scary. That would mean that the perpetrator would have to be someone with a top-secret clearance. Although that list was rather long, it included, among others, the president of the United States.

POTUS was having the White House barber cut his hair when the Whelan meeting began.

He looked grimly at the procession that filed in. Whelan, O'Shay, and surprisingly, Moynihan, with another Secret Service agent that he didn't recognize as a backup.

What is this, the O.K. Corral?

Edgar Roswell waved the barber away and snatched the cloth covering his shirt from around his neck. He stood, but didn't offer to shake their hands.

"We've got about fifteen minutes," Roswell said. He looked at Richard Whelan. "I think you've got some explaining to do."

Richard was surprised when Moynihan and his backup greeted them outside of O'Shay's office and escorted them to the Oval Office, and even more surprised when they followed them into the meeting itself.

Roswell did not look pleased to see him. POTUS was like that, running hot and cold on people depending upon the circumstances—perhaps it was what made him a politician.

"I think you've got some explaining to do," the president said, looking at him. Whelan looked at him and the Secret Service agents.

They think I'm some kind of nutcase, Richard thought, glad that he hadn't tried to get his Glock past the White House metal detectors. He'd left it in the car. Even so, one of the agents patted him down.

They sat down.

Edgar Roswell, with his television good looks, nodded warily to Richard. "First off, Monroe tells me there is no invasion of Pakistan that they can detect. The satellite images of Kashmir came back clean. On top of that, you managed to miss the brief this morning so that both Mike Monroe and I could chew your ass out."

"I don't think I was wrong, Mr. President. I'd like to examine the photos myself if I—"

"God dammit Whelan!" the president roared. "You are this close to being out on your ass! Monroe says that the photos are fine, and that's the end of it."

POTUS was amazed that his national security adviser still had the balls to pursue his theory. And that determination gave him pause when it came to Marty Jacobs. *I have to get him to back off from Jacobs, and I have to do it now*, he thought.

"I also understand you wanted to talk to me about Marty Jacobs, Richard."

He held up a hand before Whelan could respond. "I don't know what you're thinking, but you are completely out of line on that score as well. He called me last night after your little visit and I'm mortified that you're fucking around with Marty Jacobs. Of all people."

I hope the message is clear, Richard. Stay clear of Marty, he thought.

* * *

But you told me to call Marty, dammit, Richard thought. "Mr. President," Richard began, suddenly unsure of what he wanted to say, "we've known each other a long time. Ever since Skipper's untimely death."

"I know all the history, Richard," Roswell cut him off, "but this job isn't run on the past. It runs on the present, and present performances. And you haven't been performing lately."

"There is a reason for it."

"And that reason is?"

Richard took a deep breath. "I think Marty Jacobs is trying to frame me."

Edgar Roswell shook his head. "Do you know how paranoid that sounds? Why would Marty Jacobs be trying to frame you?"

"Because he's pissed that I was seeing his daughter."

"Why?"

Richard looked at him, hoping the man wouldn't make him go there. "Because he didn't like the fact that his daughter was sleeping with a black man."

Roswell leaned back, shaking his head. "Marty Jacobs a racist? Is that what this is about? What, he didn't accept you into his family with open arms?"

"Not exactly."

"And you base this on what?"

"Someone working for your buddy said that Marty had his daughter under surveillance throughout our relationship. And Marty knew things that I didn't think he knew."

"Like what?"

"Like the precise date that Mary and I became intimate."

"Did it occur to you that maybe his daughter told him?"

"Doesn't matter. He had a private detective tailing Mary. The detective told me that Marty has a footlocker full of surveillance video in his basement. Has had it for a long time."

Charles O'Shay broke in. "So, because Marty was watching his daughter, you think that he has a vendetta against you?"

"What else explains everything that's happened?"

Edgar Roswell looked at him. "Meaning?"

"The police were given an incriminating audiotape that purported to be me threatening to kill Mary Jacobs, a conversation that didn't remotely happen. And now Marty has been having me followed by this private detective."

"And the private eye told you all this?" Roswell asked, his eyebrows raised.

Richard shook his head, exasperated that he was sounding like some kind of nut. "Not all of it, no. The private eye told me about the surveillance."

"And have you seen any of these tapes?" O'Shay asked.

"Of course not. I was only told of their existence today."

"So Marty Jacobs didn't show you any home videos when you went to see him last night?" the president asked.

"No, of course not."

"So you admit that you went to see Marty Jacobs last night?" the president pressed.

"He invited me out to see him."

"That's not what he told me," Roswell said. "And if he did, doesn't that contradict your little theory about him trying to frame you?"

"Not necessarily."

O'Shay: "And you think, somehow, that Marty Jacobs has enough clout to plant evidence with the Washington police? Did Marty have his own daughter killed to spite you as well?"

"Well, something weird is going on."

"Is Marty Jacobs the reason why you missed the brief this morning?" Roswell asked.

"No, not directly."

"Explain that, please. What were you doing?"

"I was . . . ," and Richard realized that he couldn't tell them what he'd been doing and what he'd found at Mary's apartment. They were all looking at him, waiting for an answer.

"I was unavoidably detained. Responding to the *Washington Post.*" *And shooting up Rock Creek Park.*

"But you think Marty Jacobs had this story done about you."

"I'm not sure."

"But you said that the press coverage was a result of a conspiracy, did you not? In my office this morning?" O'Shay pressed.

"I may have said that, but I'm not sure that the two are necessarily connected."

The president sighed. "So what do we really have here, Richard? A lot of innuendo, a questionable relationship, questions about your role as my national security adviser, and questions about your involvement in Mary Jacobs's death. Right?"

"We have Marty Jacobs surveilling me and his daughter. And having me followed."

"According to some private detective. Did it ever occur to you that maybe Marty thinks you are implicated in his daughter's death? That you're being followed because Marty, as a grief-stricken father, is looking desperately for answers?"

"No."

"And you're suggesting that Marty Jacobs had his daughter under surveillance before you became intimate, right?"

"I'm not sure."

"But you said he knew the date you became intimate with her, and you implied that that was a result of the surveillance, right?"

"I did imply that, yes."

"But that was before you met Marty, wasn't it?"

"Yes."

"So if Marty had his daughter under surveillance before he even knew of your existence, why is any of it related to you? My God, man, Marty Jacobs does business with governments, and he deals with weapons systems. He could have been having his daughter followed for her own protection."

Richard was silent.

President Roswell looked at his watch. Whelan didn't look convinced. *Well, I'll give it one more push.*

"Gentlemen, I'm sorry, but I have pressing matters to attend to." He looked at Richard and shook his head. "I can't have you harassing campaign contributors, missing meetings, and implicated in a terrible death. You are this far," he made a pinching gesture between his thumb and forefinger, "from getting dismissed. One more incident, one more revelation about you in the papers, and I will ask for, and receive, your resignation. Am I clear?"

"Yes, sir."

Roswell paced a little. "And I don't want to hear anything more about Marty Jacobs. He has suffered a terrible loss. Do you understand what that means? I certainly do."

And Edgar Roswell hated himself for what he was doing, using the memory of his dead son to try and keep Whelan contained.

Because if Whelan couldn't be contained . . .

Roswell turned away and the meeting concluded.

"Bettina," Donna Elm, Ron Dempsey's secretary hissed in her ear. "The secretary wants you up here right away!"

Bettina was used to these calls. Most of them could be attributed to Donna's hyperactive personality.

"Slow down, Donna. What's up?"

"Just get yourself up to the secretary's office right away!"

"What, did something happen?" Bettina asked. But Donna had already clicked off.

She hustled up the stairs, not wanting to wait for the elevator. *If it's World War III, I don't want to miss it*, she thought grimly. She reached the secretary of state's office on the run, and Donna just made a windmilling motion with her arm, telling her to keep going right through to Dempsey's private office.

The door was closed, so she knocked.

"Come." She recognized Dempsey's voice. She opened the door and went in.

"I came as quickly as I could, Ron," she said. Her boss and the other occupant of the office stood to greet her.

She reached out to shake his hand from rote, and then nearly fainted as she saw who it was.

"This is a completely off-the-record visit, Bettina," Ron Dempsey said. "No one is to know that the ambassador is here."

But that's impossible, she thought. Protocol, diplomacy, chain of command . . . all were violated by this kind of impromptu visit.

She was a professional, though, and cool.

"Ambassador Liu," she nodded slightly and took his hand. *What the devil is the People's Republic's ambassador to the United States doing in the secretary of state's office? There's been no overture for this kind of a visit. What's Ron thinking?*

Then she sat down to listen to what the Chinese ambassador had to say. As she listened to him speak, she couldn't get the thought out of her head that war was coming, and that everyone in the international community knew it except the president of the United States.

Or maybe he does.

Really have to get the Porsche fixed with my severance pay, Richard thought on the way out of the White House. He glanced at his watch. It was only six-thirty. An early night for him, significant because he had the sense that he was being taken out of the loop.

He thought about his meeting with the president and shook his head. *I must've seemed like a lunatic.* Some big piece of the puzzle was missing, and he hadn't thought about how all the pieces fit together well enough to figure that out before meeting with Roswell.

And now he was almost certainly out of a job. *Dammit.* That meant that he had to get as much going as he could while he was still drawing a salary and could still represent himself as a high-ranking member of the current administration. So he was going to use every bit of his authority and position to get as much out of people as he possibly could.

There were several central mysteries, besides the basic question of what was going on.

Why was he the target?

Why had someone planted classified documents linked to him at Mary's apartment?

Who had given the D.C. police the audiotape?

Was Marty Jacobs simply a grieving old man with a prurient streak?

Was the president involved?

He had the strongbox of documents in the boot of the Porsche, not wanting to leave them in his office until he'd had a chance to look at them. *Gotta remember to get them out of the trunk,* he thought, *because if the car is stolen and the documents get stolen with it . . .*

As he pulled away from a stoplight he confronted the feeling he'd had in the Oval Office. Why hadn't the president simply dismissed him? Couldn't the president have arranged everything that he'd experienced? Why would he do that? Why the reference to Skip Roswell, dead so many years?

He'd seen firsthand the power emanating from the Oval Office. History had seen it abused, and the revelations of those abuses had probably only scratched the surface. And just how deep did Edgar Roswell's relationship with Marty Jacobs go? Clearly that was one of the president's hot buttons, and clearly his relationship with Mary Jacobs had touched a nerve in ways that he didn't quite understand yet.

One thing at a time. He'd called Marcus Blaze after his meeting with the president.

"I need you to find the two thugs who stopped me the night Mary was killed."

Blaze was silent for a moment on the phone.

"Marcus, you have your ear to the streets. Maybe there's some buzz going around about two white guys impersonating cops."

"Ear to the streets." Marcus had sounded dubious over the phone. "Yeah, Harvard, I can see where you'd think that. I can ask a few questions, Rich, but, it's not like I have a network of informants feeding me info in some shitty bar."

"I'm grasping at straws, Marcus. I need a push from your end."

"Word on the street, eh? Okay. So which one are you?"

"I'm sorry?" Whelan had said, thinking that they had a bad connection.

"Well," Marcus said chuckling. "I'm obviously supposed to be Huggy Bear. So who the fuck are you? Starsky, or Hutch?"

So it was still a couple of needles in a haystack, he thought.

Or maybe not.

What are you thinking, Whelan?

Decision making under uncertainty. That was what intelligence estimates and the related decisions always came down to. You never had perfect facts, but you could infer a lot from the facts you had, and the facts you didn't have.

Think about it, Whelan.

Finding two people who impersonated police officers is like trying to find a needle in a haystack if it's a random oc-curence.

But the deck stacked against him was anything but ran-dom.

Classified documents planted at a crime scene. Either taken from his files or from one of the original recipients.

Split-second timing required to kill Mary before I showed up. Aided by two impersonators who hear a radio call and a code that doesn't exist and then leave the scene.

Could the call have been the all clear? Could Mary have already been dead? Is that what code fourteen meant?

And a private detective working for a major campaign contributor harasses me.

Are the impostors a random element? Two needles in a haystack?

I don't think so. Either they work for Marty Jacobs, which raises the seemingly unlikely possibility that he had his daughter killed, or they work for the president, or some-one in government who wants me to take the fall.

But for what, exactly?

Detective Bobby Steinway stopped by his partner's cramped office before going home.

"You make the phone call?"

"Yup."

"What do you think? Will it be enough?"

Johnson shrugged. "Could be."

Steinway smiled. "What did Cochran say at O. J.'s trial? 'If the gloves don't fit, you must acquit'?"

Johnson, exasperated, looked at his partner. "Something like that."

"Well, I got a new one. If the tape attests, we must arrest."

"Oh, please."

"C'mon, Bill." Steinway began chanting. "If the tape attests, we must arrest. If the tape attests, we must arrest. . . ."

"Go home, Bobby. Just go home."

Patrolman Ralph Bennigan pulled up in front of the apartment building, having driven through the park to get there. This was his last stop of his watch, and it was a rather simple task. He'd gotten a late call to make this pickup, and although the ride through the park was pleasant, his tired body made him anxious to call it a day.

But there was a guy waiting for him not quite in front of the building, and Bennigan could tell he was a cop just by the way he carried himself. Detective, from the looks of him.

"Yo, you here to make a pickup?" the man asked him as Bennigan ambled toward the entrance of the building.

Ralph looked at him. Kind of a big guy. "Who wants to know?" he asked, careful not to sound disrespectful in case the guy did have a gold detective's shield.

The guy pulled a badge from his back pocket. "Relax, I'm with Homicide. My captain wants this item delivered pronto to Johnson and Steinway. They sent me to expedite things. You got paper?"

Bennigan handed him the envelope with the paperwork. "They sent a gold shield down here for an errand?"

The guy shrugged. "Rush job on that case in the papers— you know, the rich broad's murder."

Bennigan knew that there was all kinds of heat about that case. He shrugged.

"Well, it's all yours. Have a good one. Say, I've never seen you around, have I?"

But the man had already turned away and was approaching the door of the apartment building.

The doorman watched the guy come in after he hit the buzzer on the front door, immediately thinking he didn't know him. This placed the guest in one of two categories: the type who would politely stop at the desk, or the type who would assume that the nameless, faceless doormen would know them after having glimpsed them for half a second in the company of one of the tower's residences fifteen years ago.

The latter could be unpleasant. He always tried to be polite but insistent because he didn't want the super hassling him because one of the residents was hassling the super.

The big man came directly to his station. A good sign.

The man pulled a badge from his pocket. "D.C. Metro Homicide Division. I'm here to make a pickup."

Ah, yes. He checked his clipboard. "I was sort of expecting a messenger."

"Chain of evidence. From you to the police, to the courts, so a suspect can't claim there was tampering. Can I have my package, please?"

The doorman took the brown-paper-wrapped package from the shelf and handed it to the police officer. He also handed over his clipboard. "Sign here, please?"

"Sure."

The doorman watched as the man with the mustache scribbled something with the proffered pen.

"Thanks." The detective turned and walked to the door.

The doorman looked at the signature.

"Nick" and a last name that was impossible to decipher was all he could make out.

12

Frank Moynihan didn't like being out of his realm, but he found himself, at the DCI's request, paying a visit to the CIA headquarters compound in Langley, Virginia. Mike Monroe wanted to see him personally about his interview and polygraph with Richard Whelan. Although Moynihan was uneasy briefing CIA on a purely domestic issue, he was sufficiently afraid of Richard Whelan that he wanted to do everything he could to assess the threat. Including talk to the CIA about what they found. And the president wanted him to keep Monroe in the loop.

Monroe's secretary, Ida, showed him into Monroe's office. Michael Monroe favored minimalist art deco furnishings, much to Moynihan's dismay. The metal and leather chair that he sat in facing Monroe was uncomfortable enough to make Frank Moynihan think about keeping the meeting short and sweet.

Monroe was on the phone whispering, and Moynihan reflected that he'd never really liked the man; a bit too pompous and know-it-all-ish for his tastes, especially for someone who didn't have much of a background for their job. Intelligence, like the Secret Service, was the forte of the professional careerist, not the political appointee.

Monroe hung up the phone and stood, shaking Frank's hand.

"I take it national security is safe for the moment," Frank quipped.

Monroe shook his head. "China's mobilizing because of the Indian bomb thing. Say they don't like nuclear weapons detonated so close to their borders and that they will assist their client, Pakistan, in repulsing any invasion by the Indians. State has their tits in fifteen wringers over it. And we got a nutcase as a national security adviser to the president. So no, Frank, national security doesn't feel particularly secure at this point."

Moynihan groaned inwardly. Mike Monroe thought the weight of the free world rested on his shoulders. Worse, he took no joy from the ponderous weight of his "responsibilities" unless all the lesser lights knew it.

Asshole.

The two men sat down.

"What've you got?"

No preamble, just give, Moynihan thought. Well, it was CYA time.

"Let me bring you up to speed. Whelan's polygraph was interesting but not conclusive. We noted some stress over the question of whether he was involved in her death, but the experts say that it could simply be survivor's guilt. There is nothing that suggests that he was responsible for it in any of his results. If he was involved, I'd have to say that he was remarkably cool under pressure. At least in answering my questions."

Monroe sat back, playing with a pencil. "But the polygraph didn't clear him, per se, is that correct?"

Moynihan nodded. "That's correct. It didn't give him a clean bill of innocence."

Monroe continued flipping the pencil from hand to hand. "What did you think of his . . . performance?"

Moynihan shrugged. "I've known Richard Whelan for several years. He's always been a solid citizen from what I could tell."

Monroe leaned forward. "Know anything about his personal life?"

"Like what?"

Moynihan shrugged and said nothing for a moment, then spoke.

"It doesn't make him a killer. Although . . ." Monroe hesitated, as if reluctant to go on.

Frank Moynihan just looked at him.

"Look, I'm not a racist, but have you thought about how a Richard Whelan would react if his white girlfriend was seeing other people? Maybe lots of other people? This is his only entanglement, and he's got it bad for her, and then finds out that she's letting other people dip their wicks? Do you think maybe, just maybe, he snaps?"

"How do you know all this?"

"I don't. I'm just speculating. But Whelan always struck me as being too good to be true. Ivy League, shot down in Desert Storm, all the right stuff. You ever seen anyone who didn't have a dark side? Ever seen anyone who's so cocksure of himself that he runs himself and everyone around him right off a cliff? Well, maybe this is Whelan's dark side, that he's in over his head, that he's losing it. The signs are all there, Frank.

"This India thing is another symptom that he's losing it. We gather the intelligence, but we rely on the national security adviser to help process it and come up with an assessment that prevents us looking foolish when somebody explodes a weapon that they aren't supposed to be willing to deploy."

Monroe fixed him with a glare. "Now I know that the judicial system considers this man innocent until proven guilty, but we're talking about someone with close access to the president of the United States, Frank. I'm just wondering whether the man's security takes precedence over Whelan's civil rights in a criminal case."

"I've thought about it as well."

"And?"

"I talked to the president about it. You know Roswell. He won't make that kind of decision for fear that it will come back to haunt him. I guess he thinks Whelan will go to the press and create an even bigger stink if he's pulled from the inside."

"That's stupid."

Moynihan nodded. "I know, but this is how the man thinks. He's close to pulling the trigger on Whelan, but he's given him a last chance. So to answer your question, we don't have enough to move on him right now. But if we ever cross that line, then we'll evict Mr. Whelan from his post and from access to the White House and wrap the whole thing in a national security cloak so thick that not even Johnny Cochran could bullshit his way through it. Okay?"

Monroe nodded. It was what he wanted to hear.

Richard checked his messages on the way home.

Sam Hennings had called him, said it was urgent. He dialed the man's office, halfway expecting to find him there.

Hennings picked up on the first ring.

"Did the computer people find a match on the Indian blast?"

"Haven't heard anything. I was calling about your other question."

"And?"

"You're on a cell phone, right?"

"Yeah," Richard acknowledged, understanding the implication immediately.

"We should meet. There's a coffeehouse near my house. I can be there within the hour."

"Okay." Hennings gave him the address. "See you there."

* * *

Bettina Freeman left Ron Dempsey's office feeling like she had the weight of the world on her shoulders. First India explodes a bomb. Then both India and Pakistan refuse to sign the Nonproliferation Treaty. Now she and the secretary of state had just had a highly unusual visit from the Chinese ambassador.

Was this how world wars start? she wondered. She dialed Richard's office phone when she got back to her office, but he wasn't in. She tried his cell phone, but it was busy.

She didn't trust herself to leave a cryptic message. She would wait until she got to him; she needed someone in the administration who could tell her what was going on.

There was one other issue that Moynihan wanted to cover with the DCI.

"Have you heard about Whelan's meeting with the president?"

Monroe nodded. A very disturbed Edgar Roswell had called to fill him in.

"That one certainly supports your 'losing it' theory. He's paranoid that he's being set up by mysterious forces with far-reaching influence. That's why I want him out of the White House and away from the president."

Monroe shrugged. "The president feels especially vulnerable about Jacobs. And Whelan is mucking around in an area that no one in the administration wants him to muck around in."

"Why? Is this some campaign-finance issue?"

"The presidency has a strange but predictable effect on people, Frank. You've been around enough to know that. The president is concerned about his place in the history books. So whether it's fund-raising or foreign policy, the president has to be concerned with how some future historian will view him."

"What could Marty Jacobs have done that's so incriminating?"

"Nothing that I know of. But appearances can be damaging. Jacobs runs a high-tech company that furnishes weapons systems to the Pentagon and technical support to folks around the world. If he were deemed to have undue influence on the presidency, it would create a stain that wouldn't go away. There are only a handful of companies that specialize in the areas that Rocketdyne has expertise in. Hughes and Loral are the only others that have the same kind of reach."

"And they were both named in that scandal with the Chinese during the Clinton administration. Something about them inadvertently passing strategic information to the Chinese by helping them launch satellites or something, right?"

"Yup. Something like that. And since the press and Congress never got to hang Clinton, even though they sure tried like hell, there's a sense of unsatiated blood lust in the White House. And the current international situation doesn't help."

"Then it will be very tricky to remove Whelan without damaging the presidency, Mike."

Monroe nodded. "And there's nothing you can do without the president's blessing. That's my counsel, Frank. Wait."

The greasy spoon had the ambience of a misplaced truck stop and the cuisine of a culinary disaster zone. The art deco design had faded over the years into rust and taped red-vinyl stools and older, tired waitresses who served their wares with indifference. Richard saw green mold on the apple pie in the display case and was wary about even ordering coffee.

He was relieved when Sam Hennings came in. Hennings ordered coffee and a cheeseburger, and Whelan silently wished his stomach good luck.

"So what's going on?" Whelan asked as Hennings waited for his order.

"Well, my contacts in the NRO reconfirmed that Monroe

and Erskine certainly moved a Keyhole around last night to get a look at southern Asia. So that part checks out."

"Did your people analyze the images that came out of that survey?"

Hennings shook his head. "Nope. I have it on good authority that the images were passed directly to the DCI himself. All copies. So no one from our section has seen a thing."

"Damn. Is there any possibility that he could be mistaken in his assessment of the photographs?"

"Anything's possible, depending upon what he was looking for. But I can't tell; no one can tell at this point, because those images are in Monroe's safe at Langley. Or in some shredder someplace."

"Is there any other way to get access to those images?"

Hennings looked at him. "Mind telling me what this is all about?"

"I suspect that CIA's official interpretation of the events of last Sunday may be a bit incomplete. I told Monroe and Erskine that in no uncertain terms in the follow-up."

"Why?"

"Because something doesn't add up. New Delhi shouldn't have known that a Pakistani force was in the area in time to deploy a nuclear weapon to take them out that close to the Pakistan border. Unless. . . ."

"Unless what?"

"Unless India had forces in the area. Substantial forces. Like an invasion force under cover during our usual satellite passes."

Whelan paused. "What scares me is that my scenario suggests that we're on the verge of full-scale war in the region. And China has already said they won't stand idly by if Pakistan is threatened."

Hennings thought for a moment. "What I don't see is how all this fits in with your girlfriend's death."

"Neither do I. But there's a link, somewhere. I can feel it. Too many coincidences; too many things happening at the same time."

"You know, there is one way to get a look at those images. But I'd have to act quickly."

"I don't want you to put yourself at risk."

"This is a national security issue, is it not?"

"I think so."

"Then it's either Leavenworth or World War Three. And if it's a thermonuclear deal, Leavenworth won't matter."

"How is it you can get your hands on the images?"

"It's risky, but I share your feeling that something odd is going on. Everything that comes off the Keyholes is downloaded to a ground station and transmitted directly to Langley."

"Okay. How does that help?"

"There's a certain amount of redundancy built into the ground stations. In case a data dump to Langley gets garbled, they can reconstruct the data from the temporary backup that's held at the ground station that received the images."

"How long do they keep the files?"

"Forty-eight hours, tops. And that's dependent upon the volume of incoming traffic and their storage capacity."

"Could Monroe or Erskine have ordered the backups destroyed along with the original images that were delivered to them?"

Hennings shrugged. "Possible. But these guys aren't sophisticated enough to know that the ground stations keep backups. They don't know how the machinery of operations works. So I'd be surprised if they even thought about it."

"Still, how would you get your hands on the backups?"

"I'm still thinking that one through. I have friends throughout the system, but requesting backups of secure

Keyhole data is not an everyday occurrence. Somebody could alert the chain of command that I've asked for it, and then the jig would be up."

"Could we borrow the backups?"

"Whoa, Richard. I'm not a thief. It has to go through channels."

"I said 'borrow,' Sam. Not steal."

Hennings shook his head. "Doesn't matter. These are very secure installations. Perimeters are patrolled with armed guards with instructions to shoot to kill first and ask questions later, if ever. And the data are protected in a million ways and encrypted, so you can't walk in with a floppy and walk out with anything useful. This ain't *Mission: Impossible*."

"I need to see those images, Sam."

"I knew you would say that. I'm thinking about how to do it. But I don't have any answers for you just yet."

"Hmm." Richard took a sip of his coffee and made a face. "Ugh. Burnt."

Hennings took a deep swig of his own. "What, they serve you guys Starbucks in the White House? Shit, we live on lousy coffee. This isn't so bad."

Richard looked at his watch, suddenly very aware of what a long day it had been. "I gotta get some sleep. Maybe some answers will be forthcoming if I let go for a few hours."

"Yeah. I'll keep you posted."

When Richard got home there was a message from Bettina asking him to call her as soon as possible. He picked up the phone and called her.

"Richard! Thank goodness! I was afraid I was going to burst if I didn't talk to someone."

"What's going on?"

"Not over the phone. Come over. Or maybe I'll come over there."

Richard was tired, chivalry notwithstanding. "I'll put some coffee on."

"Be there in a half hour."

The one named Nick in the black van outside stopped the tape once the phone call terminated. He dialed a special number and played back the tape from Whelan's phone call to the party at the other end.

"Were you able to put anything in his house?" the voice asked.

"We decided that's not a good idea. As the national security adviser, Whelan gets his house and phones swept regularly for listening devices by the Secret Service."

"So you want to pull the taps now?"

"Absolutely." Nick nodded at Rudy, his partner. Apparently their patron had agreed to pulling the taps.

"We need to hear his conversation with her."

"I can put the team in position with a rig to cover most of the common areas of the house, but we're thin. We can't tail him afterward because we don't have the manpower or the vehicles."

"Just tell me what they discuss and pull out."

Half an hour later Nick noted the silver BMW pull up and park in front of Whelan's town house. Nick's people were already deployed because he'd anticipated that they would have to be able to pick up conversations inside the house; he'd scouted the best places to listen while it was still daylight.

He whispered into his throat microphone. "The target is entering the premises now."

There was a tall hedge that separated the property from the street. His men were posing as telephone line repairmen in a cherry picker working on the telephone lines nearly in front of Whelan's house. When they got the signal, one of them trained a nearly invisible laser beam on the bay windows of Richard Whelan's living room. It picked up the vibrations of the glass and transmitted the sound to the van.

Inside the van, Nick listened to the output even though the tapes were running. He adjusted the gain until he could hear Whelan's footsteps as he approached his front door.

"Hi."

"Hey. Coffee's ready. Still take it the same way?"

"Yup."

He could hear Whelan walk toward the kitchen and Bettina Freeman follow him.

There was a gap in the conversation because he didn't want to turn the gain up enough to hear what they were saying. Once they came back into the living room the volume would blow his eardrums if he did that.

"So the Chinese ambassador initiated a clandestine meeting with Dempsey?"

"Yeah. Highly unusual."

"How'd they get him into the office without someone noticing?"

"Unless you knew him, you wouldn't know him, if you get my drift."

"What was Dempsey's reaction?"

"Extreme caution. If something blows up and it turns out State knew about it in advance there'd be hell to pay."

"You were in the meeting?"

There was no response; Nick thought she must have nodded instead of speaking.

"So what was said?"

"He said that his government was highly disturbed by our lack of reaction to Indian aggression."

"Highly disturbed?"

"Think diplomatic terms, Richard. 'Highly disturbed'

enough to initiate an out-of-protocol meeting with the secretary without the president's knowledge means something big is about to go down."

"But he didn't say what."

"He didn't have to. He said that the Chinese military establishment was going to a heightened state of alert over this."

"Which means what?"

"I'm getting to that. He said he expected something to happen in the next several days, and that the administration knew what New Delhi was up to. And if President Roswell wasn't going to do anything about it, the Chinese would."

"I'm not sure what to read into that. Hell, they approached Dempsey, not the president directly. And Dempsey used to be our ambassador to China, so they may view him as a kindred spirit that they can manipulate."

"But they said that the U.S. knew what New Delhi was up to. Why would they say that?"

"I don't know . . . wait a minute. They must know about the satellite Monroe and Erskine moved to cover the region. Beijing tracks our birds so they can hide things when they're overhead."

"So they think our surveillance should have picked up something. Did it?"

"Not according to Monroe and Erskine."

"But that doesn't make sense."

"I agree. But why would Monroe and Erskine cover anything up?"

"Besides making you look bad?"

"Not a sufficient reason, I'm afraid."

"Could they have been mistaken in their assessment of the data?"

"Anything's possible. According to my sources, none of the intelligence analysts saw the images."

"Damn. I think the ambassador was trying to warn us."

"About what?"

"Not to get involved if war breaks out."

"We don't have any mutual defense arrangements with India. Why would the Chinese worry about us?"

"They'd worry if they thought it was going to escalate into a nuclear conflict."

"Whoa. You think that was the message being delivered?"

"Why else would they go to such great lengths to warn us?"

"Why not approach the president directly?"

"Because they think the president's part of the problem, Richard."

"You mean they think he tacitly supports whatever India is cooking up."

"Right."

"But the president doesn't appear to know."

"Right again. And someone has to tell him."

"Don't look at me. I'm this close to being canned."

"Who else, then?"

"What about your boss?"

"My boss can't exactly tell the president that he violated protocol by meeting with the Chinese without his before-the-fact approval. And if Roswell knows what's going on, my boss is out of a job, too."

"So I'm it."

"I'm afraid so."

Whelan sighed. "I'll think about it. But I need something more than my charm and good looks."

"Well, you can't tell Roswell about the visit. That's out. Dempsey would have my ass if he knew I was here."

"So I have nothing to work with."

"You have your charm and good looks."

"Very funny."

* * *

Bettina Freeman left Whelan's house shortly after that. The surveillance team pulled out after Rudy transmitted the conversation to their patron in a secured microburst that lasted less than a second.

13

Bill Johnson arrived for work the next morning hoping to put the Whelan case to bed for good. At about 11:30 he received the package that he'd been waiting for. He signed the evidence transfer slip and called Steinway over as he unwrapped it.

"This is it."

"About time. Should I go commandeer a VCR?"

Johnson hefted the videotape. "Yeah. Looks like VHS format, as we requested."

"Okay. Let's do it."

Richard Whelan was contemplating how to approach Charles O'Shay about his and Bettina's suspicions. He could just lay it out there, but he knew that he would be dismissed as nothing more than a crazy. And last night's performance wouldn't help. He needed those satellite images, and he needed to show the president that something was wrong.

Unless he's part of it. Which wouldn't be so far-fetched. He began thinking about Roswell's history and found himself questioning everything he knew about the man.

Richard was seventeen when Skip Roswell had been killed in an automobile accident. Typical of the lifestyles of the young and well-to-do, they had been at a party with most of their classmates during the final weeks of their senior year.

The house was gorgeous, and Tim Macklin, their host, thought nothing of having fifty of his closest friends trash the place while his parents were in Paris. Richard had walked into wild music played much too loud at the Short Hills, New Jersey, home of Tim's investment banker father and been handed a beer. A group of guys and girls were skinny-dipping in the indoor pool and invited him in, if he was willing to get naked, of course. The white girls were interested in checking out whether the myths were true, and Whelan, being shy, wasn't about to show them anything but his Levis.

"Where's Tim?"

Two of the girls giggled. "Upstairs with his girlfriend."

"Oh." At these parties, upstairs meant in a bedroom having sex.

"Yeah, with his new girlfriend of about two minutes," one of them said, laughing. "Hey, Richard. There's a spare bedroom up there, y'know."

He caught the looks from the other guys in the pool. Don't mess with the white women, no matter how much they throw it in your face, he thought. The ones that flirted wanted the white guys to be jealous; later it would be something they thought they could brag about, and Richard wanted no part of it.

He drank half the beer and strolled around, a stranger in a strange land, amazed at the size of the house and the advanced drunkenness of his classmates.

Tim Macklin caught up to him in the kitchen, where he was sampling some of the few chips that hadn't gotten soaked in alcohol.

"Hey, Richy, what's up?" He grabbed his hand and tried to do a brother's handshake.

"You're kind of wasted, bro." Macklin liked to think he was cool; Rich tolerated it.

"Wasted is the watchword for the evening, dude." He grabbed a joint that was making the rounds and inhaled deeply. "Good shit. Want some?"

Richard ran track and barely drank beer, much less did drugs. "Nope, I'm cool. When are your parents due back?"

"Late next week, I think."

"Aren't you kinda trashing the place?"

Macklin shrugged. "Consuelo will clean it up. I'll slip her an extra couple hundred to keep quiet about it. Ain't nothin' that a little cash can't fix."

"If you say so. How long are you going to let everyone hang out?"

"Dawn if they want. You never been to one of my parties, Richy?"

"Can't say that I have." *Never been invited before.*

"Damn, too bad. Look at what you've been missing. I'm thinking, though, that this party needs some more grub." He pulled a set of car keys from his pocket. "Wanna take a spin?"

Richard noted the Porsche emblem on the key ring. "Yours?"

"Nah," Macklin said, swaying to the beat of music only he could hear. "My dad's turbo Carrera. Mighty fine wheels, dude."

"Hey, Tim, I hope you aren't planning on driving."

"Me?" Tim pointed to himself, swaying. "Way too wasted to drive. But you can if you want. I'll come with you."

What was that, a sixty-thousand-dollar car? *I don't think so.* "Nope. But don't you drive."

"Always the Boy Scout, Rich. You ought to lighten up every once in awhile." As soon as he said it, Tim Macklin covered his mouth and started giggling.

"What's so funny?"

Macklin laughed. "I said 'lighten up' to a black guy! Shit, I must be fucked up."

"Ha-ha, Tim."

"No, man, don't get weird on me. I didn't mean it like that."

"No harm, Tim. No harm."

"You know my dad thinks we should get more people like you in the school."

There were all of two black people in his class of eighty-seven.

"And why is that?"

"Y'know, more disadvantaged black kids. Do our part to help out."

"I hardly consider myself disadvantaged." His father was a prominent physician, as was the father of his only black classmate.

"Aw, man, you know what I'm talking about. Besides, all you brothers carry switchblades and shit, right? You know how to handle yourselves in a fight. So what's the difference?"

Richard shook his head. "Whatever. I'm going into the living room."

"Oh, I fucked up, huh? No harm, though, right?"

"No harm." *What an asshole*, Richard thought.

He'd seen Skip Roswell with his arm around a pretty brunette, so he hadn't bothered to say hello. But Macklin was still on his mission to get food.

"Hey," Macklin said, "who wants pizza?"

There was a ragged chorus of generally positive response.

"Well I got the keys, here, who wants to come with me?"

Skip Roswell raised his hand. "Yo, I'll go. If you let me drive."

"No problem. You got the balls to drive this car, you can drive."

And Macklin handed the keys to Skip Roswell, and they left.

An hour later they hadn't returned. Rich Whelan was worried that something had happened, maybe they were stopped by the police. He could see Tim Macklin waving a joint at a police officer and asking him if he wanted a hit.

He fingered his car keys in his pocket. He could go looking for them.

Always the Boy Scout. He surveyed the party that he'd drifted through and decided he'd had enough "fun" for one night. He headed into the cool evening, away from the meticulously landscaped grounds and to his beat-up Volkswagen Beetle.

As he got in he wondered where to go, calculating the possibilities in his head. The nearest pizza place in Short Hills was probably closed, therefore they could have gone to Millburn. And if they'd gone to Millburn they would be back by now.

He started the Beetle with a rattle. Skip had a thing about fast cars and winding roads. They could have taken the long way, like route 509, which was bordered by woods and had lots of curves mixed in with the straights. Maybe they are dragging 509, racing some street punk with a big block Chevy.

He put the Beetle in gear and headed for the 509.

It was dark on the highway, so he had the Beetle's weak highbeams on as he carefully negotiated the curves. As he rounded a curve he saw headlights approaching, appalled at the speed with which the oncoming car was approaching him.

As the car flashed by, he recognized the distinctive shape of a Porsche.

And Tim Macklin was driving.

He turned his Volks around to pursue. By now the Porsche was a good half a mile ahead and accelerating away, even though he had the Beetle's accelerator pressed to the floor. He saw the brake lights come on ahead of him and then the Porsche fishtailed as the brake lights disappeared around a turn.

By the time Whelan slung the Beetle into the turn, the Carrera was gone.

He kept driving. After a couple of miles he turned around and doubled back, thinking he'd missed a turn somewhere. He slowed down, for a moment allowing for the possibility that the car had gone off the road. Just as he was about to make the same sharp curve where the Porsche had disappeared he spotted something, a dim red light, in the woods off to his left. He quickly slid to a stop and jumped out, leaving the Beetle's motor running.

The Porsche had gone off the road and spun, burying itself in a thicket of woods. A tree had nearly sheared off the car's tail; it was a dim red warning light from the cockpit that he'd seen. Whelan threaded his way through the torn-up ground until he reached the hulk of the sports car.

Macklin was strapped into the driver's seat, facedown over the wheel, still breathing, the sour smell of vomit coming from somewhere.

Skipper Roswell was nowhere to be seen.

It took some minutes for Richard to locate Skip. He'd been thrown from the car by the impact and had landed some yards away from the wreck. He was badly hurt, unconscious. Richard debated for a moment moving him out of the woods, but his father had trained him in first aid, and he knew that he could not risk moving the teenager. He got back to the road as quickly as he could, forced himself to climb back into the Beetle and drive until he could find a pay phone to call the police.

He was there when the police arrived. Someone took a hurried statement from him, but as more and more police and emergency vehicles arrived, Whelan was shunted to one side as the stern-faced professionals took over.

Macklin was lifted from the wreckage, placed on a stretcher, and rushed away. There was another ambulance on the scene, waiting to take Skipper Roswell to the hospital once the paramedics finished stabilizing him.

Richard watched from across the street as a second stretcher was carried from the woods and placed in the waiting ambulance. He watched as the paramedics stopped to discuss something with the Staties on the scene before mounting up. They seemed to be taking their time, he thought. He walked across the highway as the ambulance began slowly driving away without its flashing lights or siren going.

One of the Staties noticed him and waved him over.

"Is this Roswell the state senator's son?"

"Yeah."

"You know their number offhand?"

Richard knew the Roswells' home number because he'd worked with Skipper on a school term paper. He recited the number for the officer.

"Okay, son, I think you should go home," the cop said as he finished writing down the Roswells' number.

"Hey, was Skip okay? I noticed the ambulance didn't seem to leave here in much of a hurry."

The cop looked at him, seeming to debate how much to tell him. Young black kid, obviously not a troublemaker if he hung around with this crowd.

"I'm afraid not, son. Your friend's injuries were too massive. They pronounced him about fifteen minutes ago."

Whelan took a step back. "Pronounced him?"

"Sorry. As in, 'pronounced him' dead. Now why don't you go home, okay?"

There were rumors that swirled around the school after that, because Tim Macklin, with a blood alcohol level two and a half times the legal limit, was never charged in the case. Edgar Roswell, the grieving father, had announced shortly after Richard went to college that he was running for Congress with the backing, rumor had it, of Tim Macklin's father. Backing that had been secured in exchange for Roswell persuading the New Jersey State Police not to charge his son for driving while intoxicated and vehicular manslaughter.

And Roswell had won, not only because of Macklin's financial backing but also because Macklin was a heavy hitter in the state's Republican party.

And now, President Roswell was bent out of shape over another big campaign contributor.

There was something that would link all of this together, something. . . .

He just had to find it.

Bettina called and asked him if he'd approached the president yet.

"No. I have no proof. And POTUS will go through the roof if I go back to him with idle speculation." He proceeded to tell Bettina about his meeting yesterday with the president.

"Yeah, it is kinda tough. Are you free for lunch?"

Whelan snorted. "Unfortunately, the 'Great Richard Whelan' has more than enough time on his hands these days. Did you have someplace in particular in mind?"

"Yeah, but not around here. I will actually consent to a short ride in that ridiculous car of yours."

Wait till she sees the back window blown out. "When?"

"I'll swing by and get you about twelve thirty."

At about the same time Detectives Johnson and Steinway were viewing the videotape that had arrived that morning. It was short and conclusive. The two men viewed the tape several times, discussed it briefly, and prepared to visit the White House.

The surveillance van picked up Richard Whelan and Bettina Freeman as they left the White House in Whelan's battered Porsche. They followed behind in a loose tail, not wanting to give themselves away if at all possible.

Nick, with the mustache, was driving. Rudy was in the shotgun seat.

"Don't press it, man. We know he'll be back at the White House after lunch, so no need to get blown while Whelan is off chasing a little nooky."

Nick just looked at his partner. "Hopefully the cops will pull him off the street before too long."

The van had a full complement of exotic equipment and a full video-editing suite. There was barely enough for the two other muscle heads that made up the team this morning. One of them, Raoul, was eating a cheeseburger that stank up the inside with the smell of onions.

Nick's cell phone rang.

"Yeah." He listened for a moment, and Rudy could tell that whatever was being said was not making his partner happy.

"Look, this is not the way to conduct this kind of op," Nick said, raising his voice. He listened again, tried to interject something, but the voice at the other end cut him off.

"They just left the White House. Maybe it's a lunch date, I dunno. If they stop, maybe we can make the hit, but . . . yeah, I've got a piece on me that I can drop. But this is not the way to do this. We're not talking improv theater here, because when that happens, things go bad in a hurry."

Nick listened. Rudy could tell that the voice on the other end was shouting.

"Right, right, you're the boss. Okay. I'll call you back with a situation report. 'Kay. Bye."

Nick shook his head. "He just doesn't get it. Apparently the *Post* didn't get the package we planted at the girl's house, and he thinks Whelan may have intercepted it. So he's spooked, wants some immediate action."

"Action, meaning what?" Rudy asked, afraid that he already knew the answer.

"Just hand me my bag, it's in the back, Rudy," Nick said, ignoring the question. Rudy reached back and grabbed the black leather satchel behind Nick's seat. Nick swerved to avoid some traffic, checking to make sure that they were still two or three cars behind Whelan in the congested midday traffic.

"So what kind of action?" Rudy asked again, impatient. Nick found what he was looking for and pulled a Browning automatic from the bag. He showed it to Rudy.

"This kind of action."

Detectives Johnson and Steinway approached the White House and flashed their badges for the gate guard.

"Who are you going to see?" the guard asked, surprised that two of D.C.'s finest were going into the White House but weren't on anyone's guest list.

"Richard Whelan."

"Let me check. I think he just signed out." The guard ducked into a booth to make a phone call to security. He came back a minute or two later.

"Yeah, Whelan left a few minutes ago. He's expected back after lunch."

"We need to speak to someone about Whelan. Who would you suggest?"

"Uh, gee, I dunno. What's it about?"

"It's a criminal matter. Routine inquiry. But we'd rather tell someone in authority what we're here for."

"Criminal matter, huh? Let me think. Maybe you should see my sergeant."

"That's a start. Who should we ask for?"

"Just go up to the main entrance, show your credentials, and explain what you want. They'll take it from there."

So Detectives Johnson and Steinway went up to the entrance to the White House.

Off of K Street N.W. there was a courtyard restaurant that was screened from the sidewalk by an eight-foot-tall black grill fence. The fence was a permanent fixture even during the winter, and Richard had often thought that it was a waste of good solid construction when the weather wasn't warm enough to allow patrons to dine outside.

He parked his car in the underground lot, and he and Bettina made their way to the open air on the escalator. Bettina hooked his arm with hers as they cleared the escalator. Richard said nothing, mainly because it felt good. They were standing in the bright sunshine waiting for the maître d' to seat them when Richard noticed a black van pass by on K Street. He only noticed it because the van seemed to linger a little too long when traffic resumed moving.

Then Bettina whispered something in his ear, and he jumped, startled.

"Spooked ya, huh?" she said, laughing at his response.

When he turned back toward the street the van had gone.

"No joy on that one. You can't seriously be thinking about a drive-by, Nick. Too much traffic."

"Yeah, I agree, doesn't fit the mission profile, but we have to do this." Nick thought for a moment. "I tell you what. You swing over and drive and I'll get out. After I'm done I'll hop the subway and didi mau outta there. I'll call you from where I end up when I think I'm clear."

"Okay," Rudy said as Nick pulled the van to the corner. "But we'll be close by just in case something goes wrong."

Nick nodded, stuffing the Browning into his waistband. "Just don't let him make you."

Rudy nodded, and Nick opened the door and was gone.

Frank Moynihan took the phone call from the FPS desk sergeant manning security at the main entrance. He listened and said a silent prayer of thanks that the man had called him. He sent his secretary up to get the homicide detectives and shouted at one of his agents to get him a VCR, pronto.

"So when does the SECDEF get back in town?" Bettina asked.

"He's at Vandenburg doing some meetings. The president told him to stick it out rather than come right home because of the India-Pakistan thing. I think it's something to do with Star Wars." *Star Wars* was the term applied to exotic missile defense schemes that had been cooking since the Reagan years.

Bettina nodded. "You seem a little preoccupied, even for you. Something other than the obvious bothering you?"

Richard shrugged. He had his back to the entrance and was trying to scan the street for the mysterious black van, but it was tough to see through the narrowly spaced spikes of the fence that surrounded the café. "I saw a van as we were walking in."

Bettina turned to follow his gaze, but saw nothing but traffic out on the road. "So?"

"I don't know. Something about it spooked me, and I don't know what."

"Seen it before?"

"No, not really." Although there was a black van behind us for at least part of the way here, he thought. He'd seen it when its driver pulled around some traffic.

To catch up to him?

Probably nothing, he decided. He smiled, tried to put Bettina at ease as he scanned the street.

"So what do you want to talk about?" he said.

Rudy drove around the block, trying to gauge how long it would take his partner to get back to the restaurant. He was trying to calculate escape routes in his head, because he had a bad feeling about this little assignment. Nick was right. Improvisation got people caught. If something goes down, he thought, he would head down to the Washington Monument and from there out toward Ronald Reagan Airport. Any pursuit would think he was trying to get away, so if he ducked into the long-term lot. . . .

Someone had stalled out in front of him. He hit the horn, then pulled around.

Nick made sure his navy blue blazer covered the pistol before he approached the entrance to the café. The sidewalks were not particularly crowded yet, although it was still early in the lunch hour. He reconnoitered a bit, pausing to take in the high black fence that partitioned the restaurant from the sidewalk.

Only one way in, he thought. Only one way out. There was a gate for an emergency exit at the rear of the café, but it was locked.

He saw that Whelan and Freeman were seated fairly far from the entrance. A long walk in, and a long walk out. Also not very good.

The general rule of thumb was that bystanders wouldn't react to a gun and a shooting in a public place fast enough to stop a shooter from approaching his target, whacking him out, and walking swiftly out again. But that was in restaurants where the target was only located a few feet from the exit. A long walk past twenty or thirty tables was a different matter. Someone was bound to be brave enough or foolish enough to challenge him and get a bullet for his troubles. Worse, if there was a crowd of people at the entrance waiting to be seated, he'd literally have to fight his way through them to leave.

And in a crowd, some or all of them might find the collective courage to make escape difficult. Or ID him later for the police.

So that left him with one option. How high was the fence around this joint, anyway?

Frank Moynihan greeted Detectives Johnson and Steinway and showed them into his office.

"You have a videotape?"

Johnson nodded. "We requested the security camera tapes from the lobby of Twenty-seven ninety-five Wisconsin Avenue, Mary Jacobs's residence. These are from the night Mary Jacobs was murdered." He handed the tape to Frank Moynihan. "It's pretty self-explanatory."

Moynihan popped the tape into the VCR he'd had wheeled into his office, made sure that the television was turned on, and pushed the play button.

"They use time-lapse cameras to save on film. Swap the tapes pretty frequently, so the quality isn't bad."

"When did you request it?"

"Yesterday. We're lucky because they reuse the tapes. Management of the building pulled this one thinking that we would eventually want to see it."

The image on the screen was grainy black and white. It was more a succession of still images rather than a moving picture, and it took Moynihan a few seconds to get acclimated to the jerky motion.

Johnson stood up to narrate. "You can see the time code at the bottom. This is from around eight P.M., which is close to the time of the victim's death. As you know, Whelan has maintained that he did not arrive with Ms. Jacobs because of a traffic stop. So, we figured the tapes from the front lobby would either support his alibi and show us another possible suspect."

"What about the doorman?" Moynihan said.

Steinway responded. "As you'll see, the doorman was not in the lobby when Mary Jacobs and Richard Whelan entered."

The frames jumped. Moynihan saw the front doors open. He checked the time code at the bottom of the screen: 8:05.

Richard and Mary Jacobs walked into the lobby together and moved across it in stop-action jerks.

Johnson said: "This confirms Whelan's first lie. He was with her when she entered the building."

Moynihan watched the couple get on an elevator and disappear.

There was no one in the lobby for several frames. Then the doorman appeared. The time code at the bottom advanced until it was 8:15.

Steinway: "At this point, nine-one-one has just received the call from Whelan's cell phone indicating that Mary Jacobs has been murdered."

The tape advanced another few frames. 8:22.

Whelan emerged from the elevator, and as the doorman looked up, sprinted across the lobby and left the building.

Johnson reached out to turn off the VCR.

Moynihan stared as snow filled the screen. "Christ."

"The tape shows him enter the building with the deceased, then leave by himself. He was obviously in some sort of altercation, both the doorman and several other witnesses attest to that. There has never been any evidence that he was stopped by D.C. Metro Traffic patrols." Johnson paused.

"We're here to arrest Richard Whelan for the murder of Mary Jacobs. His bail has been revoked."

*   *   *

"I had a conversation with Marcus about you yesterday," Bettina said, sipping a Diet Coke.

There was a pause that Richard didn't seem to want to fill until he said, "Really."

"Well, I had to talk to someone."

"And Mr. Mojo, as you call him, only charges by the hour. A natural choice, I guess."

"You know, I asked you before—what is it between you and Marcus Blaze? Way back when I was surprised that you even knew him, and in talking to him, I was even more surprised at how well he knows you."

"We go back a ways."

"College, right?"

Richard shrugged. He'd never revealed his true relationship with Marcus to anyone, which was one of Marcus's sore points.

"Well, he did say something interesting."

Richard looked up. "Like what?"

"That I shouldn't fall in love with you all over again," she said.

Richard's eyes snapped to meet hers.

In love with him?

Again?

Rudy nursed the black van through another turn, coming up on the back side of the restaurant. He couldn't see anything through the fence, although he could make out that the place appeared to be packed with people enjoying dining in the D.C. sun. And he didn't see another exit, either, which really sucked.

Maybe he'd have to take the van through the fence if the shit hit the fan, he thought. That would certainly make for a hot LZ, though, and the thickness of the individual spikes that made up the enclosure didn't give him comfort that he could even plow the van through it without a good head of speed.

I'll just have to floor it, he thought.

Nick approached the maître d'. He shoved a ten spot in the guy's hand and said that he thought he'd noticed someone he knew in the restaurant, and could he please walk in and take a look.

He didn't wait for an answer. He could see the back of Whelan's head, thirty feet away.

"Say that again, please. Slowly."

Bettina looked down at the tablecloth.

"He said you were the kind of guy who's tough to fall in love with. Nice, caring, smart, but the kind of guy who always responds when someone breaks the glass and pulls the alarm for a fire."

She looked up at him. "You break the glass and out pops Superman Whelan to rescue the damsel in distress, whisk her away from danger, and even give her a couple of bucks to get her hair done and her clothes cleaned to boot. And the damsel always falls for this caring hero, but, according to Marcus, the hero always heads back to his fortress to wait for the next crisis.

"He said you'd give someone the shirt off your back. But that what happens—"

Bettina remembered that Marcus had shaken his head, a rueful smile on his face.

" 'You know, Bettina, what happens is that the damsel watches super nigger rush off to solve crisis after crisis, and she starts thinking, "Well, what about me? Ain't I important enough to keep him here?"

" 'And the answer, unfortunately, is no. It's not that guys like Rich can't be regular guys and take out the trash, but every woman I've seen him with eventually realizes that when the world needs saving, Rich is going to be right there, in costume. When his cell phone rings it's the president, for God's sake.

" 'He's the kind of guy who's larger than life when the shit hits the fan, and though you admire him for it, you can't get with him in any meaningful way because he makes us feel small in comparison, not by anything he thinks or says, but *because of what he is*.' "

"Marcus said all that?"

"Why so surprised? Mr. Mojo has his moments. And what he said was really true."

Bettina looked at Richard Whelan and realized that he'd zoned out on her last sentence.

"Richard?" She asked him, and then twisted around to see what he was staring at.

There was a black van on the street, passing by the restaurant.

Nick was ten paces away when Whelan got up and went toward the fence at the back of the café. He looked and saw Rudy and the van on the street beyond.

"Dammit, Rudy," Nick muttered under his breath, "I told you not to let Whelan make you."

He was five paces away from the table. Time to rock and roll.

He pulled the Browning from his waistband.

Bettina had twisted around to look at the van and didn't see the big man with the mustache pull the gun not five steps away from her. Something made her turn around, though, and she found herself staring at the barrel of a gun.

She screamed so loud her whole body shook with it and Richard turned just in time to see the muzzle flash seem to leap from Nick's gun.

* * *

Nick was an expert marksman and couldn't miss from five feet away. So he only fired once.

But Bettina had slid down in her seat when she started screaming, and the bullet cleared the top of her head by less than an inch and plowed into the back of one of the patrons behind her.

Nick was incredulous that he'd missed, but steadied the gun and squeezed the trigger again.

Whelan began sprinting back toward the table, recognizing the tall mustached man as the cop from his ill-fated traffic stop. Someone to his left caught that first round and screamed, and Bettina sort of slid out of her chair as the gunman began firing again.

He got off two shots before Richard hit him with a flying tackle.

Rudy heard the gunshots from the van and watched as the commotion began in the café. He was now a third of a block beyond the back end of the restaurant and pulled the van over next to a fire hydrant and waited anxiously.

The bitch slid under the table, and he missed with both rounds. Dammit! Then Whelan hit him, and the gun barked again, discharging uselessly into the air. With his left arm he clubbed Whelan down off of him and began looking for the target.

And couldn't find her.

The clock in his head said he was running out of time. He took a step to get a better look under the table, but Whelan grabbed his leg, sending him sprawling.

He fired twice more, into the air, and whatever panic the rest of the customers felt exploded until the place was in bedlam.

* * *

The shots deafened him, but he hung on grimly, hoping that Bettina hadn't been hit.

"Richard!" she cried out from somewhere behind him, and he relaxed his grip on the shooter's leg just a little to turn toward the sound.

"Stay down!" he screamed, and then felt the gunman pull free.

Exit, Nick thought, *stage right!* He struggled to his feet and began running directly toward the fence at the back of the restaurant. He had to time this perfectly, he thought, because he had to get out of here, even though he was sure that he hadn't hit the woman at all.

Three shots, three misses from point-blank range, he thought, furious. He got to the back fence, hopped up on a table, grabbed hold, and swung a leg over to the other side.

Rudy twisted the steering wheel as he saw Nick climbing the back fence. He put the van in reverse, not caring that the back right tire ended up on the sidewalk. Now he had an angle to just floor the thing back into traffic once Nick was aboard.

"C'mon, buddy. Let's beat feet the hell outta here," he said.

Whelan saw the shooter reach the back fence and begin to climb over. To his right, he saw the black van and heard the tires screech as the driver repositioned it to angle out into traffic. Once he's aboard, he thought, they'll be gone.

He was running toward the fence as Nick got his other leg over the spikes at the top of the fence and dropped to the other side.

As he dropped down, Nick realized that he still had the Browning in his right hand. He paused to wipe his prints off the gun, then tossed it back into the fenced-in area, and sprinted toward the van.

Whelan angled away from Nick toward the van as he ran toward the fence. He had one chance to catch this guy, he thought, and he wasn't going to do it if he stopped to climb up and over.

Well, he thought, you remember the triple jump from high school track, right? He spotted a chair and a table in just about the right position and hurtled toward them.

Hope that fence isn't higher than it looks, he thought, *'cause this is gonna be close.*

Bettina's shoulder was bleeding from where she'd been grazed, as she watched Richard running toward the fence. She heard something clatter against the concrete somewhere off to her left, turned, and saw a gun glittering in the sunlight. She could dimly see through the bars of the fence that the gunman was outside the café, sprinting toward the black van. And then she looked at Richard rushing headlong toward the fence.

He had a full head of speed, crashing through the strewn chairs left behind by the panicked diners. *Here we go.*

In full stride he planted his left foot up onto a chair, then pushed off. His right foot landed on a table next to the fence still in full stride, and he launched himself toward the fence, laying full out, hoping to sail over it.

Death from above! Whelan thought as he cleared the fence. Nick was right in front of him, angling toward the van, right in his glide path.

He hit him right between the shoulder blades, causing the gunman's breath to explode from his chest in a grunt. They tumbled to the ground, Richard grabbing Nick's blazer and using it to haul him down.

*   *   *

Bettina saw Richard hit the chair then the table perfectly and sail over the black spikes of the fence and staggered to her feet to see the result.

She heard the impact of two bodies on the sidewalk beyond her, and a shouted curse along with the ripping of fabric.

Richard had him, then he didn't. The jacket tore in two, right down a middle seam, as they tumbled to the ground, and the big man was quicker, doing a combat roll and getting back to his feet before Richard could untangle himself.

Nick got to the van in three strides, yanked open the door.

"Go, go, go!" he screamed, and Rudy gunned it, cutting off a cabby in a hail of horns.

"Did you get her?" Rudy yelled as he swerved around some traffic.

Nick shook his head. "Fucked it up. I had her, then I missed her." He slammed the plastic dashboard in disgust.

At the White House, Moynihan considered his next words carefully. "You cannot arrest Whelan here."

"What do you mean?" Steinway asked, indignant.

"I mean I will not have a ranking member of this administration 'perp walked' out of the White House in front of a mob of reporters."

"We haven't told anyone about this."

"Bullshit. If you didn't, how much you want to bet that someone from the precinct hasn't let on what's about to happen? You asked a judge to revoke his bail, didn't you?"

"Of course."

"Then it's all over the White House press corps by now, and I repeat, gentlemen, if you're thinking about parading Richard Whelan down the White House steps cuffed with a sweater thrown over his face, you can forget it."

"This is a police matter, Mr. Moynihan."

"Not in the White House it isn't. This is a matter of national security, and I dare you to provoke the president into invoking his rather broad Constitutional powers in that arena. You push me, and you'll be busting prostitutes on Avenue M for the rest of your lives."

"You have a better idea?" Johnson asked.

14

Richard came back into the restaurant, holding the two shredded halves of Nick's jacket in his hands. Blue smoke and the smell of cordite hung in the air. The one patron who had been hit, an elderly woman, lay on the ground moaning.

"Are you okay?" he said as he came up to Bettina. But he could see that she wasn't. She was shaking, and there was blood on her clothes.

"You're hit! Sit down." He urged her into a seat.

"Just got grazed," she said. She was dizzy.

Richard went to reassure the elderly woman, whose wound looked serious. He saw the metal glint of a gun lying on the ground between two tables near the black fence.

Multiple sirens wailed in the distance, approaching.

Richard jogged over to pick up the gun, a Browning automatic. He knew the gun well, he had one just like it stored in his locker at his gun club in Silver Spring.

He picked up the gun, felt the familiar weight and heft of the weapon.

Too familiar, it seemed. He looked at the bottom of the grip.

Saw the initials RW scratched there. *Uh-oh.*

He shoved the gun in his pocket and ran back towards Bettina.

He pulled out his cell phone and called Charles O'Shay.

"O'Shay."

"Chuck, it's Richard. Listen, I've got to see the president today. It's urgent. Something just happened that should convince him that he needs to launch a full-scale investigation into what's happened to me."

"Hold on a sec, Richard. I'm going to put you on speakerphone."

Richard reached down and put his arm around Bettina.

There was that blurry, tinny sound as the speakerphone engaged.

"Richard?" O'Shay sounded like he'd fallen down a well.

"I'm still here."

"Richard, I'm with Frank Moynihan and Detectives Johnson and Steinway of the Washington, D.C. police. First off, son, why don't you tell us where you are."

Something's wrong. He could hear it in O'Shay's voice.

"What's going on?" Sirens approaching, probably paramedics and police. *If this is what I think it is . . .*

Moynihan: "You need to turn yourself in to the police, Richard. We've arranged for you to go into the precinct where Detectives Johnson and Steinway first questioned you about Mary Jacobs's murder. If you go quietly and cooperate, it will spare us all a great deal of difficulty."

"Turn myself in?"

Johnson: "For Mary Jacobs's murder. We have the security camera tapes from her apartment building that show you and only you entering with her and then running out after . . . you killed her."

"That's impossible."

Moynihan: "I've seen the tape myself, Richard. So has Charles. It's absolutely conclusive."

"It's a frame-up."

O'Shay: "Richard, you have to help us out on this one. You need to turn yourself in so we can get this sorted out."

"Then I'll come back to the White House." He had to get moving. The first police cars were pulling up to the scene. He took a step away from Bettina.

"Richard," she hissed, "where are you going?" She desperately didn't want him to leave her.

Moynihan: "Under no circumstances are you to return to the White House, Richard. You have been relieved of your post and placed on indefinite administrative leave. Your IDs have been canceled and you will be arrested if you try and get anywhere near the building. So I want you to go to the police station and turn yourself in for the good of the administration and to avoid the press. Do you understand?"

A videotape? That shows me entering the lobby with Mary? Impossible. He quickened his pace until he was just below a jog.

"I don't think I can do that, fellas." He glanced back at Bettina, then turned away.

Bettina: "Richard!" But his back was turned, and he was jogging toward the exit.

O'Shay:"You realize that this only adds to the presumption of your guilt, Richard?"

"Listen, someone just tried to shoot Bettina Freeman. The gunman was the same guy who stopped me the night Mary was killed. O'Shay, listen to me. They dropped a gun at the scene; one of my guns. This is a setup, and whatever it's about it's huge."

Moynihan: "More conspiracy theories, Whelan. I don't buy it."

"I didn't kill Mary!" He was at the entrance to the café. Three police cars had pulled up, officers climbing out and moving toward the milling crowd, an ambulance squealed to a halt and paramedics . . .

Johnson: "Don't try to run, Richard. We have your town house under surveillance, and we've got an all points bulletin out on you. So just settle down and come on in. You can't get away."

"Look, I know this looks bad, but if I surrender now I'll never get to the bottom of it. I'll keep in touch."

He hung up and sprinted for the underground parking lot where he'd parked his car.

Charles O'Shay turned off the speakerphone. "Well?"

Steinway was on the phone checking. "We got him; Bell Atlantic Mobile pinpointed his location. Nice job keeping him on the phone, gentlemen. We'll take it from here."

Moynihan and O'Shay watched the detectives leave. O'Shay ran his hand through his hair. "Does the president know yet?"

Moynihan shook his head. "I came up here in case you heard from Whelan. So I haven't told him."

O'Shay popped the copy of the security camera tape from his VCR.

"I'd better show him this before he sees in on the five o'-clock news."

But Moynihan was already dialing the speakerphone. It rang once, twice . . .

"Treasury Department Special Operations Group. How may I direct your call?"

Bettina watched Richard jogging toward the exit of the restaurant, her anger rising in proportion to the pain in her shoulder. There he was, Superman, rushing off to the next crisis, the Bat signal supplied this time by a cell-phone call. She'd watched him flying over the black fence like some comic book hero, thinking that all he needed was a cape and a costume and the picture would be complete. Now she was left behind, hurt, bleeding, and traumatized because someone had chosen to point a gun at her.

And then she thought about it.

Why would someone want to kill her?

* * *

Richard was running, but he had no idea where to go. He'd retrieved the Porsche; now he was going to make a dash to his house to get money. And he would need a new set of wheels, too.

He parked the car a few blocks from his house and began walking toward home so that he could see if it was being watched before committing himself. As he walked, he did an inventory of what he had on him, besides his cell phone.

He had one hundred fifty-seven dollars and sixty-three cents in cash.

He had four major credit cards, one of which was maxed out.

He had his now-defunct White House ID.

He had the keys to the Porsche, which he would have to abandon.

He had one Browning semiautomatic pistol with seven rounds left in the clip as well as his Glock with several clips of ammo.

Not a heckuva lot. And if Moynihan was involved, then they could easily either trace or restrict his access to ATMs or his credit cards; Secret Service was part of the Treasury Department, and he had no doubt that they would bring every resource to bear to run him down.

Then he remembered the classified documents in the trunk in the hood. With all the excitement of meeting with Bettina, he'd forgotten to take them out of the car. And with no house and no office to hide them in, he was stuck with in-criminating evidence in a car that would surely be all over the police radios any second.

He shook his head in disgust. First things first. He needed some money.

He did have some money at his house. Maybe a grand he kept in a strongbox hidden in the basement. If he was going to try and evade capture, he had to have that money.

But by the time he was a block away from his house, he knew he was too late. The street was cordoned off, and police cars and television camera crews were very much in evidence.

15

Sam Hennings was in the middle of lunch when he got the phone call. It was a summons from Phil Erskine to come see him immediately.

Uh-oh, he thought. What's the sound of shit hitting the fan? It's Erskine's patrician tones summoning you to an immediate meeting.

He left his sandwich and went directly to Phil Erskine's office.

It was even worse than he thought. Erskine and Monroe together. Hennings began mentally totaling up how much emergency money he had in the bank just in case he was going to walk out of here without a job.

"Yes, Phil. You called me?"

Erskine steepled his hands under his chin. "Yes, Sam. Got a rather interesting phone call from the people at Sandia National Laboratories. Said one of their researchers was tying up a huge block of time on one of their Crays and that they thought one of our people had requested it."

"What would that have to do with me?"

Erskine smiled, and it was not pretty the way it pinched his face. "As far as we can tell, you're the only one who knows Doctor Gonzales from their ASCI computing group. So you're the obvious first choice for the connection."

Does he have anything? Or can I bluff?

"I talk to Enrique all the time," Hennings said, trying to build a later case for plausible deniability. "Did they say what it was about?"

Monroe cleared his throat. "This wouldn't have anything to do with the Indian situation, would it, Sam?"

Hennings shook his head. "I haven't talked to Enrique about that. Ever."

"So you certainly didn't ask them to do any modeling about it?"

"Nothing to model. They look at test-bed data on explosions. All we have is a few bits and pieces from the Keyholes. And what would a model prove, anyway?"

Erskine nodded. "You have a point. But there's a lot going on right now, and I wanted to make sure that everyone here is on the same team. Any requests for outside help have to come through my office, okay, Sam? No freelancing."

"Er, sure. I'll make sure that I remember to buck anything up to you if I ever get the urge. To freelance, I mean. Anything else?"

Erskine shook his head. "No. That's it for now. Thanks for stopping by."

Hennings practically ran out of the office.

Erskine turned to Monroe. "Well? What'd you think?"

Monroe shrugged. "I thought he was going to have a cow when he saw me in here. Other than that, I don't know. Maybe it's nothing. But I would keep an eye on Hennings, anyway. Sandia didn't say what they were working on?"

Erskine shook his head. "They explained it, but they could explain it a hundred times and I wouldn't get it. Some kind of exotic math that's so new nobody understands it. That's why they were curious when CIA was mentioned. What the hell would we want with this stuff?"

Monroe chuckled. "You know how these boys work. Probably some exotic way to encrypt a nudie picture into a screen saver of the Vatican or something. But Hennings was the first one on India, wasn't he?"

Erskine nodded. "Yes, he was. Why?"

"Hmm, all the more reason to keep an eye on him."

"You want the full treatment?"

"What, put him on 'watched' status? No. No need. Just keep an eye out for anything else that crosses your desk about him, that's all."

"Sure, Mike. Consider it done."

Richard Whelan retreated from the world to try and sort out his options. He didn't dare use his cell phone to call anyone, because he realized that O'Shay and Company had been trying to keep him on the phone so they could pinpoint his location. So he turned his phone off, just so it wouldn't act as a homing beacon for the police.

Where to start?

Well, it all began with Mary. He could either go back to her apartment and see if he picked up any more clues there, or . . .

He could find out just how much Marty Jacobs knew about his daughter's relationships and see if there were any clues there. All he had to do was get into Fortress Jacobs without being seen.

Hah. Maybe he should turn himself invisible while he was at it.

But first he needed some cash.

Sam Hennings was on the phone to Enrique Gonzales as soon as he reached his cubicle.

"Hey, Enrique, did I or did I not say I wanted this kept quiet?"

"What happened?"

"The Blues Brothers just questioned me as to whether I was behind some esoteric work tying up Sandia's computers because someone out there thought it had the full weight of the CIA behind it."

"Uh-oh. Did they nail you?"

"No, I denied it. But if I am now on their radar screens, I can't have someone out there confirm that it was CIA or me that was pushing for this."

"I hadn't heard anything. Let me check around."

"Okay. And Enrique?"

"Yes, Sam?"

"When we talk again, no specifics. I don't know if I'm going to be watched or not. Okay?"

"Aren't we being a bit paranoid, Sam?"

"You bet, Enrique. You bet your ass."

Frank Moynihan was in his office pacing, waiting for some word that Richard Whelan had been captured. He'd already gotten an irate phone call from the president about how the matter was handled. POTUS had chewed him tough for not letting Whelan be taken into custody at the White House when he returned from lunch, press scrutiny be damned.

When the phone buzzed he snatched it from its cradle.

"Yes?"

"Morgan Bishop, Director of the Treasury SOG. We just got a hit on Whelan."

The security guard at the First National Bank and Trust was watching the tellers when his radio squawked.

"This is Alex."

"Alex, this is Mr. Wiggins, the branch manager. I got a weird phone call from the Secret Service."

Alex began undoing the snaps on his holster. Secret Service was part of Treasury, so it could be anything, counterfeiters, bank robbers, drug-money laundering . . .

"Go ahead, Mr. Wiggins."

"Treasury is tapped into the ATM network. Seems someone's using our ATM machines. A fugitive of some sort. Don't stare, but can you see someone at unit number three?"

The automated teller machines were located in a glassed-in vestibule visible from the interior of the bank and were accessible twenty-four hours a day. There was a line to access the four machines nestled into the far wall. Alex scanned quickly, looking at unit 3.

"Black guy, yeah."

"Okay. D.C. Metro is rolling and should be here in a minute or two. Whatever you do, don't confront the man because he's considered armed and dangerous."

"Right." Alex glanced back at the tellers and the bank employees manning their desks. Everything looked normal, so it wasn't a diversion for a robbery. He clipped the microphone back to his shirt pocket.

A cash withdrawal takes about sixty seconds. Even if the man was just beginning his transaction, the police would never get to the bank in time. That would mean a deadly shootout on the street, particularly if the man was armed.

But if he could ease up behind him and stick his gun in the guy's back, well, one move and he's gut shot, *game over.*

Might even get me on the D.C. Metro police force, he thought.

Richard was in the ATM lobby, waiting patiently for the machine to complete its business. Too bad the daily limit was four hundred bucks, he thought, because he didn't dare try this stunt again.

The wad of bills came out of the dispenser, as well as his card and a receipt.

Alex eased into the vestibule. There was a man standing by the little table that held deposit slips and other supplies, but everyone else was patiently waiting to use the machines. He might get close enough to pull this off, but then again, he might not.

It's hero time, Alexy boy.

He pulled his gun.

"Everybody down!" The security guard was yelling and waving his gun. Richard hit the floor. He watched the guard's highly polished shoes with run-down heels walk past him toward the man standing at the third ATM.

"Hands up, pal," the guard said to the man standing at the ATM. The man put his hands up, one hand clutching an ATM card, the other clutching four hundred dollars.

Alex grabbed the ATM card and looked at it. He heard the wail of sirens in the distance and smiled.

"Richard Whelan, eh?"

The man turned to the guard, obviously scared witless. "Hell, no. This guy gave me his card and his pin number, and asked me to get him some cash."

"What?" Alex exploded, turning around.

But Richard was already kneeling next to the little table, the Browning automatic in his hand.

"Don't make me do this," Richard said urgently. He heard the sirens, too.

"Just give me the money and I'll be on my way." *One wrong move and the reflexes take over, show me a threat and you'll be dead before I even think about it, and you don't want to die today.*

Alex hesitated.

"Give me the money, dammit!"

There are too many people in here, Alex thought. *Too many people outside, too. A stray shot and someone gets killed, and I'm standing at the head of that particular line.*

Richard moved toward him, gun still trained on Alex's heart. He deftly snatched the wad of twenties from the guy at the ATM, then peeled off roughly half of them and stuck them in the guy's pocket.

"Hey, I don't want your damn money now."

Richard managed a weary smile.

"A deal's a deal, bro."

He backed out of the bank, then took off running down the street.

Bill Johnson had just finished interviewing Alex the security guard when Frank Moynihan pulled up.

"What the hell happened?" Moynihan asked.

"Apparently your boy pulled off a little scam. Gave someone his ATM card and pin number and asked him to make a withdrawal in exchange for half the money. The guard caught the alert from Treasury and decided to take matters into his own hands."

"So he drew down on the wrong man."

Johnson nodded. "Uh-huh. And by the time he realized his mistake, Whelan had his gun on him. Whelan took the money and then ran just as our patrol units were pulling up. They lost him in the streets."

"Shit."

"Although, I find it interesting that Whelan stopped and gave his accomplice roughly half the money."

"Which proves what?" Moynihan snorted.

Johnson shrugged. "Nothing. But it's not what I would expect of a killer."

"Then you need to study a little history. Some of the most notorious killers and thugs, particularly bank robbers, have been real charmers. Whelan is the same. That's why he was able to kill Mary Jacobs."

"I guess so," Johnson said, but for the life of him, he wasn't convinced.

* * *

Lisa was cleaning up in the kitchen of the Jacobses' Potomac, Maryland, home when she heard the knock on the door. All of the other servants were off today, and she thought Mr. and Mrs. Jacobs were out, since she hadn't heard a word from either of them since coming on duty. She looked at her watch. After five. Nearly time to go home. She hoped it wasn't those Jehovah's Witnesses making the rounds. They could talk you to death when they knocked on doors in her neighborhood.

She opened the door. "Yes?"

"UPS delivery for Mr. Jacobs. Is he here to sign for it?"

She shook her head. "I'll take it. Where do I sign?" she asked, reaching for the package.

But the driver held the package back and didn't seem to have that electronic clipboard for her to sign.

"Sorry. But Mr. Jacobs has to sign for this himself. Please check to see if he's at home."

"Wait right here, I'll use the intercom to make sure."

Lisa retreated into the house. This was certainly odd. If he was UPS, where was his truck?

She came back a few minutes later. "Sorry, Mr. Jacobs is not present. So either I sign or you'll have to come back tomorrow." She was annoyed because the man was now standing in the foyer, not at the door as she had specifically requested.

"Darn. I don't seem to have my clipboard. Do you mind if I make a phone call?"

She looked at him more closely. He had the UPS hat and brown jacket, but he was wearing . . . suit pants?

"Can I see some identification, please?"

Uh-oh, Richard thought. *The jig is up.* "Wait one second."

He tore open the package, opened the box under the wrapping, and pulled out his Browning. And pointed it at the maid.

"Just be quiet, ma'am. I don't want to hurt you. I just want to have a look around."

But Lisa panicked and ran into the kitchen screaming.

Richard had no intention of shooting her, and didn't have time to follow her. He quickly descended the stairs to the basement.

It had cost him the two hundred dollars from the ATM to buy the jacket and hat from a friendly black UPS driver. He'd driven the Porsche out to Potomac, keeping well within the speed limit, painfully aware of how conspicuous he was in the car and how exposed he was should the police arrest him with classified documents in the trunk.

Now, with the whole house alerted and the maid probably calling the police, he would have at most a few minutes to rummage through Marty's collection of videotapes before the police and the private security firm the sign on the lawn advertised would come running.

Now where, he thought, *would Marty keep a footlocker of home videos?* He hit the basement running, finding it odd that the massive television set was on with the sound turned down low. There was nothing obvious, no piece of furniture that looked like it contained a footlocker. He scanned the basement quickly and found nothing.

Maybe behind the bar somewhere? He ran over to the bar to take a look.

Lisa was trying to remember the code sequence on the alarm system that would notify the police that there was an intruder in the house. She opened the clear plastic cover that protected the keys and began studying the keyboard, hoping that she would remember what she was supposed to do just by looking.

Then she heard a single shot ring out from the basement.

"Oh, no," she said under her breath. There were three colored keys at the bottom of the control unit. One said "Police," another said "Fire," and a third said "Armed Response." She pushed all three in succession and then scurried back into the pantry and pulled the door shut.

Provident Security, Inc., had the most ex-cops and ex-FBI agents on its staff of any of the private "armed response" firms that serviced the well-to-do in Potomac, a fact that its sales brochures trumpeted. They also had the prettiest alert-desk operators, too.

At least, that's what John Miller always said to his partner, George Hilton, whenever they got a call from "one of the gals."

But not this time. "All units, all units, vicinity of Potomac Creek Drive, Jacobs residence, Five Potomac Creek Drive, multiple-alert status indicates occupants in danger, please respond."

"Shit, that's us." John cranked the late-model Camaro into gear and squealed away from the coffee shop where they had been on break from patrol duty. George picked up the mike.

"This is Five Victor on station. We'll be there in a couple of minutes."

"Say again, Five Victor, and please follow protocol."

"Roger, base. Five Victor responding, ETA two minutes."

Marty Jacobs was lying behind the bar. Behind him was a padlocked footlocker. Richard stopped, knowing even before he turned the body over that the elder Jacobs was dead.

First Mary, now her daddy.

He turned the body with the toe of his shoe. A single gunshot wound in the middle of his forehead—Marty's eyes open, sightless . . .

Whoever's behind this is cleaning up all the loose ends. So why am I still alive? he wondered.

To take the fall, dummy. They'd dropped the Browning at the café, hoping it would be found and linked to him. They'd left classified documents at Mary's apartment, all linked to him. Now Marty Jacobs, legendary money man and presidential friend was dead, and it was no secret that there was no love lost between the fugitive Whelan and Jacobs. *Especially since you told the president that Marty was setting you up.*

That plus phony audio- and videotapes conveniently delivered to the police somehow.

Without hesitating he shot the lock off the footlocker and began digging inside. But the tapes were in seemingly random order. He pawed through them, counting the seconds as sweat appeared on his forehead. Keep looking, keep looking, one of them is going to jump out at you and say "Take me!"

He kept digging until he found one that said simply "Alan" on a piece of masking tape on the face of the cassette. No more time to be choosy. He grabbed it just as he heard the squeal of tires on the gravel driveway above.

"Unit Five Victor is on scene, base. Front door is ajar. No sign of any vehicles. Request backup from Potomac PD, over."

"Roger that, Five Victor. Potomac PD estimates ETA in five, repeat ETA in five."

George looked at his partner. They were both ex-cops who'd been forced into retirement for questionable shoots in Baltimore. The doctrine of armed response was to be first and go in hot.

They both unholstered their weapons and went in the front door combat-style like they'd done a million times before in past lives.

The house was deathly quiet. John Miller whispered into his throat mike, "This is Five Victor. We're inside. Tell Potomac PD that there are friendlies on the inside, over."

He had the squelch button turned up so he couldn't hear the response. He nodded to George. The kitchen was on the right.

They went in.

Richard heard the footfalls above him as he began climbing the stairs. I have no training for this, he thought frantically. And the last thing I want to do is get into a shoot-out with the local cops. He paused at the head of the steps leading out into the foyer.

George went into the kitchen screaming "Provident Security, come out with your hands up!" and proceeded to quarter the room with his gun.

Nothing at the stove. Big Webber model, too. Hmm.

Nothing at the refrigerator. Subzero model, easily a five-figure accessory. Not to mention the marble countertops and the custom cabinetry.

There was a sound from behind the pantry door, which was closed. Something fell, and there was someone in there coughing.

John whipped open the pantry door, gun at the ready.

Lisa stumbled out, covered with flour. "Don't shoot! He's downstairs, and he has a gun! I heard a shot!"

George and John raced from the kitchen and down the steps to the basement.

Richard heard the footsteps moving toward the kitchen and the commotion as Lisa came out of the pantry. Okay, if he was going to move, it had to be now. He took off across the foyer, heading for the back door leading out to the tennis courts and pool.

George and his partner heard the back door slam just as they got to the bottom of the basement steps. John motioned to his partner to give pursuit; he wanted to check out the basement.

George thought he was in decent shape for having a boring sedentary job. He ran, puffing a little, up the stairs and toward the back, where the sound had come from. It took him a few precious seconds to locate the back door, scan the outside, and kick it open.

"Armed security. Freeze!" He yelled to anyone waiting to ambush him. He looked left and right. Nothing. He entered the yard.

Richard was hiding behind a gazebo twenty yards away. He'd taken cover as soon as he heard the back door kicked open. Now there was thirty yards of magnificent grass between him and the tennis courts, or twenty yards of magnificent grass between him and the pool. The tennis courts were behind him, but the pool was to his left. Which meant that he'd present a much better target if he went for the pool.

"I know you're out here! Potomac PD will be here in a minute, and they are going to cover the back exits. So let's just take it easy and drop your weapon."

George had retreated back into the house for cover. Richard could just barely see his gun hand peeking around the edge of the door frame. He had to get out of here.

Stay defensive. He took aim, mindful that he had only a few shots in this clip and that was it. He squeezed off two shots. Then he took off running.

The shots tore chunks out of the door frame inches from George's hand. "Shit!" he screamed, and rolled into the backyard to return fire. He got off three wild shots at the retreating back of a man dressed in a UPS uniform. Boy, what a black eye for the Brownies, he thought.

"Shots fired," he said into his throat mike. "Unit Five Victor George has shots fired in the backyard of Five Potomac Creek Road."

Then he got up to pursue.

John discovered Marty Jacobs's body behind the bar and backed away, careful not to contaminate the crime scene any more than he already had. He did notice that it was a head shot at close range, because he could see the powder burns on the victim's forehead. No other signs of a struggle.

Looked like a mob hit to him. All these rich geezers were dirty, anyway.

Richard was running as fast as he could and hurdled the center net of the main court and headed toward what he hoped was an open gate at the back of the court. He could feel the footsteps of his pursuer behind him, and every time he paused, he could feel a bullet in the back getting closer and closer. *Event cascade, that's what I called it. I'm sinking lower and lower*, he thought. *Step by step, descending into this mess until there won't be any way out.*

He punched through the back gate. Now there were, from what he remembered, a high set of hedges that maintained the privacy of the compound from the road behind the house. He would have to find a way to get through those and take off on the run.

Although if what the guy said is true, the cops may be out here already. If I come up against a uniform with a gun I'm going to lay it down, he thought. Just stay defensive before you kill someone.

He turned and fired a nuisance round at his pursuer, just to keep him honest.

George was running and stumbled when Richard's shot whistled over his head. Damn, he thought, not getting any younger. Better call in the Mounties.

"This is Five Victor George. Suspect is headed south off the property onto Court Lane. Have Potomac PD cut him off there."

He paused for a second to catch his breath, then continued on, cautiously.

*   *   *

Richard crossed the road behind the Jacobs estate at a dead run. Directly behind the Jacobs residence there was another property that was bordered by low hedges, which he hurdled easily. He didn't dare stop to think about how much ammunition he had left. Instead he kept running.

He would rely on speed, first of all. He would get clear and hope like hell he wasn't the only black man in Potomac, Maryland, driving a beat-up Porsche out of here.

He heard the sirens before he heard the squeal of the police car's tires. Potomac PD's on-duty squad car ripped around the corner onto Court Lane in a four-wheel drift that almost put the vehicle off the road. The officer screeched to a halt right at the point where George cleared the high hedges of the Jacobs property.

"Which way?" The police officer screamed at George, and George was happy that he was wearing his Provident Security looks-just-like-a-police-officer's uniform.

"He just crossed into the other property. See him?"

The cop disappeared into his cruiser for a moment and reappeared with a shotgun. "Let's go!" he yelled, and he and George took off after Richard.

George fired a warning shot, which Richard ignored. He kept running, kept under control, and fought his rising panic.

This house was smaller than Marty's and had fewer amenities. Just a pool, and a pretty small one at that. Richard disappeared around a fence for a moment, looking for a way out.

"Hey, you! Get off my property!"

Great. The homeowner was spraying pesticides on his garden and spotted Richard running toward him. Richard cut right again, hoping that the cop and the security guy hadn't split up to cut him off.

He was sprinting for the road when his luck ran out. The

cop had doubled back to his police cruiser and was waiting for Richard as he neared the edge of the property, his shotgun at the ready.

"Halt! Police!" the officer said, and pumped a shell into his shotgun.

Stay defensive, he screamed to himself. *Don't put a bullet in the cop's forehead. Rent-a-cop behind you*, even as he started to raise his gun, *reflex action*.

"Halt, dammit!" The officer fired once into the air as a warning, and pumped the shotgun again.

But Richard was too close, and accelerated, hitting the policeman square in the chest before he could bring the Remington to bear.

They went down in a heap.

Richard Whelan was a fugitive from justice. The news topped the hour at the all-news station that Sam Hennings was listening to.

Hennings sat back in his cubicle. Once again he was at a decision point. Either he could trust his instincts that Richard Whelan wasn't a crazed killer, or he could run for cover.

Well, he thought, if he isn't a killer he really needs my help now. Besides, he thought, I'm really curious now. Something about this stinks. So maybe I do some fishing for my own sake, as long as I'm safe.

He turned off the radio. There was another cubicle nearer the window, a good forty feet away in the cavernous portion of the CIA headquarters that he worked in. Hennings had an idea about how to get the backup Keyhole information without anyone knowing about it. And to do it, he needed an empty cubicle.

He grabbed a cup of coffee and made his way across the room. Several analysts had been relocated to another section of the compound, so most of the cubes here were empty of people but not of equipment. One guy in particular had left the agency in the last week or so, and he was counting on Langley's internal IT people to be as sloppy about internal security as they were about manning the PC help desk, which was an utter joke.

There was no one around. Quickly he sat down and powered up the terminal that was still sitting there at the empty desk.

As he waited for the machine to boot up, he began searching for the Holy Grail in an insecure, overly mechanized environment: a Post-it note with a list of the old user's passwords that had been inadvertently left behind.

As he was checking the drawers the PC finished booting up. He was going to do this in steps to avoid triggering any internal alarms. He clicked on the Lotus Notes icon and went into Lotus Notes Mail. This version had a simple sign-on screen that remembered the user's name; all he had to do was type in the password.

The default was the user's first name. He knew of only two people in the section that had ever changed theirs—E-mail was not considered a secure forum at the agency, so who cared if someone got access to E-mail? He was greeted with a sign-on screen with the old user's name: Virgil Szymaniski. Good thing he didn't have to type all of that in. Under password, he typed *Virgil*, then hit "enter."

Up scrolled a list of Virgil's outstanding messages. Good. That meant that for E-mail purposes, Virgil still existed. Now if he was still on the agency's secure intranet and he could locate a password . . .

Richard and the cop rolled around on the ground. He knew he had seconds, at most, to subdue the cop and get away. He punched the poor guy in the face, a good roundhouse right that had a lot behind it, but it didn't put him down.

Worse, he'd dropped his gun, and the officer was desperately trying to get his own service revolver out of its holster;

if he did that, Richard knew that one of them would get killed by an accidental discharge.

But he had leverage, he was on top. Richard could feel the Kevlar vest under the man's uniform shirt as he punched the cop again, willing the man to give in, but he could see the fear in his eyes, fear that he would die here if he let Richard get the upper hand. Richard swung to hit him again, but missed, and the cop reversed him using the momentum of the missed punch to throw him to the side. Richard rolled away, but the cop was already getting to his feet, already had his hands on the shotgun.

But Richard had rolled onto his Browning. He scooped the weapon up and rolled onto the balls of his feet, a lousy shooting position because the recoil could knock him flat on his back and all would be lost. But he pointed the pistol at the cop, his finger taking almost all the slack out of the trigger before he stopped himself.

"Drop your weapon," he growled, trying to be as menacing as possible.

"No, you drop the gun, nigger!" The cop was pointing the shotgun at Richard's face.

And just then George rambled up, completely out of breath.

Sam Hennings had located what looked to be Virgil's last password crib sheet. It was an understandable failing, because every subsystem within the agency required a unique set of passwords that had to be changed every six weeks. Some, like Virgil, had literally dozens of passwords for all the applications that he had to access, and the security system not only remembered if you'd used a password before, it also knew if you were trying to use the same password for more than one application.

And Virgil had access to downloads from the ground stations, as did Sam, but since Virgil wouldn't be around to get into trouble, he would simply make the request with Virgil's ID.

They faced each other, and Richard could hear more sirens screaming in the background. The cop had his weapon trained on him, and George, puffing and out of breath, was trying his best to do the same. Richard looked closely at the rent-a-cop. Saw the telltale bulge under his shirt, too.

"I said drop the gun, motherfucker!"

I said I wouldn't draw down on a cop, but if he takes me in, I'm finished. They'll hang me for Marty Jacobs, and they'll hang me for Mary, and there won't be a damn thing I can do about it. Bluff, he thought.

The cop's hands are shaking. He wants to go home to his wife and kids, and he thinks I'm some kind of urban nightmare come to visit his pretty little city. *How many times has he even drawn his gun in anger?*

"I've got nothing to lose, Officer! Nothing at all, and I guarantee I'll make your wife a widow before you take me down!"

He began moving closer, and the cop backed away. "Don't make me shoot you, asshole!" George was moving in from his right, ambling the way an out-of-shape man carries himself, lopsided and chest heaving, looking for all the world like a coronary was imminent. *You have one chance, Richard, God help me.*

Richard fired into the cop's chest, ducked, and fired at the rent-a-cop, hitting him about the same place he'd hit the police officer. The cop's shotgun blast sailed pellets over his head; George had just gone down in a heap.

Richard was on top of the fallen cop in an instant, making sure he was still breathing, checking for any signs of blood. There were none, and the cop was out like a light, his chest heaving as he took air into his lungs past his bruised rib cage.

Just to make sure, Richard lifted the cop's uniform shirt, felt the Kevlar vest underneath, and then gathered the shotgun into his hands.

Sirens! Gotta move quickly. He went toward the rent-a-cop, who was writhing on the ground still holding his weapon.

"Don't try anything!" Richard screamed as he approached George. "Drop your weapon! Do it! Now!"

George let his gun fall from his shaking fingers. "Can't . . . can't catch my breath! Shit . . ."

Richard picked up his gun.

"Don't shoot me! Please . . ."

Richard checked the load in George's gun. Teflon-coated bullets, designed to penetrate the body armor both George and the police officer were wearing.

Good thing I wasn't loaded out with those. Both of them would be mortally wounded.

He moved back to the cop, searching for the keys to his cruiser. He found them, then he jumped into the police cruiser and took off.

16

He circled back around toward the front of the Jacobs residence, but other Potomac PD units were responding to the scene of the crime. He'd parked almost a mile away from Marty's residence, pulled the car off the road into a copse of trees, well hidden from the road.

But the police activity on Potomac Creek Drive deterred him—he couldn't run the risk that the car would be ID'd as he drove out of Dodge.

He turned back toward the highway. He could only hope that the car would stay hidden until he could retrieve it.

Bettina Freeman was released from the hospital with a huge bandage on her shoulder, which still hurt. She'd listened to the accounts on the local news and seen the videotape footage that showed Richard Whelan entering Mary Jacobs's apartment building with her and then exiting on his own on the run. She had spent a good deal of extra time in the hospital answering questions for the police and she was tired, and she didn't want to think the unthinkable about the man who'd saved her life.

She lay down, hurting inside, because he'd abandoned her and it didn't look like he was coming back.

* * *

Two hours later Maggie Smith, who'd lived on Potomac Creek Drive since before all the new money had come in, rolled slowly past the Jacobs house, wondering about all the police activity. Such tragedy had touched that family in a matter of days, Maggie thought, that it was impossible to think that any more could happen. She resumed speed and headed home.

She saw something out of the corner of her eye as she pulled her old Mercedes diesel station wagon into her driveway. She got out, satisfied that the car door still closed with a satisfying thunk, and turned back to the woods on the other side of the street.

It looked like something had disturbed the woods. Perhaps a deer, she thought, although they were horrible creatures, Walt Disney's Bambi notwithstanding.

She went inside to call the town property maintenance division. They all knew her from her frequent phone calls, so she was sure they would have a truck out here to assess the situation promptly.

The president was in his residence taking a nap when the steward opened the bedroom door.

"Mister President, sir, you have visitors," the steward said softly, but the president was awake in an instant. He sat up, swung his legs over the side of the bed. He'd fallen asleep fully clothed; he'd cleared his schedule of meetings today to take a break from the killing pace, a habit he'd learned from studying the Reagan era of the presidency.

He went out to the sitting room just outside the bedroom.

He was not surprised to see Mike Monroe and Charles O'Shay waiting for him.

He settled into a wing chair. "I take it you have some news that isn't pleasant."

Mike Monroe spoke first. *The spook always has his ear to the ground, always the first with the dirt. Wonder what he has on me?* POTUS thought. "Mr. President, Marty Jacobs was killed this afternoon."

POTUS didn't say anything for a moment. Both men were studying his reaction.

"How?"

"We believe it was Richard Whelan, sir," Monroe said.

"You're sure it was Whelan?" He signaled to the steward to bring them some soft drinks.

"Relatively. The maid heard a shot, and Marty was killed by a single bullet to the head, execution style," O'Shay said.

"The status of the police investigation?"

"They have his house under surveillance, his description and that of his car is out on an APB. They are watching all his known acquaintances, Edgar." Mike Monroe said gently.

"I want to talk to Marty's wife. Offer my condolences. Set it up, please, Chuck."

"Certainly, sir."

"Thanks, Chuck."

No one said anything for a moment.

"Excuse me, Edgar, but you don't seem surprised," O'Shay said.

Surprise isn't quite the word I'd use, Chuck.

"I should have had Whelan removed before all this happened." He decided to change the subject. "Does the press have this?"

"If they don't they will very soon."

The president sighed. "We'll do a 'no comment' on a continuing police investigation until he's brought in. In the meantime, Chuck, get your people working on drafting a statement." He hesitated. "Two statements. One expressing regret over Marty's death for immediate release, the other about Whelan."

The president stood up. Chuck O'Shay was looking at him, probably trying to find some evidence of an emotional reaction.

No, Chuck, I'd say the word is overjoyed that Marty is dead. He looked at them expectantly, because if they had nothing else, the meeting was over. Both men turned to leave.

"Mike, could you stay a second? I'd like to talk to you for a moment about the international situation."

"Certainly, Mr. President."

He was running, and he was alone. He hit the streets after he dumped the police cruiser with the keys in it in the worst neighborhood he could find. He'd dumped the shotgun into the Potomac River.

He used most of his remaining money to buy some clothes at a surplus store, hoping that the police wouldn't release the details of how he'd been dressed to infiltrate the Jacobs home. He stuffed Marty's videotape into the waistband of his pants and set out to find a place to spend the night and plan.

He drifted, thinking, ending up near the White House in a park across the street from the JW Marriott Hotel on Pennsylvania Avenue. Call it hiding in plain sight, he thought.

He thought about the videotape he was carrying, wondering if he really wanted to see it. There are answers, and there are answers, he thought, and when the questions are this difficult, you have to wonder whether there are some things you really don't want to know.

Sitting in the park near the man-made pool he thought about Mary and about that last cocktail party for Bettina.

He'd been talking to some of the staffers working the Hill, and he'd seen her go into a back room with Desmond Havensworth, a friend of her father's. Havensworth had taken Mary's hand to lead her away from the crush of the crowd, an oddly familiar gesture that bothered Richard.

He'd gradually worked his way around the room to the door. It was the library, if he recalled correctly, and the door wasn't completely closed.

He'd been looking at Bettina, who looked radiant, when he'd heard a snippet of Mary's conversation with Havensworth.

"Your father's very concerned about your relationship with Whelan."

"If this is another of those 'Richard isn't good enough for me' conversations, I think I've heard quite enough of them."

"Your relationship puts a lot of things in jeopardy. Marty wonders if you've considered the ramifications."

"Desmond, it is so out of character for you to act as a messenger boy for my father."

"Mary, believe me, Marty has not shared with me what's bothering him so much, but he did ask me to convey the message."

"Then you can tell him that I got the message, and I continue to get the message."

"Okay. You always were the headstrong one, weren't you?"

"I have my father to thank for that."

"I have always been able to see that, Mary. You realize that I've known you almost a decade now?"

"Thank goodness that isn't long enough for you to tell me you remember me in diapers."

"No," Havensworth chuckled a bit. "But I've seen you flower, Mary. And I agreed to be the messenger boy because I wanted to deliver a message of my own. . . ."

Someone had begun braying at a joke to his immediate right, and Richard lost the thread of Mary's conversation. But within seconds, Mary had flung open the door, surprised and guilty to see him standing there, struggling to get Havensworth's arm from around her shoulders.

Things had gone rapidly downhill from there. Havensworth continued to try to hit on Mary, and she'd continued to move away from him, but interestingly, she hadn't come to Richard's side. When the door to the library had opened and she'd seen him standing there she hadn't said anything, just walked right past him as if he didn't exist. Havensworth hadn't bothered to acknowledge his presence, either, and Richard had gotten so angry. . . .

But now Mary was dead and he was a fugitive. His vaunted career had bitten him squarely in his ass. *Like Marcus always said it would*, he thought bitterly. But as he replayed Mary's conversation with Havensworth in his mind, he realized that perhaps there was a different interpretation for the words than the one he'd assumed.

"Yo, brother-man, you got a smoke?" someone asked him as they shuffled by.

"No. Don't smoke."

"Don't blame ya. Shit'll kill you."

The old man shuffled by.

"Hey, is this a good place to spend the night?" Richard asked.

The old man shook his head. "Cops sweep this area regularly. Best to get away from here unless you want to spend the night in jail."

The old man looked him up and down. "Never seen you around here before, have I?"

Hope this guy doesn't read the papers. "Nope, just got into town. My girlfriend turned me out, so I'm stuck," he said, improvising.

"Uh-huh." The man was looking at him. "Seems ta me I done seen you befo', though." He chuckled. "Don't worry, it'll come ta me. Next time I see you."

The old man shuffled off.

"There's a file I transferred," she'd said.

Why had she mentioned that at the party?

"Your father's very concerned about your relationship with Whelan."

He'd assumed that Havensworth meant that Marty Jacobs

objected to their relationship because he was black. Could there be another reason why Marty was concerned?

"Your relationship puts a lot of things in jeopardy. Marty wonders if you've considered the ramifications."

Again, he'd thought that Mary's relationship with her father was in jeopardy, and that the ramifications meant that she would be disinherited, or something.

But now Marty's dead, as well.

And she'd said to him something about a file and someone tried to plant confidential documents in her apartment.

No, actually, that wasn't exactly what she'd said. She'd said it won't work, the implication being that the file was part of the reason their relationship wouldn't work.

It was a key that didn't fit his interpretation of the night's events but did fit with his notion that Mary was hiding something from him, something that her father certainly knew about and paid for with his life. Something so profound that it made him unsuitable for her in ways that went beyond skin color or class.

And let's face it, Whelan, the only other significant attribute you have that Marty would have been keenly aware of is that you are the national security adviser to the president of the United States.

And was there anything about his job that Marty would find objectionable that didn't affect national security?

Mike Monroe sat with the president watching the last of a lengthy CNN report from the border of Pakistan and Kashmir. The CNN correspondent was with a massive buildup of Pakistani troops who were, in their words, ready to defend their border to the death from Indian troops that "wild rumors" had placed nearby in Kashmir. The camera played over the faces of the troops, some shockingly young, others old, all showing the fierce pride of an army that has yet to see the horrors of battle.

Edgar Roswell turned off the tape. "Wild rumors about a buildup of Indian forces in Kashmir, eh? CNN must be where Whelan got his insights."

"Have you been in contact with New Delhi and Islamabad?"

"Every day. But what worries me is that I haven't gotten any response from Beijing."

Monroe shrugged. "Then there's nothing, in the absence of intelligence, that you can do except maintain contact with all parties involved."

Roswell didn't respond immediately, and Monroe thought he looked tired.

"I asked you to stay behind because there's something I want you to take care of. This whole Richard Whelan–Marty Jacobs thing is going to linger like a bad smell. It has the potential to be another Vince Foster from the Clinton administration—guy commits suicide, no evidence of foul play, but the investigation into the man's personal life takes on a life of its own, and the nutty conspiracy theorists have him as everything from the Whitewater bagman to Elvis."

Roswell looked at his DCI. "There are certain things about Marty's affairs that should not become public, certain records that may or may not exist that would be, ah, very damaging if they were to come out in the wrong way. I want your people to sanitize the situation for me—" Roswell waved away Monroe's unvoiced objection—"because I've already signed a presidential finding allowing you to violate your charter, and because I personally asked you to keep Marty Jacobs clean and you didn't do it. I will discuss with his widow the transfer of Marty's personal files and other effects to government custody in the interests of national security. I want you to make sure that there's nothing else out there that can hurt us, okay?"

"How deep do you want me to search?"

"Get it all, wherever and whatever might be out there."

"Mr. President, with all due respect, it's difficult to keep something like that under wraps. The more manpower I use, the more people need to know what they're looking for. The more people who know, the more we have to baby-sit people for the rest of their careers to make sure they don't get pissed off and write a 'fictional' account of their escapades."

"Are you saying you can't do it?"

"No, Edgar. I'm not saying I can't. But keeping it quiet could require the sacrifice of lives were an extreme situation to arise."

"I don't want to know the details. And if you get caught, you'll hang by yourself. Understood?"

"Yes, Mr. President. I understand."

17

If there is no mercy, if justice isn't tempered by mercy, then the world grows cold, and hell is in the world. It was difficult to believe in the concept of mercy after you fired a missile at a convoy of Muslims invading your land and turned away before the blast. It was difficult to believe in God enough to strike down the supposedly godless, not like that, *not like that.* Orders were orders, and the enemy was the enemy, nothing more than grid coordinates on a map, a patch of land with people crawling over it that required that they be dispatched to hell expeditiously.

The pilots in the ready room were playing cards or watching the nearly nonstop CNN coverage of the Pakistani buildup and allegations of coming war. Amjad Singho had just returned from a tour of the fighter aircraft on the alert strips and looked carefully at the men in the ready room as he shook the water off his slicker.

There was a certain amount of tension in the banter, he thought, which was good. They'd been on alert for nearly three days, rotating on and off duty in twelve-hour shifts but secure in the knowledge that if the orders came they could all be ordered to scramble at a moment's notice.

"Singho probably knows, eh?" one of the newer members

of the squadron said to a group playing poker. He said it loud enough for him to hear. "He's connected."

"Yeah, Singho, what is the news from New Delhi? My wife is getting lonely."

"Your wife is never lonely when you're on alert, I'm told," Singho said with a straight face. "Your brother stands in ably for the cause. That's why your wife told you to request this assignment." There were great guffaws from the other pilots as he said this, but everyone knew he was kidding.

"Hey, fuck you, Captain. The only reason you got this assignment is because your uncle works for the prime minister. You surely weren't assigned here because you can fly."

Singho nodded good-naturedly to his opponent and laughed. "Yes, you are correct. I'm here to sweep the runways up after people like you bend airplanes crashing into them. Quite a demanding job, actually."

This brought more laughter.

"Seriously, Captain," one of the other pilots said, "do you have any news? All we get is what CNN International is saying about the Pakistanis preparing for war and the Chinese claiming that parliament is rattling its sabers."

Singho shrugged, not wanting to get into it. He was not married; his only family was his uncle who did indeed work for the prime minister. He knew more than he could tell the men because the alert could be canceled at any time. If they did indeed back away from this madness, the less said about the preparations the better. Without a family it was easier for him to keep these secrets, which was why he was in command of this particular flight of aircraft.

"He knows more than he's telling," someone yelled. "Look at him. He's practically about to burst with secrets."

"Are you ready to carry out orders if they arrive?" He said this to the room, eyeing each pilot in turn as they fell silent.

"Sure, Captain, as long as my ass isn't flat and broke

from sitting in these damn chairs and playing cards," some-one shouted, breaking the moment. Once again everyone in the room laughed.

"Is it the weather?"

"No," Singho lied. The MiG-27 ground attack fighters they flew were all-weather capable. Even the intense rain they'd had for the last two days would not stop the Bahad-hurs from operating.

"Then why the alert?"

"In case Pakistan retaliates. You may end up tail chasing Pakistani nuclear missiles."

"Then you're just the man for the job, Captain!" Again everyone chuckled, but the laughter was more subdued.

Singho moved away from his men, heading toward the tiny office he had in the ready room. He tried not to think about the meaning of his last conversation with his uncle, but as he busied himself in the paperwork, he could not help but recall and ponder the meaning of his cryptic words:

> When the weather clears, the eagle may strike. Be ready.

Sam Hennings took the call from Enrique Gonzales at his house early the next morning.

"Good news. My researcher finished his runs."

Sam hesitated. Whelan was now being accused of mur-dering Marty Jacobs. A little voice was telling him to pull back, run for cover.

But he couldn't just ignore Enrique, because then the sci-entist might start asking questions that would lead back to him. Better to just shut this avenue of inquiry down.

"And?"

"We have results. I'll send you the data file and an analy-sis by E-mail."

"You want to give me a hint as to what it shows? If anything?"

"Is there something about this exercise that you aren't telling me?"

"Why?" *Does he know about the Whelan connection?*

"The results. They scared the crap out of my researcher."

Sam Hennings called Richard's number at the White House from a pay phone near his home, hoping to get his voice mail.

"You have reached a nonworking number at the White House. Please dial zero to be connected to the White House operator."

Damn. He'd been hoping that his voice mail would still be working. He didn't dare call Richard's home phone, knowing full well that any such call would be monitored, and anything on his home machine would be damn near public knowledge. He left the pay phone, wondering about what Enrique Gonzales had told him and what it meant. First of all, it was now quite possible that Whelan possessed knowledge that made him dangerous to someone, someone potent enough to want to kill his girlfriend and discredit him.

He's going to have to contact me, somehow, he thought. And he better do it soon.

Bettina Freeman woke up sore and disoriented. The bandage on her shoulder was more of an irritant than a help, and she pulled at the soft edges until it pulled away. She didn't turn on the television, not wanting to hear other revelations about Richard Whelan.

But he saved your life, she thought. *How could he be a murderer?*

She picked up the phone and called her office to leave a message that she was not coming in today.

As soon as she hung up, the phone rang. She grabbed it, hoping somehow that it was Richard.

"Hello?"

"Bettina Freeman?"

"Yes, this is she."

"Detective Bill Johnson, Washington, D.C., homicide squad. We understand that you were assaulted by Richard Whelan yesterday and we'd like to ask you some questions."

"Who told you that?"

"Um, someone fired shots at you in an open-air restaurant yesterday, didn't they?"

"That's correct."

"Ballistics has confirmed that the same gun involved in the shooting at the café was also used to shoot a police officer and a security guard in Potomac, Maryland, and was discharged at Marty Jacobs's home."

Then it was true. Oh, God, Richard, what have you done?

"We'd like to ask you about the shooting yesterday."

"Richard didn't try to shoot me at the restaurant."

"Are you sure?"

"Yes. This man was big, with a mustache. And he was white, so this isn't a case of mistaken identity."

"Then Richard began shooting?"

"No, Richard didn't have a gun."

There was a pause. "I'm sorry, ma'am. Did you say Whelan didn't have a gun?"

"That's correct. The guy with the mustache left it at the scene. Then Richard picked it up as he was leaving."

Something didn't add up, Detective Johnson thought. "Ma'am, are you absolutely certain that Whelan wasn't carrying at the restaurant?"

"Well, this big white guy shot at me and Richard didn't pull out a pistol and fire back. So yes, I'm sure. What's wrong, anyway?"

"That math doesn't work. Two guns were used at the Jacobs residence. One, a twenty-five-caliber Beretta, was left at the scene. That gun had Richard Whelan's initials on the grip."

Bettina remembered Richard looking at the bottom of the grip of the pistol the killer had left at the restaurant. He seemed . . . surprised, now that she thought about it.

"Detective, I didn't hear anything about a security guard and a police officer being killed in Potomac. Are the police withholding information from the public for some reason?"

"No. They had him cornered, apparently, when they were hit. The cop and the security guard were wearing Kevlar vests and took hits to the chest. They were very lucky."

Shots in the chest? Richard was a target shooter and an excellent marksman. She'd seen enough movies to know that when someone has a gun on you, you go for a head shot.

"Detective, is it possible that the Beretta was planted at the scene?"

Bettina could hear Johnson sigh.

"What makes you say that?"

"Let me ask you a question. You said the gun in the Jacobs home had Richard's initials carved on the bottom of the grip?"

"Yes. Why?"

"Because Richard looked at the bottom of the grip of the pistol he picked up at the café. He seemed surprised."

"Which means what?"

"Maybe he saw his initials on that gun, too. And the killer left it behind to incriminate him in the shooting."

"That's a bit of a stretch."

"Yeah, but it makes sense to me. Did you know he is a crack shot?"

"We know he belongs to a club out in Silver Spring, but that hardly qualifies you as a marksman."

"Check with the people at the club, Detective."

"Why should we do that?"

"Because if you had two people with guns on you, would you shoot them in the chest and risk taking a bullet from someone as they're going down? Or would you kill them with a shot to the head?"

"If I could, I'd go for the kill."

"Then if Richard is an expert shooter and a killer to boot, why does he shoot two guys intent on taking him in their Kevlar vests?"

Maggie Smith woke up the next morning curious to see what had disturbed the brush across from her home. The people at the town's property maintenance department had not understood what she was talking about.

Damned immigrants. Was it so impossible to have a college graduate that spoke English in the employ of the town? She paid enough in taxes, for goodness sakes, and all she'd gotten from the foreign-sounding voice at the other end of the phone was that deer problems were animal control, not property maintenance, and the soft click of the line being disconnected.

So, bright and early she got up, put on her tennis shoes (which was her euphemism for sneakers, purchased for eleven dollars and change at K-Mart, thank you very much), and marched outside.

She immediately noticed something that she hadn't seen yesterday from the car. There were tire tracks leading into the woods from the road.

She picked up a long stick and began probing the underbrush until she clanked it against something metal.

Like a car, she thought, suddenly excited.

The old man woke up and proceeded to get about his morning routine. He had enough in his belly to last him until the Seventh Avenue Church opened its soup kitchen at around eleven. Good Baptist church, likely to have some real food, unlike the Catholics, who couldn't cook worth a damn. St. John's soup kitchen was open on Saturday, which made the old man hate the weekends.

So the first thing he needed was a newspaper. He ambled out into the sunlight, heading for a trash bin near the Metro, because the commuters always left papers in the garbage.

There were plenty of papers around. He pulled the *Washington Post* out of the trash bin.

Son of a bitch. There was a picture of that guy he'd talked to by the park yesterday. Now that he thought about it, there had been another picture of him in the paper a couple of days ago.

Maybe there's a reward, he thought, shuffling off to find a phone.

Richard woke up stiff from sleeping in a doorway down the street from the Lincoln Motel. It was amazing how the best spots seemed to be "reserved" for the "regulars." And he was careful to start moving early before he was rousted by a property owner or a cop. That was the last thing he needed, for someone in the world to recognize him.

Although he certainly felt invisible.

He began shuffling toward the White House, unaware that he was walking into a trap.

Marcus Blaze was in his office looking at a client file when the intercom buzzed.

"Yeah, Sharice?" He only hired attractive women for his office, and Sharice was the best looking of the bunch. Five foot eight, hips and tits out to there the way he liked them, which was good, because when you looked into those big brown doe eyes . . .

You could hear wind whistling between her ears because there was nothing, abso-fucking-lutely nothing in her head. Girl was dumber than most posts, for God's sake.

Damn good thing she was fine, otherwise he'd have to fire her. And it was a damn good thing that he wasn't sleeping with her, either.

"Uh, Mr. Marcus?"

"No, it's the big bad wolf, Sharice. What is it?"

"You, um, got a phone call. From somebody named . . . Sasquatch?"

"Bum spotted your client hanging around near the White House, of all places. We're mobilizing now. If you've heard from Whelan, or if you hear from him, I want him to turn himself in before any more blood is shed," Detective Johnson said.

"According to the police, Richard Whelan is an armed, brutal killer. Why the phone call and the special treatment?" Marcus asked.

"Something Bettina Freeman said. I want to question him before he gets killed."

"Little late to start doing your job, isn't it? Well, I can tell you this, Detective. Somebody wants him out of the way, because my client is innocent."

Patrolman David Titlebaum responded to Maggie Smith's call about a car hidden in the thicket across from her house.

She was probably watching him from her kitchen window, he thought as he climbed out of his patrol car. Everyone knew Maggie Smith, the pain-in-the-butt old broad who swore that the world revolved around her.

Titlebaum turned toward her house and tipped his cap, then walked into the woods to find this supposed car.

Ms. Smith had cleared as much of the brush as she could away from the back end of the car.

Well, well, well. The old bat was right. It was a car, and . . .

He recognized the license plate from the APB that had

been distributed when he came on shift. Not only was it a car, it was Richard Whelan's Porsche.

Hot damn! He'd be a hero. Every law enforcement agency in the district had a hard-on for Whelan.

He went toward the front of the car, noting that the back window was covered by a sheet of plastic.

After a few minutes of dicking around, he managed to reach in through the back window and unlock the driver's side door.

Then he pulled the hood latch and heard the front hood pop open.

The visitor's entrance to the White House was a block away, and Richard wondered whether he could chance getting something to eat. His stomach was growling. But he didn't think he could risk even stopping at a newsstand for a Twinkie.

Just ahead of him someone bent over to buy a copy of the *Washington Post* from a street machine. Richard immediately turned away.

He almost missed the D.C. Metro police car screaming past on the street behind him, lights off, siren silent.

He watched via the reflection in a shop window, as another, and another, and another patrol car raced down the street toward the Marriott Hotel and the park where he'd considered spending the night.

Titlebaum saw the strongbox in the hood trunk of Whelan's Porsche. Thinking it was cash, he reached in and pulled it out of the car.

The box was unlocked and opened easily.

His eyes got wide when he saw the papers marked TOP SECRET inside.

"Dispatch," he said into the microphone clipped to his shirt.

"This is dispatch."

"Uh, I think you better get the watch commander on the line. And have somebody call the White House or the CIA or something."

Ten minutes later the phone rang in Charles O'Shay's office.

Someone from the Potomac Police Department was on the line.

"Papers marked TOP SECRET, eh? Any idea what the subject matter is?"

It took a few minutes for them to check with the patrolman on the scene via radio.

But when they told O'Shay what the title page said, he turned pale.

He punched the hold button on the phone. Jesus H. Christ.

O'Shay started to dial the FBI director's number but thought better of it.

Gotta contain this, he thought. Wrap it up *tight*. He dialed Frank Moynihan, spoke for a few minutes, then disconnected. He then dialed Mike Monroe at CIA.

Then he got back on the line with the Potomac Police Department.

"Listen very carefully. This is a matter of national security. I want you to keep everyone away from that car and the area until Secret Service has men on the scene to secure the documents. If the press gets within a thousand yards of that car, there'll be hell to pay. Do you understand? No, no, no debate. Just tell me whether you understand, yes or no."

Frank Moynihan slammed the phone down. "Arnie!" he yelled to his number two. "Get in here!"

Arnie appeared at the door in an instant.

"I want two choppers and the agents to fill them to rendezvous with me on the south lawn of the White House in two minutes. We have a situation."

"What do I tell the troops?"

"Tell them that we're going to Potomac, Maryland, to secure a crime scene and retrieve some of the administration's dirty laundry. And when I say secure the crime scene, we're going to lock it down tight."

O'Shay stepped into the Oval Office. The president looked up from the trade delegation that he was meeting with.

"Yes, Charles? Gentlemen, this is Charles O'Shay, my chief of staff."

"We need to speak, sir, for a minute. In private." O'Shay smiled for the members of the delegation.

O'Shay raised his eyebrows just a touch. The president picked up the cue.

He cleared his throat. "Gentlemen, if you could excuse us for a few minutes?"

O'Shay watched as the last of the four-man delegation filed out of the room. He turned to the president.

"What is it, Chuck?"

"The Potomac Police Department found Whelan's car."

"And?"

"He had a strongbox of classified documents inside. One of them relates to Project Thor."

"Oh, Jesus Christ."

Detectives Johnson and Steinway pulled up to the JW Marriott Hotel on Pennsylvania Avenue and into bedlam. There were fifteen police cars out front and a van discharging a SWAT team as they stepped from the patrol car and into the morning sunshine.

Steinway looked at the scene with disgust. "Subtle, we ain't."

"Yeah, if Whelan is still in the same parsec of space, I'd be surprised."

"Who's on scene?"

"Captain Billings."

"Shit, if I were Whelan I'd have left the galaxy by now and be headed for *deep* fucking space."

The squawk of fifteen sets of radios startled them.

"All units, all units, suspect Richard Whelan has been spotted on North Executive Drive by National Park Service personnel. All units vicinity, please respond."

Two Huey gunships swung low over Maggie Smith's house, rattling the windows with their rotor wash. Frank Moynihan looked over the scene, relieved that there were no television trucks around.

"Swing around and let's see the perimeter!" he shouted at his pilot. The pilot nodded and swung the gunship around.

Half a mile up Potomac Creek Drive, Moynihan saw the police-established perimeter. There was a line of news trucks and at least five reporters trying to talk their way around the beleaguered cop standing by his car.

"Take it down, now!" Moynihan screamed. "Tell the second unit to move to the end of this street and set up!"

When Richard heard the sirens coming he turned and ran. He ran parallel to the White House grounds, past several surprised Federal Protective Services guards, and turned right onto Pennsylvania Avenue, heading back toward the Marriott Hotel.

He gave himself up to it, the rhythmic pumping of his legs and heart, willing himself not to run harder but to simply move his legs faster.

But no matter how fast he ran, he couldn't outrun a police cruiser. One parked in front of the White House squealed into a turn and gave chase.

As he crossed Fourteenth Street another cruiser pulled parallel to him, past him, then swung across the lanes of traffic until it bounced up on the sidewalk sideways, blocking his path.

"Halt! D.C. Police!" Two officers climbing out of the car, guns drawn.

Forget the pistol, Whelan, he thought. Because the rest of them will shoot you down like a dog.

He ducked into the street, bullets flying toward him, and he cut the angle more and dove under a tractor trailer from a nearby construction site, bullets spanging off the steel of the trailer.

He rolled out the other side, just managing not to get hit by another patrol car, the driver slamming his brakes at the last possible second to avoid hitting him, and then two more cops out on foot, chasing him.

He headed up to New York Avenue, hoping that he could get to the Metro Center subway stop before he was captured. He turned right down Thirteenth, heading into Chinatown, and another cruiser turned a corner in pursuit.

Forget it! he thought, and he doubled back, heading toward a building on New York and Thirteenth that was being gutted and renovated.

You're trapped, his mind screamed, give it up! But he kept running, ducking down as more bullets flew over his head.

Now he was rushing past guys in hard hats as he entered a gutted building lobby, just missing stepping into a pan of wet concrete that was being used to patch part of the sidewalk. He could hear footsteps behind him, cops on foot, he thought, and he headed into the building's basement, down the steps of a stopped escalator, hoping that the work on the building was concentrated on the higher floors.

When he got to the bottom, he was in what looked to be a storage area.

He found the back door to the storage cage that was locked from the outside, as he heard footsteps treading down the escalator steps behind him.

He pulled the Browning he'd retrieved from the café yesterday and pumped two rounds into the door lock.

One of the patrolmen behind him yelled "Shots fired!" into his radio and opened up blind because the storage area was dimly lit.

Richard felt something hot sting his left arm as he went through the door and resisted the urge to fire a volley of shots in response.

Now he was in the basement with the heating plant. One set of steps led up the stairs, and he took them two at a time, realizing that he was liable to get drilled if cops showed up at either the bottom or the top of the stairs.

He burst through the stairwell door. First floor, a side entrance, apparently, another officer coming through it. No exit out the back, he doesn't see me yet, but he will in about—

"Freeze, police!"

Combat roll under the discharged round, realizing the gun in his hand made him a shoot-first target. He relaxed his hand in the middle of the roll, the Browning clattering away, the rent-a-cop's Glock and the Potomac PD officer's service revolver nestled at his back and in his jacket pocket, respectively, gunshots following him across the floor until he bounced up and stepped into a doorway; shots now pelting him with wood from the door frame. No gun in his hand, the reflexive targeting in his head turned off.

"Don't shoot! I'm unarmed."

Steps coming from the basement. Two pairs. The entrance to the basement had closed but not latched behind him.

The cop in the entrance lobby coming toward him.

"Hands above your head where I can see them!"

He complied. *One chance, Richard, you have one chance.*

Facing a gun and a nervous police officer.

The door to the basement burst open. "Police officers, freeze!"

The patrolman's gun swerved away from him just enough as the officer turned to look at his comrades. Richard backhanded the cop's gun hand and pushed as hard as all those workouts at the gym would allow, sending him sprawling into the others. He took off running as the three cops went down in a heap, shouting.

Out the door, into the sunshine, more units rolling on him, he crossed the street, sliding over the hood of an old Plymouth that nearly killed him with its front bumper, crossing the street, into a crowd, cops and construction workers boiling from the building behind him.

Frank Moynihan jumped out of the Huey, telling the pilot to keep it wound up, and jogged over to the roadblock.

The woman arguing with the Potomac cop was short, wired real tight, and yelling about freedom of the press.

"Officer!" Moynihan yelled over the Huey's engine, "Moynihan, Secret Service." He pulled his badge and shoved it into the reporter's face.

"I want this area cleared back to the end of the street, and I want it cleared now!"

"Uh, sir, this woman is from NewsChannel . . . ," the Potomac cop started.

"I don't give a damn who any of these people are. Clear this street, now!"

The reporter got into Moynihan's face. "Who the fuck are you! The Gestapo?"

Frank Moynihan pulled his gun, grabbed the reporter by the lapels of her cheap suit jacket, and dragged her real close.

"Ma'am," he whispered in her ear in a no-bullshit tone that made the reporter go cold, "the president of the United States has authorized the use of deadly force to secure this area in the interests of national security. If you do not get in your van, turn around, and leave immediately, you will be the first casualty. Do . . . you . . . understand . . . me?"

He let go of the woman's lapels, and she nearly staggered because Moynihan had lifted her up until she was on tippytoes.

Moynihan wheeled. "I need two men to get this traffic turned around, right now!" He waved his hand at the chopper, holding up two fingers.

Two of his men clambered out and he clambered back in.

"Let's go! Take me back to where the car is!"

The Huey lifted, turned, and sped off.

Have to get away, have to get away . . .

There was a subway stop half a block in front of him. Metro Center. He chanced a look behind him.

No one yet. *But if they suspect that I'm on the train, they'll just stop it at the next station.* He stopped at the top of the long escalator leading down into the train station, a homeless man watching him intently, leaning on the waist-high retaining wall that bordered the escalator down, the strong smell of urine wafting up the escalator well to assault his nose. He felt blood trickling down within the sleeve of his jacket, hoped it wasn't serious. He left a smear of blood on the retaining wall and headed down.

Johnson and Steinway were in the next wave of the uncoordinated police response. They turned onto Thirteenth just as Whelan headed from the street into the vestibule of the underground subway station.

Steinway pointed. "He's making a run into the train station!"

Johnson aimed the car at the curb right near the escalator. "Are you sure?"

"No, but let's check it out."

They jumped out of the car as it crested the sidewalk.

* * *

Richard paid his fare and walked quickly toward the platform. The Metro Center station was large, with a long walk from the token booths to the tracks, and the walkway to the platform was divided into two separate paths. He walked as quickly as he dared toward the actual subway platform, and when he reached the tracks he went as close to the edge of the platform as he dared, making sure that there were people behind him to shield him from anyone coming up from behind.

He heard the noise of the train approaching the station, and it was music to his ears.

"You see a black guy run down this escalator? Six-two, wearing a jacket?" Johnson asked the bum leaning on the retaining wall.

The bum shrugged. "Got a quarter, mister?"

"D.C. Police," Steinway said, showing his badge. "Answer the question or visit the lockup!"

The bum just pointed down the escalator, and Johnson and Steinway ran down as fast as they could after their suspect.

People were entering the train, and Richard chanced a look behind him just as Johnson and Steinway came off the separate pathways to the platform.

Steinway immediately went toward the front of the train to try and get the engineer to hold the train in the station. Johnson cut to his right toward the rear of the train to see if he could spot Richard on the train before it pulled out.

The doors were closing.

Which way, Rich? In or out?

Steinway knew that he wasn't going to make it to the engineer, because the doors closed and the train lurched before starting to pick up speed. He skidded to a halt right at the entrance to the subway tunnel, frustrated.

Johnson jogged up to him a few seconds later.

"See him?" Steinway asked.

"No. But let's see if we can get through to transit and hold the train at the next station."

"Right."

Moynihan's gunship landed on the street as close to Whelan's Porsche as the pilot dared. Moynihan and his remaining squad of agents jumped out and ran past three Potomac PD units and headed toward the car.

Titlebaum was standing guard over the lockbox as Moynihan burst through the thicket that shielded the car from the road.

"Where is it?" Moynihan demanded.

Titlebaum was about to ask for ID, but the demeanor of the man standing in front of him strongly suggested that it wouldn't be a good idea.

Titlebaum opened the hood.

Moynihan reached in and pulled out the lockbox. He opened it, looked at the title page of the document, and snapped the lid closed.

"You two," he said to two of his agents, "set up a perimeter."

Moynihan looked at Titlebaum. "Did you look at this?" he asked, motioning to the strongbox.

"Just the top page that was stamped TOP SECRET, uh, sir."

"Okay. You're coming with me, Officer."

"Sir, I don't think that's such a good idea. . . ."

"Save it. Unless you want me to arrest you."

Titlebaum stared at Moynihan. "Yes, sir. Lead the way."

The subway doors closed in front of him. Richard could see Steinway running toward the front of the train and Johnson heading toward the other end of the platform.

There were still people waiting for a different train and

Richard made the decision he'd been leaning toward: *split the defense*.

He turned around and walked back out of the station as the train began pulling out, hoping that neither detective spotted him as he walked back along the pathway leading to the escalators out of the station.

18

President Edgar Roswell had invited Charles O'Shay and Mike Monroe to a hastily called meeting in the Oval Office.

"Moynihan has the Project Thor documents. He's taking steps to place them back in whatever godforsaken vault Whelan got them out of," POTUS said.

"Thank goodness. If that had hit the press, given the international situation . . . ," O'Shay started.

"Still, Mr. President, what disturbs me is how Whelan would have gotten access to Thor in the first place. He doesn't routinely get involved with DOE or that side of the fence, so it's not like he would have simply come across those documents in the course of his work."

"What are you saying, Mike?"

"That Whelan is part of a much bigger problem. If what we think has been happening is true, that Whelan appears to be in the employ of someone other than this administration for the purpose of stealing and passing secrets."

The president shook his head. "This is a cluster fuck to end all cluster fucks."

But O'Shay was thoughtful. "This puts a new spin on Mary Jacobs's murder, Mr. President."

"How so?"

"It may provide a way to engage in some damage control."

O'Shay described what he was thinking.

The president looked grave. "Do you realize the risks you're running with this, Chuck?"

"It's damage control, Mr. President. Did you ever see *Schindler's List*? There was a scene where the Nazis are trying to find out who stole a chicken. They line up all the prisoners, and when they refuse to talk, the Nazi camp commandant pulls out his pistol and shoots one of the prisoners, threatening to shoot them all, one at a time, until one of them talks."

The president and Mike Monroe looked dubious, wondering where this one was going.

"But before the commandant can shoot someone else," O'Shay continued, "one of the prisoners, a little kid, actually, steps forward and says something like, 'I know who stole the chicken, Commandant.'

"And the Nazi bends down to look at this kid, and asks him who stole the chicken.

"And the kid looks at the commandant and points to the guy the Nazi just shot, and says 'Him!'"

Chuck O'Shay stood up, warming to the idea. "What I'd suggest, Mr. President, is that Whelan is for all intents and purposes already a dead man and a dead weight on the administration. So in effect, what I want to do is point the finger at the dead man and blame him for all our troubles."

And the president thought, *If we can only get someone to keep Whelan from talking. . . .*

WASHINGTON, D.C., THE SAME TIME

Bettina Freeman was puttering around the house when a bright light flashed briefly through the living room window. She'd gone to work and carefully avoided the office gossip about the White House, and carefully avoided her boss. She'd come home after a day immersed in the mind-numbing paperwork of the job, the radio off, her secretary telling all callers that she was "in conference." The reports of the frantic chase downtown and the speculation that Richard had engaged in a running gun battle with police was shaking the last bit of hope she had that Richard was innocent. Certainly, the shooting at the café and the possibility that the would-be killers had planted one of Richard's guns at the scene had given her hope that she wasn't wrong about him.

But a shootout with police?

She picked up the phone and dialed Marcus Blaze's number. No matter what, she still had feelings for Richard Whelan, at least enough, she thought, that she didn't want to see him killed.

Maybe Blaze can convince him to turn himself in, she thought as she dialed.

There were police officers everywhere, and Richard could not get close to Bettina's town house. He didn't dare call her because he knew in his heart that someone would be listening to her every conversation.

Richard Whelan had jumped the fence surrounding the Washington International School and was hiding behind a tree on the downslope from the school grounds. He was facing R Street where Bettina's town house was situated, and he had been trying to shine a light through the living room window.

The street was quiet, but he'd seen at least one unmarked car with either cops or federal agents inside down the street from Bettina's white town house. He didn't dare try and walk up to her door, so he aimed the flashlight at the window again.

He'd come here after recovering from his little encounter

with half of the D.C. police force because he had no place else to go, and he needed Bettina's help.

He hoped she was still in her living room, sitting in the dark, because he was down to his last fifty dollars. He looked at the Marty Jacobs videotape he'd been carrying since yesterday.

"I hope you have some answers," he said to the cassette.

He took the high-powered flashlight he'd purchased at a local hardware store and shined it at her living room window again, just for an instant.

There was that damn light again. Not a steady light, it was flickering on and off, on and off, and it was driving her crazy. She got up to close the curtains when it hit her.

She ran into the kitchen to get a pad and a pen. C'mon, girl, she'd learned this stuff as a Girl Scout because her parents didn't qualify for Jack and Jill. She sat in the dark, watching the irregular series of flashes, writing down the letters they represented.

She knew it was Richard; Richard knew that she'd learned Morse code as a kid.

It took him a long time to send the message, because he didn't dare send a steady stream of light flashes at her windows, and he had a lengthy set of instructions that he wanted her to do. I hope you're getting this, he thought, because he didn't know how long the batteries in the flashlight were going to last, and he really didn't want to have to wait until tomorrow night to try again.

Finally he was finished, and he waited a few moments, hoping that she would acknowledge that she'd received his message.

A few minutes stretched into five, then ten. She must be in the bedroom, he thought, and there was no way to shine a light there from the street. A beat cop strolled past, and he huddled down lower on the park bench, his baseball cap pulled low over his eyes.

Time to move. He stood, stretching his aching muscles. He glanced back at Bettina's living room window, hoping against hope, and the lights flickered on once, then twice.

That was the recognition signal. And in her window was a crude hand-lettered sign.

YOU'RE MAKING ME CRAZY!!!

That actually made him chuckle. Now if he could convince her that he wasn't a serial killer, he had a slim chance to clear his name.

The plainclothes police officers assigned to baby-sit Bettina Freeman saw the sign right after the lights went out in her living room.

"I guess she made us." Terry Allen was a twenty-year veteran of the force. He noted the three exclamation points.

"Wouldn't be hard. There have been cops all over the place since she got home." Nelson Young was a spring chicken with only five years' seniority.

"Yeah, but you know how some civilians get the willies when they're being monitored. Let's just hope she doesn't come out here and go bananas on us."

Young saw the front door open. "Uh-oh, Terry. You oughta be careful what you say."

But Bettina Freeman did not head to the officer's unmarked car. Instead she walked to the silver BMW parked in the driveway.

"It's three o'clock in the morning. Where's she going?"

"Let's just see, shall we?"

She got in, buckled her seat belt, and pulled into the street. The cops followed a discreet distance behind, although the streets were empty and it was obvious that they were following her.

She made a few turns and passed through the tonier sections of Georgetown, driving at a leisurely pace. Then she turned toward downtown.

"What's she doing, slumming?" Allen asked.

"Maybe she has a thing for Seven-Eleven coffee or something."

The neighborhoods deteriorated until they were in some of the worst ghettos in the city. Bettina kept cruising, oblivious to the tail and the desolate trash-strewn streets.

Eventually she turned into a rundown establishment called the Lincoln Motel and pulled the car into one of the many empty parking spaces that lined the parking lot.

"Hang back. Let's see what she does," Young told Allen, who was driving.

She got out of the car and went in to the front desk where the clerk was snoring softly.

"Hey, Rip Van Winkle. I'd like a room for the night, please."

"Sure," the clerk said, rubbing his eyes. "Forty-two dollars if you want clean linen."

She paid cash and the desk clerk handed her a key.

"If you don't mind my saying, this doesn't look like the kind of place you should be hanging out in."

"Really?"

"We get a rough clientele sometimes."

"Maybe I'll just take a look at the room. Where is it?"

"Out the front door and down near the end of this first building here. Park your car in space forty-three and you'll be right at your front door."

"Thanks."

She went back outside and drove the BMW down to the end of the building, parked, and went inside the room.

Her tails saw her every move.

"Call it in. We might need to get a tap on the phone," Terry Allen said.

But as his partner was in the process of calling in their location, Bettina Freeman came out of the door, turned off the light, and got back into her car. She drove back to the office and went inside.

The clerk was just about to doze off again when she walked in on him. "You were right. Not my cup of tea. Maybe I'll try the Marriott," she said to the desk clerk. She handed him back the key and waited for him to count out her forty-two-dollar deposit and give it back to her. "And you should get someone in there to clean up the bathroom. It stinks," she said as an afterthought.

"That'll have to wait until morning when the crew comes in."

"Whatever."

Then she got back into her car, started it, and began to leave the parking lot.

"What do you think?" Young asked his partner.

"You got cab fare?"

"Yeah."

"You go check with the desk clerk. I'll stay with her in the car. I'll call you when she settles down."

"Gotcha." Officer Young climbed out of the unmarked car and went inside to the motel office. Terry Allen followed Bettina's BMW as she pulled into the street.

The cop flashed a badge at the desk clerk. "Police. That woman who was just here. Did she rent a room?"

"Yeah, for about a minute. She said she didn't like it, gave me back the key, and I gave back her money."

"Hmm. Interesting."

His cell phone rang. "Yeah?"

It was Allen. "Looks like she's going home. What's up with the roach motel?"

"She changed her mind. I'll catch a cab and meet up with you at her house. Bye."

The cop walked out and flagged down a lonely cabbie on the street.

The desk clerk shrugged. He saw all kinds.

Richard had taken a chance and caught a cab to the motel. He had a baseball cap pulled low over his eyes, and barely muttered to the driver the address of the Lincoln Motel. He'd told Bettina to take her time so that he could be in position when she got to the destination and he'd been watching as she pulled up in her BMW.

Richard watched the interplay between Bettina and the cops tailing her, and was relieved when the straggler got into a cab and drove away. He'd been watching Bettina as well, and went to the room that she'd briefly occupied.

The key, shorn of its key ring with the room number, was sitting on the windowsill outside the room as he'd requested. He picked it up and opened the door and went in, careful to draw the shades before he turned on a light.

He'd picked the Lincoln Motel because they still used keys, not the little plastic things that changed every time the room was let. He'd had Bettina substitute an old house key of hers on the plastic key ring with the room number; the next patron trying to use that key to open this door would get a surprise.

And it was early in the morning, even for this part of town. He'd taken the calculated risk that the real key could sit on the windowsill for a few minutes until he could come collect it because there weren't many people wandering the grounds at this hour. He'd also taken a calculated risk that her tail wouldn't become curious and check out the room she'd just changed her mind about renting.

So, he had a place to stay for a few hours, unless the desk clerk got some more business and decided to rent the room with the supposedly messed-up bathroom again tonight. That part of the ruse had been the hardest to communicate in Morse code, and he hoped that she'd gotten what he was trying to accomplish.

But best of all, the busted neon sign outside the Lincoln Motel advertised that they had the kind of cheap television sets that had a VCR built in.

Richard needed to sleep, but he woke up early, before seven. He thought he would have perhaps an hour or two left in the room before the maids began making their rounds.

He queued up the videotape, wondering if there was anything there that would justify the risk he'd taken to get it. The screen went to static, then cleared, showing Mary Jacobs leaving her apartment and getting into her car. He felt a pang seeing her again, but ultimately curious about the mysterious Alan and her relationship with him.

The tape skipped forward to a shot of Mary getting out of her car. Whoever was shooting the video (presumably Norm, Marty's private detective) made sure that he caught her in close-up to assure the viewer of who she was. She was on K Street, near Constitution. Mary Jacobs crossed the street into a small park at the corner of K and Seventeenth, it looked like.

There was a man coming toward her, a big guy by the looks of it, clean shaven and not smiling. Richard couldn't quite see his face, but maybe his face wasn't so important.

He pecked her on the cheek, and their hands brushed. They chatted for a couple of seconds and then separated.

And that was the end of the tape.

She stopped calling his number three months ago, Richard thought. I don't know when this was shot, but let's assume it was several months ago. But this Alan person called her the day she died and left a graphic message on her answering machine. Why?

Richard rewound it, and watched it again.

* * *

Richard Whelan watched the "Alan" tape for the fifth time, losing heart because he'd risked so much to get it and it proved nothing.

Perhaps he should break it down. Who was Alan? He re-wound the tape, watched Mary approach him, peck him on the cheek. Alan was only on camera for thirty seconds, approaching the rendezvous with Mary, and it was difficult to get a good look at him.

Big guy, works out. Orioles baseball cap on his head. Sunglasses.

Rewind the tape. Focus on Alan.

The man coming toward her. Anything in the background? Surveillance? Cops?

Nothing. Just people in the park, enjoying a sunny day.

Stop. Rewind.

Look closely at his face. Someone from the White House?

Swagger in his walk.

Look closely.

Square jaw, swagger, big guy, clean shaven.

Rewind the tape.

Clean shaven, maybe in his late thirties. Military bearing, almost.

Wait. He'd seen this person before. Think, Richard! Think!
Rewind.

He's easily over six feet tall, maybe six-two or -three, based on the way he towers over Mary.

Richard closed his eyes.

Imagined the face with a mustache, without the cap and the sunglasses. Jeans, maybe, dark hair from what he could remember.

"Nice car, Midnight. You out for a little joyriding?"

His eyes snapped open. *Saw the man from the café, holding a gun on Bettina.*

Rewind the tape. Look closely now. He stopped the tape when "Alan's" face was most clearly visible and took a pen and colored in a mustache on the TV screen.

He stepped back to admire his handiwork.

This was a man he knew.

The phony cop who'd roughed him up. Bettina's would-be assassin.

His partner had called him Nick.

19

THE WHITE HOUSE

The president had gotten the word from his press secretary that CNN was running with the story within the hour and would cite "unnamed sources within the White House."

He had CNN tuned in on the television in the Oval Office.

One of the anchors was talking when he was replaced with a special report—breaking news placard.

Here we go, the president thought.

THE LINCOLN MOTEL

Whelan was confused. Why was Mary mixed up with a gun-toting goon? It didn't add up.

Frustrated, he watched the tape again. And saw nothing.

He slapped the rewind button. Watched it again.

She was on K Street. There was a man coming toward her, Nick with a baseball cap and dark glasses.

He pecked her on the cheek, and their hands brushed. They exchanged a few words and then separated.

He watched again, focusing on their contact, trying to read Nick's lips, their hands brushing in greeting, but he couldn't make out what Nick was saying, so he rewound the tape, nearly crazy with frustration, because maybe the clue he was seeking wasn't on this video, maybe she was just sleeping with the guy. . . .

Who helped set me up for her murder?

Nick walked up to her, their hands brushed . . .

Wait. He rewound the tape. Looked at her hands, saw them curled as if they held something, watched his hands, they were empty . . .

Their hands brushed and they kissed, and he rewound the tape.

Looked at Nick's hands after he touched Mary's.

His fingers were curled, Mary's hands were empty.

And then it hit him.

He clicked the remote to turn off the VCR. The set was tuned to CNN, and he caught the last three seconds of the placard announcing breaking news. He was about to turn it off when he heard his name mentioned.

THE WHITE HOUSE

". . . Sources within the administration of President Edgar Roswell have confirmed to CNN that Richard Whelan, the president's national security adviser, accused of a bizarre string of murders and shootings and the object of a wild shoot-out with police yesterday in downtown Washington, may have compromised national security by selling classified documents to the highest bidder.

"We have this report from Potomac, Maryland, where Richard Whelan's car was found yesterday by police. . . ."

The picture dissolved to a stern-looking woman. The president didn't bother to read her name.

"Carolyn, Potomac, Maryland, was stunned yesterday by the murder of Martin Jacobs, legendary entrepreneur and longtime resident of this affluent town. But before residents even had a chance to digest the shooting that shattered their tranquility, another, more ominous spectacle occurred less than a mile from the Jacobs residence. . . ."

They cut to home video showing Cobra gunships sweeping low over a residential street. The reporter continued in voice-over: "Two armed helicopters containing scores of Secret Service agents descended on this sleepy town and surrounded Richard Whelan's car. From the accounts of worried residents, agents sealed off Potomac Creek Drive in order to retrieve evidence from the Porsche nine-eleven that police say Richard Whelan drove here in order to gun down Marty Jacobs. One of our colleagues, Joan Simpkins of Channel Ten, was at the police checkpoint when Secret Service agents pulled their weapons and ordered her and the other members of the press to leave the area."

Joan Simpkins was a short, unattractive woman in her forties wearing a rumpled Dior suit. "I've never seen anything like it. One minute I was discussing certain aspects of the case with Potomac police, the next thing you know, some guy hops out of a helicopter and sticks a gun up my nose and tells me to leave or else. It was the scariest thing I've ever experienced in twenty years in the broadcast news business."

CNN cut back to the live reporter who was looking down at a monitor. "As of eight A.M. this morning, Secret Service officials had a terse 'No comment' about what they found in Richard Whelan's car, Carolyn, but from sources within the Roswell administration has come the stunning news that officials now suspect that Richard Whelan may have had classified, highly sensitive documents in his automobile, and that he was using his position at the right hand of the president to steal and sell classified information to the highest bidder.

"There has also been widespread speculation that Whelan knew of and failed to inform the president of India's impending use of nuclear weapons in Kashmir in its ongoing dispute with Pakistan. Whelan's malfeasance, sources say,

has contributed to the paralysis evident in the administra
tion's handling of this affair. . . ."

The president clicked the remote.

Let the firestorm begin.

THE LINCOLN MOTEL

Richard Whelan sat stunned, his mind working the ramifica
tions of what CNN had just reported.

It made a certain kind of sense, he thought, given wha
he'd just witnessed on the videotape. It was one of the las
pieces in a brilliant campaign to discredit him, and he'd bee
a step behind all the way.

But for the administration to tell the world he was dirty
meant that his usefulness in whatever was going on wa
done. He had been identified as a scapegoat, and he knew
that whoever was behind this wouldn't want him to linger o
the headlines a moment longer than was absolutely neces
sary. And they certainly would not want him around to te
his side of the story. No, Richard Whelan would disappea
and the White House would tell the congressional hearing
that the pariah had, luckily, been stopped before any rea
damage was done.

That meant that either the president, O'Shay, or maybe
Monroe was behind all this. It had to be one of them, the
more he thought about it.

Or maybe all three.

Marty Jacobs, friend of the president, dead.

Mary Jacobs, his girlfriend, dead.

Secret documents planted on Mary and now his suppose
involvement leaked to the press.

India explodes a neutron bomb. He thought about it for
few minutes, then picked up the phone.

Marcus Blaze listened to his now-infamous client for

few minutes, nodding and taking notes. It was a short conversation and he sat back and sighed when it was over.

"I hope you know what you're doing, Harvard," he said softly to himself. "They always keep a Kryptonite rope around in case supernigger gets out of hand or looks the wrong way at a white woman.

"And you have done both, my brother. I think they got the tree for your lynching all picked out."

He put the phone on speaker and dialed.

POTOMAC, MARYLAND, CORONER'S OFFICE

Detective Bill Johnson was attending the Marty Jacobs autopsy, having asked and received permission to kibitz on Potomac PD's turf. Johnson looked down, ignoring the steady stream of commentary the coroner was making into the microphone on his lapel. Marty Jacobs had a single gunshot wound to his head, inflicted by a .25-caliber Beretta pistol that had been found at the scene.

He'd been shot at close range. Why two guns at the scene, the Browning and the Beretta?

The coroner made a standard Y incision into the victim's chest.

"When did he die? What time of day?"

The coroner looked at him, annoyed. "The lividity of the corpse suggests either late morning or early afternoon as the time of death. I covered that before, Detective. Listen more closely or be quiet."

Johnson wrote that down in his notebook. *The maid said Whelan got there in late afternoon.*

His cell phone rang. The coroner looked at him, annoyed at the interruption, so Johnson turned and stepped away from the table where Jacobs's body was laid out.

"Johnson, Homicide."

"Marcus Blaze, Detective. My client wants to turn him self in."

"Smart move."

"But he wants to do it at a time and place of his choosing Do you have a pen?"

"Sure," Johnson already had his notebook out. "Shoot."

Johnson rapidly covered the page with notes. When they finished talking, Johnson called his captain, then called the White House.

THE WHITE HOUSE

Charles O'Shay was wrapping up an early staff meeting covering what they would and would not say about the Whe lan mess when Frank Moynihan appeared at his office door O'Shay got up and went into the hallway, closing the door on his staff behind him.

"Make it quick, Frank. I'm in a hurry." O'Shay looked at his watch. Ten thirty.

"Whelan's attorney made contact with the police."

"When?"

"A few minutes ago. He wants to turn himself in."

"Where?"

"Brookhaven Mall. He wants Bettina Freeman there and D.C. cops, but no feds."

O'Shay snorted. "No feds, huh? That's a laugh."

Moynihan shrugged. "The mall bit has me concerned. I he goes berserk a lot of people could get hurt."

"True, but he probably doesn't want to catch a bullet him self. I'd do the same if I were as bent as he is. Any chance that we can pick him up on the way in?"

"I wouldn't advise it. If he burns any of our people he'll simply walk away. His lawyer made that clear to the police But given Whelan's notoriety, they called me to coordi nate."

"What do you think, Frank?"

"I think we take him into custody ourselves. The D.C. Police can be there as observers, but I think we put a group in the mall in plainclothes and take him down."

"Do you need the president to make a phone call or two?"

"I already talked to him about this, and he agreed to make the appropriate overtures."

"Fine. Anyone else we should brief?"

"No. FBI has agreed to let us handle the arrest to keep things simple."

O'Shay took a breath. The quicker Whelan was out of sight, the quicker this whole mess would die down.

"Just remember, Frank. The president wants this whole thing wrapped up quickly. It's imperative that you take Whelan down, not the police."

Frank Moynihan nodded. "We're on it."

Richard was moving again, having hurried away from the Lincoln Motel.

Twenty minutes later he called Sam Hennings from a pay phone.

"Don't say my name. Don't believe what you're hearing about me."

Hennings was silent, so Richard continued. "Do you have anything?"

"Yeah, and it's hot. But not over the phone. I'm glad you called."

"Have you noticed any surveillance? Any strange clicks on your phones?"

"No. But that doesn't mean that it isn't there."

"Okay. Where?"

"Same place we met the first time. This afternoon, about four."

"I'll be there."

* * *

Early that afternoon Bettina Freeman was about to get into her BMW when someone called her name.

"Ms. Freeman? Frank Moynihan, Secret Service."

She'd seen Moynihan many times but had never spoken to him. "Yes, what do you want, Agent Moynihan?"

"We know you're going to meet Richard Whelan. Let's go back inside and have a chat."

Bettina sat on the couch in her living room. Moynihan paced.

"Please don't misunderstand me, Ms. Freeman. I realize that Whelan contacted you through his lawyer, but I just want to make sure you understand that helping him in any way is a crime. You realize that, Ms. Freeman?"

"I understand."

"And you are aware of the serious nature of the charges against him, are you not?"

"Yes, yes of course."

"Fine. We are hoping that this will go off without incident, but I think you should consider wearing a flak jacket just in case."

She looked confused. "I thought this was to be a purely police matter?"

"That was Whelan's wish. But this is now a matter of national security. Secret Service will handle the arrest."

Bettina did not voice her disquiet. *If it was an espionage case, it should have been the purview of the FBI. Then again, if you want to kill him, if it is a conspiracy, then this is the way it would happen.*

"Are there any special instructions that his attorney told you about that were not shared with the police?"

"Just that he wanted to give me something before he was taken in. What, I don't know."

"Any reason why he wanted you to wait for him by the fountain on the main floor?"

"None that I know of."

"Okay. Rest assured, Ms. Freeman, if he makes one wrong move toward you, we'll take him down."

I bet you will, she thought.

BROOKHAVEN MALL, EARLY AFTERNOON

Through Blaze, Richard had passed Bettina explicit instructions about which entrance to use so that he could watch her enter and see if she had a tail or not. He'd shopped this mall a million times with Mary and knew it inside out.

He looked at his watch. She was late. Typical Bettina.

And then he spotted her getting out of a cab. She looked worried. She was carrying a large shopping bag that looked like it had a couple of sweaters in it. Good, Richard thought, just as Blaze had instructed.

He watched closely as she went through the revolving door, waiting to see if anyone followed her in.

He glanced at his watch again. He'd give it five minutes, then follow.

Frank Moynihan was on the second floor in an area that had a view of most of the ground floor. He had fifteen of his people in plain clothes covering the exits to the mall. He'd told them that they were authorized to use deadly force only if there was no other way to prevent Whelan from getting away or if Whelan made a move to harm Freeman. Picking a mall wasn't a bad move for a man who had no experience as an operative, he thought. Too many opportunities for hostages if it came down to a fight.

"Freeman just came in the south entrance. No sign of the suspect."

"All units, look sharp," he said into his walkie-talkie. He wondered what the D.C. police were doing.

* * *

Bill Johnson was in a Starbucks on the second floor. He and Steinway had argued with their captain about whether they wanted a SWAT HRT team to cover the mall; both Steinway and Johnson wanted the firepower.

But his captain had talked to Moynihan and that had sealed it. This was to be a federal operation. So he and Steinway had three other officers in plain clothes on the ground floor, but they were there to observe only. They weren't even tied into the feds' radio net because their equipment was incompatible with the Secret Service's. So they were supposed to stand around and play with themselves, he thought, disgusted.

Richard waited five minutes, checked his parcels to make sure he had everything, and entered the mall. His Glock and two spare clips were stuck in his waistband in the small of his back, but God help him if he started shooting in the crowded mall.

"Unit five: Suspect just came through the south entrance. Red flannel shirt, jeans, and a baseball cap."

Moynihan keyed his radio. "Units three and six, converge on Freeman, but don't get too close."

He lifted his binoculars. Whelan was dressed in a dirty flannel shirt and jeans, with a baseball cap pulled low over his forehead.

"This is unit six. I have the suspect in sight. Do you want to take him now?"

Moynihan: "Negative. Let's see what he has to say to Freeman." *Maybe she's part of it*, he thought.

Bettina was near the fountain in the middle of the ground floor. There would be a good line of sight for anyone laying crosshairs on them, but he was counting on being the target this time. He began walking swiftly toward her.

He was still thirty feet away when she spotted him. He saw the quick shake of her head, calling him off, but he kept walking toward her.

"Unit six, I'm in position."
"Unit three, in position."
"Unit five, I'm ten feet behind the suspect."

Bill Johnson's radio came alive. *"This is Edwards. I think it's about to go down by the fountain. I see her, and Whelan approaching her. Look alive, guys."*

Johnson left his decaf coffee and jogged to the nearest stairwell to go downstairs and watch the action.

Moynihan saw Whelan walk up to Bettina Freeman and hand her a package of some sort. She was wired for sound and he waited for Whelan to say something.

But Whelan didn't say a word. He went up to her and kissed her on the cheek. Then he gave her the package and kept walking around the fountain toward the exit covered by unit seven.

Interesting.

"All units, they exchanged something. Take him into custody, but do it quietly."

Three people seemed to break from the crowd and start closing in on Whelan.

Richard made all of the agents converging on him. He was in cockpit mode now, hostiles at his flight level closing, everything choreographed—altitude, attitude, airspeed, controls, weapons, *threats*—

He could feel the crosshairs on him, sure that he was the

target, the one additional shooter that he was certain was above him in the sun, certain that death was waiting in the next step or two. There. He was in the open. He could almost feel the shooter tightening his grip on the trigger, taking out the slack . . .

Bill Johnson watched the Secret Service agents converging on Whelan. *Nice and easy, guys,* he thought to himself. *Civilians all around.*

And then Whelan seemed to dive, as if for cover, and he heard the sound of a high-powered rifle; the marble floor where Whelan had been standing puffed twice with high-velocity impacts.

"Shots fired! Who the hell is shooting?"

"Somebody just tried to snuff him! Hold your fire!"

"Where's it coming from? Sounds like a sniper rifle!"

"Get down, everybody get down!"

Moynihan heard the shots, began searching the ground floor for muzzle flashes, but saw nothing.

"All units, take cover! Spotters, where is that rifle?"

He was looking up now, looking for someone with a weapon. Agent Wilkins began pointing toward the catwalk near the roof. "The shooter is up near the roof!"

"All units, there's a shooter on the catwalk near the roof. We got anyone up there?"

"Negative, negative. I'm pinned down!"

Pandemonium erupted as the shooter tried desperately to pick Whelan off. There were people running everywhere as Richard scrabbled across the marble floor. He chanced a glance back at Bettina, hoping that she was all right.

She was hiding under the winding stairwell that led to the second floor. He'd positioned her so that she would be covered by taking two steps if shooting started. And the shooter had positioned himself in the only spot where he could get into position without being observed and easily get to the roof to get away.

There was a Secret Service agent crouched in the exit doorway, gun out, looking up. An elderly matron ran toward him, frantic to get out of the door and get away from the gunshots. Once he was out of the sniper's line of fire, Richard came to his feet and joined what was now a crowd of several people rushing to safety.

The agent never had a chance. Two people tried to run through him, knocking him over, one of them smashing him over the head with a shopping bag at the sight of the agent's gun.

Richard was about to sprint into the parking lot when he saw someone draw down on him from the corner of his eye. He pulled his Glock from his waistband and turned.

Target and shoot. No, wait . . .

"Halt! Police! Drop your weapon and get on the ground, spread eagle!" Bill Johnson stood there, not twenty feet away.

Richard looked at the open door, freedom just steps away.

"Do it now or I'll shoot!" Johnson said. The detective had a shot if the people running out the exit would stay out of his way. A risky shot, but he could take him.

Richard hesitated. To get so close . . . but he couldn't fire on Johnson; it was clear that he wasn't wearing a vest under his dress shirt.

"I said, drop your weapon, Whelan, and get on the ground. Do it NOW!"

They were facing each other, seconds ticking away. More agents, more cops were running toward him. One of them would take the shot at him once the mad rush of shoppers thinned. Worse, the Secret Service agent at his feet was stirring.

Time was running out.

He looked at Johnson, his eyes pleading. Their eyes locked for a second.

"Put it all together," Richard said softly. Then he turned and sprinted through the door into the parking lot beyond, one of hundreds of people that had spilled out of the mall.

Bill Johnson did not fire a shot.

20

"You let him get away!" Moynihan thundered at Detective Bill Johnson. "My people saw it. You had a shot, you could've taken him down. Goddamned incompetents!"

Moynihan strolled away to question Bettina Freeman before Johnson could say a word.

It had taken an hour to unravel the chaos at the mall. Bettina Freeman had been detained for questioning as soon as the shooting stopped. But they had hundreds of injured shoppers and at least two agents that had been run down in the melee once the shooting started. Whelan had gotten away cleanly.

It was therefore a very angry Frank Moynihan who questioned Bettina Freeman after things began to settle down. Bill Johnson, after suffering a withering glare from Moynihan, was also in attendance.

"What just happened here, Ms. Freeman?"

"I don't know."

"We just had your boyfriend jeopardize a mall full of shoppers in order to avoid being captured. Please convince me you weren't in on it."

Bill Johnson spoke up then, angry. "What makes you think that Whelan set this up?"

"It's too convenient. A shooter in the mall, Whelan gets away in the confusion."

"Where's the shooter?" Johnson asked.

"He got away."

"What?" Johnson said, incredulous. "A mall full of you people and the shooter gets away?"

"That's what I said. The shooter's gone. So my money is that he was in cahoots with Whelan."

"Why," Bettina asked, "would he set this up?"

"Well, what did he pass you?"

"This." She handed over a package wrapped in brown paper. Moynihan took it and ripped it open.

It was a videotape.

"Get us a VCR!" Moynihan snapped.

They reconvened in an electronics store in the mall. The manager had allowed them to take over the premises once a dozen or so Secret Service and D.C. police waved their badges at him.

One of Moynihan's people put the tape into a machine and pushed the play button.

They watched in silence as Mary Jacobs met a man on K Street, pecked his cheek, and went on her way.

"What the hell does that mean?" Moynihan shouted when it was over. He angrily motioned for an agent to rewind the tape and play it again.

They watched it again. While they were watching, one of Bill Johnson's plainclothes officers whispered something in his ear.

"Is this asshole toying with us?" Moynihan asked. "This is meaningless."

"I don't know," Bettina said. "All I was told was to stand near the fountain as close to the spiral staircase as possible, and that he was going to tell me something. But he never said a word," Bettina said.

"You're looking at obstruction of justice, young lady," Moynihan said, pointing a finger at her. "Whelan set this up to make us look stupid. I want that tape analyzed! Somebody get on it!"

"Agent Moynihan?" Bill Johnson spoke up.

"What?"

"There's someone here you should talk to."

"Who?"

Johnson motioned to the teenage girl who came forward shyly.

"Who the hell is this?"

"Calm down. She saw something."

"She was here in the mall?"

"No. Outside, in the parking lot. Go ahead, young lady."

"I saw a black helicopter land on the roof of the mall after the people started running out."

"You saw a what?"

"A black helicopter. Somebody got on, then it took off."

"From the roof?"

She nodded.

"So that's how the shooter got away," Johnson said. "Courtesy of the D.C. police. At least we didn't forget to do basic police work."

Moynihan ignored the dig. "Doesn't prove anything."

"Add it up, Agent Moynihan. Someone takes shots at Whelan with a high-powered rifle, then gets away in a black helicopter, avoiding a cordon of police and federal agents."

"Your point?"

"Helicopters. High-powered rifles. If Whelan set this up, he must be some kind of fucking James Bond."

Johnson cornered Moynihan after they let Bettina Freeman go.

"I'm beginning to get a bad feeling about this."

"I'm beginning to get a bad feeling about your department, Detective."

Johnson looked like he was going to get in Moynihan's face but then wisely backed off.

"First thing is, I don't think Whelan killed Marty Jacobs."

"Preposterous."

"Hear me out. I was at the autopsy this morning. Coroner puts the time of death at no later than early afternoon. Whelan doesn't show up there until late afternoon."

"But it was Whelan's gun. The maid heard the shot."

"Yes, a Beretta pistol was the murder weapon and was found at the scene. But that videotape you just saw? Also came from Jacobs's house. He stored them in a footlocker. A locked footlocker. That lock was shot off with a Browning semiauto. That was the shot that the maid heard."

"Big deal. He carries two guns."

"Think it through, Agent Moynihan. This bothered me from the very beginning. Why shoot Jacobs with one gun and shoot the lock off the footlocker with another? Why leave the murder weapon at the scene? Is Whelan stupid?"

"Most criminals are, Detective."

"We also have Bettina Freeman's statement that Whelan saved her life, and that the shooter appeared to drop one of Whelan's weapons at that crime scene; the Browning that was used on the footlocker."

"She's got the hots for him and would say anything to clear him. What else do you have?"

"Just this. Whelan's attorney told me that he expected that an attempt would be made on his life this afternoon. He said that there was no way you guys would let someone outside of the federal government take him alive, and that he thought that you guys would be a significant presence.

"Add it up, Moynihan. Jacobs has two guns at the scene and appears to have died earlier than Whelan could have gotten there.

"He predicts that someone is going to try and kill him at the mall, here. And someone does.

"The shooter or shooters get out of here in a helicopter. That means someone with serious juice not only set this up but knew about it in advance. So I have one question, Agent Moynihan."

Johnson took a deep breath. "Who else did you tell about the operation here at the mall?"

"None of your business," Moynihan said, but he mentally ticked off the list in his head.

Charles O'Shay. And the president.

At 4:00 P.M. Richard Whelan was across the street from the greasy spoon where he'd first met Sam Hennings. He watched Hennings walk in and waited, searching for any sign that he was being followed.

After ten minutes he was convinced that if Hennings had a tail he would never see it.

He went in.

He and Hennings sat at a booth in the back of the restaurant.

"Thanks for meeting me. You're taking a huge risk."

"What the heck happened at the mall? It's all over the news."

"I had to get whoever is behind this to tip their hand. And they did."

"Why do that?"

"Because once they began to run with the 'Whelan is a spy,' and 'Whelan missed the boat on India,' I knew that I was expendable. For some reason, up until that point they preferred me as a fugitive cut off from everyone. Why, I don't know. Once they decided that I'm to blame for everything it was obvious that they would rather have me dead than let anything else come out about me. And the discovery of classified documents in my car sealed the deal. The documents were first planted in Mary Jacobs's apartment so that the *Washington Post* could 'discover' them."

"But someone with a high-powered rifle?"

Hennings didn't need to know all the gory details. "Look at it this way. If they hadn't made the attempt, I'd be in jail right now."

"And you thought all this through in advance."

Richard shrugged. He'd put Bettina in jeopardy on a hunch. He wasn't proud of any "brilliant insight" that produced that result. And he'd have to make that, and many other things, up to her. But the mall had been an important part of the plan, because he knew there was only one way for a shooter to operate in that kind of environment, and only one way to get out afterward. Not many people could put someone on the roof and get them off again. Not many at all. And that told him something.

"You have some news?"

"Yeah, like I said, I heard from the ASCI guys."

"One second. Did you bring a cell phone?"

"Yeah, why?"

"Because I need you to make a phone call. A short one."

"Okay, shoot. What's the number?"

Bettina picked up her cell phone at the first ring.

"Hello?"

"This is a friend of a friend. Did you look at the tape?" a strange voice said.

"The Secret Service took it."

There was a pause.

"My friend says look in your bag. I'll call you back in a few minutes."

She'd been carrying a shopping bag with some clothes in it for the meeting with Richard, as per his instruction. He'd said he wanted her to carry it so that she would be easier to spot.

She retrieved the bag from her foyer where she'd left it. She pulled out the old sweaters. And there, tucked against the left side of the bag, was a videotape with a Video Duplicators! No Questions Asked! sticker on it.

A few minutes later the phone rang again.

"Did you look at the tape?"

"Yes. It's a copy of the one the Secret Service took."

"What did you see?"

"Mary Jacobs kissing some guy."

There was a pause. "My friend says look at it again."

"Why?"

"Look at her hands. They weren't lovers meeting. It was what they call tradecraft in the spy business," the man said, pausing.

"It's a brush pass."

Hennings ended the call. "What was that all about?"

"My girlfriend was meeting someone and passing him something. What that something was is the key to all of this. This Nick person is the same guy who helped set me up for Mary's murder."

"Maybe the stories are half true. That Mary Jacobs was stealing secrets and selling them to the highest bidder."

"Could be. But I don't get the why part of it yet. Worse, the police showed me her phone bill. She called my office fax number once, but I never got a fax from her. I'm thinking maybe she got something off my office computer. The thing is, I don't know what it could be." Richard hesitated.

"So what's your news?"

"The ASCI guys finished the analysis on the Indian nuke."

"And?"

"They're convinced that the weapon that was detonated is based on an American design."

"What? That doesn't make any sense." *American design?* he thought. *What was the document in the lockbox? Project . . . something? Related?*

Hennings shrugged. "Scared the shit out of the Sandia guys. You have any nuclear secrets on your computer?"

Whelan shook his head. "Nothing like that. Since my machine is connected to an external phone line, anything classified that I work on is stored on an external drive that I pull whenever I'm not using the machine."

"Then it must be something, Richard. Think!"

"I've thought about it. There's nothing that would be interesting to an external party."

"Then we're stumped."

"Were you able to get the data from the satellites Monroe and Erskine had looking at Kashmir?"

"Requested it under an alias. Should get it tomorrow. Unless they arrest me."

"So I guess we wait until . . . hold it. Hold it one minute."

"What?"

"I told you that the police showed me Mary's phone bills? Well, there was a number on there that they thought might be this Alan person."

"Should we contact the police and get the number?"

"No need. I remember the number." He wrote a number down on a napkin, then motioned for Hennings's phone.

"Let me give it a try. Whoever answers the phone is in this up to their eyeballs."

Bettina Freeman watched Richard's videotape one more time.

She looked closely at Mary Jacobs's right hand; her left hand was clutching the strap to her purse.

She watched her approach "Nick."

Her right hand was not quite closed, as if she had something gripped lightly in it.

They kissed. Her right hand brushed his and opened. His hand closed.

She walked away.

Her right hand was now open.

She rewound the tape.

Now that she knew what to look for, it was obvious.

She went into her home office and began to work on the second part of Richard's request.

Richard Whelan dialed the Nick/Alan phone number. It rang once.

"Operator twenty-two."

He was so startled he hung up.

"Wrong number?" Hennings asked.

"I'm not sure. You try it." He handed him the phone. Hennings hit the redial button.

Hennings listened briefly, then hung up.

"Man, that's weird."

"Operator twenty-two?"

"Well for me it was 'Operator seventeen.'"

"Very strange."

"Hmm. Did you say that the police couldn't trace this number?"

"They said that Bell Atlantic couldn't immediately provide the subscriber."

"Holy shit."

"What's wrong?"

"That's the kind of set up that NSA or CIA uses for its field operatives. It's a message board so you can pass messages back and forth. It also functions as an untraceable number whenever the operative wants to leave a phone number. So of course Bell Atlantic can't give the police a subscriber's name, because the subscriber is the United States government, and nobody needs to know anything more without someone cloaking it in national security."

"NSA or CIA? Are you sure?"

"Nearly. That still doesn't explain why Mary was killed. Unless the government was spying on itself."

"Doesn't make sense. Unless . . . ," Whelan snapped his fingers. "Damn! How could I have been so stupid?"

"What do you mean?"

"What if Mary didn't steal something from my computer? What if she put something on it? Something that whoever is behind this didn't want me to see?"

"You mean she was killed to keep from spilling the beans about this?"

"Right."

"So Mary Jacobs is passing information to someone with connections to the U.S. intelligence community. The two of you start going out. She continues to do whatever she's doing, gets a guilty conscience, and then starts toying with telling you what's happening. And then she's killed."

"Then I have to find what it was she put on my office computer."

"And you can't just walk into the White House and boot up."

"Right."

Hennings smiled. "There might be another way."

21

The president of the United States woke up the next morning and lay in bed for a moment, not wishing to start another day. Not quite yet.

Marty Jacobs was dead. Skipper was dead. He'd built a career on the bodies of people close to him, and he was finally tired of it.

He sat up in bed and his wife stirred next to him, but he didn't wake her up. Not just yet. Not to share the sacrifices and the blood that it took to land in the White House; those he bore himself in the early mornings, before the start of the day.

Bettina Freeman went to work early that day. She had an envelope full of papers in her hand as she made her way to her BMW. She looked around, but the police had pulled their people the night before. If anyone was following her, she couldn't see them.

She took her regular route to the State Department's offices. She parked her car the way she normally did, exited the parking lot the same way she had for the last seven years.

The only difference was that today she bumped into a man and dropped her envelope. She bent over to pick it up and instead picked up a smaller envelope that felt like it had a set of diskettes in it.

The "stranger" picked up her envelope and continued on his way.

Susan Hennings watched Richard Whelan pour milk on a bowl of Cheerios and make a face. She loved her husband and had her misgivings about his decision to let a fugitive stay in their house, but she found his reaction to her husband's choice of breakfast cereal amusing.

"It's good for you," she said, smiling.

"No wonder I don't like the way these taste."

She gave him a cup of coffee and began her daily routine.

It wasn't until late morning that Bettina Freeman had an excuse to go to the White House. She was a floor below the Oval Office, the same floor that Richard's office was on.

She waited until the corridor was clear. Richard's secretary was on indefinite leave, disgraced because her boss was disgraced. She went to his office door and retrieved the key that had been in the envelope passed to her by Sam Hennings.

She partially closed the door behind her and turned on Richard's PC. She was relieved that it was still here and still intact. She checked all the connections while she waited for the machine to run through its initial self-tests. Everything appeared to be in order. Just to make sure, she picked up the phone on Richard's fax machine.

Dial tone. She'd tested it last night to make sure that they hadn't disconnected the outside line Richard used for his fax. Now she was ready.

She placed the diskette from the package into the floppy disk drive and executed a command.

The drive light came on and it began grinding. She wanted

to get out of here, but there was one other thing that she was supposed to do.

Good. Almost done. Her fingers were poised over the keyboard when the door opened.

"Ms. Freeman?"

She looked up, surprised at who was standing there.

"Would you mind coming with me, please?"

"I'm not doing anything wrong," she said, too defensively.

"You are violating national security just by being here. Let's go."

She stood up. Richard's monitor said, Reboot Now? Press Enter or ESC.

She let her finger drag over the enter key at the edge of the keyboard as she stepped away.

"Give me the diskettes you were using."

She extracted the diskette from the drive and handed it to him. He crushed it and threw it into the wastebasket, then motioned toward the door.

Sam Hennings came home. Richard greeted him at the door.

"How did it go?"

"Fine. We exchanged packages. She continued on. No surveillance on me at all."

"Good. This came for you."

He handed him a FedEx package addressed to Virgil Szymaniski, c/o Sam Hennings.

"Cool! These are the satellite images."

"Can't someone trace the request to you?"

"The c/o field on the address isn't searchable. It's text only, not a data field. So, nope!"

"Can you look at them here?"

"Yeah. They were downloaded to a PDF file."

"Okay. Give me Bettina's info, and we'll wait for her call."

* * *

Richard spread the articles that Bettina had pulled down
from the Internet on the kitchen table. He'd asked her to do
some research on Rocketdyne Systems.

As he began reading, he recalled his own research about
technology transfers to the Chinese. During the early 1990s,
the Chinese had suffered a series of launch failures in their
commercial satellite business. Hughes Corporation, along
with Loral, had provided information to the Chinese concerning certain esoteric aspects of missile nose-cone design
to help them correct the failures.

There had been a great deal of speculation about how the
information was passed, because the license to provide the
information to the Chinese had been granted by the Com-
merce Department, which was only involved because the
Clinton administration had changed the licensing process
and taken responsibility for it away from the State Department. State had maintained that they would never have
granted the authority to give the Chinese sophisticated missile design information because the knowledge could be applied to ballistic missiles.

A congressional investigation into the matter, combined
with reports of widespread and effective espionage against
American weapons laboratories, had started a firestorm of
speculation that the Clinton administration had allowed the
Chinese to steal American nuclear secrets in exchange for
questionable campaign donations.

While the Chinese theft of nuclear secrets, as well as the
transfer of sensitive design information, appeared to be
facts, the connection between the Clinton administration,
fund-raising, and the espionage had never moved beyond the
realm of right-wing speculation.

Loral and Hughes, he recalled, had shrunk away from
work with the Chinese.

It was then that Marty Jacobs's Rocketdyne Systems had stepped into the void. A year before the Roswell presidency, Rocketdyne had bid on and won a series of highly lucrative high-technology contracts with companies in the People's Republic. This was where Bettina's research was helpful, because it gave him dates and news stories from sources as diverse as *Business Week* and *Jane's Defense Weekly*.

He pulled a pad of paper close and began sketching out a timeline on Rocketdyne.

What immediately struck him was that Rocketdyne did no business with India. Never had. Which didn't support the beginnings of his theory of what was going on.

He next noticed that over the last year Rocketdyne had been on a spectacular losing streak with the People's Republic; they'd lost nearly every single contract that had been up for renewal during that period of time.

That was interesting. But still no tie to India.

He recalled what research he'd done on India's development of nuclear weapons. In May 1998, they tested a thermonuclear device. Then some time later, they'd announced that they had developed a neutron bomb.

How much later? It was about fourteen months ago, he recalled. It had been in the *Wall Street Journal*. China, if he recalled correctly, already had an enhanced radiation weapon. They'd announced theirs eighteen months ago. Give or take.

He paused to check on Sam Hennings, who was carefully decompressing the PDF files from the CD-ROM he'd had delivered.

"Anything?"

"Not yet. Looking at a lot of empty Kashmiri landscape. But there are fifty images on this disk, and they each take time."

"Bettina hasn't called yet?"

"Nope."

"Think we should try it? She has to have been in and out by now."

Hennings shrugged. "Sure. At least we should test my theory. You did say that you have a Hitachi fax machine on that line, didn't you?"

"Yup."

Hennings chuckled. "Love those Japanese gadgets. You can send a tone to your fax machine that tells it not to pick up. Pretty common knowledge to hackers, and it's probably the way Mary Jacobs got past it to get into your PC. Let me get out of this and give it a whirl. But if she hasn't gotten to your machine and turned it on, then we'll only be able to defeat the fax machine."

"Let's give it a try."

Hennings exited the viewer that he'd been using to look at the satellite images and brought up his own communications menu.

"What's the number?"

"202-456-5505."

"Okay."

He made sure his modem was on, then keyed-in the telephone number followed by a series of symbols.

"Here goes."

Richard heard the modem dialing out. The phone rang once, twice, and then picked up. He heard the tone from the fax machine, looking for an electronic handshake. Sam's machine sent a series of tones, and the fax machine went silent.

"See? It works."

The monitor said, *Connecting to remote terminal . . .*

Inside Richard's office, the program that Bettina had installed came up on his display. It was a "Terminate and Stay Resident" program, or TSR, that allowed users to access and control their desktops remotely. This was a failsafe in case Bettina couldn't find and retrieve Mary's mysterious file.

On Sam's computer, the screen changed and a logo came up: *Remote Access PC*.

And then Richard saw his desktop icons appear as if by magic on Sam's machine.

"All right!" Hennings gave Richard a high five. "We're in!"

It took twenty minutes of sophisticated searching to find the one file that had been created on his computer on the date Mary had dialed in.

"This looks like it. She hid it pretty well."

"Can you print it out here and get out? I don't want someone stumbling on this in the middle of the session."

"Sure. Printout, coming right up."

Sam gave Richard the printouts and went back to screening Keyhole satellite data. Richard went back to the kitchen and sat down. They were close to unraveling the mystery. Or so he hoped.

He looked at the pages. There were six in all. Mostly graphs of spectrographic and other data, and some seismic data as well. Well, he was no seismologist. He felt the letdown wash over him.

But Mary gave this to me as a key to what was going on. Maybe as insurance to keep anything from happening to her. But she didn't let anyone know about it, maybe to protect me.

He looked more closely at the sheets. They were labeled in small print in the upper-right-hand corner. He was holding them up to the light to try and see the labels better when it dawned on him what he was really looking at.

The first set of graphs was labeled: *U.S. Neutron Bomb Test, July 1974.*

The second set was labeled: *People's Republic of China Neutron Bomb Test.*

The third set was labeled: *Indian Neutron Bomb Test.*

He held all three sets up to the light, sandwiched together.

Now isn't that interesting.

All three results were almost identical.

"Hey, Richard. C'mere."

"What have you got?"

Sam Hennings turned away from the screen. "Take a look at this."

The image on the screen was deep in Kashmir near the Pakistani border from the latitude and longitude on the image.

"And this." He hit a button to bring up another image.

Richard looked at the positional data. This was from deep within India.

"And this."

Again, from within Kashmir, but closer to the Indian border.

"Am I seeing this right?"

"Oh, you're seeing it right. Unless I miss my guess, this is a huge Indian military force aimed right at Pakistan. They were caught in the open by the satellite Monroe had retasked."

Richard's mind was reeling. "Wait, wait, let's put this all together."

They were in the kitchen where Richard had his materials spread out.

"Is there any chance that Monroe misread the photos?"

"If he was blind, sure. Otherwise, no. There's too many troops and support vehicles, and the supply lines stretch practically all the way to New Delhi."

"Why haven't they moved? If an invasion was what they had in mind?"

"Weather, probably. But the weather's clearing, if I recall correctly. They've had a couple of days to consolidate their forces. And they blasted the troops that Pakistan had sent out to probe. A military expert could give you a better estimate, but I'd say they could be ready to jump off in the next twenty-four hours."

"And Monroe deliberately misled the president."

"It would appear." Neither of them said it, but what they thought was—*unless the president knows.*

"So the question is why?"

"Yeah. Maybe he wants to go to hell and doesn't want to wait on line."

"More complex than that. Look at this."

He showed Hennings the printouts from Mary.

"We already know the bomb India detonated in Kashmir is from an American design. But this shows that the Chinese have the same design."

Richard began pacing. "And Mary is seen passing information to someone with some connection to the U.S. intelligence community. She could have been doing it any number of times. So the question is, what was she passing?"

"And how did she come to be in possession of classified data like this?"

Richard picked up his timeline on Rocketdyne Systems.

"Up to a year ago, Rocketdyne was the People's Republic's favorite American firm. Then, all of a sudden, they begin losing contracts. Why?"

The answer was there, somewhere, he just had to sort it out.

And he recalled something Bettina had said early on: "*It seems like Monroe has the ear of the president on foreign policy on this one, which is bullshit.*"

"Look at this timeline. Rocketdyne is king until a year ago. Eighteen months ago, the Chinese successfully test a neutron bomb. Fourteen months ago, India tests a neutron bomb. Both designs identical copies of an American design. Then Rocketdyne starts losing contracts with the Chinese."

Think, Richard, think. Mary said you were the smartest guy she'd ever met. She was counting on you to figure it out.

Rumors and innuendo about selling the Chinese nuclear secrets. Mary passing something to an "operative" who then sets me up while someone kills her. The president is sensitive about Marty Jacobs, big campaign contributor.

Mary is killed, and someone in the government is behind it. Someone with enough "assets" to put a man on the roof of a shopping mall and get him off again and have a van full of electronics equipment sophisticated enough to fake an audiotape and alter a surveillance video.

Monroe influencing foreign policy decisions on Southeast Asia.

India tests a bomb, and Rocketdyne falls out of favor.

And then something he'd seen on the test results began bothering him. What the hell was it that he should remember?

He went back to the printouts of the test results. Looked at the Chinese test, and the Indian test.

Then he looked at the American test. At the bottom-right-hand corner of the graph, on the other side of the date.

PROJECT THOR

And the administration freaked out when someone found Project Thor data in my car, sending in Secret Service agents, not the FBI, to secure the data.

And then they decide to blame me for everything. Were they going to leak the part about Thor, too?

And then it all clicked.

"Oh, no," Richard said. "Your boss is playing God."

"You want to explain that one?"

But Sam's cell phone rang, and Richard dove for it, hoping it was Bettina.

They were in a CIA safe house somewhere in Virginia. Bettina was tied to a chair, her hands and feet bound with tape.

Nick was on the porch, making sure his partner, Rudy, and one of their extras, Raoul, were positioned properly out in the high grass bordering the property.

Mike Monroe, director of Central Intelligence, dialed the number Bettina had given him.

"That you, Whelan?"

She couldn't hear the response.

"I have your girlfriend. What I propose is a trade. Your life for hers."

Again she couldn't hear the response.

"I'm going to give you my location. If I hear anything out of the ordinary, if I get the slightest inclination that anyone but you is out there, I will put a bullet in her brain. Do you understand?"

Monroe paused, then chuckled. "I've already gotten away with it. I'm just going to make sure that you don't spoil the party. Oh, and by the way, I'm still in touch with my office. So if I hear anything about you spilling the beans about what you suspect but can't prove, she dies."

Monroe listened, then held the phone in front of Bettina Freeman's face. "Say something for lover boy."

"Richard," she sobbed, but Monroe terminated the call.

Richard closed the cell phone. "That was Monroe. He has Bettina and is threatening to kill her."

"Call the police!"

Richard shook his head. "No, the police will only get her killed. After they arrest me, for all I know. This has to play out in a different way." *This is the endgame, Richard. You up for it?*

"You haven't explained what's going on."

Richard got up and began pacing.

"Bear with me, Sam. This takes a great leap of faith, but somehow, it all fits together.

"Someone in the administration passed nuclear secrets to

the Chinese. Weapons design information, thermonuclear warhead design, and the design for Project Thor, which was the U.S. neutron bomb. In exchange, Roswell gets campaign contributions and other funding funneled through Rocketdyne, Marty Jacobs's company.

"They would have needed a secure link to pass the data. CIA provides the operatives and the infrastructure, but Monroe doesn't want to get his hands dirty with the actual exchange. Marty doesn't want any traces of sensitive information flowing to the Chinese through Rocketdyne, either, because that's how Loral and Hughes got burned. So they passed the information through Marty, who passed it to a CIA cutout through Mary."

"There were limits to what she could do for the company." *Marty Jacobs had said that, hadn't he?*

"What's in it for Rocketdyne?"

"Business. Big business. They stepped in where Hughes and Loral were afraid to tread. The profits from those contracts must have been enormous, much more than whatever trickled into the president's coffers."

"That still doesn't explain how India gets a U.S.-designed weapon."

"They got it because your boss got scared. He's military intelligence from the the post–Vietnam era. Think domino theory, Sam. So when the Chinese upgrade their launching systems and couple them with sophisticated weapons of U.S. design, Monroe realizes that he's created a monster that threatens the security of the U.S."

Hennings snapped his fingers. "So they give the same stuff to India, right at China's back door. India tests weapons that look the same as the ones the Chinese have, and China figures that if they needed to buy this information, India must have bought it, too. And they figure it came from the same source: Rocketdyne."

"Right. And Rocketdyne starts to get cut off from all the lucrative business that was part of the deal. Meanwhile, Mary gets scared of the implications of what she's doing. She asks her father for details, maybe, and Marty tells his little girl some of the big picture. Then she starts dating me and begins to get an attack of conscience.

"So Monroe has her killed. Mary may have threatened them with some sort of drop-dead tell-all letter, so Monroe has to figure out how to kill her and how to discredit me, because he suspects that she may have told me, or that information I would come to possess would unravel the whole scheme. They even go so far as to plant Project Thor documents in Mary's house for the *Washington Post*, so that I could take the blame for everything."

Sam looked disturbed. "Then why wouldn't Monroe tell the president about India's invasion force?"

"Because he wants it to happen. He wants China distracted by a nuclear exchange in her own backyard. He's using India to fight a proxy war so that the Chinese will focus on southern Asia, not on its ability to wage war with the United States."

"Shit. Do you think the president knows?"

Whelan shrugged. "That's what I intend to find out. What scares me is that the Chinese think that he must know, and since he's done nothing, that the president condones this whole thing."

Richard borrowed Sam's car to make the drive into the Virginia countryside, all the time his mind working, putting more of the details together, figuring all the angles. The address was a farmhouse on a dirt road somewhere in Virginia. It was so isolated that Richard spotted it from three miles away; it had to be the address he was looking for because there wasn't another structure around for miles.

As he came closer he could see that the main road ran through the edge of the property, and that a dirt road bordered by high grass connected the house to the street.

He slowed the car. Naturally, he thought, Monroe doesn't want me to get anywhere near him. His shooters are probably nestled somewhere in the grass, waiting for me.

Richard pulled to the right side of the road and reached over and opened the passenger door, carefully steering so that he was halfway on the gravel shoulder. He looked at the farmhouse, the dirt road, and the street, his mind calculating the angles and distances. They would take him as soon as he turned into the dirt track, he thought.

That put limits on where they could be hiding, since he was assuming they would have automatic weapons, like the latest greatest offering from Heckler and Koch preferred by law enforcement.

Ass-kicking time, he thought. He remembered shooting at the private detective in the park and the seamless way that he'd handled his gun.

No restrictions this time. Anyone shows a threat and they are *gone*.

He turned into the dirt track leading to the farmhouse.

The shooters, Rudy and Raoul, were in staggered positions in the high grass so that they wouldn't kill each other if the vehicle came abreast of them. The idea was to destroy the occupant before then, and as the car turned onto the track they opened fire. The windshield splintered, then caved in, and the motor coughed and died as round after round smashed into the engine. The gas tank was toward the rear of the car and didn't catch a stray round.

Lifeless, the car rolled to the left side of the dirt road and came to a stop half in, half out of the bordering grass.

The shooters waited a few minutes, concentrating on whether anyone climbed out of the driver's side alive. The late summer breezes moved the grass back and forth, and there was no sound except for the tortured ticks and pops of coolant running out of the hot engine.

There was no movement.

"Clear!" Rudy yelled. Both stood up and moved cautiously forward toward the car, looking closely at the driver's side for any sign of blood.

This is for Mary, Richard thought. He popped up from behind the trunk, and shot both men.

"Rudy, shit, man, I'm hit," Raoul said as he went down in a heap, blood leaking from a shoulder. Rudy was silent, and when Raoul looked over at his companion, he saw why.

Rudy was dead; one of Whelan's bullets had smashed through the bridge of his nose and into his brain.

Then Raoul's radio squawked. "What's happening?"

"Rudy is dead, and Whelan is somewhere in the grass."

Shit, Nick thought. He turned to Monroe. "He got Rudy and is somewhere on the grounds." If he felt any remorse, he didn't show any.

"Get the rifle and get ready," Monroe said. "If he gets past Raoul, take him when he's in the clear."

Nick grabbed the rifle, an Israeli-manufactured Galil sniping rifle, and went upstairs to the bedroom that faced the dirt road. He thought briefly about his dead partner, but partners came and went in this business. He hugged the rifle to his side.

A good gun, he thought, a good gun is a keeper.

He set up, scanning the field with his binoculars.

Raoul rolled swiftly away from where he lay, wanting to get out of Whelan's kill zone. He scanned the car for any movement, but there was none.

Maybe Rudy got off a lucky round, Raoul thought. But I'll just wait it out here.

* * *

The voice in the grass didn't sound like Nick's. That meant that the other phony cop was somewhere around. Whelan surveyed the scene.

He looked at the farmhouse. There was an upstairs window that had a good, unobstructed view of the grassy field. I bet the son of a bitch is up there with a sniper rifle.

And they know I'm here. That means time is running out for Bettina.

For some reason he remembered a scene from *The Dirty Dozen*, the one where Jimmy Brown has to sprint away from the Nazi fortress at full speed while pulling the pins out of grenades and dropping them into the vents feeding the underground bunker. He remembered the groan from the film festival audience when a Nazi took him out with a machine gun.

A shooter in the grass, almost certainly another one with a scope in the upstairs window. Time running out.

He put a full clip in the Glock. Jimmy zigged when he should have zagged. Remember that, Whelan.

Remember it. One-hundred-yard dash to the door of the house; the upstairs shooter won't be able to draw a bead on me once I get close because the roof slopes out to cover the porch. One hundred yards and I won't hear a thing if there's a bullet with my name on it, won't feel a thing if he goes for a head shot.

But he'll no doubt try and slow me down.

One hundred fucking yards.

Shoot to kill.

One.

Two.

Three.

Richard Whelan jumped up and started running.

Nick saw the figure jump up and fire off a volley of shots to his right to try and keep Raoul pinned down. He put down the binoculars and picked up the sniper rifle.

Deep, easy breaths. Set up his position as best he could. Plenty of time. Stock of the rifle to his shoulder, his body braced against a chair. Eye to the scope.

Whelan had zigged and he was looking at tall grass. He swept the rifle around to try and pick him up.

Ninety yards to go. Whelan cut left, hoping his angle would give the shooter in the grass a bad angle. Full stride, concentrating on keeping his muscles calm and his legs pumping faster and faster, and faster.

No shots yet. Any moment now he'll have me in his sights. . . .

Nick found him, running diagonally to Nick's right. Applied pressure to the trigger . . .

Monroe heard the report of the rifle and the tinkle of glass as the bullet smashed through the upstairs window. Then a series of shots. He looked at Bettina and smiled.

"Guess your boyfriend tried to make a run for it. Too bad."

Monroe turned towards the stairs. "You get him, Nick?"

Whelan cut back to his right as the bullets flew. He was too far away to actually hit the shooter, but he aimed the Glock in the general direction of the farmhouse and fired. His foot hit a burr of dirt hidden by the grass and he stumbled.

Raoul was up and moving once he realized that Whelan was running toward the house. He saw him cut to his left, then reverse and cut right, always on a diagonal, always moving closer to the farmhouse. He began running, too, staying well to the right of Whelan's position lest he catch a stray round, and fired a burst of his own at Whelan's back.

But Whelan stumbled. *Shit*, Raoul thought. *Missed*.

Nick's first bullet shattered the pane of glass in front of him, but Whelan had cut back to Nick's right. Nick followed, cutting loose a fusillade of shots, still calm, professional, still trying to reacquire Whelan in the telescopic sights.

Damn, the bastard could run! he thought, but then Whelan stumbled, and Nick marked the spot with the crosshairs.

That's all she wrote—*bro*. Nick began pumping rounds into the grass where Whelan had gone down.

He stumbled, and was conscious of the fact that the shooter behind him had opened up. Now there were bullets spraying dirt in his face as Nick's rounds walked in on him.

Whelan rolled away, then crawled forward, desperately trying to get out of the shooter's line of fire, but the damn grass revealed his every move like the wake of a boat.

Two guns on me now, he thought, as he heard the HK open up behind him again.

Raoul sprayed shells into the grass, then flinched as he saw the muzzle flash of Whelan's weapon send a bullet back in his direction. Missed me, motherfucker, he thought. But the gunshot gave him a precise location, and Raoul swept the HK in that direction.

Whelan fired back at the shooter in the grass, but it was a wild shot, because he immediately jumped to his left. A stream of lead tore up the ground he'd just vacated, and Richard moved again, again to his left, not daring to try and put a bullet into the second shooter until he had shaken his aim.

Nick stopped shooting because he'd lost Whelan's position. He swept the scope around, waiting for the grass to move, and missed Whelan's gunshot at Raoul.

Raoul thought the target must have moved after firing at him. He swept the HK to his left, but then saw the grass move to his right. Wrong way.

He swung the HK around and let go another burst, conscious that he would have to change the clip soon.

Whelan caught a round in his shoulder as he moved right, the bullet twisting him around in the middle of the air. He thudded to the ground leaking blood.

You see that! That Nazi motherfucker shot Jimmy Brown with a machine gun! Damn, nigger, get up!

Get up!

Damn, this hurts.

Got his ass! Raoul thought. He saw blood spray from the body and slap the high grass like crimson rain. He waved at the farmhouse, hoping to get Nick to cool it so he could check the body. But first he slammed a fresh clip into his Heckler and Koch.

Nick saw the wave. He picked up his radio.

"You get him?"

Raoul took a second to respond. "Saw blood. Chill out till I check on him."

"Right."

A breeze moved through the grass, hiding his movement for a second as he crawled away from where he'd fallen. If they pick me up again, I'm a dead man, he thought.

The breeze died down, and Whelan lay still, waiting, his mind on automatic.

Inside the farmhouse, Bettina Freeman heard the echoes from the last shots die away. Monroe smiled at her again, then called upstairs.

"You get him, Nick?"

Nick called down. "I think so, but sit tight. Raoul's going to check."

And Bettina put her head down, thinking, *please, please don't die, Richard, please . . .*

Raoul sprayed a burst at the blood-soaked grass just in case. He walked forward cautiously, his finger curled around the HK's trigger.

"Come out, come out, wherever you are," he whispered. He reached the bloody grass.

Oh, shit. No body and a trail of blood leading . . .

He turned to his right.

Richard waited, knowing that his shots would give away his position. Waited until the target was in the box, waited until he could hit him so damn hard he'd be dead before he hit the ground.

Raoul spotted the blood trail, turned to his right.

He was looking at Richard's gun barrel when it exploded, Richard pulling the trigger, punching holes into him, one, two, three . . . until the Glock's hammer fell on an empty chamber.

Nick saw Raoul stagger as the sound of the gunshots reached the farmhouse. He turned the rifle, sighting on Whelan as he leaped toward Raoul, swung the rifle, caressed the trigger, and the rifle bucked against his shoulder, then again . . .

And he saw Raoul's head explode right at the center of his crosshairs.

"Shit," he muttered, then looked over, wide eyed, as the radio squawked.

"Nice shot, asshole. Now I'm coming for you," Whelan said.

Another gust of wind, stronger this time, was waving the grass back and forth. Grimacing from his wound, Whelan grabbed Raoul's HK and moved away as quickly as he could.

* * *

Monroe heard Nick cursing a blue streak upstairs and shook his head. Time to take matters into his own hands.

"Get up, honey," he said, roughly hoisting Bettina Freeman out of her chair. "Time to put that little tushy to work."

Whelan was about thirty yards away from the farmhouse and feeling closer to fainting with every step when the front door burst open and Monroe appeared, practically dragging Bettina out onto the covered porch.

"Hey, Whelan! I got something here that belongs to you! Show yourself or the girl dies!"

He was far to the left of the porch, hopefully well out of the sniper's range. He pulled out his cell phone and dialed a number, then put the phone back into his pocket, still on and connected to the call.

He stood up, feeling his legs go wobbly.

"I'm right here, Monroe."

Nick could hear Whelan, but couldn't see him. He'd have to climb out of the window onto where the roof covered the porch to get a shot. He'd be exposed while he did it, but then again, Whelan only had a pistol, right? If Monroe could get him talking, he'd step out and put a bullet in Whelan's brain.

"Hey, Rich, can I call you Rich? You look like shit," Monroe said, laughing.

"Not as bad as you're going to look when I'm done with you, *Mike*."

"Well, Whelan still has those *cojones*, eh? Too bad Ms. Freeman here is going to take a bullet because of them."

"Why'd you do it, Mike?" Whelan asked, conscious of the cell phone in his pocket.

Monroe chuckled. "You familiar with the term *blowback*, Richard?"

Richard shook his head, no.

"Blowback is the worst nightmare of intelligence work, Rich. It's what happens when you run an op in Spain to penetrate certain leftist publications to whip up antigovernment sentiment and Congress gets wind of it and starts having hearings on why the Spanish press is out of control. Well, it was our op, Rich, but we don't want Congress mucking around investigating something that eventually leads back to us. It's what happens when the repercussions of one action spin out of control."

He paused to point the gun at Bettina Freeman's head. "It was a beautiful scheme, all those dead people with valid Social Security numbers writing thousand-dollar checks to the president's PACs, big money, Rich, from the Chinese. But there was a problem, both with the Chinks and with your dead girlfriend, and I had to blame it all on you."

"And now India is about to go to war."

"Hey, tough shit. Gives the Chinese something to think about."

"So you set it all up. Mary's murder, the documents, all to cover up your double dealing. Did you know about India's plans? The invasion?"

"Yup. HUMINT assets gave me some of it. Brilliant, don't you think?"

"So the question is, Mike, how much did the president know?"

"You certainly would like to know that, huh? Well, the man isn't dumb. But the beauty of it is that the things I don't tell him, Rich, *he doesn't want to know*. He knows that I have a 'black' operations budget. Couple of guys with some toys, and you're in business protecting national security. With the president's blessing."

"But why not tell the president about the invasion plans?"

"Because if there's a dustup in southern Asia it isn't our concern. Think of it as an opportunity to complicate things in the region and give the Chinese pause."

"So that's why the Chinese have been having backchannel communications with State. They think the president must know about India's plans, and endorses them, because they think he must have endorsed the transfer of nuclear secrets to India in the first place."

"The Chinese won't do anything but sit and watch. And worry. But I couldn't have your girlfriend here telling you secrets, and I couldn't have you running to the president to tell your tales. Takes away the man's plausible deniability. So Ms. Freeman was expendable. Lucky for me we didn't whack her at the restaurant, because she proved useful in baiting you here."

"What if it escalates? What if India executes a credible first strike against Pakistan? Think the Chinese will sit back and watch then?"

"I've encouraged the president to stay in close touch with everyone in the region. It'll calm down."

"Bullshit."

Nick had one leg over the windowsill, then carefully climbed out onto the roof over the shards of broken glass held in place by the frame. He could see Whelan to his right.

He knelt down, bringing the rifle to his shoulder . . .

Reflex. Richard saw the movement on the roof, brought the HK up and fired a quick burst that caught Nick in the chest and toppled him backward. He dropped the barrel of the gun so it was on Monroe who had turned back toward Bettina when Richard brought the gun up.

"Don't move, Mike."

Nick was down, bleeding like a stuck pig, wind whistling from a sucking chest wound. "I'm hit!" he screamed weakly. "I'm hit!"

Monroe pointed his gun straight up into the air and fired three quick rounds into the roof that punched nice big holes in it. "Shut the fuck up, Nick." Blood was dripping onto the porch from the roof holes as he pointed the gun at Whelan. "So where were we? Ah. I was about to shoot your girl-friend."

He smiled. "Unless you'd like to be first."

Richard relaxed, no longer dizzy, as he focused on the barrel of Mike's gun.

"If you think you can hit me, go right ahead." *Because I know you can't.*

Monroe brought his left hand up to steady his gun. "So long, nigger."

And pulled the trigger.

Bettina heard Monroe's gun roar like a freight train, and saw winking flashes from the barrel of Richard's borrowed HK. And then Richard went down, and Mike Monroe seemed to stumble backward into her, knocking her off balance until she went down hard and blacked out.

Frank Moynihan passed Sam Hennings's bullet-ridden sedan in a Secret Service Chevy Suburban.

"Christ," he said to no one in particular. "Looks like the taxpayers owe somebody a new car."

They passed Rudy, the first shooter, lying in a pool of his own blood in the middle of the dirt road, and the springs on the heavy Suburban groaned as they drove through the high grass around the prone figure.

They could see two bodies sprawled on the front porch of the farmhouse. He recognized Bettina Freeman covered in blood; the other he presumed to be Mike Monroe. Someone else lay on the roof extension, dead, from all appearances, a sniper rifle clutched in cold hands.

"See if we can match that weapon on the roof there to the one used at the mall," Moynihan said.

There was no immediate sign of Whelan. Moynihan's truck rolled to a stop and agents piled out. Another Suburban blocked the entrance to the dirt road. His forensics people would arrive shortly.

"Find Whelan," Moynihan barked as he climbed the three short steps to the farmhouse porch.

He looked at Monroe, still breathing although not likely for very long, a gun still in his hand. Moynihan worked the pistol free of Monroe's hand with his foot. The DCI groaned.

Then he looked more closely at Bettina Freeman.

She was covered with blood, all right, but she was still breathing, and he couldn't see any wounds on her, except her shoulder, which was bleeding a bit into her bandage. He pulled a handkerchief from his pocket to wipe the worst of it away.

As soon as he touched her forehead, her eyes snapped open.

"Richard?" she asked tightly. Moynihan shook his head and helped her sit up.

"I've got a body!" one of his men sang out from the grass in front of the house and Bettina's heart sank.

"Male, multiple gunshot wounds. He's gone." The agent continued walking toward the farmhouse, eyes searching.

Bettina watched the agent move forward then stop. He pointed off to his left. "Over here! Looks like Whelan, sir!"

Moynihan and Bettina were off the porch in a flash. The agent was kneeling over Richard's prone form.

"How is he?" Moynihan asked.

"He's hit, sir. Shoulder wound, also a graze in his side."

Bettina saw the blood oozing from Richard's head and turned away sobbing. Moynihan bent down to see for himself, then turned and hugged Bettina Freeman.

"It's a scalp wound, Ms. Freeman. That's why it's bleeding so much."

"Is he . . . ," she asked, not wanting to know the answer.

But Richard answered himself. He groaned.

"Did you . . . get it all?" Richard asked Moynihan after they revived him.

Moynihan showed him his cell phone. "Hennings clued me in to wait for the call. I heard Monroe take credit for this mess and a few other things that shouldn't have gone out over an unsecured phone, but I'm still clueless about all this."

And Bettina saw Sam Hennings's cell phone peeking out of Richard's pants pocket. It was on, and had been sending every word to Moynihan.

"Monroe?"

"He's about done. He's up there on the porch."

"Help me up. I've got to ask him something."

Moynihan looked at Bettina, then at Whelan. "We should take you to a hospital, Richard."

"No! Monroe first, then the White House."

"Richard, you've been shot!" Bettina said.

"I'll live. Help me up, dammit."

Whelan bent over Monroe. The DCI's eyes were glazing over, his chest heaving as his body shut down.

"Monroe! Monroe! You have to tell me! What did the president know? Does the president know about India?"

Monroe looked at him, eyes dull.

Then he smiled.

"Figure it out, Whelan."

And then he died.

"Okay, Richard. Now you're going to a hospital."

"No. Call O'Shay and take me to the White House. Have paramedics meet me there, just keep me conscious long enough to tell the president about India."

"Richard," Bettina began, "you can't be serious."

Richard turned to look at her. "He won't believe anyone else. Not Moynihan, not O'Shay. When he sees me, he'll believe me. And he has to believe me, Bettina. He has to get on the phone to the Chinese and New Delhi."

Whelan turned to Moynihan. "Let's get the hell out of here."

Moynihan started to protest, but Whelan's look silenced him.

Bettina leaned against the house, watching as the Secret Service agents held Richard Whelan upright between them and began walking to the nearest Suburban.

Well, at least he's alive, she thought. But there he goes again, rushing off to save the world and leaving me alone.

Damn him, she thought, even though she knew that he was doing the right thing.

Still, she blinked back a tear.

"Wait a minute," Whelan said to the agents supporting him. "I nearly forgot something. Turn me around. Back to the porch."

Bettina didn't turn when the procession mounted the steps, thinking that it was Secret Service walking the crime scene. She was hurting again, because of . . . him.

"Hey," Richard Whelan said, and she turned around.

Whelan moved closer under his own power, the Secret Service agents letting him take two shaky steps toward her.

"You're hurt," he said, noting the fresh blood from her old wounds. She simply nodded.

And then, amazingly enough, Richard Whelan put his arms around her and kissed her.

"And if," he said when their lips parted, "they don't put me in the hospital room right next to yours, there's gonna be hell to pay, okay? Tell them the 'Great Richard Whelan' said so."

She nodded, afraid that if she opened her mouth she'd start crying.

Richard caressed her face one last time. And then he

turned away, nodded to the Secret Service agents who managed to catch him before he fell out, and she watched Superman limp to the Chevy, off again to save the world.

Bettina Freeman wiped her eyes.

Damn, I love that man, she thought.

EPILOGUE

SOMEWHERE NEAR NEW DELHI, INDIA

Amjad Singho smelled the sour rubber, metallic scent of his oxygen mask dangling in front of his face as he completed his engine-start checklist. He was sitting in an Indian Air Force MiG-27, and as he glanced out of the cockpit he saw one of the grounds crew raise his hand in the air and make a circular motion.

Wind 'em up.

They were parked three abreast on the tarmac at one of India's most secret airbases, three airplanes armed with a special strike package that Singho's nation had never before deployed. He snapped the switches to start the fighter's engines, feeling the turbines turn over and come to life with a roar.

It was early morning, several hours before dawn. The skies were clear; a prerequisite for them to launch. Even though the Bahadhur was an all-weather air-to-ground capable bird, command had mandated that the weather be absolutely clear in order for Talon flight to launch. There could be no mistakes about their targets, and they needed good weather to be absolutely sure.

He completed his preflight checklist and began to taxi out

to the runway as soon as his inertial guidance system got its bearings.

As the jet roared down the runway he could not help but feel that no payload, no ordnance he'd ever carried, weighed as much as the plastic packet of cyanide pills zippered into the breast pocket of his Nomex flight suit.

Duty Before Self.

THE WHITE HOUSE, SEVERAL HOURS LATER

"The president is sleeping, and I don't want him wakened for this," Charles O'Shay said. They were in a conference room, the same conference room that Johnson and Steinway had questioned Richard in eons ago, it seemed.

Richard Whelan was covered in bandages and was receiving blood from a packet hanging from a stand next to him. The White House had extensive medical facilities in case the president needed them in an emergency, and even now one of the staff physicians was outside the door in case Whelan collapsed.

O'Shay looked at Whelan with some distaste. "But this incident could precipitate a Constitutional crisis if it ever gets out that the president used laundered Chinese money to win his campaign. I need to think about this, and how to present it before we wake POTUS."

Whelan spoke in a voice that was weary. "We're talking about war, Chuck, and you're talking about politics. Either we wake the president or I go public." He saw O'Shay's look of alarm. "That's right. These bastards used the press to smear me, and I will not hesitate to hit back. Now either we go with you to see the president, or I'm going alone. Which is it?"

"Secret Service has been instructed not to disturb the president, Richard. You'll never get through."

"He will if I take him, Chuck. And I intend to take him up

to the residence myself. With you or without you. Now which is it going to be?" Moynihan said.

There was a long silence as O'Shay measured his options. Can't put this genie back in its bottle, he thought, resigned. Even though the revelations had shocked him, he didn't put any of it past Edgar Roswell; he knew the man too well, knew what it took to gain the presidency.

"Fine," O'Shay said finally. "Let's go."

They made their way to the residential quarters in the White House, O'Shay in the lead, Moynihan, and a weak and limping Richard Whelan.

They were surprised to meet Steadman Dennis, chairman of the Joint Chiefs, and a Marine Corps major, in the corridor on the way to the president's bedroom.

"What the hell are you doing here?"

"I might ask the same of you, Chuck." Steadman raised his eyebrows at the sight of Richard Whelan, but said nothing.

"I've got something to tell the president that can't wait," O'Shay said, but Dennis turned and was walking so quickly that O'Shay could barely keep up. Richard was trailing behind.

Dennis turned to O'Shay, and the look in his eyes turned O'Shay's stomach to ice. "Whatever it is, it's going to have to wait."

As he went to the bedroom door and threw it open, Whelan noticed that the marine major was carrying something that he'd hoped he'd never see. It's called the football. It contains the launch codes for the nation's nuclear weapons.

Edgar Roswell was dreaming of his son, Skipper, as a boy. They were playing football on the front lawn of the house he had in Bernardsville Township in New Jersey, a million years ago.

Dennis shook him awake more roughly than was necessary. His wife was at a dinner and wouldn't be back in the residence for some hours.

"Mr. President, you must wake up."

Edgar Roswell blinked, and the dream image of his son catching a pass faded.

"Are you awake, sir?"

The president mumbled a response. He's out of it, Whelan thought.

Dennis plunged on; he had no choice.

"We have a situation, sir. Approximately forty-five minutes ago elite units of the Indian military crossed the border between Kashmir and Pakistan in force. Details are sketchy, but it looks like damn near all of India's ground forces are committed to this push."

We're too late! Whelan thought.

Dennis took a breath and continued.

"This assault was timed to coincide with a strike against Pakistan's nuclear forces. Indian MiG-27s armed with what we think were tactical nuclear weapons swept into Pakistani air space thirty minutes ago. Two strikes were successful in delivering what we are guessing were nuclear devices in the two- to ten-kiloton range against Pakistani nuclear-capable installations. Are you with me so far?"

The president nodded, but the look in his eyes suggested that he hadn't caught up.

"The Chinese must have seen this coming. Two hours ago we detected heightened activity at many of the People's Republic's strategic missile bases. I was alerted because we've never seen this kind of activity before.

"As promised, the Chinese retaliated. A single missile, a modified Long March ballistic missile, was launched fifteen minutes ago. The flight time was less than ten minutes, Mr. President."

Dennis's voice dropped to a whisper. "The target was New Delhi, sir. We think New Delhi may have been hit."

He put his hand on the president's shoulder and looked in his eyes. The president was confused, unfocused.

"Mr. President, I am recommending that we immediately upgrade to Defcon One. I have Major Stewart here with the nuclear launch codes. Protocol requires that we get you out of the capital and onto one of the airborne command centers, but I also need some direction as to how to respond. I need some orders, Mr. President."

But Edgar Roswell just looked at him, not wanting to comprehend what he was hearing. China? India?

And Richard wondered just how much the president knew. He searched the man, looking for clues, remembering Monroe's last words: "Figure it out, Whelan."

"Mr. President?"

Edgar Roswell blinked, a million thoughts pulsing through his mind, the military response, the diplomatic response, all of them swept from his mind by the image of his personal hell populated by the incinerated bodies of several million people, *the money, oh the fucking money, how could it have been worth it?*

"Mr. President?"